DEATH
of a
PERFECT MAN

Second Edition

Death of a Perfect Man

A Red Rock City Mystery

M. M. Gornell

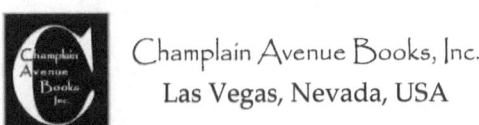

Champlain Avenue Books, Inc.
Las Vegas, Nevada, USA

Published by
Champlain Avenue Books, Inc., Las Vegas, Nevada

Copyright © 2009 by M. M. Gornell

International Standard Book Number 978-1-943063-24-6

Library of Congress LCN: 2016931633

Cover by *LAWRENCE*

SECOND EDITION
2016

Printed in the United States of America

For Trisha

PREFACE

The Red Rock Inn & Café, Red Rock City itself, and the inhabitants, visitors, and locations therein, exist only in author's imagination. But Red Rock Canyon State Park and the surrounding Mojave Desert terrain are magnificently real. There is a particularly magical spot on California Interstate 14 south of Inyokern, where if you stop and take in the sunset over the Sierra Nevada Range—fanciful tales of love, revenge, and murder come to life.

PART ONE
The Gathering

Chapter One

Sunday

Sunday evening was fast closing in and Jada Beaudine found herself battling escalating fatigue and apprehension. What seemed so right in Seattle a couple days earlier, was now feeling like an ill-conceived and dreadful mistake.

Since leaving Washington, she had driven over a thousand-plus miles through diverse and often breathtaking West Coast scenery—providing more than adequate unencumbered time and space in which to ponder her past, future, and present circumstances.

Now, late into what had been an exceedingly long second day of relentless driving, Jada could no longer ignore the self-doubt edging its way to the forefront of her thoughts and emotions.

She opened her side window and cool dry desert air rushed in—touched with a faint scent of eucalyptus. Except for an abandoned shack in the distance, Jada saw neither humans nor dwellings on either side of the road. She also didn't see any other cars on the highway, and her own minivan suddenly felt

Lilliputian and inconsequential against the vast and seemingly desolate Mojave Desert landscape. So different from home. *And scary.*

A few miles back, ten minutes or so before, she had driven down out of the mountains from Tehachapi on Route 58 and had had her first glimpse of the desert as it stretched before her. At that point, road signs and accommodations had been few and modest—but enough that she could have easily stopped for the night. Instead, she had inexplicably taken the turnoff heading north onto Interstate 14.

Why? No easy answer came to her. Was it because the landscape was so different? Alien even. And fearful of being engulfed into the foreboding surroundings, she had headed north in an unconscious attempt to go back home?

Out loud she said, "No, just another bad decision."

Jada took a long deep breath, then slowly blew out an exaggerated sigh. Of course she would eventually have to stop for the night. *Why prolong the inevitable?* Again, her rational mind provided no adequate answer.

True enough, when she initially turned onto I-14, she had been partially enraptured by a grand sunset featuring Sierra foothills capped with brilliant streaks of burnished red and deep tangerine, with the in-betweens and edges lightly washed with powder blue and pink.

Jada had never seen anything like it, and the unexpected beauty had momentarily awed, intrigued, and revitalized her. But now, just a few more miles and minutes later, her hands were clamped tight around the steering wheel and her teeth clinched to the point of pain. Beautiful sunset notwithstanding, she was in trouble.

She snatched a quick glance at her gas gauge. The needle hovered close to empty. "All my fault," she accused with hindsight clarity. Next she glanced in the mirror on her visor.

And I look as awful as I'm beginning to feel.

Indeed, Jada's overly large and deep-set brown eyes had lost both their inner vitality and their surface luster; and the corners of her full mouth were drooping. In concert, her high forehead was furrowed into a frown, and her eyes burned from fatigue and glare. She had gotten a haircut right before heading out—having her frizzy red locks sheered down to almost nothing. Remembering how the overly zealous beautician had gone a little crazy, Jada rubbed her hand over the stubble covering her head—it felt like rough peach fuzz.

If she had just left Bakersfield earlier in the morning, *if* she had foregone that unnecessary side-trip to Lake Isabella, and if she had just stopped to get gas in Tehachapi, or even Mojave— she would not now be in this mess.

Not another car for miles...well, maybe one set of headlights, a couple curves back. Out of gas, freezing, alone—desert creatures surrounding me—snakes, scorpions, coyotes? She wasn't sure what animals prowled the Mojave nights.

Dusk was advancing quickly. And once again, with the luxury of current knowledge with which to judge her past actions, Jada evaluated her trip provisioning, and found it also wanting.

Her attitude had been cavalier, and as she now realized, irresponsible and potentially dangerous. She had left everything in storage except one small suitcase, a toiletry bag, a box of pottery books, and a binder of glaze recipes—all four items now in a neat row on her minivan backseat. That was it. *Now I don't have any food left and only half a bottle of water. Maybe a flashlight. Fresh batteries? Probably not.*

With a longing that surprised and bewildered her in its intensity and contradictory implications, Jada wished for the old comforts of Seattle—familiar surroundings, established friends, comfortable patterns and routines—and the all-encompassing feel and smell of damp coastal air. Blessed humanity all around— suffocating yet reassuring.

At the same time, something from within was compelling her to escape Puget Sound. *Away from* the waters that had taken her husband, Terry, a year ago in that horrible and unforeseen sailing accident. *Away from* all the places, sights, and sounds they'd experienced together. *Away from* all the friends they'd shared. *Away from* that horrid insurance investigator and his lies about collusion and fraud.

Jada knew anxiety was now affecting her thinking and compromising her judgement. She forced herself to take another long and slow deep breath, willing her hands to relax. Then she stretched her jaw and slowly rotated her head—back and forth, side to side.

Besides, it was too late to turn around. She switched the heater to full blast—illogical and silly, given the car's interior warmth. Her chill was of the spirit, not the body.

There. In the distance Jada thought she saw a sign—a small green highway placard. She accelerated slightly—it was a sign, barely readable. It said "Kern 5, Red Rock City 12, Bishop 150." She had heard of Bishop, but the other two?

She drove on, more miles, maybe five—seemed like a hundred. Finally, on the left side of the road, a string of dull yellow lights materialized, surrealistic in import as they swayed rhythmically in the night wind.

She slowed down and looked for a signboard. Squinting, Jada read a bleached-out sign on a small adobe structure. The sign confided softly in washed-out lettering, "Red Rock Inn and Café." But all she could make out in the diminished light were two vintage gas pumps, ten or so rickety 1940s era resort cabins, a café maybe, and some kind of structure out back. However, it was enough for her to stop, and she pulled in next to the first pump to appraise up close what she had glimpsed from the highway.

Her hopes evaporated.

The pump was an antique, and it would be a miracle if it functioned. An old beat-up white station wagon with several flat tires sat dejectedly by the office entrance. "Red Rock Inn Limousine" had been painted on its side ages earlier; now the words, in faded black letters were barely recognizable. There were a few dim yellowish lights glowing in the cabins around the property—but the whole place, like the pump, seemed to be down-and-out-and-dead.

Someone tapped on her car window. Startled, Jada felt her heart jump from surprise. And apprehension.

"Gas?" A thin-faced middle-aged looking woman with longish brown hair pulled back in a tight ponytail appeared from nowhere and stood with her face inches from Jada's car window—staring at her and waiting for a response.

The woman was wearing unflattering faded blue overalls and a jeans-type work jacket that was ill-fitting and hung stiffly on her bony body as you sometimes see with mannequins. Her eyes though were dark green and luminous. reflecting a contrasting softness and comfortability—a fortunate asset in the current situation.

Those eyes helped Jada gain her composure, manage a tentative smile, and lower her window. "Yes, filler-up please. I wasn't sure you were open."

The woman continued to stare at her curiously; and Jada, under such intense scrutiny, felt the impulse to shift into drive, stomp on the accelerator, and get the hell out of there. She didn't. *Where would I go anyway? It's dark, I'm alone, out of gas...I guess I could call, but that would be admitting defeat...*

Finally the woman said, "You should stop driving now. I have a vacancy. I'll fix you a sandwich." Then she added with a small explanatory smile that made her angular face seem softer, and less threatening. "I'm psychic, sometimes."

Psychic? Jada shivered. *Bleak place, weird woman.* But still, she decided to stay the night.

* * * * *

In Ally King's mind, her decision process was complete, and her resolve firm.

Yes. She now knew in every pore of her body and in every cranny of her mind that she would kill the Beaudine woman.

In fact, she would look straight into Jada's eyes—so she would know who her killer was—then shoot her point blank in the head. If there were problems, she'd be easy to overpower. Ally's good would give her strength to overcome Jada's evil.

Where was it in the Bible that her mother—when in one of her drunken stupors—was always going on about? *Smiting* everybody who got in their way. Ally couldn't remember the quote exactly, but she could still clearly see her mother's face, ravaged from drink and irate with anger at imagined persecutors. The exact quotation didn't matter anyway. She knew what needed to be done, now didn't she?

Ally also knew she had the determination necessary to accomplish her mission. *Got it from dad.* Terry had remarked several times—once even while making love—her eyes might be powder blue, but they were hard as steel. She knew he had meant it as a compliment—Terry liked her tough-girl attitude and mannerisms—especially in contrast to her little-girl pouty facial features. And most of all, he had liked her unabated approach to love making. She smiled, remembering.

For two days now she had followed the "evil woman" from Seattle—and Ally had used every minute of that driving time to think, plan, and plan again—always keeping Jada's blue minivan in sight. She figured her own ubiquitous white Ford was fairly inconspicuous. Still, she was careful.

Ally knew this area; her retired Uncle Phillip lived in Lone Pine. So as soon as Jada headed north, she figured Evil-

Woman would have to stop in Red Rock City. Jada surprised her though by pulling into that dump before the town proper.

When Jada stopped at the Red Rock Inn & Café, Ally slowed, turned off her lights, and pulled over on the highway shoulder—waiting to see what she was going to do.

Dumbfounded, but eventually acquiescent to Jada's inexplicable decision to stay overnight, Ally drove on into the town of Red Rock City where she knew there were several decent hotels. *No matter*, all the better for her, now wasn't it? She knew where to find Jada in the morning.

Ally smiled and patted the revolver on the seat next to her. The touch of cool hard stainless steel was reassuring. Her gun was a Smith and Wesson Special Hogue Bantam .44 with a 3 1/8 inch barrel—she knew its specs and unwieldy name verbatim. She had remarked to Terry at a gun show how she thought it was "cute." He had bought the gun for her on the spot. Soon now, it would be over. The perfect time and place would present itself in the desert to use her cute little Bantam. *Yes*, Jada Beaudine would die in the Mojave.

The rich snooty witch certainly deserved to die. It was because of Jada her Terry had gotten killed—and Terry had been the best thing that had ever happened to Ally. He had been handsome, sexy, smart, and had truly cared about her.

She knew herself to also be sexy-attractive, and considered her perky femininity far superior to "plain-Jane-Jada." It still amazed her how Terry could have ever stayed with a woman like that. Now he was gone, and she would have to be his avenging angel.

"Oh, my darling," she said to his memory. "Don't worry. She'll pay, she'll pay."

Ally patted the gun again, her expertly done blood-red fingernails tapping against its matte grey surface. In line with her intentions, it was fully loaded and ready.

7

Chapter Two

Twixt Night and Day

Lyle Elliott found his meager motel room desk adequate, but hardly comfortable. He was neither surprised nor put out. For he learned a long time ago the physical world was designed to accommodate average sizes, shapes, and proportions—and Lyle was not average in most respects.

He shifted his hefty form around in his chair a bit, trying for an optimum fit of body and furniture.

"At least the seat's padded," he said to his empty room.

Tall, around 6'5" and solidly built, Lyle was often caught off-guard when catching the occasional store window reflection of himself next to a shorter and slighter companion. Not that Lyle didn't know how he looked—physically that is—but he felt he didn't have any real idea of how others viewed him, or his import in the world, either physically or as a person. But when he was working and in disguise, it was so much easier—he knew what others were seeing.

Still, those occasionally snatched and comparative images would invariably bring back memories from his teenage years, his mother Gerty encouraging him. "Tall people are usually successful people," she had liked to say. Her words still rang vividly in his psyche, but Lyle was a middle-aged man now and aware his size was sometimes intimidating—and consequently ineffective in cajoling information from reluctant participants, except by force—which was not his forte or general inclination.

Invariably, Gerty Elliott had always finished her little mother-to-son pep-talks with a kiss on his cheek and the words, "And you're such a handsome boy too."

These days, Lyle did acknowledge he was somewhat handsome, in a craggy experienced-looking way only a man beyond his fiftieth year could be. Yet, handsome or not, he remained unmarried and unattached as time swept him faster and faster into midlife. Gerty blamed her son's perpetual single-state on being "too darned picky."

Tonight, alone and thinking about his mother, Lyle smiled to himself at the irony of this particular circumstance. He would never be able to tell his mother how wrong much of her advice and conclusions had been over the years—or how lonely he now was.

He sighed from tiredness, got up from the desk, walked over to his room's one window, and closed the heavy drapes— his large but perfectly manicured fingers holding them partially open for just a moment to snatch a quick peek of the night. What he saw outside was blackness, what he heard was silence.

Next he unlocked and checked his special overnighter. His employer-issued .38 Smith and Wesson was tucked in safe and sound. Lyle re-locked his case with a sigh. He didn't like carrying the gun—but it was part of the job these days—and Gillian and James Insurance Agency didn't believe in taking chances.

A few hours earlier he had emailed his boss, Hamilton Wolfe. But now at 4:00 A.M. and still unable to fall asleep, he decided he needed a sleeping potion—writing, sans computer. Lyle knew from past experience that putting it to paper would send him off faster than any pill ever could—something to do with the pen to paper ritual that cleared out the synaptic connections and put his brain to rest.

January 6—Early Monday morning
Hand written report to: Hamilton Wolfe

    Following up on my email, I took a room at the Best Western in Red Rock City. I've got a feeling this could be what we've been waiting for. Why else would she detour to this out of the way place if not to connect with Terrence? She was driving by herself all day, then she pulled into a dump of a motel off the highway that's at least 10 miles outside of town. I'm guessing they picked it because the place is so run down and isolated. There's not going to be much traffic moving through there. Little chance of being noticed.

    I almost lost her once. You know how we discussed I should hang back, not risk being spotted? And of course I was in disguise. I thought for sure she'd be heading to Barstow on 58 out of Tehachapi, but then for no reason she headed north up to a place called Lake Isabella. The roads were crap, let me tell you, Ham, and I thought she caught sight of me on a couple of the curves and was trying to lose me, but now that she's stopped at this Red Rock Inn joint I think she was just killing time going to Isabella, because she didn't stop, just headed north up I-14, probably wanting to pull in after dark.

Lyle didn't mention the white Ford he'd seen a couple times. On that, he'd just wait and see.

Chapter Three

Monday

Someone was banging hard on cabin number-two's door. Her door.

Jada's waking thoughts were scattered, and she could only guess at the time. She could, however, see the sun rising above the horizon through a small window by her bed. The window was hazy-white from age, and bent, dingy yellow blinds hung crookedly in its frame. But neither the haze nor the blinds were adequate to keep the sun from angling straight in on her face. Surprising she wasn't already awake.

The knocking continued, more insistent now, forcing her into full consciousness. Her sleep had been uneven anyway, fitful and spotty. *I need to wake up and deal with this.*

"Who is it?" she called out petulantly. Morning had arrived far too soon, and immensely brighter than expected. In fact, she couldn't remember a morning sunlight ever assaulting her like this in Washington. More often it had been the sound of rain on her windows welcoming her to a new day.

No one responded—just more knocking. Resignedly she rolled out of bed, a squeaky ancient wire—spring contraption she had gratefully welcomed last night. A pain shot through her lower back, causing her now to curse the bed's lumps, bumps, and noisiness.

"How could I have been so stupid to stop here?" She rubbed her also-aching neck. Then she tested the worn linoleum floor with one toe and found it stone-cold. "What a god-awful dump." *No one to blame but myself.*

The knocking stopped as she reached the door, and Jada looked for a peephole to see who was there. Then she remembered where she had landed and quickly adjusted her expectations back about sixty years. There would be no peepholes in the doors at the Red Rock Inn.

She opened the ill-fitting door a sliver. Irina Hughes, the woman she'd met last night, stood before Jada, her large green eyes again strangely luminescent, even in daylight—and wide with shock. Or, was it fear Jada thought she saw?

"I need your help, Mrs. Beaudine." In contrast to her rambunctious door pounding, Irina spoke almost in a whisper.

"Ms. Hughes?"

"Please," Irina implored. "Can you come with me? And it's 'Rina.'"

Jada couldn't fathom why a woman she had barely met the night before thought she needed her help. And what did this strange woman need her help *with*? Cooking at the café? Pumping gas for goodness sakes?

Oh yes, and why was there sand on the floor underneath her door? *This is ridiculous.*

Despite all her questions and doubts, Jada nonetheless said, "Hang on a bit. You can come in while I get dressed." She had slept in most of her clothes and only needed to put on socks and shoes. So fatigued the previous night, she'd left her toiletry bag in the minivan before stumbling into the room, finding the bathroom, checking the sheets were clean, and making a barely coherent call to her sister-in-law, Solina Beaudine Chambers, in Atlanta. Then she had fallen into bed. Now, Jada wished mightily for her toothbrush and toothpaste.

"I know you think it's strange I've come to you." Irina stepped in and stood just inside Jada's cabin door. Like last night, she was dressed in a long sleeve shirt and overalls, faded and oversized, topped with a jean jacket. She hugged herself tightly, an identical jacket slung over one arm. "I was just BS'n you last night with that psychic crap. Actually I recognized you."

Caught off guard for a second, Jada caught her breath, but quickly regained her composure. Fortunately her back was to Irina. *Damn.*

"You know," Irina continued, her tone less assured. "Your recent tragedy, and before that, those murders and stuff. You were on all the networks. And cable too."

Jada turned and stared at Irina, long and hard, giving herself time not to respond with her characteristic knee-jerk anger. This move was supposed to be about change. Her world, and herself. Indeed, this woman was a stranger. How could she know how crappy this last year had been? How tired she was of being recognized, stared at, whispered about.

"You must be mistaken," Jada lied. "But I'll come with you anyway."

"Thanks." Irina handed her the jacket she was carrying. "It's still cold out."

Once faced with chilly desert air, Jada gratefully put the jacket on. In full morning light, what had seemed mysterious and ominous the previous night, now merely looked ramshackle and seedy. The buildings were faded pink stucco, sand dirty in spots, and in much need of repair. In addition to the office-café building near the two pumps, there were eight to ten one room cabin "things" appearing to have been haphazardly dropped from the sky, landing where they would around the place. Her cabin, number-two, was near the rear of the café building.

This gathering of rag-tag dwellings—isolated and rundown—fronted the highway and formed a dejected little cluster on the way to somewhere else. *For sure, somewhere else for me. Atlanta and the bosom of Terry's relatives.*

As Jada hurried to keep pace with Irina's short, quick strides—and even underneath the protection of a jacket—she shivered from the chilly morning air and the psychological impact of the desolate landscape surrounding her. They were headed toward the rear of the property, out into flat open desert—except for one incongruous flat-topped bump of a hill maybe a mile to the west—with the Sierras, now gray in morning light, providing a distant yet dramatic end-of-the-earth demarcation. And all Jada could see to her side and rear were miles and miles of tract-less desert, pockmarked with sagebrush and creosote bushes—with a few surprisingly elegant Joshua Trees to remind the viewer of Mother Nature's tenacity and durability. *You could disappear out there and no one would ever find you.*

The mountains did have an evocative charm, and for sure the air smelled pleasantly poignant and fresh. But why oh why would anyone want to live in such a god-forsaken place? Evidently, Irina Hughes did.

The terrain below her feet consisted of dirt, sand, dirt, dead sagebrush, dirt, "sticker bugs," dirt, and more sand. Jada stumbled several times, stirring up whirls of dust around her feet and causing her to further bemoan getting caught up in this insanity. Still, she followed, even as they walked farther away from the main group of buildings. *Out into no-man's land.*

Finally, about fifty feet ahead, two structures appeared she had not been able to see from the road last night, or from her cabin this morning. One was a small tower-shaped building, leaning a bit, but in fairly good condition. As they walked around the structure, Jada could see front and rear doors and large windows on the sides of the tower. The other building was a sizable one-story octagon, and the two buildings were connected by a long covered walkway. There was also a small parking lot in front of the octagon accessed by a dirt road coming from...Jada had no idea where.

This morning there were two cars in the lot, a newer model white Ford truck and a blue Toyota sedan.

Irina headed to the back door of the mini-tower, then when inches away, hesitated for a second, took a quick look to make sure Jada was still with her, squared her shoulders and resolutely entered the building.

Jada followed close behind, and at the door, even before she entered, she sensed a familiarity of some kind; and once inside she immediately recognized the feel and smell of closed-in humidity and damp clay. *A ceramic studio? Weird.* Well, an intriguing coincidence at the least. She stopped, then stepped to the side of the door opening, out of the sun streaming in from behind, and squinted into the dimness ahead. Slowly her eyes adjusted and she could make out bags of clay and shelves lined with pottery in the making.

Then she saw him—slumped over his pottery wheel, his head turned sideways and smashed into a large cylinder he had been throwing. It looked like he had been shot in the head through the eye now buried in clay, and a single stream of dried blood ran down the side of his nose. The back of his skull where the bullet had exited was shattered, ugly, bloody. Jada wanted to turn away. But she didn't, couldn't.

From the part of his face she could see, he had been a handsome man in a pretty-boy sort of way with dark brown hair. He also looked to be thin in build. She guessed his age maybe around forty-five or so. He was dressed in jeans, blue work shirt, and was sock-less in aged brown loafers. One of his hands rested on the wheel surface—his long thin fingers—now still covered with drying clay.

Jada sighed sadly for the dead man, and wondered what this stranger had been doing and thinking when the bullet hit. Had he been pulling his cylinder up, imagining what great vessel it would become, ignorant his time was over? Or, had he looked up in time to recognize his killer—lock eyes—and in horror, seen his end?

A long moment later she forced her gaze away from the dead man's face, abruptly turned around and left the studio.

Back out in cool dry air, she took a couple deep breaths to re-orient herself and squelch resurfacing memories of that ghastly night the authorities had come to tell her Terry was dead. Her husband of fifteen years gone—her world destroyed in seconds. Revisiting death, be it stranger or beloved, was not something Jada wanted to deal with. *No*, this trip was to move forward, not go backward.

Irina Hughes came out of the studio and stood next to her. "I can't believe he's gone." Her voice was clear, but obviously upset. "Nick was a perfect man, you know."

What an odd way to describe him. "We need to call the police," Jada said. Not comforting words, but what else could she say or do?

"I already did."

"And then you came to get me?"

"Yes."

"Why?"

Irina sighed sadly. "I wanted you to see what I saw. Before anything changed."

She echoed Irina's sigh with one of her own. "I guess I'll have to stay until the police come." In the background Jada heard a woman's laugh from the direction of the octagon building. Ignoring this sound of life beyond her own space and moment, she turned to Irina and added, "Then I'll be checking out." She started walking back toward her cabin. *I need to get the hell out of here.*

"Please..."

Jada barely heard Irina, but she stopped, waited, and rubbed her forehead, trying to forestall a headache in the making. It was incomprehensible how this could be happening again.

Murder that is—intrusive and unwelcome.

Irina took a step forward toward Jada's back. "I *do* know who you are. I read all about you in the newspapers, followed everything about your husband."

Jada stood still, and when she didn't move or answer, Irina was evidently emboldened by her silence.

"And I was intrigued by what happened to your husband." Irina quickly cleared her throat. "And then the other stuff—murders—right? And you're a potter too, right? And the money..."

Jada turned and faced the woman she perceived as callously trying to invade her life, her mind, her emotions. "And because you read about me in the newspapers you think it gives you the right to involve me in..." Jada was at a loss there, not knowing what was going on. So she waved her hand in a sweeping angry gesture. "All this?"

Irina looked appropriately taken aback, but held her ground. "I know I'm assuming—"

The sound of ear piercing wails—approaching sirens— instantly changed the moment and brought a man and a woman out of the octagon building. Jada saw curiosity, but no real concern in their faces. In fact, both were smiling and exchanging comments, seemingly unaware the bell was tolling for their little slice of the world. *Don't they know there's a friggin' dead man less than one-hundred feet from them?*

"Early birds for Nick's class," Irina explained. "Corissa McNichols-James and Hal Morton. I better let them know what's going on."

Jada desperately wanted to run to her cabin, toss her stuff in the car, and high-tail it to Atlanta before anyone could stop her. Instead, and yet again, she followed along behind Irina as she headed toward the man and woman. She could feel a mild wind brushing her cheeks and see small swirls of sand dancing around her. A storm to come? Or the status quo in this god-forsaken dustbowl?

"What's up, Rina?" Hal Morton called out as they approached. He was trim with white hair, salt-and-pepper mustache, and deeply creased skin. Jada thought he had an interesting face with a touch of cunning playing in his eyes. Maybe five-ten or so, maybe in his sixties, dressed in slacks, shirt, and a shop apron, he was absently sanding a small clay figurine. She thought sanding unfired pottery was a bad thing, but in this dustbowl, what the hell?

"Do you hear those sirens?" Hal looked toward the road. "Coming this way I think."

"Nick's dead," Irina announced without ceremony. "Don't go near his studio."

Jada was surprised at Irina's apparent lack of sensitivity in breaking the news of Nick's murder. Then momentarily mesmerized, she watched as Hal let go his small statue—an angel it looked like—as it fell through the air, seemingly in exaggerated slow-motion, before shattering into pieces on faded patio flagstone below their feet.

"Sorry, guess I should have been gentler," Irina apologized in a tone that said she was anything but sorry.

She does not like this man. Jada figured Hal must also sense Irina's distaste.

Hal, however, seemingly had not taken offense. "You're kidding, right?" He tilted his head and peered into Irina's eyes, as if searching for assurance she was not making some kind of sick joke. Jada recognized his reaction and knew the feeling first hand. Time had not blurred her memory of that moment over a year ago when the policeman's words just hadn't made any sense.

Corissa, drying her hands with a paper towel, stepped forward, closer within earshot of Hal and Irina, and direct eyesight of Jada. "What's happened?' She looked down at the scattered pieces of Hal's statue. "Something bad has happened, hasn't it?" Corissa's words were demanding, but her voice was weak, hesitant, nervous. She was young, an oval-faced brunette, with large dark-brown expressive eyes. *Cute,* Jada thought. Almost pretty, but just missing the mark.

The sirens were getting louder.

"Yes, something has happened to Nick," Hal said turning to Corissa. "Cori." He put his hand on the young woman's shoulder. "Rina says Nick is dead." He said it like he still couldn't believe it himself.

The sirens came to an abrupt stop. Jada looked toward the approaching flashing lights and saw a patrol car moving fast toward them, creating a whirlwind in its wake of spitted gravel and sand. An ambulance followed, barely visible in the dust.

"But that's crazy," Corissa said. "When did it happen? Not this morning? Couldn't be."

Jada stepped forward next to Irina and looked at the young woman. "Why?"

"Because Hal and I have been here together. Right, Hal? We would have seen, or heard..." She stopped talking and stared at Jada, curiosity and apprehension overtaking her expression.

Jada was about to introduce herself, but thought better of it. Waste of time. She would be moving on to Atlanta before nightfall. *Besides, the "Mounties" have arrived.* She almost smiled in response to the incongruous picture her flippant thought had conjured up—Canadian Mounties in full-dress uniforms charging across the desert on horses, for goodness sakes. But *no,* this wasn't a smiling occasion.

Red Rock City's Chief of Police Josia Rhodes stood five-eleven, was solidly built with rugged features—which Jada knew would be considered attractive by some—and had a great voice, deep and resonant. Nonetheless, Jada didn't like him from the start. She also had a niggling feeling she had seen him somewhere before. *But that's impossible.*

As to the source of her immediate aversion, Jada guessed something about his body language—which she saw as an arrogant swagger—had immediately put her on the defensive. And coming out of the year she'd just experienced, a year peppered with unfriendly cops, reporters, and investigators, it would have been hard for anyone in those occupations to win with her. *Bad timing for him, but I can't help how I feel.*

His initial actions deepened her antipathy. For it was not until *after* he and the medical examiner Doctor Beach took an initial look; and not until *after* he called into Bakersfield for the loan of a full forensics team; and not until *after* he sent the ambulance on back to Red Rock City; that Josia finally allowed her little group to step inside—out of the sun and rising temperature—and into the cool ceramics lab. Even that concession, he unabashedly explained, was "So *I* can get the events straight."

While all this was going on, Jada waited, watched, waited some more—and fumed. The man was not only arrogant, but also high-handed and rude. Besides, it was after 9:00 A.M., she hadn't had breakfast, not even a cup of tea. She toyed with telling him to go straight to hell right off, but like a good little schoolgirl, she buckled up, and when permitted, marched into the lab with the others and took a seat on a stool at a worktable near the entrance door.

A quick glance around the facility favorably surprised her. The lab was well equipped—ten or so electric pottery wheels, a slab roller, an extruder, a pug-mill, lots of windows— and two lovely large skylights nestled in an open post-and-beam octagon ceiling. Who would have thought? Out here at the end of the earth. Indeed, despite the circumstances, and despite her immediate aversion to Josia, it felt rather "nice" being in such a place. Fleetingly, she wished she had met the man who had created such a space.

As soon as their little "suspect" group arranged themselves on stools around the table, Josia—surveying the room from the door—asked, "What is this place, Rina? And who is the corpse I've got on my hands in that tower building? All these years and I didn't even know you had either of these buildings back here."

"You don't remember Nick?" Irina's tone was sharp, accusatory. "He started the lab and classes almost as soon as he rented number-ten for his studio. You *should* remember. I even sent you and Helen a flyer about the classes."

"Oh yeah," he admitted, seemingly unperturbed. "Forgot. Wasn't Mother in one of his first classes? And there was some claptrap about all the women liking him—some kind of 'perfect guy?'" His facial expression clearly showed what he thought of that concept.

Irina didn't respond, but Jada was positive her eyes watered from anger, or grief, or both, and she figured Irina was barely holding back some choice words. *Well, good.* Hopefully she would tell the arrogant butt off.

Another officer entered the lab—pleasant faced, shorter, younger, and not as road-weary or swaggering in his demeanor as Josia. "Ms. Hughes," he nodded to Irina.

"Come on in, Gabe," Josia said. "Got your pad?"

"Yes, Sir." Eagerly the young man pulled up a stool next to Irina, whipped open his notepad, and poised his pencil. His features were well defined, sharp, yet baby-faced, and his hair was cut even shorter than her own in a military "buzz cut."

We look like a scene straight out of a forties movie, Jada mused. *Black and white, of course. And if you ignore the hair styles.* Her anger had subsided an iota or two. Maybe she could get through this.

Unfortunately Josia abruptly turned directly to her. "Okay, who are you?"

"My name is Jada Beaudine, Mrs." She heard her voice sounding calm and steady. *Good so far.*

"Great, Mrs. Beaudine. Now I've got your name, but *who* are you? And why are you here?"

"Excuse me?" *Not so good.*

"Look, nobody stays here unless they're crazy." He shot a quick and meaningful look in Irina's direction. "I've got a dead body and I see a nice new mini-van in the parking lot with Washington plates, and here sits a woman I don't know, so I have to ask questions." Then he smiled, big and toothy. "You understand, I'm sure."

Without forethought, Jada leapt right into telling Josia—whom she was now sure was an arrogant SOB—what she thought of his interrogation methods. "I don't have to tell—"

Irina quickly cut her off, "Si, *I* asked Mrs. Beaudine to stay. And *I* asked her to come see Nick's body this morning. She's an innocent stranger."

Jada interpreted the look Josia bestowed upon her as containing equal portions of disbelief and disappointment their little test of wills was over. *Only round one, Chief Rhodes, only round one.*

Whatever *his* inward thoughts, Josia shrugged and moved on. "Okay then, Rina, you tell me what you know. Gabe? You getting all this?"

"Yes sir."

Irina straightened herself in her chair and stared directly at Josia. "I get up early every morning," she said. "You might remember that's my habit, might not. This time of year it's starting to lighten up around six-thirty or so. I always take a morning walk as soon as I can see well enough to walk back in the flats." She looked away for a moment, up toward the ceiling, as if collecting her thoughts. "You might also remember that, or might not. First though, I went over and opened up the café and started getting stuff ready for Manny to do breakfast. I was going to cook for Mrs. Beaudine myself, make her some coffee at least, maybe some eggs. Manny hadn't come over to the café yet..." She cleared her throat and shifted on her stool. "After I got everything prepared to cook I went walking out back. I remember thinking how I was going to have to do something about that dog that's been hanging around, build a dog house, or something, when I noticed the light was on in Nick's tower. Then I remembered this was a class morning, and I thought I'd stop by and say hi, and..." She wiped away a solitary escaping tear. "I stopped, the back door was open, and there he was, there he was." More tears materialized and Irina wiped her eyes with the back of her hand.

Jada dug in her pockets looking for Kleenex then remembered it wasn't her jacket. Her right hand, however, found a folded piece of paper stuck in Irina's jacket pocket. Intuition stopped her from pulling it out. *Not now.*

"Fond of this guy, Rina?" Josia asked.

It sounded to Jada like he was asking a question he already knew the answer to. Maybe she was reaching, but she guessed Irina and Josia had a significant shared past.

Irina took her time to fully re-compose herself, turning her gaze out the window toward the parking lot. "Nick was a nice guy, that's all. Everyone liked him."

"Did you touch anything?"

"No. I wanted to, but I realized when I saw the hole in his head, and the blood that..."

Corissa caught her breath audibly. "He was shot?" she whispered.

Some emotion in Corissa's voice caught Jada's attention and made her wonder at the young woman's sincerity. She couldn't, however, put her finger on what she had sensed.

Hal cleared his throat. "I think Cori and I are thinking the same thing. We didn't hear anything this morning, and we were here." He looked directly into Corissa's eyes for confirmation. "What would you say, around seven?"

"You both arrived together?" Josia was now walking back and forth, forcing all of them to move their heads to keep up with him.

Hal again spoke for Corissa and himself, "Yes."

"Are those your cars over there?" Josia motioned out toward the parking lot. "The truck?" He looked to Hal.

Corissa said, "That's mine, Chief Rhodes."

"Both of you live in the area?"

They nodded.

"Make sure you leave your address info with Gabe." Then returning to Jada, he asked, "You hear anything?"

"No I didn't," she answered politely.

"Are you sure? What woke you up so early if you didn't hear anything?"

"Ms. Hughes woke me." Jada took a slow deep breath, a temper-control technique she acquired during the dark times after Terry's death. "Are you calling me a liar?" she asked sweetly with a forced smile. Underneath, she felt ready to pounce if pushed another millimeter.

"Now don't go getting upset. Just doing my job, Mrs. Beaudine." Josia was evidently intuitive enough to back off for the moment, and turned his attention back to Corissa and Hal. "Almost forgot, what were you two doing here so early?"

"We started getting our stuff together. Class seems to go by so fast." Again it was Hal speaking, both for himself and Corissa.

"What *exactly* did you do when you got here?"

"Well," Hal said. "I went and got my dry figurines to sand and Cori washed her hands and got started wedging clay."

An automobile could be heard approaching outside with the accompanying sound of tires again crunching gravel. Irina stood up and walked over to the window. "More students are arriving."

"Gabe," Josia directed. "Go outside, will ya? Get those folk's names and addresses and some quickie prelim statements if you can. Then send them home."

Gabe eagerly hopped to it.

Josia's cell phone rang. He answered, and while listening, gave Jada several curious looks. Then he rung off without ceremony or comment to the caller.

She held her breath. *It's starting again.*

"Mrs. Beaudine," he said. "Could you stop by my office in town in a couple hours? We're near the Post Office. I'm sure Rina can give you directions."

Jada knew this was an order, not a request, but she was not prepared for a full out battle. Not yet.

"Sure," she answered casually. *And it's only 10:00 A.M.*

Later, back in cabin number-two, Jada pulled out the note in Irina's jacket pocket and unashamedly read it. Handwritten in big childish scroll, it read, *Meet me at dawn tomorrow. I need you. Nick.* She stuffed the note back from whence it had come and flopped backward onto her unmade and squeaky bed.

"Maid service at the Red Rock sucks," she informed the water-stained ceiling.

27

Even though she was making every effort to stay calm, her brain hurt and she could feel acid building in her stomach. If she could just take a little nap, but Jada doubted she would be able to drop off. Not after seeing that dead man and having to deal with Josia Rhodes.

But she had to do *something* to keep her mind distracted until she had to talk to the SOB again. At least two hours to kill. She sat back up on the edge of her bed, causing the springs to again sing their irritating off-key tune.

TV? There was a small one on a rolling cart, with a remote control, no less—and it was color. When she gave it a try, however, reception was atrocious—the static and "snow" taking her for a moment back to a childhood time sitting in front of the family's first set—Jada quite proudly having the job of moving and turning the rabbit ears. Eons ago.

What the hell. The crappy TV didn't make any difference anyway. Her plans definitely did not include another night in this wretched place. But then her attention was caught by someone, or something scratching on the door. *Coyote? No, not in the middle of the day? Rat? Oh Christ.*

Fortunately, next came a real live knock followed by, "Can I come in? It's Rina."

"Sure. It's open." What other option did she have? She hadn't yet figured out how to make the knob-lock work, and there wasn't a bolt.

As Irina entered, Jada watched in amazement as more sand blew in, followed by a scroungey-looking black dog that charged into the room, jumped up on the bed next to Jada, then put its head down complacently on her lap while simultaneously thumping its tail.

"What the...?" Jada was more startled than scared.

"I wondered who she was waiting for," Irina said.

"I've never seen this dog before in my life." The dog weighed about sixty pounds, and on closer look was relatively clean and recently trimmed.

"You're connected somehow. She's been coming here every morning for a week now." Unasked, Irina sat down in the one scarred and scratched wooden chair. "I've tried to get her to come into my cabin, tried tempting her with hot-dogs. But she'd only hang around outside the café, waiting, watching. I did manage to give her a bath with a hose, and cut some of that hair. I even got her in the car and to the vet." Irina took a quick breath. "The vet said she's about three, been fixed, no major problems she could find. Gave her shots. She's got funny black spots on her tongue." She smiled with fondness. "Her eyes are great aren't they?"

"Must be part chow," Jada found herself saying. "Her eyes *are* nice, and gentle." She rubbed the dog's head. "Soft fur."

"Can we talk?" Irina pulled her chair closer to the bed. "I owe you some explanations."

Now that's an understatement. "I'm all ears." Jada was curious as to what she had on her mind and took a couple seconds for a more considered look at the woman. Irina's face was long and rather austere, and her eyes were really quite penetrating. They were intelligent eyes—but were they also trustworthy?

"I didn't mean to offend you this morning," Irina said. "But I do feel like I know you. Pictures of you and your husband were in the paper almost every day." She finally dropped her eyes, releasing Jada from her intense scrutiny. "I know you said I was mistaken. And I understand you probably have gotten tired of people bothering you."

But you still think you can intrude into my life like this? Jada forced a polite smile, and waited.

"I'm sorry for your loss. I should have said that earlier."

"Thank you."

"Anyway," Irina continued. "I was intrigued by what had happened, then later by you specifically. I've read a lot of mysteries." She said the last little bit like it should explain a lot about her behavior.

Alright, she did have a modicum of sympathy with the fascination Irina was trying to justify. "In real life," Jada candidly admitted, "murder isn't an intellectual exercise. I've read my share of mysteries too." She took a deep breath and shook her head. "But *death,* the real kind, not the literary kind," she sighed, "especially when it's violent and bloody, is horrid and sickening. Dead bodies..." Jada again saw Nick, drooped over his pottery wheel, a life gone, just like that. He'd gotten up that morning, like any other morning, expecting life as usual. "...aren't nice," she inadequately concluded. Looking back at Irina's face she saw tears.

"Nick was..." Irina started, but couldn't finish.

Jada remembered her earlier words. "A perfect man?"

Irina composed herself through a deep breath, then a hearty nose blow. "Sounds silly when you say it."

Jada scooted back on the bed, leaning her back against its rickety headboard. The dog again put her head on Jada's lap like she had known her new friend all her doggy life. "So tell me about Nick. Like, who was he, why was he here?"

"I'll try," Irina said resolutely. "But first, I need to finish explaining why the hell I came to get you this morning. I think I knew last night when you pulled in there was a cosmic reason for you to stop here." She smiled wryly for a second. "Christsakes, look around, I'm not exactly running a spa here. Then this morning when I found Nick, I knew you were here for a reason."

Jada was finding the essence of Irina illusive. What with her rough "country western" style and sometimes gritty language—juxtaposed with a shyness usually reserved for girl-next-door-types—and throwing in her reluctant mystic connection to the cosmos—Jada didn't have a neat little box to tuck this woman into.

"I met Nick about three years ago," Irina said. He came around looking for a studio away from home. He lives in Red Rock City. He's got a wife, Darcie, and two kids, a boy and a girl. Said he couldn't afford much, but then he proposed he use the tower shed as his studio and give classes in the old octagon." She stopped for a breath and looked out through the cabin's hazy front window. "He even said he'd build a connecting covered walkway for free and split the class fees with me." She shrugged. "It sounded great, anything to get some work done on this place." A flicker of a smile crossed her face even though her eyes were still teary. "So I said sure, what the hell, isn't like I'd be giving up anything. Besides, he cleaned up the whole place, set up tables and shelves, got second hand wheels on ebay."

"Whoa," Jada interrupted. "You have cable or satellite here?"

"Hell no. Phone line." Irina managed a real smile. "The class thing worked right from the start. We had five for the first class, and the numbers have held around five to eight showing up every class. Not everyone comes every session, but there's never been less than three or four."

"How often is class?"

"Once a week, every Monday morning. Then there's open lab Tuesday through Thursday from nine until noon. And Nick's there…was there…to answer questions."

"So," Jada looked up at the ceiling as she spoke. "Nick worked in his own studio whenever he wanted, then was in the octagon building Monday through Thursday for about three or four hours a day?"

"Yeah." Irina smiled. "He said if you didn't treat doing pottery as a full time job you were just fooling around and not a serious artist."

Hogwash, Jada thought. She had known a lot of excellent potters who didn't have the luxury of potting full time, but she held her opinion to herself. "Hmm. What's his last name by the way?" *Had Josia asked?* She couldn't remember.

"Williams. Nick Williams."

Irina said his name with such apparent fondness, Jada went with a hunch. "You were having an affair with him."

Irina inhaled sharply. "I *did*." Then she was silent for a long moment. "Hell," she eventually continued, "it was over soon after it started. But how did you know?" Before Jada could reply, she said, "I guess it's obvious. And that's what I'm afraid of—Si's gonna figure out real soon Nick and I had something going."

Jada pulled out the note she found and handed it to Irina. "This was in your jacket pocket. I read it."

"Damn it." She sighed with irritation. "Si's gonna think I killed him. I know it. Shi—" Irina caught herself mid- profanity. "Dang it." She got up, walked over to the window by the front door, pulled back a faded piece of green and red plaid cotton curtain, and stared outside. "I broke it off with Nick a couple months ago. I have no idea why he sent me this note."

Jada asked quietly, "Why did you break up?"

Irina turned back and looked at Jada straight on, green eyes now puffy from held-back tears and pleading to be believed and understood. "I couldn't stand the thought of his wife. What he was doing to her. And the kids."

The dog had gone to sleep and was snoring lightly. Irina went on, her voice cracking. "I also found out I wasn't the first, and I figured I wouldn't be the last. Hell, I wasn't even the *only* current. Not so perfect after all." Regaining control, she added, "But, Nick didn't deserve to die. Especially not like that."

"Do you know who else he was fooling around with?"

"No. Don't think so." Irina sniffed and swiped at her nose with her jacket sleeve.

Jada didn't press her, though she was sure Irina did *know*. "Did you notice how nervous Corissa seemed? What's going on with her?"

Irina seemed glad for the change in subject. "I don't know her well, but she's shy, kind of unsure of herself. She's young."

"Too timid and too young to have an affair with Nick Williams?"

Irina smiled slightly, then "tsk-tsked" out the side of her mouth and shook her head. "I knew you'd be good at this. Will you help me, Mrs. Beaudine?" She gave Jada the full force of her bewitching green-eyed gaze. "I didn't kill Nick. But I know as soon as Si starts digging I'm gonna be his number one suspect."

Ignoring her request for help, Jada asked, "How do I get to Red Rock City? I have a date with the Police Chief."

"It's only about twelve miles—" Irina was interrupted by a knock on the door. "Come in," she called out.

Jada cleared her throat loudly and shot a meaningful glance Irina's way. *For Pete's sake, this is my cabin.* The dog lifted her head and twitched her nostrils.

"Ms. Hughes, Rina," said a soft male voice with a toff English accent. "It's Hilary Giles. From class."

"Oh." Irina quickly opened the door. "Hilary, come in."

"I don't want to disturb." Cautiously, Hilary peered into the cabin, then evidently deciding propriety dictated he remain on the stoop, did not enter. "Manny said I might find you here," he explained. "He also said it would be suitable if I came around. I was late for class, but there are police at the lab, and an ambulance, and the studio is locked, and there's yellow tape."

"I'm sorry," Irina said. "You haven't heard yet, right?" Her tone was gentle, protective.

"Heard what?"

Jada felt foolish and awkward just sitting there listening, so she got up and walked over to the door, hoping to introduce

33

herself and get a better look at Hilary Giles. What she saw was a slight man, older than she had expected from his voice, dressed in a casual shirt, slacks, and slip-on loafers. Hilary also had hollow dead eyes, sunken into a very sorrowful countenance, and Jada was caught unawares by the emotion his face conveyed. Immense sadness.

"Hilary," Irina said, in a much more compassionate voice than she had used with Hal. "Nick is dead."

"Mr. Williams is dead? No, Ms. Hughes, quite impossible. Not for a man of his age. He never mentioned any serious ailments."

"He was murdered."

Jada didn't want to hear or see anymore. She did wonder what a fragile-looking English gent was doing out in the middle of the Mojave. Nonetheless, she hurriedly grabbed her canvas bag and left Irina and Hilary in the doorway of her cabin, teary-eyed and consoling each other.

Within moments, she was off to Red Rock City to see Josia Rhodes. Maybe the dog would be gone when she got back? *More likely*, she thought, the mutt would be fast asleep in the middle of a still unmade bed.

"Come in, Mrs. Beaudine, do come in. I've been expecting you. I'm Madge Lee, Si's mother." She was wearing East-Indian sandals, a floor length skirt made out of crinkled red material, an oversized hand painted cotton shirt, and an infectious smile Jada found hard to resist.

Jada couldn't help but return the woman's smile and step into Madge Lee's world. Madge Lee's other personal adornments included a Native-American design beaded headband, long silver and jade earrings, and a gaggle of rings — gathered, perched, and nesting on all her fingers. Atop all this confusion of colors and styles, wisps of soft curly gray hair escaped in a crown fashion from underneath her headband.

She spoke with precise pronunciation, and Jada thought she detected the remnants of yet another English accent, this time very mild. "Si is not in at the moment." She took Jada's hands affectionately. "But please, come in. I don't bite." Then with a quirky tilt of her head and a pleasingly amused smile, Madge Lee added, "What an interesting face you have. I have sandwiches and tea prepared. Scones and cookies also."

Dogs were barking somewhere on the property.

Jada was starved; she still hadn't eaten breakfast. *Okay, okay, I'll play along with this nutty woman for a bit.* She followed Madge Lee through the foyer of a two- story geodesic dome, the enticing aroma of freshly brewed tea and bakery goods leading the way.

"I suppose Gabe gave you directions here?" She gracefully ushered Jada into a large open room, the main part of the dome. The center ceiling ridges seemed at least thirty feet high.

"Yes he did." Indeed, Deputy Gabe Spriggs had been waiting for Jada at the Red Rock City Police office with a "request" from Josia. Quoting, "Could you please meet me at my home?" he had repeated Josia's words with care. "And, sorry for the inconvenience, but police business, you know."

Jada knew she was being taken advantage of. Still, she had thought it wise to stay on the good side of the law long enough to get out of town. Hard—considering Josia's personality—but probably worth the effort. Consequently, she drove out to his house, carefully following Gabe's directions—"Go five miles north of Kern on 395 then west about ten miles down a dirt road. Then make a left by the large Joshua tree, a right by the brick fireplace ruins." All the while, Jada found the terrain alien to her aesthetic, and the isolation downright scary. *No man's land.*

Having survived Gabe's directions, and now standing in Josia and Madge Lee's home, she had to admit this unusual woman and her obnoxious son had built a spiffy place, wherever the heck in the Mojave they were.

Madge Lee continued to make a big deal of getting her comfortable; and in return, Jada acquiesced. In a way, it was nice being fussed over, and Madge Lee wasn't that bad, even if she was related to the Police Chief, and helped him lure unsuspecting strangers into their lair. The two women ended up sitting at a modern wrought- iron and glass table in a cozy little breakfast nook corner off a sparkling modern kitchen that was brightly lit from skylights. And several sets of French doors brought in additional light from a garden area. The round glass tabletop between them was covered with scrumptious-looking goodies.

While Madge Lee did the honors, pouring tea and serving sandwiches and little iced cakes, Jada was content to let her play the gracious host while she enjoyed the feast, quietly British in its selection and presentation. She could hold her curiosity at bay a little longer.

Eventually, several cups of tea and numerous sandwiches and *petit-fours* later, Madge Lee finally explained in rather quick order how she and "Mr. Rhodes," as she called Josia's father, had met at the new Heathrow airport at the end of World War II, how it had been love at first sight, how she had followed him to Chicago, then to San Francisco, then finally to Red Rock City where he had worked for over twenty-five years as a research scientist at the naval base in town.

"Mr. Rhodes, my dear, died three years back."

"Lee" was her maiden name, and Mr. Rhodes, contrary to the conventions of the fifties, had called her Madge Lee all through their marriage and she wasn't about to change now — even though her son still thought it the proper thing to do.

Jada found Madge Lee lively, emphatic in her pronouncements, physically demonstrative, and warm in her interactions. All in all, extremely likable. She was even beginning to enjoy her visit until Madge Lee got to the reason why Jada was now sitting in her home and genteelly sipping English breakfast tea imported from Harrods of London.

Josia, in his quest for truth, had run her plates and license, talked to a buddy back in Seattle, and asked his pal on the *Red Rock Tribune* to pull up some back articles. Result—Josia knew much more about her than she would have wished. The topper though, and what galled Jada the most, was Josia's outlandish and unprofessional tactic of asking his mother to size her up.

"Now, Mrs. Beaudine," Madge Lee said refilling their china tea cups. "Don't think too badly of Josia. There's a very good reason why he wanted us to talk. He fancies I'm a bit psychic." She raised her hands in mock surrender. "I helped in a couple cases, and now—"

Jada couldn't hold back any longer, no matter how delightful Josia's mother was. "And exactly what are you supposed to 'psyche' out?" she asked. "Whether or not I killed a man I never met before?" The harshness of her own tone surprised Jada.

She wanted to be reasonable—it wasn't Madge Lee's fault her son had grown up to be a jerk—and her own flashes of anger were terribly revealing, telling others much more about herself than Jada wanted. *I'm supposed to be changing.* But the nerve of these people.

Still, she didn't mean to hurt Madge Lee so she attempted a half-hearted apology, "I'm sorry, Mrs. Rhodes—I mean Ms. Lee—it's just that...." How could she explain what the last year had been like, how tired she was of the constant scrutiny?

"It's just that you're sick of living public," Madge Lee said as if she had known Jada all her life. "Feeling like you're always on a stage, feeling like everyone is viewing you skeptically, while you just want to be anonymous…want to turn the clock back."

"Yes." Jada was not about to go through the horrors of the last year with a stranger, no matter how likable. But yes, she would be civil.

Madge Lee cleared her throat and said brightly, "Well, I know you'll find it hard to forgive Josia, but I'm sure you will eventually. You have a kind heart, I can tell. And he means well, he really does." She edged a silver platter of goodies closer to Jada. "More cookies?"

It was a nice spot where they sat, with the French doors opening onto the deck and garden area where two German Shepherds, who had at first put up a big fuss on seeing a stranger in their home, were now laying down quietly in the shade. Under other circumstances Jada would have been quite comfortable. But with the murder and Josia nosing around, she couldn't completely shake off her emotional tiredness and anger.

"Are you really psychic?" Not that she really cared, just wanted to move the conversation on.

"Well," Madge Lee demurred. "Maybe, maybe not. Now, Rina, that sweet lady, has a real gift. She doesn't think so, pooh-poohs me whenever I say it. But she does."

"Everybody around here seems to know each other." For a moment, Jada saw herself as the stranger looking into their little world, and the sense of isolation caused by that flash of insight produced a feeling of longing that didn't make sense. She barely knew these people.

"Might seem that way to an outsider, but we're not as inbred and closed-circle as it might seem at first." Madge Lee nudged her tea service to the side a bit, reached across the table, and before Jada could object, again took her hands in hers. "What I do know is Josia is way out on a limb if he thinks you or Rina had anything to do with murdering Nick Williams."

"Thank you." Obviously Madge Lee was far more intelligent than her son. And to Jada's chagrin, she realized Madge Lee was scrutinizing her hands more closely, rubbing her fingers over Jada's unpolished, uneven, and ragged-edged nails.

"You're a potter too, I see." She looked up at Jada. "Rina said you were, and I can tell by your nails." Madge Lee let her hands go with a little sigh. "I was in one of Nick Williams's first classes you know." She smiled wryly. "Charming young man, but I've seen a lot of the world, my dear, and I know a womanizer when I see one." She looked out toward the patio. "He was a good teacher though, and his work is excellent, by my standards at least. But some evil bastard decided to kill him." She tsked decidedly, and returned her gaze to Jada. "Not right you know, people can't go around taking matters into their own hands. That's what civilization is all about by my way of thinking." Madge Lee looked at her intently. "So, you're going to need my help to clear this matter up. Yes, you are going to need my help."

She didn't have the heart to tell Madge Lee she wouldn't be hanging around Red Rock City any longer than she had to. They wouldn't be clearing up anything together. By this afternoon she would be long gone.

Ally had timed it just so.

She sped up to the rear of Jada's minivan on Highway 395 until their cars were only inches apart. She planned on hitting Jada's back bumper as hard as she could without loosing control herself—forcing Jada onto the shoulder at sixty-plus miles-per-hour and causing her car to spin uncontrollably onto the highway's soft shoulder. Then she would pull off right in back of her and wait.

Wait until the shaken and trembling witch stumbled out of her car. Then she'd shoot her in the head and get the hell out of there. Of course if Jada wasn't wearing a seatbelt, or crossed over into oncoming traffic—maybe Jada would do the world a favor and kill herself without any further help from Ally.

At the last second, however, even with Ally so close, Jada managed to slowdown dramatically while simultaneously pulling off the road in a controlled stop.

Jada's surprisingly skillful maneuver caught Ally unawares, and she had no choice but to keep going past the evil woman and her stupid minivan.

Ally cursed, her words entering the world wrapped in an exasperated and angry hiss. But there was no way around it, she would just have to let Jada out of her sight yet again. She had first tried following Jada all the way to that weird-looking house, and ending it. Once there, however, she had felt so darned exposed.

If there had just been a few trees, or a bunch of bushes—anything or anyplace where she could have hidden the car within eyesight of the house. But there had been nothing she could use for cover. All around, just sand, a few rocks, scrub brush, and more sand. Too much openness, now wasn't it?

Yet, her Uncle Phillip had told her many a time how much he liked living in Lone Pine. Of course he had a lot more trees.

"He's crazy." Ally had been alone in her car the whole trip—her only company whatever local Country-Western station was available. But occasionally she talked to herself out loud. Partly, she liked hearing her own voice, and partly she desired the practice. She wanted her speech to be more refined, more "educated," as Terry had suggested. "Nothing to do, no place to go," she said, finishing her thought about her uncle.

When following Jada to that ugly house, Ally also thought she caught the sound of barking dogs. For her to hear their barking from as far behind Jada as she was, her mind envisioned huge monstrous canines with flared nostrils and bared saliva-dripping teeth. She was terrified of dogs. *No*, she wouldn't chance it. So she had turned around and headed back to Highway 395 where she waited it out at a gas-station-market—Mack's Quickie Mart. She was sure Jada would be returning on the same route—there really was no other way back—and she would have a second opportunity this morning to kill her. She had been right. Jada had headed back on the same route, and Ally had tried to force her off the road. *Two chances to kill her today—on the road, and at the house— both failures!*

Ally was not happy, and as she drove back into Red Rock City, last night came back to her in rushes of memory.

When Jada pulled into the Red Rock Inn and Café Sunday night, she had driven on into Red Rock City and stayed at the Best Western. She had noticed the rental car belonging to that fool insurance chump who was also following Jada in the motel's parking lot. Since he was most assuredly on an expense account, she decided the Best Western ought to be okay. Spending money to kill the evil woman was money well used.

Once checked in and guessing Jada was also tucked in until morning, Ally had thought it would be nice for a few hours not to have to keep the woman constantly in her sight. So she decided to treat herself and actually eat a restaurant meal.

The motel had a small diner attached and Ally had easily found a booth in the back where she could just sit, eat, and unwind. Not that she could really relax, not until Jada Beaudine was dead and buried. She ordered a nondescript entrée, a stew of some kind, a beer, and a slice of apple pie that caught her eye on the diner dessert-carousel. She had eaten slowly, trying unsuccessfully to enjoy the food.

She ended up staying in the diner for a couple hours while a steady stream of customers came, ate, then departed—back to their daily lives. Mostly couples, she had noticed, and as usual since Terry's death, these strangers' relationships and interactions stabbed at her continuing raw emotions.

What pierced her heart the most was the way they looked at each other. Then there were the discreet, and indiscreet touches, the shared smiles—even a couple modest kisses—all gut wrenching reminders of what she and Terry had had together. She almost cried several times.

Her Terry had been so vibrant, so full of wild ideas and plans, a dreamer, a doer—her man. What a "couple" they had been. If she closed her eyes tight enough and for long enough she could still clearly see his face. That wonderful smile, slightly crooked, so sexy.

Why oh why had he ever married that horrid woman?

Consequently, this afternoon, Ally hadn't given a damn how long she had to sit and wait in Mack's Quickie Mart while Jada was at that house. She also hadn't given second thought to trying to run her off the road when she had left.

Nothing mattered but killing Jada Beaudine.

It was near three o'clock when Jada headed back to the Red Rock Inn, and the sun was already in descent toward the western horizon. Winter in the Mojave was shortening the desert days.

"At least I can see the sun here," she said to herself. No doubt it was raining back home. *No, not home anymore.*

She needed to pick up her stuff and get back on track to Atlanta where Solina and Neal were waiting. But it would be dark soon, and checkout time was long past. Maybe she should spend one more night here, then get back on the road in the morning? Jada sighed several times while bemoaning her plight, weighing her options, and blaming Josia Rhodes.

After a few moments, and inescapably aware of the practicality of not driving through unknown areas at night, Jada decided there was no need to continue rushing, and reluctantly surrendered to the inevitable. One more night.

Accordingly, as she approached the Inn from the north--a different direction, a different perspective—she took the time to look at the place with a more objective eye. However, a different geographical point of view and a stab at aesthetic objectivity did not change things. The Red Rock Inn & Café remained a motley collection of buildings, really not more than the barest of shelters; all in desperate need of repair and purpose.

A place to get completely lost in. A place to forget the past. Was that why Irina Hughes was here? Had she needed to begin anew? And Nick Williams? Why had he decided to set up a studio in this rundown god-forsaken place?

Instead of pulling into the main drive, on a whim, or maybe on purpose, Jada took the side road back to the ceramics studio. It was bumpy and dusty, but gratefully short. Hilary had said the lab was locked up; and indeed, a strip of yellow crime scene tape was tacked across the front door. Deputy Spriggs had been a busy boy.

Undeterred by the tape, Jada got out of her minivan, walked around to the rear, under the walkway, and looked for a back door. On the back patio she found a large gas kiln and a propane tank tucked away under a modest but seemingly well constructed loggia. A gust of wind caught her unawares and swirls of sand danced around her feet.

Looking behind her, she could see Nick Williams's studio at the other end of the patio. It was surrounded by a white canvas structure, a covered scaffolding evidently erected by Bakersfield's forensic team. In the fading light, Nick's mini-tower looked peculiarly eerie, shrouded in white as it was, makeshift walls flapping gently in wind-driven swirling sand, and the very top of the tower barely peeking up and out.

Jada could also hear the sound of voices inside, just mumbles really, but her mind easily attributed and inferred words and purpose. Oddly, the murder scene canopy and human activity made Jada's surroundings feel more familiar. She had been at murder scenes before, been through the protocol of gathering forensic evidence. This she understood.

She further looked around, trying to think like the murderer; and indeed, she couldn't see the Café or cabins from where she stood. The angle was wrong. And conversely, *no one can see me from the main buildings*. Also the door to Nick Williams's studio, now under the canvas, was just at the other end of the patio. Easy for a murderer to slip between the lab and the studio without being observed.

Next, Jada stealthily edged closer to the lab's back door. Oddly, given the outside temperature, the doorknob was cool to Jada's touch; and with an apparent piece of good luck, the knob turned under her tentative try. For an instant the feel of the cool antiquated brass lock swept Jada back in time. She was suddenly a young girl on her grandmother's back porch in the middle of a frigid Chicago winter—rushing ahead of her parents to open Grandma Kat's back kitchen door, then feeling the hard coldness of the knob penetrating right through her mitten.

Jada shivered, and as quickly as it had come, that tiny fleck of remembrance vanished—but not without leaving an unexpected sweet aftertaste of familial warmth and longing. *They're all gone now.* She was an only child, and all her elder family members had passed on, leaving Terry's relatives as he only family connections Jada had left. There were a couple distant cousins she barely knew in the Midwest. But that was it.

She forced herself to ignore these stray bits of remembrance and emotion, and refocused her attention again down the patio toward the tower where the forensic team was working. Still, no one moved about outside—just muffled and disconnected voices under the white canopy. She turned the knob farther and slipped in.

The smell of damp clay in Nick's studio earlier that morning had been pleasantly familiar. Now, standing alone in his actual classroom building, Jada found the all-encompassing aroma of clay even more poignant, more inviting. And why hadn't she noticed during this morning's interviews? The answer was obvious. Dealing with Josia had stolen all her sensory perceptions.

She squinted into what seemed to be a dimly lit backroom, a small window up high her only source of light. Instinctively Jada's hand found a switch on the wall to the left, and after a quick flip, a meager overhead light revealed shelves lining all the walls in the small room, and a door straight in front leading to another backroom.

Pottery creations still on bats and covered in plastic filled the shelves to her left and to her right and thick sheets of heavy plastic hung like doors in front of similar shelves, creating what Jada figured was a primitive damp box. The plastic was opaque with age, but Jada could still make out shadowy silhouettes of pots and sculptures beckoning from behind.

Motionless, she stood for a moment, enjoying several slow deep breaths. She found these few moments of personal quiet—just her and the clay—extremely pleasant. Unfortunately, they also evoked a longing for a past time in her life, a time she would never be able to reclaim. And there was something else. *What? Did it have to do with Nick's murder?* She wondered. For from the moment Jada had surreptitiously entered the lab— Nick's lab—she had also felt a foreboding presence hanging in the air.

She was, however, not fearful and moved forward through the next room, a kiln area containing two medium sized round electric kilns, shelves, boxes of shelf posts—all crammed together with barely room to pass through. Again Jada stopped for a couple moments, taking in her surroundings.

Finally, she progressed into the large open workroom where she had been interviewed that morning. This time she took a more encompassing look. Besides all the equipment she had noticed earlier, there were several sinks, a wedging area, and lots of work tables. She ran her hand over the polyurethane surface of one work table—dusty but smooth, and again cool.

The temperature in the lab was perfect, and Jada wondered how. A noiseless air-conditioner somewhere? Sure, it was winter, but a Mojave Desert winter was not a Chicago winter, and so far it certainly didn't seem that cold to her—except at night and in the early morning hours.

Nick Williams hadn't missed a beat setting up his lab, and Jada wondered about the classes he had taught. *Had he been a good teacher? Had the equipment worked well? Was it ever too hot, too cold, like studios often are?*

"Jada." An urgent whisper. Immediately she was afraid. It was a man's voice—from her rear she thought. Then a quick scuffling noise.

She jumped and turned around. No one was there. *Maybe just the wind?* "Who is it!" she demanded.

The front door opened, allowing in the afternoon sun and a blast of heat and dust—followed by Irina Hughes. "Mrs. Beaudine?" she called out. "I saw your car. Are you alright? And who are you talking to?" She was heading toward Jada carrying two large Styrofoam food containers, happy aromas proceeding her. Garlic. Pepper. Asian spices. "I figured you'd be getting hungry. I let your dog out to relieve herself. She came right back in, seems happy just laying around on your bed all day."

Jada forced her racing heart into submission. "Chinese?"

"No, Thai."

"How'd you get in?" Jada asked. "The door's locked and there's tape across it." Maybe Irina saw the person calling out to her. "Did you see anyone prowling around here at the lab building?"

"I have a key, so I just tore the tape off," she said. "This is my place, not Si Rhodes's. No one at the tower took any notice, too busy doing whatever cops do. And no, I didn't see anyone."

It must have been the wind and my mind playing tricks. "I didn't know you cooked Thai food at the café."

"Got it in Red Rock City." Irina pulled paper towels and two cans of pop out of her jeans-jacket pockets. "Don't know anything Manny can't cook, but he's off tonight. I got enough for everyone here at the Red Rock." She smiled, apparently at some private amusement. "I thought you might be a shrimp person. Garlic shrimp okay? The other one is vegetarian, tofu and eggplant in a hot chili sauce, if you prefer."

"Shrimp." *Lucky guess on her part, knowing I like shrimp.*

"Thanks, Ms. Hughes."

"Rina, *please*."

The two women pulled up stools and dug in. Jada was suddenly ravenous and it was a few minutes before she was inclined to converse. When she did speak again it was to ask, "Who's everyone? You mentioned a 'Manny?' This is really good, by the way."

"Manny Chacon. He's my cook, maintenance man, handyman, and damn good friend. He lives in the cabin number-three, right next to the café. You can see it from your cabin. I'm in number-one."

"Who does the rooms?"

"Manny's mother comes in once a day, most days. Usually brings a ton of food with her, claims Manny doesn't eat enough."

"But he's the cook…"

"She has her own ideas about things."

Jada thoughtfully returned to eating for a few moments. "This rice is great and they made the sauce really hot." She put down her plastic fork and said through a resigned sigh, "Guess I'll be staying another night, checking out in the morning if that's okay with you." Jada heard herself finish her declaration in an apologetic tone and was immediately peeved. She didn't need to justify her actions to Irina Hughes.

"Did Si change his mind?" Irina asked. "Say you could go?"

"Chief Rhodes doesn't have anything to say about my comings and goings," she answered sharply.

"Pissed you off too?"

Jada laughed despite her anger. "You could say that." Then she took a long steadying swallow of Coke. "What do you mean, 'changed his mind?'"

"He called up before you got back, asked to speak to you. When you didn't answer he said for me to make sure I tell you not to leave town before he talked to you again. In person."

"I'll go see him in the morning," Jada said in as measured a tone as she could muster up. It was time to change the subject before she got really angry. "Tell me about Hilary Giles. Such a sad looking man."

"He's not happy, easy to tell." Irina's voice softened, "Will never be a happy man again."

"What happened?"

"His son was killed. In an auto accident, hit by a drunken driver running a stop sign. William was a college freshman, intelligent with a bright future I'm told."

Jada agreed, Hilary Giles would never recover. Not from something like that. "His wife? Other children?"

"She never leaves the house anymore. Their other son is off to college now, don't know how it's affected him. Hilary is in the class because his shrink told him to take up a hobby as therapy. I like him, he's a good man."

"What's with the English accent?"

48

"He came to Red Rock City as a researcher out on the base. Never left. Don't know if he became a citizen, probably did. His wife is American. Texan, if I remember right."

"Any other regulars besides Manny?" Just making conversation, Jada told herself, she didn't really want to know. She would only be here until the next morning. Then off to Atlanta.

"Just Linda in number-five and Mrs. Shoecraft way back in number-eight." Irina finished off her pop. "So, what happened with Si?"

Jada preferred to leave that topic alone, but what the hell, the good chow had mellowed her so she went ahead and told Irina about the run-around Josia had engineered, and about "Tea" with Madge Lee.

Irina chuckled. "Sounds just like something Si would cook up. Tries to be a devious SOB sometimes. Speaking of devious, how did you get in here?"

"Through the back. Either Deputy Spriggs missed the unlocked door, or they figured nobody would get past their team. There's a lot of ceramic work back there drying. A lot of sculptures. Any of it yours?"

"Me? Hell, no. Don't have an ounce of artistic ability."

"Do you know who made those two big heads back there, the ones with the spikes? They're covered with plastic, drying. I've never seen anything quite like them."

"No, I don't know. You like them?"

"Ah, no, don't think so. But I was surprised to see something so avant-garde out here—" Jada caught herself.

"Out here in the middle of nowhere?" Irina smiled encouragingly at Jada. "Would you stay, Mrs. Beaudine, and find out who killed Nick Williams?"

No, this was not her business. Jada was nosey though. "Do you still love Nick ?"

"Funny you ask, I've been thinking about that all day." Irina closed her food container; she had barely eaten half. "The answer is no. But still, like I said, he didn't deserve to die, now did he?" She got up, walked over to a side window, leaned against its sill as if for emotional support, and looked out toward the Sierras. "Hell, I guess to some, fooling around on your wife is pretty bad. And I guess I probably agree." She turned back to Jada. "But isn't that what the divorce laws and child support are all about?"

"So you think his wife killed him?"

Irina tilted her head, considering. "Well, I guess I do." Then she shook her head emphatically and said, "No, can't be. From everything I know about her, I can't imagine Darcie killing anyone."

"Someone killed Nick Williams." Jada closed her empty carton and drained her Coke. "Thanks again for the food. It was pretty good. I'm going to turn in early so I can get on the road tomorrow morning right after I see Rhodes. I can't stay to help."

The two women walked back as far as Jada's cabin, where Jada stopped at her minivan for her toiletry and overnight bags. Irina was quiet during the walk.

Jada knew Irina was disappointed. But what could she do? She felt very sorry a man had died, a man Irina cared for, but it wasn't her problem. Sure, murder was abhorrent, but she couldn't fight every battle, even if she wanted to. In truth, she was barely getting back on her own feet—no time for a detour. On the other hand, Jada couldn't deny she certainly would like to be involved in nabbing Nick's murderer.

By way of a final goodnight, Jada attempted to satisfy a more personal curiosity. "Why do you stay here?" she asked. "There's nothing here, no one around for miles and miles."

"I imagine, Mrs. Beaudine, some folks need more of an audience for their lives than I do."

For a few seconds, a bemused smile graced the corners of Jada mouth, then she said, "Goodnight, Ms. Hughes."

"Rina, please."

Jada caved. "Goodnight, Rina," she said, then watched a bit as Irina headed for the main building. Interesting woman, she concluded. And in some ways, surprisingly likable.

She took in a long slow deep breath of desert night air. Dry and cool, and again laced with a hint of eucalyptus. When she turned the doorknob of number-two, it opened without benefit of a key. Clearly, the lock was useless. The dog was waiting for her, a fact Jada found equally comforting and disturbing.

A dog. Was she up to the emotional commitment required to take care of a pet? *Heck no.* Her life, until the last couple years, had been filled with pets, mostly strays; and she had loved and cared for them all. Since the last had passed, a cat named Black-Jack, she had not regained the heart and strength to take on another. In addition, when her husband Terry had drowned, her world, her life, her mind—all had flip-flopped in directions she was still recovering from—and Jada questioned whether she was now standing straight enough herself to take on a dog. *Not yet.*

The bed had been made. Manny's mother had visited at last. Jada figured it was too early to actually "go-to-bed," but a short nap would work. Then she would get up and watch TV before really hitting the sack. If she was lucky, she would sleep right through the night and get up refreshed in the morning. Then after a quick chat with Josia Rhodes, head back south down I-14, back on track for Atlanta.

To that end, she brushed her teeth, took off her jeans, and packed up everything except fresh underwear, socks, and a T-shirt for in the morning.

The sky had been clear and sunny all day, no clouds, so she didn't expect much of a sunset. Besides, she figured Mother

Nature would have a hard time beating the previous night's painting. Nonetheless, as she lay on her bed, again looking through crooked blinds and wondering if Irina, Hal, Corissa, or even Hilary had shot a fellow potter in the head, she watched an evening sky develop and crescendo that rivaled yesterday's—brush stroke by brush stroke. *Beautiful.*

She wondered what Nick Williams, the *perfect* man, would have thought about tonight's *perfect* sunset. Sadly, he would never experience another sunset in this world. *Neither would Terry.*

Tears came, but Jada was used to that.

Marie Shipley's hair, dark brown in her youth, was now snow-white, but her dark brown eyes were still intense and often questioning. Her face was plain and pleasant. She knew she looked like the type of woman you'd love to claim as your grandmother. Penny Berry had called her that once, and it had taken a great deal of will power on Marie's part not to rebuke her.

But who could get mad at Penny? Inane but lovable Penny. Well, not so insubstantial tonight, she had been the one to get the ball rolling. *Good for Penny.* Marie smiled to herself as she got out of her car and walked down the dark, but fortunately short, path to the Berrys' well-lit entryway.

Penny and Timothy Berry lived in a modest rambler on twenty or so acres at the end of Brown Road in Inyokern. It was an isolated spot, even for the desert, and very dark at such a late hour. Nonetheless, when Penny had called around earlier in the day, suggesting they all get together that evening, Marie hadn't demurred, and she guessed no one else had refused either.

Yes, even on such short notice and so late in the evening, members of Nick's little class would rearrange schedules and trudge out to the far reaches of Inyokern for a confab.

Marie Shipley knew she had been the first Penny had called, but now wanted to be the last to arrive. She recognized the cars already parked at the house and knew she'd achieved her goal of wanting to wait until after Penny—in the past a fluttery and anxious host—had everything set up and the others had arrived. Marie was definitely interested in this meeting, but too tired to endure a lot of preliminary, and most probably, quite silly chitchat.

Indeed, once inside, she saw Penny had made chocolate chip cookies with pecans and walnuts for the occasion. And as expected, she immediately started twittering on to Marie about how Hilary arrived just as she had finished putting refreshments on the dining room table, and that Leroy Ames had knocked on the door within minutes of Hilary. Hal Morton had been next, followed by Corissa and Star Thomas.

"Now that you're here, we can start." Penny bubbled. "Now we can start," her husband Timothy echoed, his face twitching with delight.

We're an interesting bunch, Marie reflected about her fellow classmates as they selected their refreshments and situated themselves around the Berrys' frilly, overstuffed, yet comfortable living room. For starters, there were the Berrys themselves, twin bundles of elfin energy, physical proportions, and gleeful nosiness; Hilary Giles, clueless and terminally traumatized; Leroy Ames, with his stiff military carriage, presence, and didactic verbal mannerisms; and Star Thomas.

Marie considered Star unique in her attractively precise yet hard to verbalize style—somewhere between Grace Kelly and Lena Horne features-wise—but of course nowhere near their glamour and beauty. Marie still considered Star an unknown quantity.

Then there was Hal Morton. At first glance, seemingly quite ordinary and pleasant, but upon knowing him better, Marie found him overly pompous and distastefully sleazy. Marie almost visibly shuddered—but caught herself in time.

Corissa, Marie preferred not to think about, and not for the first time. She was fearful that the young woman's personality and habits, once analyzed and possibly understood, would not provide happiness. She was not yet ready to deal with the source of Corissa's easy excitability and nervous ways, no matter how much she cared about Corissa's mother Ruth.

Marie knew Leroy to be a man used to taking control. So she wasn't surprised when after everyone got their cup of whatever, and snagged a couple cookies, he got right to the point. "I think it was very wise of you," he said, and looked pointedly at Penny, then Timothy. "To get us together like this, that is. I think we all got off easy today."

"What do you mean?" Corissa asked. Quite predictably, she was in an excitable frame of mind, her gaze flitting among the group and her hands evidently so unsteady she hadn't even attempted to hold a cup of tea.

Marie, as she often did, put a verbal arm of comfort around the young woman. "I'm sure Mr. Ames is referring to the fact Deputy Spriggs let us off quite easy in the questioning department." Corissa didn't seem reassured, and Marie thought, as she had done many times in the past, Corissa had such a pleasant face, and could actually be considered pretty if she'd just smile occasionally.

"Exactly," Leroy said. "And we," he said, and looked around their little group as if to ensure they were grasping the import of his remarks, "are prime suspects in Nick's untimely death."

Marie again felt the need to clarify. "Murder." It was no time to mince words.

"Yes, murder. You're quite right, Mrs. Shipley. Murder. So I expect tomorrow will be different. From what I've heard of the man, Chief Josia Rhodes is no schmuck and not easily put off."

Marie, thinking of her friend Madge Lee, smiled to herself. Son like mother.

"So I expect," Leroy continued in a knowing voice. "Questioning tomorrow will be much more thorough."

"My, my," Timothy tsked while making notes in his diary which was open on the table in front of him.

"My, my," Penny agreed. "Maybe Tim and I can figure out who the murderer is. Now wouldn't that be grand?"

Marie was genuinely fond of Penny and Timothy, despite their penchant for dressing in identical outfits, but did wonder sometimes at the silliness they occasionally spouted.

"Mrs. Berry," Hilary pointed out somberly. "You do realize one of us could have murdered poor Mr. Williams."

"Of course not," Hal Morton retorted a little too loudly. "It's usually the wife, you know."

Something about the look in Hal's eyes, or was it more the undertones she heard in his voice, but Marie was sure Hal Morton didn't think Darcie had murdered her husband at all. In fact, she speculated, he might know who had killed Nick. Or at the minimum, was nurturing a darned good hunch. Knowing Hal, he'd probably pursue the matter.

Before she could voice a caution his way Star Thomas spoke for the first time. "Well whoever did it gets applause from me." She made a clicking sound out the side of her mouth indicating her short and direct declaration was all that need be said on the matter. Then she looked at her watch and added, "Hope this won't last too much longer. I'm scheduled for the night shift and I'm cutting it close."

"Now, now, Mrs. Thomas," Leroy said, quick to take control again. "That's just why we're here tonight. I think we all need to think and talk about just what we're going to tell the police tomorrow. Statements like that might just get you in a lot of trouble."

"Well I'm not telling them anything." Corissa looked defiant, but her voice revealed an underlying timidity.

And fear? Marie wondered.

"Well…" Hilary said.

"We should help," Penny almost shouted.

"We have a lot of class notes," Timothy said, tapping his diary. "We may be able to help the police."

Leroy looked to Marie and she sensed he wanted her accordance. She said, "I think, if asked, one must tell the truth." Then with a nod of deference to Leroy, she added, "Some things we might think we know, possibly heard as casual gossip, if not asked, should probably be left alone and untold." Indeed, she had heard, overheard, and been told tidbits that sent her mind in several unpleasant directions when it came to Nick's murder.

However, Marie was not sure of the wisdom of that strategy and almost immediately regretted her statement. She also wondered who the woman was with the extremely short hair she had glimpsed this morning at the ceramics studio. A stranger for sure. Madge Lee probably knew. She'd have to call her.

In the end that night, when Marie—the first to leave after Star—headed home, she was regretfully aware nothing had been settled among her pottery class members. They were all still left on their own to explore the intricacies of their individual consciences on what to do next.

Lyle was becoming physically more comfortable in his Best Western room. But as he scrunched his legs underneath his continuing to-be-irksome desk, he was struck with—and not for the first time recently—how much of his life had been spent in motel and hotel rooms, snooping into other people's lives. While his own life, the personal part of it for sure, just limped sadly along. Other people's lives were interesting. His wasn't.

He sighed, turned on his laptop, connected to the internet, and started his daily email to Hamilton Wolfe.

Extract from Lyle Elliott's email to his home office:
January 6, Monday Evening

I tried calling you Ham, but Tiffany explained you're under the weather. You won't believe what's happened. This woman has gotten involved in another murder. I know, I know, it's like she's a magnet.

And you wouldn't believe where she's staying. I'm in a decent motel here in Red Rock City proper, but the place she's at barely has running water, no lie Ham.

I checked in with Marshall the adjuster at our local office here, and I also got hold of Phillip, he's the contact I was telling you about at the Red Rock Tribune. I had a long lunch with both of them and I now have the scoop on a few of these folks.

The guy who got knocked off, shot in the head it seems, is Nick Williams. He's a local, a pottery teacher. Forty-five, well-liked, especially with the ladies it's rumored. He has a wife who's an engineer at the base. Marshall's wife is in a book club with her and says Darcie Williams is a real nice lady and was devoted to her husband. (Of course we've heard that before!) Phillip didn't add much more about the victim, just that he had put a couple ads in the paper for his class. Thinks he's been in town about five years or so.

So, this guy gets himself shot in his studio out at this place where the Beaudine woman is staying. Like I said, the place is a dump, but people actually drive out there for his classes. The lady who owns the place is thought to be psychic in some local loony-toon circles. She's lived out there well over twenty years. Actually everyone at the Red Rock Inn sounds a little off center. At least that's what Marshall tells me. There's a young handyman who cooks at the café when the few folks staying there want to eat, Marshall doesn't know why he stays. Then there's a real old German woman who's been there for years and some young woman named Linda who's scared to be around people.

I didn't push him for more info right now. There's a strong "live and let live" sentiment around here. I think the only reason he gave me what he did was because of the murder. People don't get knocked off here that often.

The Chief of Police is a local curiosity too. Tell you more about him next time, it's getting late. So far he hasn't hauled her in. I doubt if she's involved in this murder and it could be a bad break for the Beaudines, and for us, because I'm sure they were planning to make contact and this murder might scare Terrence off.

Chapter Four

Tuesday

Jada woke up mad.

Here she was way out in the middle of the Mojave, and damnit if a potter hadn't gone and gotten himself murdered right under her nose—a fact that made her commensurately sad and pissed.

Add to that the existence of Josia Rhodes, whom she believed had a damn lot of nerve having her "inspected" by his mother—then telling her through a third party she couldn't leave town. She planned on telling him exactly what she thought of his arrogant personality and unprofessional methods on her way out of town. He hadn't charged her with anything, and she figured he would be stupid to try it. How could she have let him get away with all that yesterday?

Then there was last night itself. It had been rough. With the setting sun she had finally drifted off into a light sleep, the dog hogging a lot of the bed. Then sometime later, she slipped into a dream state where Nick Williams's face played and replayed itself across her subconscious, accompanied by background sound effects—wind-driven sand beating on her cabin windows.

A couple times she fell into what seemed a deeper sleep where unwanted images from her own past, most involving Terry—some good, most bad—paraded in and out of uncontrollable dream situations that left her anxious and annoyed upon awakening.

But now it was morning and the world had to be faced. After taking care of the dog, she would take care of her body— breakfast. Then she would take care of Chief Josia Rhodes.

Josia also woke up mad, walked his dogs mad, had his first cup of coffee still mad, and started his morning shower-shave ritual even madder.

Mainly, he was PO'd at the world because he didn't know what the hell was going on. How could this type of thing happen in Red Rock City for Christ's sake? Partly though, he was mad at himself for letting Rina and that Beaudine woman get to him. Josia was well aware of the rough edges jagging his personality; but he should have handled yesterday better.

And his mother, unusual for her, was sleeping in this morning just to further irritate him. He would have liked her opinion over coffee. Well, maybe later today he'd drag her back into this.

Josia liked his showers hot, soapy, and aromatic. Consequently, he used Head & Shoulders over his whole body because he liked the way it lathered and smelled. Showering was also his time to think.

Vehicular problems—now that was more like Red Rock City. The only way to get into town was on two-lane highways; and a significant number of the town's fast-driving young navy guys spent a significant amount of their time either speeding down the back roads or cruising down Red Rock City's main drag. Add to that the double-whammy of heavy truck traffic bound for Bishop or Reno, and the myriad RV or motorcycle caravans passing through. Most homicides Josia had to deal with were from crashes of motor-propelled and idiot-driven vehicles of some sort.

Sure, there had been a couple actual murders in Red Rock City over the years he'd been Police Chief—but this one was different. Indeed, those two previous incidents had gotten him on TV. The murderers, however, had been strangers in town with strangers' motives and strangers' ways.

No, this one was definitely personal. Personal to the town, personal to Rina, and by extension, personal to him. Josia slathered more shampoo over his inordinately hairy chest and turned the water hotter.

He sure would like to hang this murder on that smart-ass Beaudine woman. and briefly wondered why. But Nick was a local, most assuredly killed by a local; and damnit, like it or not, the murder happened on Rina's property, with Rina probably being his number one suspect.

On top of that, what leads or evidence did he have to point the finger at anyone? Not one damn thing. The Kern County forensics team just might find something, but he doubted it, and he wasn't eager to set off too many alarm bells with Bakersfield law enforcement. He needed to wrap this one up himself.

"Damn," he cursed out loud while shaving—directed not at the sizable stubble he grew on a daily basis—but at this latest mess fate had dropped in his lap.

Josia knew he wasn't a slouch in evidence-gathering himself, and he hadn't seen one damn thing lying around where Williams had gotten himself killed. No telltale cigarette butt, no spent cartridges from a one-of-a-kind pistol, not even the hackneyed broken watch fixing the time of death.

Fortunately, by the time Josia finished his morning lavations he felt better; and he attributed that lightening of his mood to having verbally vented his frustration and anger at his bathroom fixtures. In fact, by the time he left the house, he was whistling the Colonel Bogey March from "Bridge on the River Kwai."

The sun was just barely inching above the horizon, and the distance between his place and the Red Rock Inn & Café was shorter than to his office, so he headed to the Inn first thing — short cutting along a couple pit-pocked dirt roads few dared traverse.

He smiled to himself. So what if he'd gone through three patrol cars in as many years? He'd done some damn good work for Red Rock City, and he knew the Mayor and his buddies weren't about to complain. Besides, even though the ride was hellishly bumpy until he hit Highway 395, the morning was beautiful. And though he would never admit it if asked, Josia was enjoying a familiar euphoria.

He had the world to himself. It was an illusion, he knew — the vast stretches of uncompromising open desert creating a mirage of infinite distance. For a few moments though, it was his desert alone.

However, when he eventually arrived at the Red Rock Inn and found out someone had torn down the yellow police tape on his crime scene, Josia was back to cursing. "Damn." He was fuming again, and just like a kid, felt like kicking the dirt outside the ceramics lab. Most assuredly tearing the tape down was Rina's work — probably in league with that confounded Beaudine woman.

"Good morning, Mrs. Beaudine. Would you like some breakfast?" Manuel "Manny" Chacon greeted Jada cheerfully as soon as she entered—even though he was seemingly occupied topping up sugar-shakers on the café counter. Manny was of medium height and build, tending toward stocky, with a pleasantly round face complemented and accentuated by eager eyes, moderately attractive features, smooth clear complexion, thick dark brown hair, and an easy manner. He wore a sparkling clean and crisp chef's apron over what looked like jeans and a polo shirt.

"I'd love some," Jada said, and sat down at the counter. "You must be Manny." She refrained from asking how he knew her name. Irina's doing, no doubt.

He nodded, then smiled broadly and handed her a handwritten menu.

She guessed him to be in his late twenties or early thirties and liked him immediately. For sure, his infectious smile was hard to resist.

The Café part of the Red Rock Inn was modest—a three person counter, three booths in the rear, three tables along the windows—and she observed, the current patron count, also three. *Décor* was desert-dilapidated with mismatched chairs and tables, windows just on the front, and minimal-wattage lighting. On the plus side, entry into the café was through an antique and quaint looking glass-paned door, and the predominant café aromas were bacon grease and coffee. Very good news since her stomach was at the growling stage.

It took Jada barely a moment to select the "Breakfast Special," and after Manny took her order, he blithely introduced her—long distance-like—to Mrs. Shoecraft, a tiny wisp of a woman crouched over her meal in the farthest back booth.

"Mrs. Shoecraft," he called out loudly in a tone and style reserved for the hard of hearing. "This is Mrs. Beaudine, a new resident."

Jada didn't bother to correct him about her transitory status, just smiled and nodded to the old lady. She received in return, a delicate little hand wave from Mrs. Shoecraft's shadowy corner.

"We're having a surprise birthday party for her tonight," Manny then informed Jada. "Ninety." He shook his head in amazement. "She came over at the end of World War two and has some fantastic stories. We'll be starting around five. She doesn't usually stay up real late." He paused for a few seconds as if to give Jada time to assimilate all this new information. "I'm making a red velvet cake, we've already gotten the ice cream, and you don't need to bring a present." He smiled. "Let me get your eggs started."

Jada mumbled something about liking red velvet cake and again didn't have the heart to tell him she wouldn't be around. While she waited, a tall thin young woman also sitting in Mrs. Shoecraft's booth—who couldn't have been much over twenty-one—sent a shy smile Jada's way. Then avoiding any further eye contact, she got up, walked through, and left the café.

"Who was the young woman who just left?" Jada asked Manny's back.

"Linda Lowry. Nice kid. She'll come around one day. I'm helping her you know." Jada didn't know what he was talking about, but was amused by the thought of the *old*, possibly thirty-something kid, helping the young twenty-something kid.

Her wait for breakfast wasn't very long and when Manny turned back around and presented her with a platter-sized plate holding three beautifully cooked eggs-over-easy, homemade hash browned potatoes, an English muffin, several slices of honey-dew melon, and a parsley sprig for garnish, Jada was impressed, and quite grateful.

She took her time eating, slowly overcoming the funk her earlier thoughts of Josia and overnight dreams had brought on. Finally, after a second cup of coffee and having politely listened to Manny expound on the various desert climates in the US, she asked for her check.

He explained breakfast was complimentary with the room. She left him a sizeable tip.

Jada got out of her minivan and stood for a moment in front of the Red Rock City Police Office for the second day in a row. It was a modest one-story affair, looking more like a storefront business than a police station. She could see Gabe through the front window in the cramped front waiting area talking to a woman who was nicely dressed in a pantsuit, linen blouse, and pumps. She couldn't make out her features clearly, but she could see the woman was a brunette with thick and unusually long hair, braided and pinned up attractively around her head in a crown fashion. It was a style Jada remembered was popular for a period in her childhood—and an incongruous choice for what appeared from the distance to be such a young woman.

As she entered and walked up to the front counter, the woman turned toward her, and Jada was surprised to see puffy and tender-looking light brown eyes, surrounded by a tear-stained face full of grief.

"Check back in an hour, Mrs. Williams," Gabe said to the woman's back.

Jada knew instantly the woman was Nick Williams's widow Darcie. "Mrs. Williams," Jada offered her hand. "You don't know me, but I want to express my condolences. I'm so sorry for your loss." Hollow, useless words she knew, but at least she wouldn't be letting it go unnoticed that Nick had left this world. Something very tragic had happened.

Darcie shifted a wet handkerchief from her right hand to her left before accepting Jada's. "Thank you, Mrs...?" Her voice, though tight with emotion, was deep timbered and melodic.

"Beaudine, Jada Beaudine."

"Beaudine?" She paused for a couple seconds. "You found Nick, didn't you? You and Rina."

Jada nodded.

"You found..." her voice cracked.

And Jada, thinking Darcie might collapse, grabbed her arm and called out, "Deputy Spriggs."

Quickly from around the counter, Gabe rushed to Darcie's other side. "Here, Mrs. Williams, let me help you. How about you have a seat over there..." He indicated several wooden chairs squeezed in against the wall next to the counter.

"No, no, please. I'm fine. I just want to leave now."

On an impulse spawned from empathy, Jada asked, "Is there a place we could go for a cup of coffee or tea, Deputy?"

Gabe nodded his approval. "The Milton House. Like I said, I should have an answer back from the coroner in about an hour. I'm sorry Chief Rhodes isn't here himself."

"It would be nice to have some tea," Darcie agreed. "Then I could come back."

"Where's Chief Rhodes?" Jada asked Gabe.

"He's at the ceramics lab at Rina's."

"I'll catch him later." Her need to confront Josia was strong, but at the moment, Darcie's need for companionship was more important.

As the two women left the office Darcie said, "You look so familiar. It's like I've seen your face before."

"I'm new to town."

Jada drove with a promise to bring Darcie back to Josia's office and her car afterwards.

The Milton House, its window sign proclaiming it to be the best restaurant in town, looked comfortable and offered afternoon tea.

After they had ordered tea and scones, freshly made, according to their waitress—a friendly middle aged woman with an open face, too much bright red lipstick, and short tightly curled brown hair, Jada more formally introduced herself. She also provided Darcie a thin scenario, part truth, part fabrication, of how she had ended up at the scene of her husband's murder.

As she talked, Jada was able to look more directly into Darcie's brown eyes, the whites now almost blood red from crying. She not only saw a woman suffering from shock, but also a woman who had yet to realize what had *really* happened. Jada knew from her own painful experience Darcie didn't yet understand—her husband was dead—never to return. "Nick was a pottery teacher?" she said, trying to start Darcie talking.

"Yes," Darcie answered with a meager smile. "He liked to be called a 'Ceramic Artist.'"

"Are you an artist too?"

"Oh no, I'm an Engineer," she answered with a bit more life and energy, and in a tone indicating she considered "artists" and "engineers" two separate species of humans. "I work at the base." Darcue sniffed and blew her nose again. "You know, I got dressed this morning, just like I was going to work. Like nothing had changed. I was in my car to take Marta and Devlin to school and head off to work before I realized I wouldn't be going to work today. Couldn't. My neighbor called the base and school yesterday...but...."

"But it isn't real yet."

Her eyes opened wide as she stared quizzically at Jada. "Yes. You understand. You must..."

"Have lost someone close. Yes, my husband. It's been a year now."

"I'm sorry."

Jada feared their conversation was deteriorating into a wake. Inevitable, she guessed, when you're talking about dead

67

people. "Are you waiting to hear when they'll release your husband's body?"

"Yes. Deputy Spriggs didn't know much. He called Dr. Beach for me, but he didn't know." She drew in a deep long breath and let it out. "They're completing an autopsy." Her eyes watered but she kept her composure.

Even under the effects of shock and grief, Jada thought Darcie an attractive woman, probably ten or so years younger than her husband, clear, healthy looking skin, and a full sensuous mouth. In better times, she suspected, Darcie had also had a nice smile.

Their friendly, and evidently quite competent waitress, brought tea, two pots—black and green, and a plate of appetizing-looking sandwiches and scones. After she left, Darcie said, "You know Nick worked here at this restaurant for about six months when we first moved to Red Rock City. I got a job at the base right away."

"How long ago was that?" Jada's black tea was hot and good.

"About five years ago." Her shoulders relaxed a bit; seemingly Darcie was glad for someone to talk to. "Nick and I had just gotten married."

"Where did you move here from?"

"Oakland. Well, Berkeley, actually. I was finishing my Ph.D. and Nick was running a ceramics gift shop on Telegraph." Through the sadness, her eyes lit up for a second. "I know a lot of people say it, but it was true for me. I loved him from the first moment I saw him."

"So Nick was already a potter when you met him?"

"Yes. He had a hard time getting established here. It took a couple years. And he couldn't work at the base. At least he didn't think so because of some minor juvenile offense. We have very tight screening and security at the base." She finished a mini-creampuff. "These little puff things are good. What do you think the filling is, cream cheese?" She wiped a couple recalcitrant tears from her eyes and selected another from their tea-tray. "I didn't think I was hungry."

They talked for maybe half-an-hour more, Jada reluctant to leave her, even though Darcie said her sister Joan would be spending the afternoon with her and the children. Darcie wouldn't be alone, but still. So they talked longer than Jada had initially intended. Hopefully Darcie would take some comfort from the socialization. For her part, Jada learned Nick was a perfect dad, a great artist, and everybody liked him.

Eventually, the delicacies ran out and their conversation petered to an end. As planned, Jada drove her back to Josia's office to discuss the depressing realities of obtaining her husband's body.

As soon as he saw them pull in and park, Gabe came running out of the office. "Chief Rhodes is still out at the crime scene," he said. Then he gulped a breath before reading from a handwritten note he'd taken. "Quote, 'Tell Mrs. Beaudine I would like to talk to her. Tell her not to leave town until she does.' End quote."

When he looked up from reading and saw Jada's face, Gabe was very sorry indeed he would not be there when Mrs. Beaudine and Chief Rhodes next met.

It took Jada twenty minutes or so to get Darcie safely in her car and headed home, then drive the distance from the Sheriff's Office to Highway 395, and finally drive the seven miles south to the Red Rock Inn & Café. She passed the time fussing and fuming.

Her plan was to immediately confront Josia on his imperious, high-handed, and peremptory antics. How dare he try making her a prisoner in Red Rock City without ever making himself available to talk to her?

Once at the Inn, now that she knew where to look, Jada saw a patrol car at the end of the dirt road leading to the ceramics lab. First instinct was to head there straight off, but on second thought, she decided to pack and check out first. Josia could wait a few minutes. Paid up and with her bag in the car, she could just head out of town after talking to the jerk. No looking back. She drove on for a couple hundred feet more to the main drive and found Manny standing by the side of the road waving at her.

"Mrs. Beaudine," he announced excitedly when she stopped and opened her window. "I want you to come and see my cake. Didn't you say red velvet was a favorite of yours?" He sounded like a kid.

"Not exactly, and how did you know?"

"That you'd be coming now?" He laughed, which made Jada smile in response despite her displeasure with Josia. Manny's child-like good humor was becoming almost impossible to resist. "Gabe called wanting to know if Si was still here. He also said you had left the office heading back here. I connected Gabe back to the lab and came out here to wait for you." He grabbed her door handle. "Pleeease. Nobody else cares much."

Jeez. The kid could even twinkle his eyes on cue. Oh heck, she would only be delayed a few more minutes.

Once parked and inside the café, Manny waved her back into his miniscule kitchen where a magnificently frosted red velvet cake—full-sheet size—stood on his prep-table with expert writing atop in a rich burgundy icing. It read, "Happy Birthday Mrs. Shoecraft."

"I'm sure she'll be pleased. And all that lettering. You've done a great job, Manny."

He smiled broadly.

"Is Ms. Hughes around?"

"She's out at the lab with Si."

He'd told her already, but she asked again, "Does Mrs. Shoecraft know about her party?"

"Yeah, but she doesn't know about the cake."

On her way to cabin number-two Jada wondered again how old Manny really was, how and why he maintained such a high level of youthful optimism and exuberance, and why he had buried himself and his talent at this place. She was sure there was more to Manny Chacon than the "kid" act. *Everybody has a story.*

For some reason the dog wasn't waiting for her at the door of number-two. Jada sighed from guilty relief, and with heart-tugging regret. To her further dismay, the reason the dog wasn't waiting for her at the door was because she was fast asleep in the center of her bed, legs in the air, snout cocked to the side, snoring.

Jada gave her a pat on the head. She would miss the sweet mutt, but it couldn't be helped. Then Jada saw the note.

The bed had been made before the dog claimed her spot in the middle, evidently without disturbing the pillow where the note so innocently rested. It was a full page of paper, with big magic marker block printing. She stared at it for a couple seconds before really comprehending its import.

"LEAVE NOW!" She shook her head as if it would clear everything up. *Not really a warning. No, more a threat. But who? And why?*

Jada looked around anxiously and said out loud, "What the hell is going on?" No one else was in the room to answer, but someone had been. It didn't make sense. Why bother? She was leaving anyway. Still, she was shaken.

Quickly she folded the note and put it in her pocket. Of course she couldn't leave without giving the dog another pat on the head to convey a fond, yet unfortunate farewell. However, finding herself surprisingly moved, Jada succumbed to a full-out hug for the dog. Teary-eyed, she finally dumped her stuff in the minivan and headed back to the ceramics lab on foot.

Irina was sitting sullenly on a stool just inside the front door of the octagon building, while Josia sat rigidly on another stool a couple worktables away. The room was bright with midday sun streaming in from all sides. In stark contrast, the atmosphere, however, was dark and frigid. Evidently Irina and Josia were at loggerheads.

Jada cleared her throat and announced louder than need be, "Ms. Hughes, I'm ready to check out."

Irina scowled in return. "People have been calling me all day about the next friggin' class and I can't get hold of Hal to see if he'll monitor the classes for awhile. On top of that Si says I can't use the lab. And now you're leaving." She crossed her arms across her chest. "Sucks." Then she turned her face away from both Josia and Jada, preferring to stare out the window.

"Now, Rina," Josia said in an exasperated tone. "I'm not saying you can't, just that it would make it easier for us to get in and out. Just because you had a special relationship with Nick Williams doesn't mean you can be—"

"Be what?" Irina turned back to glare at him.

"A butt." He crossed his arms in like-fashion to Irina. "I can tape the whole damn place if you push me, Rina."

Jada cleared her throat a second time. "Chief Rhodes, I understand you want to talk to me."

His features quickly morphed into a smile, a big toothy variety. "Yes, Mrs. Beaudine, I wanted to thank you for hanging around so long. If you could just leave a forwarding address with Deputy Spriggs, I'd certainly appreciate it." The smile broadened. "And hopefully the rest of your journey will be less eventful."

This turn of events took Jada by surprise, though she hoped it didn't show. *The man is crazy. One minute I better not leave town—now, hit the road.*

"Sure," Irina interjected sarcastically. "Just let her go like that."

This woman is also crazy. I don't owe her anything, I just stopped for the night. Jada craved seeing the Red Rock Inn and Café getting smaller and smaller in her rearview mirror. Still, she was curious, and that curiosity prompted her to ask, "Chief, did you ever find a murder weapon?"

Too easily he played along. "You don't happen to have any ideas about what happened to the gun, do you?"

"No. The killer must have taken it with him, or her. Do you know the time of death yet?"

He snickered inside a smug smile, got up, and stretched nonchalantly. "Now, you don't expect me to blab police business to a passing stranger, now do you?"

Jada shrugged, and he threw her a crumb. "Doc Beach says sometime between three and eight in the morning."

"And Corissa and Hal arrived for class around eight?"

"They claim around seven."

"Oh yeah." Hal Morton *had* said that. Hal and Corissa, each other's alibis.

Irina softened enough to contribute. "There are always a couple students who show up early," she said. "Nick usually stayed in his studio though until time for class."

"Which was?" Jada asked.

"Nine. But," she said and scowled again, "you wouldn't be interested. You're going to Atlanta. You're checking out."

"Ms. Hughes, Rina, I'm sorry. But I really do need to check out." Jada pulled the note out of her jacket pocket and handed it to Josia. "Here, Chief, I found this on my pillow. I don't know what it means or if it's important."

He read it, then handed the note to Irina. "You got any ideas on this? Like who could have access to the cabins besides Mrs. Chacon?" Then he asked Jada, "You have any ideas who left this?"

Jada shook her head.

"Well, it sure as hell doesn't make sense," he said.

"No," Irina agreed. "It doesn't make sense. But, you're leaving anyway." She handed the note back to Josia and said to Jada, "I guess I can't stop you from going. And after that note, why would you want to stay? Let's walk back to the café and I'll run your credit card through." Her hostile attitude was gone, replaced with defeat.

Josia said, "I'm going to have this looked at, Mrs. Beaudine. If you leave your forwarding info, I'll get back to you if we can get anything off it." He turned the note over, then back. "Of course we've all handled it now. Still, the lab people are damn good. It is curious. It's like—" he stopped abruptly, then smiled ironically at something, or someone, in the doorway behind Jada.

From that doorway a female voice said, "It's like someone doesn't want her here because they know who she is, right?" Jada had heard that voice before. "They know about you Mrs. Beaudine."

Jada turned to see Madge Lee standing in the doorway wagging her finger at the three of them. "You listen to me, Josia, there are strange things going on here. Don't you sense it too, Rina?"

Irina, the reluctant psychic, clamped her lips tight and let Madge Lee's question sit on dead air.

"Anybody hungry?" Josia rubbed his hands together in anticipation, an enigmatic expression now filling his face. "I wonder what Manny is putting together for lunch today."

*   *   *   *   *

Once they all trudged over to the café, Josia asked Jada to wait, "just a couple more minutes" before she checked out. She was given little time or chance to object; and before she knew it, she, Irina, Josia, and Madge Lee were all crowded into an untidy cubbyhole behind the check-in counter.

Irina's office. Piles of papers had to be shoved off a couple chairs and a stool before they were all able to uncomfortably squeeze in. Jada did a quick look around. Rummage-sale décor predominated, but her eye also caught a tastefully framed Japanese print on the wall facing Irina's desk; and once again she marveled at the enigma that was Irina Hughes.

Josia didn't waste time taking the lead. "I think we've gotten off to a cockeyed start here. I've got a murder to solve, and Rina, no matter how annoyed you may be with me, you're gonna have to cooperate with us if you want to find out who murdered your precious Nicky." He raised his hand toward Irina. "I'm sorry. I want to mend fences here, not build higher ones. 'Precious' was a poor choice of words on my part."

Jada thought her eyes must have given her thoughts away, for he next said, "Yes, Mrs. Beaudine, Rina and I have been friends for a lotta years. We even dated in high school. I married someone else."

"Fool," Madge Lee said.

Ignoring his mother, Josia continued, "And Rina, for some reason only known to her," he shook his head in amazement, "has decided to live the life of a 'desert-rat.'" He straightened his posture and looked directly and earnestly at Jada. "I also think you and I have gotten off to a bad start."

Again, Madge Lee was to be heard. "I told him to apologize to you," she said.

75

For the first time, Jada noticed Josia's eyes were a peculiar shade of hazel. Off-putting to say the least. He said, "So, consider what I just said my official apology. That done—after I talked to mother and did a little more 'research'—it looks like you've been going through hell this last year with your husband dying like that. So I can understand how you wouldn't take to more grilling from me."

Okay, Jada conceded, he's not a *total* ass. She remained silent though, figuring she would let him say what he wanted to say, check out, and still have time to get darned close to Arizona by night fall.

"Mother may or may not be psychic," he continued, holding up his hand again, this time in Madge Lee's direction. "But she is a damn good judge of character. She says you're okay. I accept that." He paused for a breath before continuing, "I also understand from friends up north in King County that you've had some successes, 'helping out' is how they put it, with a couple murder investigations before your husband died. I don't have much patience with 'amateurs,' but I don't argue with success." He looked at his mother. "I assume my mother mentioned she's 'helped out' on a couple occasions also."

Jada nodded.

"And she probably also mentioned I have sort of a reputation in this area?"

That's it. The light bulb finally blinked on for Jada. Chief of Police Josia Rhodes. *Yes.* She had seen him a couple times in those TV specials focusing on real life murder mysteries. He was the one she thought was such an arrogant SOB. Again, her face must have reflected her thoughts quite clearly.

Josia laughed outright. "So, you saw the shows?"

"He was an arrogant butt," Madge Lee said. "Right? Patted himself on the back constantly, didn't give anyone else any credit."

"I've seen the tapes," he said. "I know I made a fool of myself, but can we get back to this murder?"

Embarrassed at her own apparent transparency when it came to Josia, Jada quickly agreed. "Good idea. You were asking me about the gun earlier in the lab. Anything from ballistics yet?"

"No. By tomorrow I expect."

"He died from the gunshot wound?"

"Doc is saying 'yes,' but the autopsy report isn't official."

Jada thought about Darcie waiting for her husband's body and wondered if she'd had to identify him. Gunshot wounds to the head weren't pretty, even when it was small caliber, and Nick was no exception. "I met Mrs. Williams today. The gun is a twenty-two, do you think?"

Out of nowhere, Madge Lee said, "Darcie's pregnant."

Irina took a step toward Josia's mother. "How do you know that?" she demanded in a rather harsh and prickly tone.

Jada surmised it had been technically "over" between her and Nick, but not completely. Irina obviously cared that another woman, albeit Nick's wife, was having his baby.

"You couldn't tell?" Madge Lee asked.

Irina said, "I thought maybe."

"You have to follow your instincts."

Plainly deciding to ignore the two "psychics," Josia addressed Jada's question on the gun. "Yep, I figure a twenty-two." An enigmatic look Jada couldn't decipher passed across his face. "Premeditated. Whoever shot Williams came prepared and knew he'd be alone that time of the morning. And they must have taken the gun with them. I'll be damned lucky to find it."

"What are you going to do now?" Jada asked.

"I'm planning on talking to everyone in that class. Gabe got preliminary statements but I've got them all coming in 'up close and personal-like' to my office in the morning. That's the soonest I could round them up unless I charge somebody with something. And I don't have any evidence to do that."

The door opened and Manny stuck his head in. Irina's cubby-hole was so cramped his whole body wouldn't have fitted even if he had wanted to join the party. "I've got a big pot of spaghetti, salad, and warm bread if anybody's hungry. Linda's taking a tray out to Mrs. Shoecraft. Nobody else around, so there's plenty."

"By the way," Irina informed Jada as they left her closet-sized office. "You've missed check-out time for today."

Peeved at herself and the Josia-Irina-Madge Lee trio, Jada consented to pay for, but not stay another day; and since she had the room still, opted for a quick after-lunch-nap before hitting the road. *Atlanta bound at last.*

The dog was waiting inside number-two and charged past Jada to go relieve herself as soon as the door opened.

"Sorry, pooch, I didn't think about you being stuck in here. I should have left you outside." Someone had filled a food dish and a bucket of water and placed them in the bathroom. The illusive Mrs. Chacon? At least the poor thing had eaten.

Some dog mother I'd be.

Moments later the dog was back at the door, tail wagging, scratching to get in. Maybe she could take her. After all, there was plenty of room in the minivan.

She let the dog in, then plopped down on her back on the bed. The dog jumped up next to her and scooted around on her back while Jada stared at the dingy ceiling—wondering what Nick had been like and why the heck would anyone want to kill a potter, for goodness sake?

Jada's ruminations surrounding Nick didn't last long. Within minutes she dozed off and her next memory was of Manny Chacon playing at town-crier outside her door.

"Party time," he was calling out. "Party time!"

It was dark, and again Jada didn't want to drive two-lane highways at night. She sighed heavily into her dark room. Why couldn't she get herself out of this place?

"What the hell," she said out loud to herself and the dog, then yelled out into the night, "Thanks, Manny."

She dragged herself into a fully awake state, took a quick shower, donned a clean T-shirt and a fresh pair of jeans, and headed to the café for the big birthday shindig. She was running out of clean clothes. Hopefully there was a Laundromat in Red Rock City.

Before she left her cabin, Jada turned the TV on as company for the dog, who in turn seemed content to continue hanging out in the middle of her bed, staring at the screen— evidently enamored with TV static.

At the café Manny had pulled the three tables together in the center of the room to make one long party table and covered their beat-up Formica tops with burgundy and white linen table cloths. He also had laid out linen napkins, real silverware, and real glasses—no plastic junk.

His luscious looking Red Velvet Cake took center stage, accompanied by platters of buffalo-wings, veggies and dip, cold cuts, cheeses, party meat balls, and assorted hors d'oeuvres like mini-quiches and shrimp balls. To drink, there was punch, and plenty of wine and beer.

Besides Mrs. Shoecraft, Irina, Manny, and Jada, Josia and Madge Lee had both returned. Or, as far as Jada knew, they had never left.

Young Linda Lowry was also there, and several new faces, one of which was Manny's mom, Mrs. Chacon. No one seemed to know Mrs. Chacon's first name, and Manny wasn't offering to tell. She refused to speak anything but Spanish, spent a lot of time patting Manny on the head and kissing him on the cheeks while presumably proclaiming his praises. The rest of her time was spent wagging her finger at Irina, again presumably, setting her straight on important matters concerning her son's well being. Jada's high school Spanish was rusty, but Irina seemed to be understanding Mrs. Chacon quite well.

There was also one new paying customer for the night. *So*, Jada did a sanity check—she wasn't the only traveler idiotic enough to overnight at the Red Rock Inn & Café. It was a comforting happening. She might as well relax. In addition, the wine and beer flowed easily—the group friendly and convivial. Manny placed her near the head of the table, next to Irina who was next to Linda, who was next to the guest of honor. Madge Lee sat on the other side of Mrs. Shoecraft.

The most enjoyable part of the evening for Jada was when everyone focused on Mrs. Shoecraft who recounted the "early days," as she called them. She told about her parents— teachers in Cologne, Germany—moving to England at the start of the war. They weren't Jewish, but her father had loathed Hitler. He considered himself lucky to have gotten his family out.

Surprisingly, Jada found herself captivated, hearing about Mrs. Shoecraft's younger days, especially in context of things that weren't yet around, like TV, computers, SUVs—no time to play your life away—working and keeping food on the table took all their time. Before the war, to take a picnic in the park was a special treat for the Shoecrafts; and after the war, the joy of being alive was enough. Nothing else special was required. She'd seen a lot of world-forming changes, and from the sound of it, had weathered them all quite well.

Jada noticed Madge Lee also offered some collaborating life-evolving comments, but mainly, quite generously and courteously Jada thought, demurred. This was Mrs. Shoecraft's night to shine. Again, Jada found herself taking a liking to Madge Lee. Despite her offending progeny.

Next, Mrs. Shoecraft told about meeting a handsome young soldier in London, of their trip to America on the giant boat, their settling in Chicago and raising two children, and much later moving out west to stay with her daughter after her "beloved Joe" had passed on. Now neither of her children came to visit and Mrs. Shoecraft had disinherited both of them.

Jada was overcome with a sudden and unexpectedly profound sadness after that bit of information—until Irina whispered, "Mrs. Shoecraft has the last laugh there. She's an embarrassment to her kids living out here at the Red Rock, so they don't care if she's disinherited them, figure she doesn't have a 'pot-to-pee-in.'" She leaned in close to Jada and lowered her voice even further. "Truth is, she can live any place she wants. She's worth a few million. Leaving it all to some animal refuge place in Kanub, Utah."

Jada's sadness and disappointment evaporated as quickly as it had appeared, leaving her trying to hold back a smile. She couldn't however. Of course by then she was half a bottle of vino to the good; not smiling took too much effort.

Mrs. Shoecraft seemed pleased with the party and Jada found it charmingly cute the way Linda Lowry had taken to being the old dear's protector—and not to forget, Manny was Linda's "guide." Jada chuckled to herself at their quirky little relationship chain.

In a low voice, Irina also provided Jada with more background information on Linda. She was twenty-one years old and unfortunately hadn't finished high school. Somewhere in her late teens Linda had turned morose, lethargic, sullen. That was followed by bouts of severe depression. Her studies went down the toilet and her social life deteriorated into nothing. She never wanted to leave the house. No friends. No associates. Not what her parents, both physicians, had envisioned. Clearly they were not pleased. Linda's older brother, Phil, was in college, and so eventually, her parents refocused all their efforts and resources on him.

"Not that they just gave up on Linda, I don't think," Irina whispered. "They did try for a long while. I met them once. They sprung for a series of tutors, then doctors, and even a hospital stay." Irina shook her head. "She's been diagnosed alternately as schizophrenic and bi-polar, and the poor kid's on a lot of heavy-duty medication."

Linda certainly hadn't said much all evening, and had avoided eye contact whenever Jada looked her way.

Irina's summation was, "She's very sensitive—an artistic type—needs a focus in her life."

She found Irina's statement simplistic, uncomplicated, and most probably grossly incomplete and inadequate. Terry's mother had been bi-polar, so Jada was somewhat familiar with that possible aspect of Linda's personality. But she had no experience and little knowledge when it came to schizophrenia.

Jada barely moved the entire evening, and her overall impression was one of being constantly plied with food and drink, while simultaneously flooded with unsolicited information and annoying questions. Still, enjoyable all in all.

On the murder front, somewhere between the first toast to Mrs. Shoecraft and Manny cutting the cake, Madge Lee squeezed in a chair next to Jada and informed her, "There's troubled waters ahead, my dear." Like Irina, Madge Lee resorted to whispering and talking almost directly into her ear. "But not to worry, I'll make myself available, starting tomorrow morning to do legwork for you." She straightened up and with a euphoric smile added, "I'm far too tipsy tonight, my dear, to help anyone. But tomorrow, that will be a different story." She nodded her head knowingly. "I know how to get information. Look at this face. Wouldn't you confide in me?"

Jada had to agree. Madge Lee had a perfect "Miss Marple" countenance housed in hippie wrappings.

Late in the party evening, Jada eavesdropped as Manny excitedly explained to the new overnighter sitting on the other side of the table, a guy dressed in black with a huge beard looking almost like a caricature of an Hasidic rabbi, how wonderful the desert was, how beautiful the sunrises and sunsets were, and how all the stuff about snakes and spiders and Gila monsters was highly exaggerated. On top of that, the solitude was just "super."

"You believe all that crap Manny's dishing out?"

While Jada was listening to the young cook expound, Josia had surreptitiously pulled up a chair between her and Irina. "All that bull about how wonderful the desert is?" He was out of uniform and drinking beer straight from the bottle, giving him a touch of humanness. In addition, a light stubble covered his lower face— hinting at a raw masculinity that Jada found disconcerting.

"Sure, don't you?"

"Hell, I've been here all my life. I don't know any difference. Just a place like any other place."

She thought Josia's claim to territorial nonchalance was a lie, but unable to guess at its reason or necessity, let it pass.

Irina got up. "I need to make more punch," she said. "And Manny's not the one BS-ing you. Ask Josia what he does every morning."

He stretched his legs out underneath Irina's vacant chair and looked at Jada. "You got any ideas?"

"About the murder?" she asked. "And I'll take Irina's bait. What do you do every morning?"

"I walk my dogs, that's all." He emptied the remainder of his bottle in one swallow. "The way I see it anyone had access to Williams's studio anytime during the night, or in the morning.

But since he was doing that pottin' stuff it probably happened right before Hal Morton and Corissa McNichols-James arrived."

"McNichols-James? Married?"

"Yep."

"She looks so young," she said. "You know, it's not uncommon for a potter to get up in the middle of the night and go throw a few pots. Beats..." She almost let slip, *crying over a dead husband.* "...counting sheep."

"Like I told you, Doc said it could have happened as early as three A.M."

"Damn." Jada straightened her back. "I should have felt that clay to see how dry it was." She tried visualizing what she had seen that awful morning. Was it just yesterday? "I think, I remember the edges of the mound and the slip on the wheel head were dry."

"Which means?" He pulled his legs back in and leaned forward. "Time wise?"

She sighed. "I don't know what it means because I'm guessing clay dries much faster here than in Washington, and I don't know what kind of clay he was using." She turned and looked Josia straight on. "Do you really think Irina killed Nick? I mean you've known her for years."

There were those hazel eyes again, looking mischievously back at her. He took a long moment, putting his empty bottle on the table, then wiping his mouth with his hand. "Mrs. Beaudine," he said at last, "if I thought Rina had killed Williams I'd have brought her in. She certainly had access, could have done it anytime, just walk over there and shoot him." He cleared his throat. "What I *do* think is she was having an affair with the guy, which in my book ain't motive for murder—just the opposite." He leaned in so close she could smell the beer on his breath. "I think I'm going to find out Nick Williams was not such a 'perfect man,' and when I find out what those imperfections were, I'll have my killer."

Since he seemed to be in a talkative mood, beer-induced no doubt, Jada asked, "Anything more on the gun since we talked earlier?"

Manny appeared, topped off her wineglass, winked, and moved on. She knew she'd had too much already, but, what the heck?

Josia asked, "Bugs ya, right, not having the gun?"

"Yes," she said. "If either Hal or Corissa shot Nick they didn't have a chance to get rid of it."

"But if someone shot him earlier, possible according to Doc, and what you said about potter habits. Whoever shot him could have easily taken the gun with him, or her."

Irina returned and handed Josia a fresh beer. She looked worried. "I still can't get hold of Hal." She chewed on her lower lip. "I've called him all day. I guess I'll just let everybody come for lab tomorrow, maybe I can keep them busy." Her frown turned into a smile, and her green eyes twinkled. Irina had turned the charm on—in Jada's direction. "Of course it sure would be wonderful if you stayed at least a couple hours in the morning, Mrs. Beaudine, to get everyone started. Maybe you'd even want to throw a few pots?"

"Well, if Chief Rhodes wouldn't mind me sitting in on his interviews later." Even as she spoke, Jada couldn't quite figure out why she was agreeing to Irina's request. Clearly too much wine. "I might be interested in hanging around until then. And monitoring the lab would be okay, I guess." She looked to Josia for agreement on the interview part. "I could still get out of town by afternoon."

He shrugged.

"I gather Hal Morton has been in classes for awhile," Jada said. "That's why you want him to teach?"

"Hal was here from the beginning. He knows where everything is and how to run the kilns and stuff. I don't think he

85

can teach, but maybe he can. Right now I just need someone to keep things going until we get all this sorted out."

Josia asked. "What's your put on Morton?"

"Don't like him, don't trust him either."

"Facts or psychic mumbo jumbo?"

Irina gave him a menacing look.

He smirked in return, got up and stretched. "Gotta head out. See ya tomorrow morning, Mrs. Beaudine." Then he went over to Mrs. Shoecraft to say his good-byes.

"Such a jackass," Irina mumbled. "And his mother is so wonderful. If it weren't for her...." She let the rest of her thought drop. "By the way, I heard Madge Lee fussing at him again, telling him to continue being nice to you and make sure he suggests you come to the interviews."

"So that's why the Mister-Nice-Guy, just agreeably shrugging his shoulders. You're right, Irina, he is a jackass."

Manny appeared again, this time looking a tad tipsy himself, and again a bottle in hand, wanting to refill glasses. Jada let him. So did Irina.

"You seem to really like it here," Jada said to Irina.

"Yep."

Manny chimed in, "Why wouldn't she like it, Mrs. Beaudine?"

"It's so isolated. Almost desolate."

"Yep." Irina agreed again.

"So, why do you stay?" Jada asked. "Besides not needing an 'audience' as you say. It has to be more than that."

Irina drained her just refilled glass. "I spent a lot of time 'looking for something,'" she said slowly. "Then I stopped for a moment, more like a year, looked at myself, and looked around me. And holy-Hannah, low and behold, I realized I didn't need to keep searching. I'd already found 'something,' and it was pretty damn special." She said it easily, as if it were the simplest thing in the world. Then she held up her glass for Manny to refill. He obliged with an accompanying inebriated burp.

Later—another half bottle of wine later—Jada lugged her overnight bag back into number-two, gave the dog some meat and cheese treats from the party, called her sister-in-law Solina again, and stayed another night.

Extract from Lyle Elliott's Email to his Home Office
Tuesday—January 7—Almost midnight

Didn't get a chance to call you today, Hamilton. Too busy.

Well, here's what's going on now. I think I spotted a white Ford Explorer several times hanging back behind the Beaudine woman as she drove back and forth to town. It's got to be Terrence. Both times, though, it kept on straight past the Red Rock. Unfortunately I couldn't get a plate number on him. He's probably thinking to bide his time until this murder thing blows over to meet up with her. If I were him, I'd try contacting her and setting up another meet place.

I can't tell if the Police Chief is trying to hold her here or not. I'm thinking he wants her long gone. Seems there were a couple grizzly murders around here a couple years back and he solved them both. The scuttlebutt is his mother helped him! Can you imagine? I think he's probably the type who wants to grab all the glory for himself. Wouldn't want to share the limelight with the Beaudine woman. Anyway, can't tell if he's confiding in her, or she's sticking her nose in, or what. I'm guessing she's poking her nose in, unasked. She even tried chatting up the Williams widow today in a restaurant. I was a couple booths away, couldn't tell what

Beaudine was asking her, but they hung around at least half an hour.

I decided I needed a closer look. So I'm keeping my decent room at the Best Western (I need their wireless internet), but I also checked into the Red Rock Inn and Café. I'm planning on keeping out of the Beaudine woman's path, but just in case, I'm wearing Hasidic get up. Nobody can see a damn thing through all that hair. I know, I know, you think it's silly. But be honest, Hamilton, if it weren't for my "dress up" as you call it, would we have gotten the goods on the Parkers? Or the Neilsons? I saved the company a mil on the Parkers alone.

Anyway, when I checked in they were having a party for an old German lady who lives there. Don't think I was noticed at all. Didn't learn much except she's planning on hanging around another day. She and Rhodes were getting real cozy. I'm guessing she's still waiting to hear from Terrence.

It's weird around here, Ham. No trees, no bushes, just dirt and sagebrush. There are some scrubby things they call trees, but they don't fit what we call a "tree" by a long shot. Great sunrises and sunsets if you're into that kind of stuff. It's also damn cold at night.

I'll try calling you in the morning.
Lyle

After sending his email and before heading back, Lyle took a few minutes to replenish the small overnighter he always carried, and check that his gun was safely in the car. Funny how his Best Western room now felt like a palace compared to his cabin at the Red Rock Inn and Café.

Chapter Five

Wednesday

Quite possibly it was the wine.

Whatever the cause, Tuesday night Jada slept soundly. However, with that deep sleep, again came dreams of Terry.

In the early days, right after his death, she had dreamed of him every night. Fortunately, in the last few months, a switch somewhere in her psyche had finally flipped and permitted her—she had thought—to move on. Nick's murder had evidently adversely affected her progress.

Last night's dreams were kaleidoscopes of small happenings—the routine occurrences that make up the day-to-day of life. Mostly happy times. In fact, the only times they ever argued in her dreams were the replays of his gambling days.

Terry had not been perfect, neither had their marriage; she didn't kid herself there. Over the years she finally recognized Terry had an inner compulsion to be somebody special, and unfortunately, he thought hitting it big at the casinos was the best way to achieve that dream. That had been the worst of times. But happily, he had eventually licked the gambling thing a couple years back, and they had moved on.

Occasionally since his death—in real life and in her dreams—Jada was still angry and resentful. For although understanding was there, and to some extent, acceptance, she had never really gotten over the hurt accompanying the knowledge that her love alone had not been enough for him.

"Well," she said to the dog who woke up as soon as she did. "No point dwelling on what I can't change, now is there?" She yawned, then stretched to exorcise any dreamland residue. "Dream time is over, puppy dog. Now, back to reality." And what a reality it was—Terry still dead, and she, alone and still longing for him.

Jada could tell from the thin shafts of light angling their way through her blinds it was still early. She pushed a yellowed slat down anyway to get a better look at the morning. The blind felt cool and dusty to her touch, but not really dirty. Mojave sand was clearly omnipresent and unstoppable.

The eastern horizon she peeked at was blood-red from end to end—underpinned with a swath of contrasting tangerine orange. "Jeez." The vividness and saturation of the colors caused Jada to blink, and for a second, doubt the reality of what she was looking at.

Last night at Mrs. Shoecraft's party, Manny had gone on and on about his wonderful desert, the fantastic sunrises and sunsets, and the marvelous abundance of critters—friendly and not so friendly. Jada was not overjoyed with the not so friendly critters, but this sunrise was breathtaking. Impulsively, she decided to give Manny's beloved Mojave a try. Yes, she would take the dog for a short walk— snakes, scorpions, and all the rest of the creepy crawlers be damned.

As she got out of bed Jada caught what she thought was the wail of fire engines in the far distance; and the dog, now sitting up on the bed, gave a short pitiful cry. She held her breath, listening for a moment. They were receding, not coming closer. Nonetheless, the fire sirens reminded her of the police sirens yesterday, which in turn reminded her of the foolish promise she had made to Irina to open the lab this morning.

"Damnit," she informed the dog. "I must have been temporarily insane, or flat-out drunk." The dog evidently thought Jada was trying to impart some valuable information for she cocked her head, twitched her ears, and thumped her bushy black tail on the bed. Immediately Jada's self-recrimination over her questionable party behavior morphed into a smile. *Okay*, there was still enough time to take the dog for a short walk, shower, eat, and make it to the ceramics lab on time. Maybe.

Before she could get started, however, the phone rang: it was Manny offering to bring her breakfast at the lab. Jada's smile grew broader, for in the background she could hear Irina pulling the strings, prodding him. The woman had not forgotten her pound of ceramic-class flesh. Jada accepted Manny's offer, which included fresh blueberry waffles, and agreed to meet him at the lab in half an hour.

She next showered, dressed, and with the dog at her side, headed out into the great expanse. On her way out the door she informed the dog, "Okay, I've decided to give you a name."

With another quizzical turn of the head, dark hazel eyes looked inquiringly back at Jada.

"I just don't know what it is yet."

Her plan was to walk about half a mile west, then circle around back to the lab instead of her cabin. If the timing worked out right, Manny would be arriving about then.

The air felt cold to her skin and barely tolerable since she hadn't thought to bring a jacket, hat, or mittens. Fortunately, as she and the dog walked, Jada found her body warming and her spirit lightening even more. The dog evidently loved it, running circles around her and sniffing under sagebrush, finding nothing—thank goodness—except multi-pointed sticker-bug-seeds that seemed to be magnetized to her thick Chow-like coat.

Despite the beautiful sunrise and the frolicking dog, Jada kept her eyes focused downward. The sandy ground was pockmarked with burrow holes and not as level as it looked. But surprisingly, after about ten minutes or so, she found her body and psyche becoming more comfortable with the terrain; and though still not sure-footed, her mind felt free enough to wander—landing predictably on Nick Williams.

Someone had surprised him at the wheel. Someone who knew him well enough to expect he would be working before class and so engrossed in his throwing as not to pay attention. Maybe a trusted friend? Someone he would never expect to shoot him in the head.

She was sure Nick had been shot from the front, yet they had found him slumped forward onto his wheel, his face smashed into his pot. The killer must have walked around Nick's dead body, then pushed him forward. If that was true, why the added malice? Whatever the circumstances, it had been premeditated, calculated, and cold. Irina had complained Nick had not deserved to die. She also had called him a "perfect man." But even though she hated to admit it, Jada agreed more with Josia. Nick Williams had imperfections, alright, and whatever those imperfections, they were the key to his murder.

She shot a quick look back to see how far they had gone and was surprised at the distance covered out into no-man's land. She turned around immediately and headed for the lab. On the way back, the dog hung close by, adventure over. They were about fifty feet from the west side of the lab, hidden from the road, when the dog started barking—urgent and loud. It took Jada a few seconds to figure out what was going on. Then she saw the body.

Cautiously, hardly daring to breathe, she walked closer, the dog instinctively staying at her side.

He was flat on his back, arms and legs flayed outward, dried blood on his forehead and on his chest around his heart. *Flies swarming all over.* Jada fought back bile rising in her throat. Someone had shot Hal Morton.

Urgently she shushed the dog, continued forward even closer, then carefully bent over the body to check for a pulse. There was none, of course, and the flesh around his wrist was cold and waxy.

Jesus Christ. Another dead body.

"Come on, pup. We need to get help. Quickly." Jada backtracked to the patio connecting Nick's studio and the lab and entered through the rear door where she thought she remembered seeing a phone. The dog followed along obligingly. Yes, the phone was there, a wall-mount next to a drying-table filled with completed work ready to be loaded into the electric kilns for bisque firing. Pieces that would probably be waiting a long time.

She called 911, then called Manny at the office. The required wheels were set into motion. Then she sat down on the stool by the phone and waited, feeling unreasonably guilty and inadequate. Nothing could be done for Hal Morton now, yet she felt someone should be keeping watch over him. She did not, however, have the fortitude to go back outside and sit by his lifeless body.

Manny and Irina arrived at the lab together. He was carrying a gigantic tray laden with coffee and tea service, silverware, and napkins, while Irina was lugging a picnic basket, presumably full of food.

Once their load had been dumped on a worktable in the lab proper, Irina insisted on seeing the body herself before she would accept Jada's statement that Hal was dead and lying on the ground right out back. Consequently, Jada sucked in a deep breath and led Irina to Hal—then accompanied her back as soon as Irina reconciled herself to reality.

Another body. Another death.

In their absence, Manny had poured three large mugs of steaming hot coffee and spread out croissants and Danish. He had dropped the plan for blueberry waffles. *Wisely so*, Jada thought, given the circumstances. There was something psychologically festive about "blueberry waffles" that didn't fit current circumstances. She was beginning to appreciate Manny as quite a treasure. Irina was lucky to have him at her side. Terry had not been so sensitive to the nuances of life.

"I can't believe this, I just *can't* believe it." Irina pulled up a stool at the worktable, grabbed a mug, and inhaled a slug of coffee. "Christ. First Nick, and now Hal. What the f...," she caught herself with an apologetic look in Manny's direction. "What the heck's going on? It's just a little ceramics class, for Christ's sake. You called Si directly, right Manny?"

"Yep. On his way."

"What did he say?"

He hesitated.

"Manny," Irina said, "I want to know."

He sighed. "Well, he cursed."

"He would."

"And then he said 'Something's going on out there, and I don't like it.'"

Jada said, "He's right, Irina, something is going on here. Someone killed Nick for a reason still unknown; and I'm guessing Hal knew what that was, and that's what made him a danger to the murderer." She sat down at the work-table next to Irina. "Josia is going to have to clamp down on everyone involved with this place and your little pottery class. Believe me, I know what you're in for." She pulled a mug of coffee over for herself. The dog laid down patiently next to her feet.

Jada preferred her caffeine delivered in tea, but went with Manny's suggestion to provide a stronger jolt of caffeine than "English Breakfast" could deliver. After a fortifying sip of hot and strong French Roast, she asked, "Irina, do you know anything about Hal that might play into this? And if you know anything about the women Nick might have been involved with, past and present, you need to tell Josia." She took a deep breath. "Otherwise, well otherwise, he's just going to keep banging away at everybody here."

Looking pissed, baffled, and maybe a little in shock, Irina shook her head miserably.

Manny cleared his throat and said, "You know a few of that class lot come to the café for coffee or donuts, sometimes even a full breakfast, before class. And there's one lady, Star, I think her name is, often stops for a burger before she heads home. I remember her because she only gets onions and mustard, no fries—and a chocolate shake. Always the same." He cleared his throat. "And she's a 'looker.'"

Jada waited expectantly as Manny sat down across the table from her and Irina, put cream and sugar in his coffee, then pulled a huge Danish covered with icing and nuts his way.

Finally he continued, "Anyway, I heard a couple of the morning bunch talking about Mr. Morton. He wasn't well liked. I got the impression under all that politeness crap...well, you know how he was, Rina."

"Solicitous." Irina's voice still sounded mystified, and her face clearly said she hadn't yet taken in Hal's murder. "Yeah, solicitous. And behind all that nicey-nicey there was, you know, what do the Brits say? Madge Lee uses it all the time." Manny looked to the ceiling for a second. "Oh yeah, 'a nasty piece of work.'"

So, Jada marveled, cheerful Manny with the childlike demeanor was not just a pretty-faced gofer and a great cook sensitive to the requirements of the occasion—he was also an observant and intelligent watchdog.

"What I remember," he said, "was the morning gang talking about how they suspected Hal was being particularly nasty to Star—that's the hamburger lady. So one of them, don't remember which, said yeah, maybe he was blackmailing her. I hate blackmailers."

Jada was surprised by the edge of anger in Manny's last words.

He looked to Irina, and evidently reading approval in her face, continued, "My mother came to the United States from Mexico. Illegally. She paid a thousand dollars to a 'coyote' for a seat in the back of a truck. She's a citizen now. But then, she was in constant fear she'd be caught and sent back." He stopped for a few seconds to catch his breath. "Eventually, she married my father, filled out papers, took the test, all that stuff. But my father, before he died, told me how for five long years while my mother worked as a housekeeper in Brentwood, the bastard who brought her across the border blackmailed her. Fifty dollars a week. Doesn't sound like much now, but at the time it was a lot of money for my mother. I was so mad when I found out, I went looking for him." Remembering, his face flushed. "I was going to kill him. And you know, I actually found him. But when I did, he had become a shriveled up old man living in a squalid room tacked onto the back of his nephew's auto-body shop."

"What did you do?" Jada asked softly.

Manny laughed, short and cheerlessly. "Looked like he was barely making it, probably not even enough to eat, so I gave him fifty dollars and left. Didn't even mention who I was or why I was there. You see in the end, my mother became a citizen, had me, and according to her, is one happy *Señora*. And that old bastard died a few years back, sick, unhappy, and penniless. 'Evil don't pay,' Mamma always says. She's right on that one."

Irina said, "Hal was evil."

"Physic insight?" Jada was skeptical.

"Yes," she answered quite seriously. "I felt it that first day he arrived. Didn't say anything, of course. Hell, didn't really know anything, just that he was one to stay away from."

Sirens wailed in the distance again—*police and ambulance this time—and what a commentary on my life that I can tell the difference.* Jada fought a wave of melancholy. *Not now.*

The dog sat up, ears perked, tail high. She could visualize Josia's face, probably annoyed, arrogant for sure. She knew he would give her a line of crap for finding a second body. And he would probably try his "don't leave town" bit again. She steeled herself. And when the sound of footsteps crunching gravel eventually reached Jada's ears, she looked to Irina, who in turn sighed dejectedly and gestured to her and Manny not to get up. Irina then went outside by herself to meet Josia.

Manny leaned over toward Jada. "I'm really glad you came to us."

"Manny, I appreciate the sentiment, but I'm leaving this afternoon." He had to know.

He looked heartbroken, but offered to refill her mug just the same. They heard Irina greet Josia, then Gabe, then Dr. Beach. It would be a long morning; and Jada knew even then, that she had just lied to Manny. She wouldn't be leaving until tomorrow.

It felt to Jada like she and Manny had waited hours; but the lab clock, a round schoolhouse type with big black numbers, clearly showed only twenty minutes had lapsed, and barely that.

Occasionally they caught voices, snippets of conversation—Josia, Gabe, Dr. Beach, Irina—mostly it was a jumble. Eventually they could hear Irina and Josia closer, near the door. Still it was hard to make out what actually was being said, then Jada caught the word "Okay," clearly said by Irina, then a glimpse of her through the window heading to the café.

I'm next. Jada prepared herself. On cue, Josia came in. She expected him to be PO'd, to swagger, to try to bully her.

He pulled up a stool across the table from her and Manny, just about where Irina had been sitting, smiled and said very politely, "Mrs. Beaudine, thanks for hanging around until we had a preliminary look at the scene." He eyed the coffee and goodies. "Mind if I..."

"Here, Josia," Manny said. "Let me pour you a mug. These carafes keep the coffee real hot. The Danish are from my mother, dropped off fresh this morning."

"Thanks," Josia said and accepted a steaming mug. "Manny," he sounded apologetic and his eyes betrayed weariness. "Could I interview you a little later, back at the diner? I'd like to talk to Mrs. Beaudine alone if you don't mind."

Manny looked to Jada, his eyes asking if he should leave her. She smiled and said, "I'll be okay. I don't think Chief Rhodes is going to haul me off to jail. At least I hope not."

With a reluctant glance, Manny nodded and departed.

"Look," Josia said, putting his cup down on the table and leaning forward. "I know you think I'm an ass, maybe justifiably, I don't know." He cleared his throat quietly. "But what's important is there have been two murders here at the Red Rock and despite appearances, I consider Rina a friend. I know she looks tough, but she's actually a pretty fragile little lady. You, on the other hand..." He stopped for a moment, clearly taking time to choose his words before continuing. "You're strong. I've seen it in your face. Now I'm a damn good detective, and my mother is a damn good investigator, but I don't know if I'm gonna get the time to bring this one on home."

Put off guard by his unexpected change in approach—and admittedly intrigued and psychologically softened—Jada took the bait. "What do you mean about not having the time?"

"The County, or the State guys, or both, are gonna want to take this over real soon. Right now, it's local with a resource assist from the county because the Williams murder hasn't hit the big city papers. No big political career is on the line." He grunted world-wisely. "And I have friends, if you get my drift. Now, with a double murder, well I figure I've got a few days, maybe a week if I'm lucky, then this isn't gonna be my case. Cases, I should say." He reclaimed his cup and took a healthy swallow. "I don't think Rina killed Nick or Hal. But this is *her* place, and it's not easy for someone to come and go here unnoticed, and they could make a motive with a little digging. Jilted lover crap." He sighed. "But I'll be honest with you, it's not just that I'm concerned for Rina."

When he hesitated, Jada picked up the thread of his thought. "You don't like having your case taken over by somebody else."

"Egotistical, huh?"

She left his question unanswered. "Chief, you're right about politics and the media. I know, I've been there. Once these murders of yours get on the nightly news it's going to be a circus no matter how many 'favors' you have out there. But I'm not sure where you're going with this."

"Where I'm going," he let out a puff of air, "is I would like for you to hang around for awhile. My mother thinks you can add some insight into this case."

Jada looked out the window. This was not what she expected, nor was it what she wanted. Still unsure what to do, she said, "I understand what you're saying." She took a deep breath. "I'd like to help but I really don't see how I can. I've already said I'd hang around through your interviews this morning."

"But then you want to get the hell out of here as fast as you can. Right?"

She gave it a few seconds. "It's been a long bad year for me," she said carefully. "My sister-in-law is waiting for me in Atlanta. I feel I need to get there."

He leaned back and waited.

Turning back to him, she said, "But I guess I could hang around for a couple more days." There. Foolishly, she realized, in a matter of minutes she had let him outmaneuver her. Or had he?

Maybe Josia had merely offered her a carrot she didn't want to refuse? His face was unrevealing.

"Any news on Hal?" she asked.

"Doc won't tell me anything about the time of death yet. Because of the cold. The dryness makes it tricky too. You think it's warmer than it really is."

He was right, her walking had kept her warm, and she had probably overestimated the temperature.

"So what did you see?" he asked.

"When the dog and I came upon Hal we were heading to the lab so I could look things over and get ready for the students Irina is expecting this morning. I kind of promised her I'd monitor them. I think the dog saw his body first. Or maybe she smelled it."

"Where's the dog now?"

Jada pointed to the lump of fur lying on the floor hidden under the table next to her stool—her ears up as if listening and understanding what they were talking about. "I was surprised," Jada continued. "One body was enough, but two? I was also surprised *how* he was laying there."

"Like he'd been blasted back, flat on his back."

"Yes. But it was gun shots, right?"

"Looks like it so far. But a larger caliber than used on Nick, .45 maybe. Head and heart."

Jada said thoughtfully, "I've heard that phrase before. That caliber can knock a man back like that, right? Especially if he's not expecting it."

"Sure can. I've been hit with a .45 testing a bulletproof vest and was damn near knocked off my feet. Professional assassins, mobsters, that's where you've heard 'head and heart.'"

"You don't suspect? Do you?"

"Doubt a paid assassin came out here to the Red Rock and plugged Hal Morton. No. I'm guessing it's local and personal."

"The other thing that hit me was his shoes."

He raised an eyebrow. "Shoes?"

"The only other time I met Hal was right outside this building getting ready for class after we found Nick's body. I remember he was neatly dressed, had on a shop apron, but he was wearing cruddy sport shoes. Often potters do that, or wear flip-flops. Especially if you're on the messy side. I didn't think anything of it. But this morning, he has on nice shiny loafers that look new. I don't know if it's important, but it makes me think, well, maybe Hal could have been here all night, or from real early this morning." Jada looked to some spot past Josia, not really seeing, just speculating. "Maybe meeting someone? An appointment? He wasn't here to do pottery. Unless he has some shoes stored away."

"Doc's gonna try to give me an estimate on time of death this afternoon. Are you still coming to my office? Rina's making me up a new list of people in this damn class. Asked her to make notes. I'm not waiting until this afternoon to talk to these folks. As soon as they start arriving here, I'm having Gabe make immediate appointments at my office." He stood up as if getting ready to leave. "Meanwhile I'm getting the county forensics team in again. Now the county will know as much about all this as I do, and they're going to be on my ass before I can blink." He shook his head, made a sucking sound through his teeth, then blew out a long, slow stream of air. "And so far I don't have a damn thing. Nothing. Not even a shell casing to run with."

Jada read behind his words, and partly agreed—this was going to be one of those squirrelly cases where forensics weren't going to be much help. *Motives, personalities, the past—that's what he needed to find out.*

The front door to the lab burst open. "Thank God, You're okay!"

Unbelievable. "Mel?"

Terry's brother Melvin Beaudine, nattily attired in a three piece pinstriped charcoal-grey suit, rushed through the front door straight to Jada—his ebony eyes apprehensive and the cut of his broad mouth firm. He wrapped his arms around Jada and lifted her off the ground in one of his trademark bone- crushing hugs.

"We've been so worried. Solina and Neal have been going crazy about what's taking you so long. They thought someone had kidnapped you, or worse. I was beginning to wonder myself."

Jada managed a look in Josia's direction, a plea for help. But he just stood there, a smirk on his face.

"So, what the heck's going on here?" Melvin insisted, then planted a big fat kiss on her forehead.

She extricated herself, kindly and slowly; she liked Melvin a lot. "I did call a couple times you know. I assume that's how you knew where to find me." She turned to Josia. "Chief Rhodes, this is my brother-in-law, Melvin Beaudine, my deceased husband's brother. Solina Beaudine-Chambers is their sister. Neal Chambers is Solina's husband." She didn't elaborate Melvin was a retired CPA now running his own in-home consulting business.

The two men, though dressed quite differently, were both about the same height and build. They shook hands and Melvin said, "The young man at the café said it would be okay to come on out here. Jada, will you please tell me what's going on?"

She grimaced; she had a lot of explaining to do. She also needed another cup of coffee, and a croissant was a definite possibility. But in a blink, her world flip-flopped yet again. Shotgun blasts—three in a row.

Josia immediately drew his gun and charged outside, with Melvin following at full gallop.

"Are they crazy?" Jada demanded of the dog. "Suppose there's a crazed killer out there?" It didn't make sense, running out like that without knowing what was going on. Well, maybe for Josia—that was his job. But Melvin? What could possibly have gotten into him?

Then the dog deserted her too, preferring to join the chase. "What the heck?" Jada demanded anew. But there was no one left to answer.

It took a couple more minutes without further shots for Jada to also venture out. Cautiously, and wisely she thought, she left out the back door and gave a quick look toward the spot where Hal's body lay.

Doctor Beach was peering into Hal's head wound, and a cop was talking on his radio—not Gabe and in a different jurisdiction's uniform. Doctor Beach looked up at Jada, and they exchanged the slightest of shrugs, but no words. Both men looked concerned and were definitely on alert.

Satisfied Hal hadn't been deserted, and praying there weren't any shots headed her way, she ran toward the café where she could hear shouting. Josia? Manny? Melvin? As she got closer she saw Josia and Melvin running south through the desert, chasing someone she couldn't see, but presumed was there. Dust from their running feet clouded the air and caused her to wonder if she was seeing right. *Melvin running after a man with a gun?*

Then fear hit her hard and intense. *This is real*, someone had been shooting, and that same someone was being chased across the desert—by her brother-in-law. The air was still chilly, but not cold enough to produce the shiver that shot through her body. Again, it wasn't even 10:00 A.M. and all hell had broken loose at the Red Rock Inn and Café.

The dog, breathing heavily and tail limp, returned after about five minutes to find her mistress in the café anxiously chewing on already ragged fingernails and pacing from door, to windows, to counter—then all over again. Jada was listening to Manny fill everyone in on what had happened. "Everyone" consisted of Jada, Irina, Mrs. Chacon, and the new paying guest.

Manny was saying, "I went outside to help Mr. Tolmin with his luggage. He was checking out."

Tolmin, the rabbi-looking man Jada had seen at Mrs. Shoecraft's party, was sitting at the front table by himself, staring intently out the window, his back to their little gathering. Jada still couldn't imagine why he would stop at the Red Rock Inn; and even more peculiarly, why his back seemed so ramrod stiff, insinuating tension—obvious even through his thick black rabbinical-looking suit jacket. Surely, his interest was only as a happenstance and casual observer?

"While I was putting his suitcase in the trunk," Manny continued, "I noticed this man standing by your door looking around suspiciously."

Manny had moved and taken station at a window next to the second table—a long-barreled shotgun ready at his side. Irina sat at the counter, and Mrs. Chacon stared at her son anxiously from behind the counter. Several times Mrs. Chacon made the sign-of-the-cross while muttering words Jada took to have religious significance.

"A man was hanging around number-two?" Jada demanded.

"That's right. So—"

"It was my brother-in-law, Melvin, right?"

"No, Mrs. Beaudine," Manny insisted, pulling his gaze from outside for a moment. "I'd already met your brother-in-law and directed him back to the lab. This was some dude I've never seen before, and he was acting real suspicious-like." He looked back outside. "He was, you know, looking around nervously. And I know our locks aren't the greatest, so I yelled out, you know, trying to get his attention. Mr. Tolmin can tell you the same thing. Then the dude pulled a gun." Remembering, Manny first shuddered, then shook his head, clearly in amazement at the audacity of such an act. "So I yelled to Mr. Tolmin to keep his eye on the bum and I ran in here and grabbed my shotgun from underneath the counter."

The story Jada was hearing sounded incredible. "It looked to me like he was going to shoot at Mr. Tolmin." Manny inclined his head toward Tolmin. "And Mr. Tolmin looked like he was going to go after him. So I shot a couple rounds off at the bum, but not actually at him, you know. I wasn't really trying to kill him." Manny's voice turned apologetic and he gave Jada another quick look. "But it stopped him from shooting I think, 'cause he stuck the gun in his jacket pocket and took off. That's when Si and your brother-in-law came running and started chasing him.

"I sure wish I'd gotten a better look at him," Manny continued. "You know, they could do one of those sketch things like you see on TV, couldn't they? But all I could tell was it was a man." He rubbed his forehead. "At least I'm almost sure it was a man."

The loud squeal of tires, then the wail of a police siren moving away sent a further jolt of incredulity through Jada's senses. She just couldn't believe her retired accountant brother-in-law was participating in a California car-chase. In response to that disbelief, she felt her stomach starting to pump acid.

She said, "Manny, you probably saw Mr. Morton's killer trying to get in my cabin." Jada hugged herself for comfort as Irina came to her side.

Mrs. Chacon had turned silent, but Jada noticed her eyes were now closed and she was noiselessly moving her lips. Praying, she was sure.

Tolmin got up and went to the front door, evidently to get a better look through the larger door-glass. And Jada stared at his back for several long moments.

Manny then left his post and joined Tolmin at the door and said loud enough for everyone to hear, "Looks like Si is still chasing the dude in his police car, but your brother-in-law is headed back this way."

Thank God.

As soon as Melvin stepped into the café, Jada pushed past Tolmin and Manny and grabbed him by his jacket sleeves at the shoulders. "My God, Mel, are you alright?" She was ineffectively trying to shake a two hundred-pound man. Finally, realizing the ridiculousness of her actions, she quit and gave him a big hug instead. "Are you crazy running after a gunman? You might have been shot." She almost added, *"In a three piece suit."*

"Nah, Sis, I wasn't in any real danger." He extricated himself from her bear-hug. "That Police buddy of yours was way out in front of me. I was just tagging along in case he needed any help. When we got back to the lab parking lot, he jumped in his car and told me to get back here." Melvin looked exhilarated, and his tone reverberated the excitement he was experiencing. "You know, you certainly live an interesting life. Are you going into the Chief's office now and wait for him to get there with the gunman? I'm confident he'll catch him."

"Ah…"

"Do you need some help?" Mel asked. "I think I should hang around awhile."

"What have you told Solina and Neal? And what are you planning on telling them now?"

"I told them that I'd find you and find out what was going on here." He paused thoughtfully for a couple seconds. "I guess now I'm going to tell them I need some time to figure it all out."

They looked at each other, calculating. "Are you calling them or am I?" Jada asked. "And what should we tell them about why I'm still here? Of course it's not that important anymore, because I'm only planning on staying a couple more days."

"I'll call," he offered. "And let's just wait and see what we tell them about your arrival in Atlanta." Then with a wink and discerning look, Melvin made himself a co-conspirator in— Jada didn't want to say the words out loud—a murder investigation. Two murders in fact. *Oh yeah, and maybe an attempt on my life.*

In an atypically refined and deceptively soft tone, Irina said to no one in particular, "I can't believe this is happening at my little place."

Indeed, Jada could feel Irina's outrage. Undeniably, Irina's little piece of the Mojave was being violated. Big time.

Gabe handed Jada a copy of the list Irina had prepared. "As far as we know, Mrs. Beaudine, this is everyone in the class."

It wasn't much, but she took it, and in a show of comradeship requested Gabe start calling her "Jada." She liked the deputy's pleasant and polite manner, and even though he willingly played the Poncho role to Josia's Cisco Kid, she was finding him an intelligent and competent young man in his own right. And his wide eyed eagerness was indeed refreshing.

Eight names, one dead, seven left—all suspects.

Hilary Giles	52	Son killed by drunk driver—ceramic therapy
Hal Morton	57	In startup class—experienced—dead
Leroy Ames	72+	Retired—makes bonsai pots—gardener
Corissa McNichols-James	25?	Young housewife—acts squirrelly
Star Thomas	40	Married (Phillip), works nights at base—pretty
Penny and Timothy Berry	62/63	Retired couple—come for socialization—gossips
Marie Shipling	67	??? first class—quiet, stays to herself—sharp

"Chief Rhodes says you're going to sit in on the interviews, right?"

"If you don't mind." She looked around inquiringly. "I'll try to stay out of the way. Do you have an interview room somewhere?"

"We don't have an interview room as such, Mrs. Beaudine, Jada," Gabe said. "We have a break-room down the hall, we call it the 'everything-room.' You know, refrig, microwave, sink. It's got a table and chairs and we use it for interviews when needed."

"Great."

They were talking in a large office behind the front counter. The office wall facing the entrance was all glass and provided an unobstructed view of the front entrance and counter. Inside there was space for a worktable and two large desks with accompanying wooden swivel armchairs.

Right inside the office door on the wall was a small corkboard with a few haphazardly displayed announcements and APBs. Not exactly high-tech.

One faxed picture flyer caught Jada's eye for a second, a mobster of some sort—"Tommy Max" she thought the smeared print read—on the run and wanted for some reason. Something about his mug-shot reminded her of Terry. Similar occurrences had been many in the early days after Terry's death, but she had thought this type of inexplicable emotional excursion had disappeared. Surprised, she forced her thoughts back to the present.

If desktops were an indication of anything, Gabe's desk, which faced the front counter, was covered with papers, folders, stray pens and pencils—accessorized with a couple old Styrofoam cups, a dingy water glass, and a circa 1970s typewriter. On one corner of his desk, a fairly current-looking personal computer sat covered and gathering what Jada now knew to be ubiquitous desert-dust.

Josia's desk faced a side wall where a gigantic poster of a wave-washed Big Sur covered most of the wall. The top of his desk was neat and clean, surface uncluttered, no dust—all office paraphernalia in their proper places, and an ultra-thin laptop computer open and running a screensaver picture of two German Shepherd dogs.

There were also a couple file cabinets and two butt-numbing wooden chairs between Josia's desk and a worktable. Jada was sitting uncomfortably on such a chair, a fact causing her mild irritation, since her posterior was quickly becoming sore. While Gabe was ensconced in his swivel chair with an orthopedic pad, further embellished with a pillow on top. Interestingly enough, a quick peek at Josia's chair revealed no such pillow luxury.

A backdoor slammed, the sound coming down a short corridor leading back and away from the office, toward what Jada thought could be a small cellblock.

"Must be the Chief now." Gabe got up and stuck his head out just far enough to look around the corner and down the hall. "Yep, that's him. Looks like he's gone into the everything-room to set up. You can go on back if you want. I have to stay out here and cover."

Jada did indeed find Josia in the everything-room. His back to the door, he was pouring coffee into a large ceramic mug. "This is nice," she said to his back, referring to the room.

The walls were a soothing blue and tastefully adorned with numerous framed *Sumi-e* prints, two of which Jada instantly liked a lot. One was of bamboo and leaves, and one was of a cat climbing through vines. "Lovely," she added, this time, referring to the prints in particular.

On the practical side, a tile kitchen counter ran most of the length of one wall, where a microwave, an espresso machine, and a toaster were available. Next to the counter stood a two-door black refrigerator.

A large rectangular wooden table dominated the center of the room, and the six accompanying chairs weren't the typical government-issue jobs, but stylish wooden dinette chairs on wheels and upholstered in a blue print pattern with tones that matched the walls. Pretty, functional, and probably comfortable.

Josia had evidently heard her come in and wasn't startled by a woman talking behind his back. Proceeding with the task at hand, he asked, "You're talking about the room, right?" He was pouring a crystalline river of sugar into his mug. "Not the usual, is it?" Finally satisfied with his brew, he turned toward Jada.

He looked awful, his face drawn and haggard, his eyes, bloodshot. She hadn't noticed earlier—maybe something happened since she had last seen him at the Red Rock Inn & Café? He said, "You know, you must be a terrible poker player. I know I look like shit. But I had a crappy night and this hasn't been a wonderful morning, as you well know."

He started to sit down at the table, grimaced and hesitated, then with a hop-limp kind of motion, managed to lower himself into a chair.

Jada sat down across from him. "Are you alright?" she asked. "Did you sprain something while you were chasing that gunman?"

"Now, now, don't you go getting soft on me. I'm counting on your no-nonsense attitude."

She grunted and shook her head. "I don't know if that's a compliment or a dig. In the interest of camaraderie I'm going with compliment." *That darn toothy smile again.*

"My mother decorated the room," he said with fondness. "Always sticking her nose into my business. Claims I'll get more out of people if they feel comfortable. You know — non-threatening kind of crap."

"And you prefer the grab 'em by the collar and beat their head against the wall approach?"

He stretched his right leg out underneath the table and grimaced again. "What I prefer, Mrs. Beaudine, is what works. That's why I let my mother do whatever damn foolish thing she wants to, and why I've asked you here. I know my mother 'works,' and I hear from reliable sources other than my mother, that you do too."

Jada decided to also take that as a compliment. "I don't like threatening notes," she said. "And I certainly don't like strangers looking for me carrying a gun. I guess that's to say, I'm interested." *Pull back, Jada. Remember, you're leaving this in a couple days.* She modified her statement. "Interested enough at least to hang around through the interviews."

"Nosey, huh?"

"'Curious' is how I'd put it."

He laughed. "Whatever."

"Chief Rhodes?" Hilary Giles stood at the door, looking in hesitantly. "The deputy said I should come back here."

Josia straightened up smartly. The tiredness and frustration she had seen earlier were gone — it was show time. He stood — no grimace — and extended his hand. "Come in, please, Mr. Giles. Have a seat."

With a wan smile, Hilary nodded a greeting Jada's way and went around Josia to sit in a chair facing the doorway, his back to the far wall. Hilary Giles watched his backside. She had seen that behavior before, but it didn't fit the persona she had postulated so far. Or did it? Maybe losing your son does that to a man.

"I really appreciate you coming by," Josia said. "You know I've got a double murder on my hands now. Mr. Williams and Mr. Morton."

Hilary's eyes widened and his long sad face fell even farther. "I heard, but...." He sighed and spread his hands on the table. "I didn't want to believe. It all seems so incredible."

A young woman appeared at the door and coughed politely. "Chief, you said you needed me this morning," she said.

"Yes," Josia said, going over to her. "Come on in Beth, have a seat next to Mrs. Beaudine." To Jada and Hilary he said, "Beth Armstrong is a Kern County Law Enforcement Training Academy graduate and is currently interning with us."

Jada wondered why "intern," then figured it must be more like a tryout before Beth selected a final assignment. She almost smiled thinking about Josia having to be on good behavior for a prospective employee. Or maybe a departmental spy?

From down the hall behind Beth came a loud clinkety-clank. All four of them in the room fell silent and waited as the noise grew in approach. Beth gave Jada a confident smile, Hilary quickly cast his eyes downward when Jada looked his way, and Josia, *damn his butt,* winked at her. Finally, an old metal cart-table, pushed by Gabe, appeared in the doorway. On it was a portable stenography machine—Jada hadn't seen one like it in decades and was amazed a working one still existed—a slightly more modern tape recorder, and a box of donuts.

Evidently Beth was going to take all this down for posterity—and so was the recorder. Gabe got Beth set up while Jada wondered who was watching the front desk. Or did it even matter?

"Despite appearances, Mr. Giles, this isn't an interrogation, but I don't want to miss any information. Beth will be recording and so will the tape recorder." Josia then sat down again at the other end of the table facing Giles, his back to the open door, fearless of an approaching enemy. Jada had seen that behavior before also—in people who don't know any better, and cocky, small town Police Chiefs.

For herself, Jada selected a chair in the middle of the table where she could see the door and everyone in the room, and not be in the line of fire.

"You see," Josia continued. "I believe our only hope of finding out why Mr. Williams and Mr. Morton were murdered lies with you guys in that class."

Hilary didn't seem offended by the implication he might be a murderer. "You think one of us killed those two poor men." Said quietly, it was a statement, not a question.

"What I think is one of you might have heard or seen something that will help me figure out why, and who murdered them."

Jada was listening intently, but for some reason Beth's activities momentarily fascinated her. The young woman had evidently done this a few times already, for her face, looking freshly scrubbed and unfortunately chubby and plain, was blank as her fingers moved. And while the steno machine *whizzed*, the recorder, an older cassette job it now appeared, *whirred* in steady accompaniment. Amazing she knew how to operate the two ancient contraptions.

Refocusing her attention, Jada smoothed out her piece of paper containing class member names on the table and pulled a pencil out of her canvas carryall bag. My technologies of pencil and paper, she mentally rebuked herself, are even more archaic than Red Rock City's.

"When did you join the class, Mr. Giles?" Josia asked.

"About two years ago." Hilary's voice was forthcoming and calm; his face, however, betrayed his reluctance to rehash such painful memories. "My doctor referred me. Actually, he insisted I take up something using my hands. He suggested woodworking, but the idea didn't appeal to me." He blew a puff of air out the corner of his thin lips. "My wife saw the ad for the ceramic class. Good man, my doctor, and an outstanding woman, my wife." His eyes shifted off to some point in time and space only he could see and feel. "I guess I need to tell you about 'why.'"

Jada was sure Josia already knew about Hilary's loss, but she also understood his need to have the poor man go through all that pain again—for the record. Patiently, they waited for Hilary to continue.

"My son was killed, five years back now, in an auto accident down on Highway 138 out of Palmdale. It was in the middle of the day, roads were dry, air was clear. There was a stop sign at a curve in the road." His gaze came back and landed on Josia. "Should not have happened," he said, his accent a tad thicker than before. "No indeed, I dare say. The driver of the other car was quite inebriated. She'd had a DUI once before."

"I'm sorry, Mr. Giles." Josia's condolence sounded genuine to Jada's ear—not just the prescribed words. "Is she in jail?"

"Sadly, no. Last we heard she had been released and moved to Northern California. My wife…" he dropped whatever he was about to say. "You don't think our misfortune has anything to do with these murders, do you?"

"No, I don't," Josia said easily. "What I was hoping is since you're relatively new to the group, you might have picked up some vibes, you know, seen something strange?" He leaned back and clasped his hands behind his head. "Hell, I don't know, like somebody fooling around with somebody else?"

"Now Chief Rhodes, no need to be oblique." Hilary smiled slightly, something Jada doubted he did much nowadays. "I'm sure you've already been appraised that Mr. Williams was something of a ladies man."

Josia dipped his head in acknowledgement and raised a "please-continue" eyebrow, real empathetic and polite-like. Jada hadn't warmed to Josia, but she was beginning, albeit begrudgingly, to appreciate his ability not to be just a one-note charge-ahead cowboy. She had liked it better when she had had him neatly stuffed in a little box with the ribbon tied tight on top.

"There are times in the ceramics lab, my good Chief, when you end up, for instructional purposes, in a group with a number of your classmates." Jada liked the way Hilary talked. His word choices were mostly American, but the rhythm and cadence of his delivery and the properness of his pronunciation and word usage were to her, downright charming. "I'm afraid I haven't been much of a conversationalist these last couple years. But yes, one does hear things." Again Hilary looked to a distant place. "Nothing concrete, mind you, but I understood from the gossip Mr. Williams has had several affairs over the years."

Josia leaned forward, interested. "Yes?"

"Well, Penny and Timothy Berry are, shall I say, congenial sorts? They were quite sure Mr. Williams was having an affair with Ms. Hughes. You know, the kind lady who runs the place?"

Josia nodded encouragingly, but Jada noticed a muscle in his right forearm twitch at the mention of Irina bedding down with Nick. She speculated there was still a connection between Josia and Irina, but since he was married—and Irina was still mooning over the perfect-man-potter—it didn't seem like a hopeful situation for either of them.

"I also heard, maybe a month ago...," Hilary said, then paused thoughtfully for a few seconds before continuing. "They were sure that affair was over. They believed he had taken up with a younger woman. And before you ask—no, they didn't say who it was."

"And before Ms. Hughes?"

"I wish I could be more helpful, but that's all I heard them say."

Hilary reached into his sport jacket pocket and pulled out a neatly folded handkerchief with a thin embroidered border. Jada hadn't seen one of those in eons either. After blowing his nose, elegantly if such a thing was possible, he then asked if there was water available.

Jada voiced the same request and Beth wanted a Root Beer. As it turned out, the refrigerator held a stash of bottled water, various soda pops, orange and cranberry juice, and milk. Josia did the honors, and while he was up, poured himself another cup of coffee sludge which he promptly doctored up with his customary over abundance of cream and sugar. No wonder he looked like hell, Jada mused, almost out loud, restraining her tongue at the last second.

"How about you, Mrs. Beaudine? Anything hit you that Mr. Giles could help us with? Oh yeah," he belatedly explained to Hilary. "I've asked Mrs. Beaudine to sit in this morning. She's had some experience in these matters." On the surface, one could take his deference to her as an example of courtesy. Jada figured he just wanted a couple minutes to get a hefty shot of caffeine into his blood stream.

Hilary looked at her kindly and said, "I understand. I've seen your pictures in the newspapers."

Jada forced herself to let Hilary's comment roll off into oblivion. "Did you ever hear any talk about Hal Morton being a blackmailer?" she asked.

His eyes widened in a childlike way. "Heavens no. I can't imagine that." Then with a resigned expulsion of air and a bewildered shake of the head, he amended, "I suppose I wouldn't be surprised, though. My wife Emily claims I'm not very observant—claims I wouldn't notice a snake unless it bit me in the posterior." He chuckled before coming back—back to the pain he would never be able to bury with his son. "I must be honest. Mr. Morton and I were not comrades."

Again, Hal Morton was not coming across as a likable guy. "Any special reason why?" Jada asked.

"Oh, that's quite easy to explain. He was arrogant and rather rude. Not a gentleman at all."

Having drained his cup, Josia was back. "And what about Nick Williams, Mr. Giles? Did you like him?"

"Ah, now Mr. Williams, like I said before, was what we would have called a rapscallion back in the old days."

"Except this 'rapscallion' was married," Jada said.

"Most true. However, that doesn't seem such a consideration nowadays, does it?"

"You have me there."

Josia asked Hilary a couple more questions, like where he was at the time of both murders, and did he own a gun? The sad answer to the first was, Hilary, a Catholic, went to dawn mass and confession every morning. Father Maurice had pleaded with him not to come *every* morning. There was no need. But Hilary explained how he had to. His sin was immense; he had to keep asking for forgiveness. You see, his son had been on an errand for him when he had been killed. Hilary figured it would take God a long, long time to forgive him for that. Regarding the gun, he said, "Heavens no. Emily wouldn't stand for it." End of story.

"And how did you find out Hal Morton was shot this morning?"

"Penny Berry called Emily with the news."

Hilary left with a promise made that he would go over in his mind his class experiences; and if anything at all broke through to his consciousness he would call the Chief immediately. Jada was sorry to see Hilary go. She liked him.

"Leroy Ames is next. Due in about ten minutes," Josia informed Jada and Beth as he stood, stretched, and rubbed his leg. "Damn chairs."

Beth cleared her throat, and Josia apologized, "Sorry, I know I need to clean up my language. My mother regularly gets on my ass about being a potty mouth."

Beth laughed uncomfortably. "Sir, would this be a good time to use the restroom?"

"Sure, sure, we won't start without you."

After she left, Josia confided to Jada, "Damn, I gotta watch my mouth. All I need is another one complaining to the Mayor about my language."

Jada stood up and also stretched her back. "These chairs aren't that bad, I've seen and felt worse. Madge Lee did a good job."

He went for yet another cup of coffee. "Refill on the water?"

"Thanks, I'll pass for now. What do you think about Hilary?" She didn't wait for an answer. "I can't believe he's a cold blooded murderer."

"Yeah, I like him too. But..."

"Yeah." She knew they both had seen "sweetheart" killers before. People you would never imagine could hurt a fly. The "darlings of hell" Jada called them. And she had quickly learned her personal likes and dislikes didn't matter for squat. Not that she had been involved with murderers a lot, but enough to know her judgement was suspect when it came to "nice." It had almost gotten her killed once, and she hoped not to make that mistake again.

When Beth returned, Jada went off to the restroom herself. When she got back, Leroy Ames had arrived and was sitting in the same seat Hilary had occupied, evidently the designated hot seat. She was introduced from the doorway and then Josia did a preparatory "poor bumpkin cop needing help" speech.

Jada could not restrain herself from staring at Leroy Ames. She needed to recheck her list. She thought Irina had written seventy-two for his age. She must have screwed up because the stiff-backed gent she was looking at couldn't be that old. For starters, his short cropped hair was a natural looking dark brown with only touches of gray in his temples; and from what she could see of it, his body looked trim and in excellent shape. His face, rather nondescript, was of a man in his fifties, sixties, tops; though it did reflect the unavoidable creases of life, the tattletale fine lines of age around the eyes and mouth were nonexistent. No age spots, no sagging jowls.

Jada squeezed past Beth so she could again sit in the middle seat.

"Beth, would you turn the machine back on and we'll get started?" Josia said.

Leroy Ames stood up snappily and extended his hand. "Mrs. Beaudine, Leroy Ames. Glad to meet you." He was tall, his hand shake firm, and his speech, crisp and clear.

Ex-military Jada speculated. "Same here," she said and sat down. "Sorry to keep you waiting."

"No problem." He sat back down, his back straight as a board, and didn't wait for Josia to say more. "I assume, from what you've said so far you're bringing all the class members in for questioning to find out if we can shed some light on the two murders you have on your hands. That is the 'help' you're talking about, is it not?"

"On the head, Mr. Ames." Josia switched his approach to match Ames's no nonsense manner. "Can you tell me how you got involved in the class, how well you knew Mr. Williams and Mr. Morton, and is there anything you noticed or heard that might help me put their killer or killers behind bars?"

Leroy chuckled. "What about the part where you ask me where and what I was doing during the time the two men were killed?"

"There's that, too." A hint of a smile flickered in the corners of Josia's mouth, but he held a straight face. "I appreciate your candor and direct approach. So, what can you tell me?"

"I'll tell you everything I can and let you decide if any of it has any relevance." He cleared his throat. "I moved back to Red Rock City fifteen years ago when I retired from the Navy," he said. "I had a brief stint of duty here earlier in my career. I liked it, so I came back." He cleared his throat once again and pulled himself up even straighter. "The problem with retirement is one needs focus in one's life. I found that out quickly. My wife, Cynthia, had no problem adjusting. She joined charity groups, book clubs, and other organizations. It took me longer finding my way. I ended up opening a communications company."

Once more, Leroy cleared his throat. Jada surmised the mannerism was his way of assuring his words entered the world as crisp and clear as his demeanor.

He continued, "At first it was just the large satellite dishes, but now there's more choices. It's kept me busy. But the last few years I've left the business more and more to my grandson who's into all the latest gizmos. I also decided there was a piece of me that I hadn't yet explored. 'My creative side,' Cynthia calls it. Too make this long story short, I decided to take up pottery."

Josia asked, "What did you do in the Navy?"

"Destroyer Captain. You a Navy man?"

Josia cleared *his* throat combined with a short cough and shot Jada a glance. "Airforce. Ancient history now."

She wondered what he didn't want her to know. "Ah," was Ames's enigmatic response as he exchanged a "knowing" look with Josia. Then he was quickly back to business. "My first class was two years ago. I have enjoyed it immensely. Throwing pots requires coordination, determination, skill, creativity, and at my age, those abilities are increasingly more important to me."

Neither Josia nor Jada asked, but the question hung in the air between them. How old was Leroy Ames?

"I'm seventy-five, to answer the question I know you want to ask. I've done nothing special. Genes."

Beth's wide-eyed expression and intake of breath showed even she was impressed.

"What I've seen myself," he continued, "is Nick Williams flirting with every woman in our class, young or old. But I took it as a charming Lothario act, not that he looked the part. A little too soft if you know what I mean." Leroy waited for Josia to nod. "Everyone knew he was married, so it was more like a joke. At least that's what I thought until sometime last year."

"What happened to change your mind?"

"I find the lady that owns the Red Rock, Ms. Hughes, an interesting person. I make a point to chat with her whenever time permits, such as if I arrive early or stay late and she's around. Over the last two years I've even come to like her—no—more like respect her." He took a moment for thought. "The Red Rock is an unusual venture in an unusual place run by what I consider an unusual woman. I even asked Cynthia to come out and meet Ms. Hughes, and then give me her opinion. Unfortunately my wife's opinion wasn't as sympathetic as mine. But she did concede Ms. Hughes was unusual."

Jada wondered what Cynthia, the military wife, had actually said about Irina, the I-could-give-a-damn part time psychic?

Leroy continued, "Back to what changed my mind, was my witnessing Nick Williams and Ms. Hughes having an argument. I hadn't meant to be there, I'm not a snoop. Find my own life quite enough to handle." He stopped and looked to Josia, then Jada, as if waiting for them to fully appreciate his comments. "Unfortunately I smoked as a younger man and occasionally I succumb to the pull of nicotine and puff away on a cigar. Class had gotten out early that day, and a friend had given me a hand-rolled cigar from Cuba. I know, I know..." He raised his hand in a "guilty as charged" gesture. "So I decided to give it a try out back of the lab, toward the open desert. I had barely lit up when Williams and Ms. Hughes came around the corner. Of course when they saw me, it was all smiles again. But for a few moments, when they thought they were alone, some rather nasty words were exchanged that made it obvious to me I was witnessing the end of an affair." He coughed lightly. "I would prefer not to quote them exactly, if you don't mind. Ms. Hughes, to my surprise, could match tit for tat with some of my old buddies in the Navy in the swear-word arena. Quite an off-color vocabulary for such a diminutive little woman."

Jada laughed outright. Quickly, she covered her *faux pas* with a fake coughing fit, but while digging for a Kleenex in her canvas bag she noticed Josia had covered his mouth with his hand.

Beth-the-sensible looked at both Jada and Josia with disapproval.

Leroy seemed not to notice. "Then there was the incident with Corissa about a month ago. I forget her last name, it's hyphenated and long."

"McNichols-James," Josia provided.

"Yes. Exactly. I overheard Williams ask Mrs. McNichols-James if she wanted to go to a bar with him in Mojave that night. I remember him explaining *Mojave*, because they wouldn't be recognized."

Now that was a surprise. "And what did she say?" Jada asked.

"Sorry to say, Mrs. Beaudine, I don't know. Now I wish I had hung around, but at the time I just wanted to get out of there."

"Too distasteful?" Jada suggested.

"Exactly."

Now, Jada thought, we might be getting somewhere. So, Nick was hitting on Corissa. Corissa was married—maybe she told her husband. Maybe he didn't like that one bit. Enough for murder? For some, definitely.

From there Leroy finished up quickly. He and Cynthia had been on the road heading to Bakersfield with their son during the time Nick was killed. They had turned around and returned when Timothy Berry called them on their cell phone. And this morning, when Morton met his demise, they were at home planning for a camping trip in Death Valley.

Why anyone would want to go camping at a place named "Death Valley" was beyond Jada.

Leroy explained he had never heard mention of Hal Morton being a blackmailer, but like everyone else so far, had not liked the man. "Sleaze bag," were his exact words. "You do plan to interview Penny and Timothy Berry?" he asked.

"Everyone in that class is going to have an 'opportunity' to talk to me, Mr. Ames. Why do you mention them specifically?"

"Because they are nosey, gossipy chatter boxes. If Morton was a blackmailer those two are most likely to know about it."

"Do you own a gun?"

"Yes, two. A twenty-two long rifle, and a nine-millimeter Beretta. Both registered and accounted for in a locked cabinet in my home. You are welcome to see them if you care to."

After asking Jada if she had any other questions for Leroy, which she didn't, Josia walked him out to the front office. Some kind of kindred spirits, Jada wondered? Personalities weren't a darned bit alike, but something was—maybe a military connection, she conjectured.

Beth decided she needed another potty break and Jada was left alone. She yawned, stretched, and thought about Hilary Giles and Leroy Ames. Both men seemed from a bygone era; but when she tried pinpointing what it was about them generating that perception, she had a difficult time. Their words, their speech, their forthright manner? She couldn't nail it down. However, she *did* think she was beginning to get a picture of Red Rock City culture; yet she simultaneously knew that whatever she postulated would likely be wrong.

Nothing, nowhere, or no one is ever that simple. "Jada?" Melvin stuck his head in the door. "Oh great, there you are."

She had forgotten he wanted to sit in—her accountant brother-in-law, nouveau detective. "Hi, you made it," she said cautiously; for an amazing and incongruous sight stood before her. Melvin without a tie.

The only other time she had seen Terry's brother in anything other than a suit, usually three piece, a white or light blue shirt and a conservative tie—typically a subtle maroon or dark blue print—was on a trip to Walt Disney World eons ago.

At the time, Solina and Neal's three kids were all still under ten, it was eighty-five-plus degrees in Atlanta, and rumored to be ninety-five degrees in Orlando. Humidity was at drizzle level in both places; and they were all going to have to pack into a minivan for the four-hundred-plus mile drive. Only then, had Melvin, the Iron-Man, finally broken and donned a print sports shirt, slacks, and sandals.

She could still picture that day, that time. Everyone else in the family was ready to go, all of them standing in the driveway, waiting for Melvin. When he finally walked out of the house, they stared at him like he was an apparition—even the kids had been struck silent. Terry had, of course, made some kind of wisecrack, and they had all laughed. Jada smiled, remembering, *happy memories, fleeting moments.*

"Hey, Sis, I'm really sorry, but I'm going to have to beg off."

Hallelujah! She stammered something about being disappointed and how she understood.

He explained, "You see, I ran into this lady at the front desk, she's the Police Chief's mother. Mrs. Madge Lee?"

Jada nodded that she knew the lady in question.

"And I'm going out to her house for lunch," he said. "Seems we have some similar interests when it comes to financial markets. She's also got some ideas on how to help you kids solve these damnable murders and I'm planning on helping her."

His eyes were prancing in a way Jada would have not believed possible. Terry had often remarked how it usually took a stick of dynamite to move Melvin forward or backward—phrased a little more crudely.

Jada was nearly speechless. "Sure, great. See you later?"

"Don't look for me until late this afternoon. I'll see you back at the Inn." He smiled, anticipation twinkling his eyes. "After lunch Madge Lee is taking me to Wal-Mart to pick up some more casual clothes. Ta!"

Ta? "Ah..." He had nearly struck her mute. Melvin was twelve years older than Terry. He had worked for thirty years as the controller for a fairly prestigious manufacturing firm in Atlanta, then—bam—forced into early-retirement. "Thank you very much, but we've got a 'new direction' for the future and a new set of hot shots who'll be leading us there." He could have been bitter, but not Melvin. Just went into retirement with a smile on his face and started trading stocks over the Internet in his garage converted into an office.

Solina reported from her visits to Melvin's home in Dunwoody, Georgia, that he would still get up early, have breakfast, shave, shower, put on his suit, then "go to work" out in the garage.

After Melvin left, Josia returned, plopped down with a sigh in the same chair he'd been sitting in before, and dropped a sheet of paper on the table. "Too bad about your brother-in-law," he said. Again he stretched his legs out underneath the adjacent chair with a grimace. "Are you ready for more?"

"Yeah, I'm ready." She got up and opened the refrigerator to help herself to more water. "But what do you mean 'too bad?'"

"My mother's taken hold of him." The grimace was gone, replaced with a smart-alec grin. "God only knows what you'll get back. Is he married? 'Cause you might want to notify his wife."

"Are you thinking something romantic?" Jada scrunched up her face in a fashion evidently ridiculous enough to make Josia laugh.

"You find that hard to believe?" he said. "Just because my mother is one-hundred-thirty years old, give or take a decade, and your brother-in-law is a young pup, doesn't mean they couldn't, ah, what should I say, *meld*, to pervert a Star Trek term."

Jada was a tad embarrassed, *but darn it*, he wasn't going to know. "I was not casting aspersions on Madge Lee's age. I was just surprised at how quickly they've hooked up together. And no, Mel's been a bachelor all his life."

"Not surprising." He still wore a grin.

"Are you baiting me? And if you are, why?" She had gotten past the picture of Melvin and Madge Lee making-out in the back of his rented Ford. Something more was going on with Josia.

"You're right, Jada."

In an instant he's slipped into calling me Jada.

"It's nothing to do with you, or your brother-in-law," he admitted. "Just tired. And old." He rubbed his leg under the table. "And PO'd. Not getting anywhere fast on this damn case. Bakersfield boys just faxed over the ballistics prelims." He motioned toward the sheet of paper in front him. "Nothing we hadn't already guessed."

"A twenty-two used to kill Nick, and a thirty-eight or forty-five used to kill Hal?"

He checked the report. "Right. With Williams, looks like a North American Arms Black Widow twenty-two magnum. Our killer used a copper-jacketed bullet which entered through the eye, and lodged itself in the back of his skull. Looks like it was face to face, close range, personal. Like we thought." He dropped the sheet of paper back on his desk and added, "You were right by the way. He did fall back against his chair. Whoever murdered him took the time to push him forward. Hard."

Poor Nick. "Went through soft tissue." Jada could still see what was left of his lifeless face smashed into his pot, one dead eye visible, staring into oblivion. She grimaced with her entire body. "You know the chair he was sitting in?"

Josia nodded.

"It's a high-end ergonomic job. If he hadn't been using that, his body probably would have ended up on the floor."

"Maybe Beach can tell us more."

"Someone," she speculated more to herself than Josia, "was really mad at Nick. Shooting him wasn't enough."

"Wanted to humiliate him too."

"Yeah. And what about with Hal?"

"One to the head, and one to the heart just like we thought. And they're saying the gun is a Smith & Wesson forty-five Colt. This time, slugs. Both bullets penetrated, did their job, then exited our victim almost straight through. Slight angle of exit out the back for the one through his heart." He expelled a long breath. "They found both bullets, one arced about one hundred yards out, and the other two hundred yards. Lucky there—it's a damn big desert. Actually, I'm really surprised they were able to identify the weapon without shell casings, but they're good at this stuff nowadays.

"They're also speculating Hal was shot straight on from about sixty feet away. CSI thinks both our murderer and our victim were about the same height."

Like her, Josia fell silent for a bit, thoughtful. "Two different people?" she offered.

"Could be."

"No, these two murders had to be connected, we just haven't figured it out yet," she said.

"We?"

"A manner of speech only. Did you and Gabe find anything at Nick's home to help?"

"Nope."

"Hal Morton's house?"

"Haven't been there yet, have to get these interviews done. I called Mojave to send Bill Hope over, but he's out with his sick wife, and Malcolm in California City is in Reno."

Jada didn't mention he probably could have gotten some more help from the County. But that would have been like rubbing salt into an open wound.

Gabe stuck his head in the door. "Chief, I'm on my way to the Thomas house now. She's home and ready to talk to me. Madge Lee and Mr. Beaudine have left, so I'll leave the bell on the counter if you need Beth to come back here and transcribe."

"Sounds good, Gabe. I expect your interview will be routine, but if anything pops up, call me right away. Okay?"

"Yes sir." Excitement rang in his voice and shone in his eyes. "Beth's sitting out there until your next interview."

Once again, events other than those planned took hold of their destinies. Beth came running in, breathless with urgency. "Deputy Spriggs, Chief Rhodes," she said quickly. "It's Uncle Charlie on the phone; he just heard about Mr. Morton and he says get out to Mr. Morton's place immediately. He's been there since way early this morning. Somebody torched his house." She took a calming deep breath. "Oh yeah, and he wanted to know why you don't ever check," she hesitated for a second, then obviously paraphrasing, "the gall-darned emergency band."

The sirens I heard this morning.

Josia was instantly up from his chair. "Charlton McNeal is the Fire Chief," he threw Jada's way. "And a smart-ass."

Gabe cleared his throat and looked pointedly toward Beth.

"No offense, Beth," Josia apologized half-heartedly while pushing his way through the door. "Forget Star Thomas for now, Gabe, I want you with me." From his disappearing back Jada heard, "You can tag along Beaudine, if you want."

First "Jada," now "Beaudine?"

Beth followed the two men out of the room. Hurrying to catch up, Jada grabbed her canvas bag, a fresh bottle of water, and grumbled, "Rhodes and I will never be friends."

No one was left in the room to hear her.

Cantil, a few miles south of Red Rock Canyon Park and a few miles north of California City, consisted of several small clusters of homes out in the middle of another vast expanse of dirt and sand held together with creosote bushes and sagebrush. They rode there at ninety-plus mph, sirens blaring, lights flashing— Josia and Gabe in the front seat of the patrol car, and Jada in the back.

Once off the main highway, Josia headed toward a thin, but still sickening grey plume of smoke rising ugly and alone on the horizon. Finally, after several miles down a dirt road they saw the fire trucks.

Josia parked a few hundred feet before a driveway that led to the smoldering remains of what Hal Morton had called home. The three got out and walked toward a group of weary looking firefighters. The wind was nearly overpowering, and Jada thought it must have been hell to fight the flames.

The smell of wet ashes was pervasive and awful, and Jada wanted to gag. But she forced back bile and hurried to keep up as Josia and Gabe strode toward a particular fireman, a large man rolling up hose. Soot lines masked his face where protective gear had been, and he'd taken off his helmet, releasing a huge shock of crinkly red hair yet untouched by the ash floating in the air around them. His appearance could have been comical under different circumstances.

"Charlie," Josia called as soon as they came into hailing distance. "What the hell?"

"About time, Si." He had a deep voice and a cheeky delivery. "I understand you got a homicide tied to this. The owner, right?"

"Hal Morton. Shot sometime this morning. What time did you guys get called out on this?"

The big fireman gave Jada a brazen once-over while answering Josia. "If you and Gabe give me a hand with this hose so truck number one can get wrapped up and get out of here, I'll fill you in right away. You won't have to wait for my report."

From the sidelines, Jada watched as Josia and Gabe helped where they could, rolling up, wrapping up, cleaning up—getting wet and dirty themselves. All around her, tired mud-encrusted firemen were silently packing up. In fact, for a moment there, the world seemed ominously silent. Not a peep.

She hugged herself to keep warm, wishing she could go sit in the squad car and turn on the heat and shake the eerie mood that had suddenly come over her.

She could have, she guessed, actually done just that— hunkered down in the car—but everybody else was working so hard, she felt rather foolish, like the weak little woman. Then she noticed several women among the firefighters—*so much for my sexist thoughts*. Encouraged, she decided to do what she could do. Use her brain.

The plume of smoke that had directed them there was actually a wisp compared to what the original blaze must have been, and the now smoldering remains of Hal Morton's house indicated it had been a modest affair. Still, Jada didn't want to slop through the sludge covering the ground around the foundation, so she tried visualizing what it had been. From the remains of the foundation she could see two bedrooms, one bathroom, a living room, modest dining area, some kind of enclosed porch for laundry, and a fireplace. It was mostly surmise, as all the walls and doors were gone and the roof burnt out or collapsed.

The brick fireplace, though, still standing, intact, and looking rather elegant, was a symbol of some kind. Jada didn't take the time to go philosophical.

Whoever had killed Hal had also wanted to silence his home. Make sure *something* would never be discovered. The obvious conclusion—Morton was indeed a blackmailer. And following that train of thought, Jada visually scrutinized the rubble before her more carefully. It was pretty easy to figure out the room with the metal bed frame, now twisted and contorted from intense heat, was where Morton had slept. If he had some sort of office, it would probably have been in the other small room, the second bedroom.

Coughing, she rubbed her eyes. And given the density of residual smoke hanging in the air, Jada figured she would not last much longer so close to the house. She would have to hurry her inspection. Morton's whole world was right out there for her to see, but what did it say? No safe, no metal file cabinet, no desk drawers in sight. The things she did see on the ground—black, smoldering, and crippled—spoke of a simple man living a modest life. Curious, for a blackmailer. The tightening in her throat and the tearing in her eyes told Jada it was past time to walk back toward the squad car.

It wasn't long before the three men, Josia, Gabe, and the Fire Chief, joined her.

"I'd offer you my hand, Ma'am," Charlton said through a wickedly sexy smile. "But it takes a special soap to get this crap off."

Jada took an instant liking to Charlton and smiled in return. *Hard not to like the man.*"No problem. Looks like you had a bad one to deal with."

"That's for sure, Ma'am. I'll make this quick so I can get back and help my number two truck crew." He rubbed the back of his hand across his forehead smearing the soot into a ribbon of black. "What I wanted you to know, Si, is there's no doubt in my mind this was arson. The bastards didn't even make an effort to try and cover it up. Can of gasoline and an oily rag. Got the can bagged for forensics. The rag is a guess and got some dirt samples from around the can, etc. It'll all be sent to the lab."

"Damn it," Josia cursed.

Charlton winked Jada's way. "Remember there's a lady present, Si."

Josia rolled his eyes.

"But I know wherewith you're alluding my friend. It's not a comforting feeling having the likes of this bloke running around our desert, now is it?"

Gabe nodded his agreement and said, "He's a nasty one alright."

Jada asked, "What will happen now? What I'm getting at is when I look around the site, not much is left. I'm thinking this wasn't just done for kicks. It was done to cover up or destroy something. Maybe blackmail evidence. But I don't see any file cabinets, or desks, or safes."

"I think we better get a full one on this," Josia said, taking up her thread. "Don't you think, Charlie? Get an onsite forensic team to sift through this mess? But keep it low profile, you know, go through that friend of yours, Samuels, right?" He took a step forward. "I don't want the Bakersfield gang to connect this to my murders just yet."

"Yep, I'm agreed. I'll go make the call now," Charlton said. Then he turned to Jada. "Ma'am, certainly has been a pleasure meeting you." With his remark he touched a dirt encrusted finger to his forehead in a farewell gesture. He also flashed her a big fat smile and an audacious wink.

The man has moxie.

When they got back to the patrol car, Josia opened the door for Jada and quipped, "Watch out for McNeal, he's full of it, and I don't mean blarney."

Gabe added *sotto voce*, "He's a nice man. The Chief's just razzing you."

Josia wasn't finished, though, and when they were all in the car, he said, "McNeal is married with six kids, so don't get your hopes up." He didn't turn around but Jada could see him watching her through his rearview mirror, smiling. She smiled back. Maybe it was because of the dismal fire aftermath, or maybe she just needed to lighten up for one little moment in time. For sure, as they headed back to Red Rock City, she didn't look back at what was left of Hal Morton's home.

Jada and Josia sat for a couple moments in his office parking lot. He wanted to continue his marathon interviews; she however was hungry, and disagreed. Peacemaker Gabe suggested they order something in, while he went off to see Star Thomas as planned earlier. Beth could continue to monitor the front desk.

Indeed, Beth was at her post when they entered the office. And while Josia and Gabe headed to the two-stall unisex bathroom-locker-room next to the back door behind the water heater and furnace—Jada headed for the everything-room to call for burgers or pizza, or whatever somebody would deliver fast. She looked at her watch. Two-thirty.

It only took her a few moments to find the phone book, call for fish, shrimp, and chips for four, and a couple sides of coleslaw and potato salad. They promised fifteen minutes, max. She then grabbed a Coke from the refrigerator and plopped down in a blue upholstered armchair in the corner by the only window in the room. *Madge Lee, you did well.*

She took an additional moment to muse how easily she'd made herself at home in the Red Rock City Police Office. A transient circumstance. Only a few days more, that was all.

After a long grateful swallow of Coke, Jada noticed her hands were involuntarily shaking. So she forced herself to take mental stock, realign her emotions. To that end, she took a long deep breath, then another, and another.

It had only been this morning when she and the dog had walked out into the desert behind cabin number-two and found Hal's dead body. But since then, someone with a gun had tried to break into her room, and someone else, or maybe the same person, had torched Hal's house. Now she was in a marathon interview session with a sore throat, burning eyes, and a stomach yelling "Feed me! Feed me!" No wonder her hands were shaking.

For the moment, she needed to at least focus her mind away from food, so she dug out the few notes she had made on Irina's list during their earlier interviews. She saw nothing worthwhile and her mind wandered to Josia. He wanted to wrap this up before he was forced to turn the case over to Bakersfield. She understood that, even empathized, but so far he didn't have anything solid. Which meant, all he could do was plod—interviewing everybody he could think of that might be connected—reading and re-reading interview records—reading and re-reading the official reports—sitting and thinking—and oh yeah, she almost forgot, getting "psychic" help from his mother. Jada could hear Josia and Gabe coming down the hall, evidently coordinating. Reverie time was up. They had both changed into fresh uniforms and when the two got closer, she heard Gabe say he was heading out to the Thomas house.

She got up and stopped him at the door. "Gabe, I've ordered some food," she said. "You want to eat before you head out?"

"Thanks, Mrs. Beaudine," he answered. "But I'll pick up a drive-through burger on my way out." He kept going, intent on his mission. *Evidently, it was still Mrs. Beaudine when Josia was around.*

Josia said, "I'm starved. What did you order? Hope you got a lot."

"Fish, shrimp, and chips, enough for four. I was thinking Gabe and Beth would be eating, too. Should be plenty since Gabe's gone. You like seafood?"

"Yeah, seafood's fine. Thanks for calling by the way." He followed her back inside the room and started cleaning out the coffeepot, preface to making a new batch of brew.

She sat down near the door. Josia, however, once he got the pot going, paced back and forth in front of the counter and Jada, waiting for his sleek black machine to do its magic.

"Whoever killed Morton torched his place," he said. "I'd bet my badge Morton was a blackmailer and the murderer couldn't find what he was looking for in the house. So he set the whole damn place on fire to make sure." He wasn't looking at Jada and seemed to be talking more to himself than her. "But from what I can see, McNeal and his guys aren't going to come up with much from the ashes."

"It's still early," she offered. "And you never know when that one piece of information will pop-up that brings it all together."

"Yeah, yeah, but I've only got a couple more days, max."

They were silent for a bit, listening to the coffeepot gurgle, thinking. Eventually Jada asked, "Do you have anything on the background of Hilary Giles or Leroy Ames? Like where they were born or lived in the past?"

"Some. Why? You think what?"

"I don't know what I think. But Nick's murder is personal. And if it's personal, it could have started before this class."

Josia walked over and pushed an intercom button on a speakerphone in the middle of the table. "Beth, could you grab the Williams's folder out of my lower desk drawer and bring it on back?" The coffeepot beeped and he turned and looked at Jada. "You want a cup?"

She shook her head and wondered how the man could possibly drink so much coffee. The acid must be destroying his stomach.

"Gabe and Beth ran some checks on everyone the day Williams was killed."

"Including me?" A gratuitous jab; Madge Lee had already told her as much.

He sat down across from her, a freshly brewed steaming cup finally in hand. "Including you."

"You're taking it black this time?"

"Yeah, got to watch the calories." He patted his fairly flat stomach.

"But you're okay with the caffeine?"

"Yeah, well, they say it's bad for you, but you gotta 'go' someway." He took a hefty swallow. "Now, that's the way I like it, fresh, hot, and strong." He smiled, clearly satisfied with his brew. "Regarding the class members, surprising how much information you can get from public records."

Beth brought both the folder and the delivery lady back. After Jada tipped the delivery lady she insisted Beth take some food back to the front desk. Beth demurred. Jada insisted some more, and Josia watched the whole exchange from behind an impudent grin.

"So, you have a nurturing side," he teased, after Beth left with food and drink on a tray.

She ignored him and helped herself to a shrimp basket and cole slaw. "Who's up next?"

"Well," he answered while choosing a fish basket and potato salad. "If I'm remembering right, McNichols-James, then the Berry couple."

After devouring several shirmp, Jada wiped her greasy hands with a napkin and dug her class list out again. "Gabe is interviewing Star Thomas, right?"

"Yep."

"And Marie Shipley?"

"Maybe this evening if it works out." His expression indicated talking to Marie today was probably not doable.

"This day will never end…"

"Too much for you?"

As if I'd ever admit that to you. "Hardly, I was thinking about you, you know, your injury from this morning."

"Humph."

Fortunately Corissa McNichols-James was late. They had barely finished eating and cleaning up the table and themselves when Beth brought her back, then reclaimed her seat at the steno machine.

As on their first meeting, Jada was immediately struck by the timid persona Corissa projected. Such a pretty young woman, she thought—no need to be self-conscious. Of course she could be misreading her; maybe it was fear she was picking up. She hadn't had time to go over Josia's background notes and would have liked to have known more about her before the interview.

Josia slid back into professional gear, and Jada, guessing his leg still ached and knowing how tired he was—they both were—was mildly impressed with the fresh energy he mustered up.

After being introduced to Jada, Corissa gave her a theatrical double take, and when recognition hit, her eyes widened. "I knew I'd seen you before yesterday morning at the lab. In the newspapers right?"

Jada forced a smile and nodded obligingly, and to her relief, it ended there. Corissa quickly moved on.

"You don't have to use the McNichols-James if you don't want." An apologetic little smile followed her words. "I've sort of dropped that. James is fine."

Josia asked, "James is your husband's last name, right?"

"We were married two years ago. I think at first I was scared to give up my name." She laughed nervously. "Mother claims it was my 'identity' that I was actually scared of losing. But now, I don't mind being Ted's wife."

Odd way of putting it, Jada thought.

Josia reached for the folder at the other end of the table. This time he'd taken the seat Hilary Giles had preferred, his back protected. Jada was again on the side, albeit the other side, and Corissa had her back to the door.

Josia said, "I've read the statement you gave Deputy Spriggs the morning Nick Williams was killed. But could you please go over the basics again real quick for us? You see, now that Mr. Morton has also been murdered I'm looking for anything you might have noticed, and didn't mention earlier. Anything that might have relevance now. Like I said, now that Mr. Morton is dead." He didn't open the folder, just let it sit innocently in front of him, and looked at her expectantly, his face hard and uncompromising.

Corissa shrank back, almost imperceptibly, but enough for Jada to notice. She and Hal had been the first ones on the scene, and now he was dead. Corissa knew she was on the hot seat—and Jada knew she knew—and Josia evidently was not above using what Jada considered bullying tactics.

"You think I lied to you?" Her voice quivered.

He didn't let up on the intensity of his gaze. "It's possible you may have missed something. And it's also possible Mr. Morton was killed because he saw or knew something he shouldn't have. Now if you saw whatever he saw..." He let the obvious conclusion sit on quiet air between them.

"They would try to kill me," Corissa whispered.

"Think, Mrs. James, please. Is there anything you didn't mention that morning that might help us?"

"I've gone over it hundreds of times in my mind." She clasped her hands together tightly on the table. "There isn't that much to tell. I arrived early and started getting my stuff together, and minutes afterwards Hal arrived. I didn't see anyone else and I didn't hear anything special." Corissa switched to nervously rubbing her hands together. "Then it wasn't much longer before we heard the sirens and came outside. I think Hal had started sanding one of his little statues."

Jada asked, "Did you have time to start working on anything?"

"Ah, let me think...no, no, I remember now, I was still getting all my stuff together." Then to Josia, "I wish I knew more." Corissa offered another thin little smile. "But there just isn't that much to tell."

"Do you own a gun, Mrs. James?" he asked.

"No I don't." She gave Jada a hesitant glance. "I'm scared of them."

"Can you tell me where you were last night and this morning?" Josia pushed.

Jada understood where he was coming from: someone, sometime, would give them something to go on. Just a matter of persistence and time. Unfortunately, time was a meager commodity with Josia.

"Oh sure," Corissa said, drawing her shoulders up. "I was at home last night, and this morning I went to the airport to pick up my husband Theodore. He's at the dentist right now." Again, she looked Jada's way, as if seeking her approval. "Poor Hal."

"Who told you Mr. Morton had been killed this morning?" Josia asked.

"Oh, that's easy." She exhaled a small breath of relief. "Penny called me this morning before I left for Ontario airport with the news. She and her husband always seem to know everything before anyone else."

Jada was fascinated. Corissa McNichols-James appeared to be an odd mix of child and woman, strength and weakness, and something else she couldn't yet put her finger on. And despite his frontal attack, she didn't think Josia was getting much out of her.

He next brought out his full toothy smile, dropped back into his chair in a more relaxed posture, and softened his tone a notch or two. "You'll have to pardon me, Mrs. James," he crooned. "If I seem to be pushin' on you. It's just that I've got two men dead and I want to bring in the murderer, real fast like, before he can do any more damage. I'm sure you understand?"

In turn, Corissa's shoulders relaxed a bit.

Fear. Jada was sure now, that's what she had seen in her eyes, heard in her voice.

Slowly and casually Josia continued trying to gather as much information as he could. Married for two years, Corissa and Theodore had no children, and she didn't work, but he did. Mr. James was an archeologist, loosely associated with the University of California, but mainly a man of his own choosing.

"Theodore's not wealthy," she insisted. "But his family left him with enough money to pursue his dream."

"Which is?" Josia asked with a raised eyebrow.

She answered proudly, "Tracing the migration of 'man' into the Americas."

"So your husband travels a lot?"

"Yes, I've gone with him a couple times, but..."

"But?"

"I'm not college educated." She said it flatly.

But Jada caught an undertow of resentment. Directed at her husband? His colleagues?

Josia pushed, "And?"

"And I don't always fit in. I could have gone to college." She finally stopped fiddling with her hands and put them in her lap. "If the money had been there. My mother, you see, was a single parent. I didn't have the advantages of some." She forced a light laugh. "Not that it matters to my husband. He's always trying to get me to come along."

"What can you tell us about Nick Williams? In particular, what was he like?"

She hesitated too long. Jada was sure Corissa was about to "massage" her answer, maybe even lie outright.

"He was alright, I guess."

"Come now, Mrs. James, we've already heard he was a 'ladies-man.'"

Showing her spunky side, Corissa shot back haughtily, "I wouldn't know about that. I go to class to learn pottery, not to gossip."

"Did Mr. Williams ever ask you to go to a bar in Mojave with him?"

"Of course not."

Josia smiled and raised his hands. "Okay, okay. So, Nick Williams was 'alright' and he never hit on you. What about Hal Morton? Was he alright too?"

She lowered her voice, and Jada barely heard her answer. "No."

"Because?" Josia persisted.

"He just wasn't nice. That's all."

She looked up, and though speaking to Josia, her imploring eyes were glued on Jada. "I'm really feeling tired, not well actually. Are you about finished with me?"

"I think so, for now," he said. "But we need to talk again. How about I drop by your home? Maybe tomorrow. And maybe also get a chance to talk to your husband."

Corissa had already started to get up and looked like she was about to puke. "Oh yeah, sure."

Jada stood also. "The bathroom is to your right. Do you need help?"

"No, no, I mean, no, thank you. I'm alright." Corissa grabbed her purse, ready for flight. "I just need to get some air, that's all." Her chair almost tipped over as she pushed it back and aside.

Josia stood up, but didn't try to stop her. "I'll be out to see you and your husband tomorrow. Please let us know if you're not going to be available."

"Yes, yes, of course." Head down, she rushed past him.

Jada listened to Corissa's rapid footsteps progress down the hallway, a quick mumbled exchange with Beth, the slam of a car door, and finally, the urgent roar of a car engine being gunned.

"Seems to me," she said, "you've touched a couple tender spots."

"She's lying."

"Agreed. About what, though? Seeing something she shouldn't have? Having a gun? Having an affair with Williams?"

He sighed wearily and flopped down in the chair Corissa had occupied. "Christ. I hate squirrelly dames like that. Don't know if you're beating up on a butterfly or trying to bag a coyote."

"The word 'dame' really dates you, on several fronts, and your animal imagery sucks."

"She's bugging you too, isn't she? Otherwise you wouldn't be beatin' up on me."

"I'm definitely interested in meeting the archeologist husband, and seeing them interact with each other."

He looked into his now empty cup, then longingly at the coffee pot. "Yeah, me too. Meeting James that is. But I want to talk to him alone, without Corissa."

Jada started to give him grief about yet another cup of coffee, but decided to back off. If was becoming a very long day, for both of them.

"Are you going to take a look at Leroy Ames's guns?"

"Yep. The ballistics weren't final and Ames could be lying about what he has."

"Of course they're probably all clean. If he used them he didn't hit me as that stupid."

"Nope."

His monosyllabic responses touched on worn nerves, so Jada, wisely she believed, stopped trying to talk to Red Rock City's finest and went down the hall and through the backdoor to get some fresh air before the Berrys arrived; which is where and when she next ran into Melvin and Irina, getting out of his white Ford rental.

"Jada Marie Beaudine, I was hoping to catch you still here." Melvin headed straight toward Jada, his features animated with fervor, arms outstretched.

Seldom did anyone in the Beaudine family—all known for their proclivity to nicknames—address anyone by their full given name. If it could be shortened, chopped, or mangled, a Beaudine would do it. Jada knew something was up. Before she could figure out what that something was, he embraced her in another bear-hug, this time, followed with a big wet smack on the cheek.

"Mel," she blurted. Mercifully, he quickly let her go.

"Now, I know my behavior may seem a little bizarre," he grinned sheepishly. "And truth be told, I'm not sure what to make of it myself. But, hot darn, I feel like a different person."

He packed a lot of oomph in his hugs for an ex-accountant, causing Jada to give herself a good shake, hoping to pop back into form. Then she stared at him in amazement and heard herself mutter, "Ah."

"If I'd known you and Terry, God rest his soul," he said while making a quickie sign-of-the-cross, "lived such exciting lives, I would have visited more often."

During Melvin's exhibition Irina had extricated herself from the passenger side of the car and was now standing beside him. Waif-like next to Mel, she nonetheless looked like a beacon of sanity to Jada.

"Irina?" she pleaded, her expression and tone importing her bewilderment and desire for explanation.

"Madge Lee," Irina mouthed almost silently. She then proceeded to cross her arms across her chest, shrug, and smile pleasantly.

"So," Melvin jabbered on. "We've had a very interesting lunch at Madge Lee's. And after I drop Rina off at the motel, I'm going back to Madge Lee's house so we can strategize. We'll tell you all about it when you come by later."

He's calling her Rina already. "Mel," Jada said in a warning tone. She needed to explain to him she had no plans of going by anyone's after she and Josia were through. She was going back to the Red Rock, take care of the dog, then hit the sack.

Maddeningly, before she could finish her sentence and say all of that, Irina butted in. "I'll be sure to feed and walk your dog when I get back," she said brightly. "By the way, have you given her a name yet?"

Jada wanted to scream. She wanted to yell at the top of her voice how infuriating they were being, and how much they were complicating an already impossible situation.

Irina must have sensed the earth below Jada was about to tilt. Quickly, she abandoned her stance and came over and put her arm around Jada's shoulder. "You look tired. Why don't we talk tonight? I'll tell you all about lunch with Madge Lee. In fact, I'll have Manny fix you a nice plate of tonight's special and when you get in, I'll heat it up for you." She released her and asked, "Have you talked to everyone in class yet? I bet Josia has been his regular obnoxious self."

Jada felt herself relax a bit. "It has been a long day, and we still haven't talked to everyone. The fire pushed everything back."

"What fire?" Irina demanded, stepping back so she could look Jada in the eye. "There was a fire? Here?"

Melvin stepped toward Jada. "Are you alright?"

To ward off another well meaning smothering, she quickly filled him and Irina in on everything she knew about the torching of Hal's house. It wasn't much.

"My, God," Irina proclaimed when Jada had finished. "What an awful day. First Hal gets killed, then his house gets burned down."

"Or," Melvin reflected out loud. "His house got burned down, then he gets killed."

Jada said, "I have to go back in. Josia is waiting for me and it looks like a car is pulling in." The three looked toward the street where an ancient blue Volvo station wagon was entering the parking lot.

"Oh, yeah," Irina confirmed. "That's the Berrys." She gave Jada a wink. "Have fun, they're interesting to say the least."

Melvin grabbed both of Jada's hands. "If you can, stop by Madge Lee's on your way back to the motel and bring the interview transcripts. We want to talk to you."

"At a minimum," she conceded. "I'll try to bring transcripts back to the Inn tonight."

"Great," Irina and Melvin both said, almost in unison. Irina additionally gave her a reassuring look and said, "See you tonight."

However, in the blink of a humming bird's eye, instead of moving toward Melvin's car as expected, Irina gasped and brought her hands to her face, her change in demeanor hardly believable in its speed. Luckily, Jada saw Irina's knees start to buckle and called out, "Mel. Help me grab her. I think she's going to faint." They caught her before she collapsed.

"Irina," Jada demanded sternly. "What's the matter with you? Are you epileptic? Do we need to call 911? Speak to me!" They managed to get the door of Melvin's car open and lower her onto the seat, awkwardly and on an angle, but seated nonetheless.

Her green eyes had glazed over and her voice took on a surreal quality. "Last night, I had an awful dream. A terrible fire. And I couldn't put it out no matter how hard I tried. We were all there." She swept her arms in a broad nonspecific all-encompassing manner. "We couldn't escape. It was horrible."

Then she turned her face up to Jada, her eyes stronger, but moist with emotion as she peered into Jada's, as if willing her to see what she had seen.

"I was going to tell you about it this morning, but then you found Hal's body, then there was the shooting, and the car chase. So I just figured it was just a bad dream. I had forgotten, but just now I remembered."

Melvin nodded his head in knowing affirmation. "Madge Lee says sometimes it's like that."

Before Jada could stop what she considered unbridled silliness, Irina grabbed her hand tightly. "When you come back to the Inn I'll tell you about the other dream I had. It was about you and a man."

Jada wanted to hear about the dream right then, get it over with. But Beth was calling her from the backdoor. "Mrs. Beaudine, the Chief is ready to start."

Irina's second psychic revelation would have to wait.

Penny and Timothy Berry sprang into Josia's interview room with eager glints in their eyes, and half smiles twitching their mouths.

Husband and wife were wearing identical flowered shirts of the kind island-smitten tourists get at Hawaiian luaus. Their sandals, socks, and knee long forest-green shorts were also unisex identical. Timothy was a little taller than Penny, and Jada guessed him around five-six. Both were thin, had short cut brown hair, and chubby-cheeked elfin faces that housed twinkling and curious eyes.

As the Berrys bounded into the interrogation room, Timothy proclaimed in an unexpectedly booming and gregarious voice, "Hope we're not too early, Chief Rhodes!"

Penny echoed, "Not too early, we hope."

Timothy continued without missing a verbal beat, "It's just that we wanted to get our information to you as soon as possible. We—"

"Didn't want you to wait," Penny finished. "Oh, Mrs. Beaudine. How wonderful you're here." She rushed over to Jada and grabbed both her hands, shaking them with considerable vigor. "You know we get the *Seattle Times* delivered to us here in Red Rock City. Our son, Matthew lives on Queen Anne, you know. We—"

"Have to keep up with what's happening in his world, don't you know. So sorry for your loss," Timothy finished.

Jada hoped her jaw wasn't hanging from disbelief, and prayed everything the Berrys said wouldn't be in joint high-spirited exclamations.

Even Josia appeared momentarily taken aback. "Ah, yes." He rubbed his chin while he fumbled for an appropriate response. "I appreciate your good citizenship in this matter."

She was unable to make eye contact with Josia and wondered if the Berrys had actually thrown him off? *No*, she quickly realized, she need not have worried. When he next spoke, his voice was firm, his demeanor more demanding. "And," he held up a restraining hand and looked directly at Timothy. "I appreciate that you have a lot to tell me, and I'm sure it's all helpful information, but I need to get it all down in an orderly fashion."

Timothy and Penny bobbed their heads eagerly and took seats next to each other across from Josia.

Jada had experienced husband and wife "matched sets" before—couples who over the years began to look alike, talk alike, and even think alike. Only one small evolutionary step, she figured, from dressing alike. There had been a time when she could have imagined Terry and herself in that way—two separate souls happily and unavoidably growing closer and closer over time. Dressing alike as oversized pineapples, however, seemed a mite excessive no matter the quantity of years together and amount of love shared.

Josia asked, "Could you start by telling me where you both were the morning Nick Williams was killed? And, where were you last night and this morning?"

Both Timothy and Penny's eyes widened as they exchanged identical knowing sparkles. Timothy spoke first, and with pride. "Alibis? Right, Chief? I told you, Penny, we're suspects." Then leaning forward and squinting his eyes earnestly, Timothy continued, "We thought you might want to know our whereabouts."

On cue, and with dramatic flurry, Penny conjured up a piece of paper from nowhere, for Jada hadn't noticed her carrying a purse or bag. "Our whereabouts."

Josia quickly scanned the paper then handed it to Jada.

Timothy wiggled in his seat. "You see Sunday nights are always special for us. It's the night we work on our diaries. At first we tried writing every night, but the routine was just too much."

Penny nodded in agreement. "Just too much."

"So we sit down at nine every Sunday night, put on some Bach or Vivaldi, make a pot of tea and catch up on the week's events in our diaries. We've done it for years. We almost never miss. This Sunday was no exception." Timothy allowed a frown to cross his brow for a second. "The problem is we have class first thing Monday morning, and we work on our diaries sometimes to eleven, even midnight when it's been a particularly interesting week. And even though we do love our pottery—"

"We do love our pottery. Doing our diaries is so exciting."

"We're often a little late for class the next morning."

Jada didn't want to break the flow and refrained from asking why the heck they didn't start their diaries earlier so they could get to class on time. Or better still, why not just pick another day to scribble?

Josia summed up their pitiful alibi, "So Monday morning when Mr. Williams was being murdered, you were both at home, sleeping. Is that right?"

They nodded. "And we're heavy sleepers, both of us," Penny emphasized. "Even during our afternoon naps."

"And last night?"

"Last night was scrabble night," Timothy said. "We didn't play long though." He rubbed his elfin chin for insight. "I'd say we retired around nine or so. Is that right, Dear?"

"Nine or so. Exactly right, Tim."

149

"And this morning?"

Timothy answered, "It's only Mondays we sleep in. This morning we arose at six on the dot. But I can assure you we were not out murdering Hal Morton! No, Wednesday morning is always pancakes. One of my Penny's specialties."

"How did you know that Hal Morton was killed this morning?"

"We heard about it on the police band. You see, it's another little tradition of ours. Penny and I listen to the radio, or the police band, or the emergency band, whichever one seems the most promising in the morning while we eat. We used to watch the stock market reports, but it was just too nerve racking, watching our money vanish into thin air like that."

Penny added, "We've helped a couple stranded motorists, you know."

Jada remembered Fire Chief McNeal's admonishment to Josia via Beth that very morning about listening to the emergency band. *Feels like a century ago. What a long, long day.*

"We heard the police dispatch sending you to the Red Rock and we also heard a fire dispatch to Cantil. Hal lives in Cantil. Do you know that?"

Josia cleared his throat in a way that made Jada know Timothy and Penny were most assuredly beginning to irk Red Rock City's constable. "So after you heard about Mr. Morton on the radio," Josia said while shifting his weight in his chair. "You decided to call around to all your fellow class members with the news?"

"Exactly," Timothy proudly proclaimed. "Hal may not have been the most endearing of men, but he had been one of us. I took it as a duty to inform the others in our little group about his untimely demise."

Penny added, "You see, we're sort of a family."

Josia sat back and rolled his shoulders. Clearly this interview was exacting a toll on his weary sensibilities. But just as obviously, he wasn't ready to give up. "I see," he said. "Well, can either of you tell me *anything* you might know about Mr. Williams?"

"You're looking for a motive for murder, right?"

"Yes, Mr. Berry, as you put it, a motive for murder. I need to know all the bits and pieces you might know, regardless of their seeming importance."

Timothy scooted his chair up as close as he could to the table. His whole body looked alert, taut—all his energy focused on Josia and the task at hand. And Penny, sitting as close to Timothy as their two chairs would allow, mimicked his actions and body language.

He said, "We did a lot of thinking and talking this morning. We figured we might know something helpful. You see Penny and I are the kind of people who pay attention to things. You know, we see things, we hear things others might not."

"Observant," Penny supplied.

"Exactly. Now we've been in the morning ceramic class almost from the beginning. Three or four years. Is that right, Dear?"

"Three or four years. Right."

"And there's a lot of opportunity to 'observe' in a ceramics class. Do you know anything about pottery, Chief?"

"Very little." Josia fingered his coffee cup like he needed a refill. It wasn't, however, a good time to take a break.

"Well," Timothy continued. "There are activities required that afford one the opportunity to 'take in' their environment, if you get my point." He looked to the ceiling for a second. "For example, there's watching the demonstrations, good time to gauge the interactions among your fellow students. Then there's painting and glazing, good time to look around. And loading the kiln. For some reason everyone goes in the kiln room for privacy."

Penny said, "Heaven knows why. It's always dirty back there and sometimes it's so hot you just want to faint. And the space is so tight." She rolled her eyes.

"True enough, my dear, but you know that's where we heard Nick and the Thomas girl having that fight."

"True," she conceded.

"And, that's where we saw Ms. Hughes and Nick kissing. He's had several affairs, we're sure, since the start of class. And, he's married!" Timothy seemed genuinely affronted. "Fortunately his affair with Ms. Hughes didn't last long. She's too smart of a woman for that."

"Why do you say 'fortunately'?" Josia asked.

Penny said, "Because we like her."

Timothy echoed, "Because we like her."

Jada too was growing weary of the Berrys. What had started as cute and affectionate little mannerisms had quickly turned into grating peculiarities. They may or may not know something, but all she now wanted was for Josia to wrap the interview up and send these two home so she could go back to the Red Rock and crash.

Josia, however, was clearly not through. "Is there anything else you picked up that might help our investigation?"

"Well." Timothy again rubbed his chin thoughtfully.

While he was thinking, Penny talked. "Nick was raised, maybe born, in Chicago, his wife was born in San Francisco, he went to school somewhere in Illinois, and he's at least ten years older than he claims." Again she conjured up a piece of paper from underneath the table and handed it to Josia. "We wrote it all down."

Jada asked, "Did all this come out during class demonstrations?"

"Not exactly."

"Not exactly?"

"I deduced it all." Penny sounded quite proud of herself.

Timothy explained, "Penny is remarkably clever you know."

Penny leaned toward Jada, her eyes proclaiming her eagerness to explain. "We were talking about what to bring for one of our potluck lunches, we do that occasionally after class, and someone, I think it was Leroy Ames, mentioned he would bring his wife's rye bread, as good as anything you'd get in New York or Chicago. And Nick said, he sure would like to taste that because he hadn't had good rye bread since he was a kid on the South Side." She smiled. "I'm sure he meant the South Side of Chicago. Then," Penny continued, "Once I heard him whispering with Star Thomas a couple tables away. I have extremely good ears. She was saying she wished they had corn fields out here like back in Iowa because you can do a lot of things out in the corn fields and no one knows the better. I'm sure she was talking about sex. And Nick responded that he had the same thing in Illinois when he was in college. Finally, I once remarked how wonderful I thought the Beatles were, and he let slip he saw them on TV in 1965 when he was in College. That would make him substantially older than what he tried to appear.

"And for Darcie," Penny batted her eyelids demurely. "I met her several times and she told me she was born in the 'City by the Bay.'"

"You're quite the detective," Jada complimented. "Were you able to deduce any information about Hal Morton?"

"Oh, that horrid man," she said vehemently. "I didn't have to deduce a thing about him. He was a blackmailer, pure and simple. I despise blackmailers, so slimy, don't you think?" Then she looked to Timothy. "Should I tell them Dear, or you?"

"You go ahead, you're doing quite well."

"Hal Morton tried to blackmail us, you see. That's how we know what a despicable person he was. I *am* sorry he's dead. But sometimes there is justice in this world."

Josia didn't hesitate, "What was Mr. Morton attempting to blackmail you about?"

"We're second cousins," she answered simply. "We didn't know it when we got married, of course. But we found out soon enough. I don't know how Morton found out, but he said he'd spread it around. Said it was illegal some places." She smiled at her husband. "Timothy of course told him to go to hell."

"And?" Jada prodded after a couple seconds elapsed.

"That was that, didn't hear a peep out of him again."

"You think he blackmailed others?" Jada asked.

"Undoubtedly," they proclaimed in unison.

The Berrys, as knowledgeable and unique as they were, had not only physically worn Jada out, but had also left her mentally feeling like a whirlybird-toy gone berserk. So before heading back to the Red Rock, she just sat in the car a few minutes—returning to equilibrium.

Then she looked over Irina's class list, the notes she had scribbled herself, and the Berrys' two offerings. Beth had also promised transcripts of all interviews, but they wouldn't be ready until the end of the day. Jada was impressed with Beth's abilities and diligence, and was singularly unimpressed with her own meager notes. On impulse, initiated by her seeming lack of progress, Jada decided to stop by Madge Lee's and see what she and Melvin were up to before calling it a day.

This time she found the drive to the dome-house quicker and easier, only taking about fifteen minutes; and some of that mileage and time she would have had to expend anyway to get to the Red Rock. And traffic was light, allowing her to relax a little, freeing part of her brain to marvel anew at the vastness of the Mojave Desert, and wonder at mankind's audacity, past and present, to settle in such a place. The immensity of it all, and the fortitude of the people who had decided this would be home, were truly astonishing.

Madge Lee greeted her with gushing warmth and hospitality; and Melvin insisted on upping Jada's welcome with several all encompassing bear-hugs. Just what her exhausted mind and body needed.

Two cups of tea and several miniature cakes later, she felt remarkably better. Still weary, but not burnt-out exhausted. Jada even managed to recount what she could remember from the interviews and tell them Beth was bringing out transcripts as soon as she could.

Then Jada hinted heavily via body language, squirming, rubbing her head, and looking at her watch, that she was ready to leave. It was ungracious, she knew, to eat and run. However, even though she felt decidedly better, and even though the interaction between Madge Lee and Melvin was charming—*who would have guessed or even imagined*—it had become an extremely long day that just wouldn't end. But it took more than antsy movements to dissuade Madge Lee. Indeed, to Jada's dismay, she seemed energized by her meager information and ready for action.

"You see, Mel," Madge Lee expounded eagerly. "I knew we'd be able to help."

"You had one of your 'insights?'" Melvin asked in the adoring voice of the newly-smitten.

Madge Lee patted his hand. "Well, partly, Dear, but mostly, I just assumed something would materialize out of all those interviews. Si is quite good at questioning, and with your sister-in-law helping," she said, now gesturing with open hands, "we were almost certain to get something of import."

What remained of Madge Lee's accent after living in the United States so many years was quite different from Hilary's, and much toned down, but Jada could still hear it. She knew from watching the BBC, British accents came in many flavors, just like in the USA, if you listened. She still remembered with a fond ear, the lyrical accent of one of her college roommates, Cheryl, from Cambridge, UK. *So many years ago.* Cheryl had introduced her to Terry.

Upon arrival at Madge Lee's, Jada had collapsed in a winged armchairs across the coffee table from the cooing duo, and there she remained. "And what exactly is this 'something' you're talking about?"

"The Chicago and San Francisco connections of course."

"Which is?" Jada refilled her teacup. Darn good stuff. Warming and restorative.

"Then there's the age problem."

"Which is?" Jada asked again, this time helping herself to another petit four, this one shining with thick strawberry glaze.

"I had what I call a 'feeling' last night, my dear Jada. A rather strong one in fact. Often I'm uncertain if it's something significant or too many onions at suppertime. There seems to be a chemical in onions that does unusual things to my brain chemistry."

Jada chomped away on cake. What else could she do, she rationalized, but eat? Madge Lee was crazy. In fact, just about everyone she had met connected with Irina and Josia—in town and at the motel—were crazy. Something in the drinking water? Fleetingly, she wondered what Terry would have made of these people, this place.

Madge Lee continued, "But no, I'm sure this insight was significant."

"Which is?"

"That the key to all this lies outside of Red Rock City."

"And we're going to figure it out?" Melvin said, more as a question than a conclusion.

"Who's going to figure out what?" A lot of "w" words had piled up. *What's left? "Where" and "why"*? Jada's brain felt fuzzy.

"We'll have to go to San Francisco tomorrow, Melvin. Then Chicago after that. I'll get us tickets and reservations. I know a couple fantastic hotels you'll just love."

"I can pack tonight."

"Beth can fax us the transcripts. I have a machine in my study."

"I'm ready."

"Whoa," Jada demanded. "Did I just hear you both say you're heading to San Francisco in the morning?"

"Yes, Jada, dear, you heard right. Would you like some more tea?"

Ally was angry Jada had driven out to the dome house again. She wanted to kill the evil woman so badly she could almost taste it. But it was so open around that house, that she again didn't want to follow all the way. This time fortunately, she found a short pull-off near a clump of desert pines where she could see the house, but was fairly well hidden herself. She wouldn't have to go back and wait at Mack's Quickie Mart.

Though, if she had to kill Jada Beaudine right in front of the Police Chief's nose, she would.

Ally also knew about the insurance agent, but he didn't follow as closely as she did. And she wasn't afraid of him anyway. She would get to Jada before him—he was just a stupid insurance grunt. It should make his company happy though, not having to pay out money to that evil woman.

Terry had said he was going to make Ally his beneficiary, but he hadn't been able to do it before his horrid wife had killed him.

"You won't get away from me, Jada Beaudine."

Jada finally returned to the Red Rock Inn and Café and Irina immediately insisted she have something to eat. She wasn't hungry—in fact, she was feeling rather queasy—too many teacakes on top of a layer of shrimp and chips grease. But Irina insisted, and in the end, she was too pooped to argue.

So, wondrous Manny prepared her pasta with a light fresh tomato and Thai basil sauce, homemade French bread, and an avocado salad, which, despite her protestations, she ate ravenously.

Her next sin in the health category was to head straight to number-two, and after giving the dog a whopping big hug, flop into bed. A sure recipe for indigestion she knew, but her fatigue had taken her beyond caring, and as she floated off, the red digital numbers on her bedside clock read 4:30 P.M.

Jada's sleep, instead of refreshing her body, turned ragged and mean, peppered with angst-driven dreams; the last of which, memorable for its vivid realism, remained with her as she awoke—choking and gasping for air and soaked in sweat. The dog was sitting at attention next to her, motionless, staring at her face.

Her dream had been of Terry and herself, on their boat during a wretched storm in Rosario Straits, in the San Juan Islands—maybe near James Island—her perspective shifting often as it does in dreams, from looking down, looking out, and looking in. Cold rain, sheeting in the wind, beat against their bodies as ten-foot waves crashed against their thirty-five-foot

Catalina. She and Terry clung to each other as they ever so surely sank into frigid swirling water, drowning, dying.

Now awake, she still felt the need to escape. Out into fresh air. Quickly, she got up and grabbed a jacket on her way out the door, the dog at her heels. Her bedside clock now read 6:00 P.M.

Each cabin at the Red Rock had a small veranda, nothing grand, a narrow concrete slab across the front and side, protected by a roof overhang. On these little pieces of gentility, Irina had provided each guest with an eclectic selection of chairs and tables. Number-two had two splotchy-white wicker armchairs and a small round wicker table.

Her dream had been horrid, extending what had turned out to be the longest of days. She needed to calm her body and mind, so she and the dog sat for awhile on the small veranda. A gentle breeze of dry air caressed her cheeks, and she fancied she could see a hint of orange beginning to brush the western sky. Sunset in the making.

Unfortunately, she could also still envision the day's events: Hal's lifeless body laying among the mesquite—just another piece of abandoned desert trash; Josia and Melvin running after a crazed gunman into the horizon; Hilary's sad eyes; Leroy's no-nonsense demeanor; and skittish Corissa scared of something. *But what?*

Then there was the charred remains of Hal Morton's house and the Fire Chief's soot-stained face and arson suspicions. Add to that the loony antics of psychic Irina and Madge Lee. Finally, the chattering Berrys, whom she was sure knew something. But how to separate the wheat from the chaff with those two?

The only touch of lightness in it all was the mystifying kismet between Melvin and Madge Lee.

The dog got up and retrieved a ragged rubber ball—with bits and pieces missing—her tail wagging at full throttle. Might her mistress play chase-the-ball? Josia's words, *bits and pieces*. That's all Jada had so far, without the "ball" to fit them into. And she doubted Josia was any closer. Willingly manipulated by the dog's pleading eyes, she threw the ball and watched as she sauntered off at a relaxed walk to retrieve it. The canine was also goofy.

Jada sighed, one of those long deep existential sighs, and waited for *her* dog to return. She had decided. Yes, goofy or not, she would take the mutt along to Atlanta. *What the heck.*

Still dead tired, she wasn't eager to return to the land of dreams. So on a whim, she decided to take Irina up on her offer to use the lab. Odd and incongruous, she reflected, she wasn't afraid to go out into no-man's-land at this time of the evening. "I'll most likely regret this later. When it's *really* dark," she told her dog.

They walked directly there, for though momentarily brave, she had no wish to retrace this morning's walk-about. Who knew what she might find next? Indeed, looking upon two bodies in three days was enough. And once started, the walking felt good. But again, she couldn't help but think about Nick and Hal.

Even after she arrived at the lab and selected a wheel to use, the *bits and pieces* of the last few days remained in her mind, jostling against each other, trying, but failing to fit themselves together. She gathered all the pottery stuff she needed, sponges and tools, a brick from the patio to prop up her foot, and a stool that fit her height. Everything had to be just in the right place. She smiled to herself. *Potting rituals.*

Her dog stretched out on the floor by her wheel.

While she wedged a hunk of clay the back door to the lab opened. "Don't be frightened," Irina called out. "It's just me. Can I watch you make a pot?" Before Jada could say yea or nay, Irina had walked up next to her. Her dog took no notice.

With a friendly nod, Jada indicated she didn't mind the company. Might even relish it, given the mood she was in and her inability to shake Nick and Hal from her thoughts.

"I was sitting on my stoop when I saw you heading this way," Irina said. "Thought you might want some company. I use to love watching Nick. Sometimes he'd take this huge lump of clay and smash it on the wheel. He'd kind of smooth it out all around, then he'd just work on the top part, making little bowls and cups."

"Working off the hump," Jada murmured, remembering happier days while situating herself at the wheel. After she had centered the clay and started coning, the clay started feeling good rising through her hands. She started off with a modest hunk, three pounds or so, enough to push her, but not too much. It had been awhile. "I can't do that. It takes more skill than I have. Nick must have been an experienced potter." She remembered Darcie explaining how he was already a ceramic artist when they married and moved to Red Rock City five years ago.

Irina pulled up her own stool, sat, and stared at Jada's hands. "I thought he was experienced. He never really said how long he'd been doing it. We all assumed it was a lot of years."

Jada was using clay new to her, but it felt good, strong, as she pulled it up and down, making it smooth—no lumps, no air bubbles. Nick had several types of clay, all "high fire." This particular clay was greyish-white stoneware.

Irina continued, "But he had a hard time getting started. Did you know he worked at the Milton House as a waiter for awhile?"

Jada nodded.

"Do you like that clay? Nick had them all mixed special."

"I think so, it feels nice." Smooth, almost as buttery as porcelain, yet sturdy as stoneware should be, and without a lot of grit.

Irina said dreamily and with a touch of nostalgia, "I didn't meet him until he came out here looking for a studio. He seemed to know a lot about ceramics. Have you looked at his work?"

"Yes." She had looked at all the pieces out back and figured the professional-looking stuff was his. Nick's work had an English feel. His pitchers especially brought to mind the work of a well-known potter, Phil Rogers. To Jada's artistic mind and taste, Nick had been a good craftsman and artisan. Her hands wanted to make a vase, so she coned the clay up a last time, pushed it back down, opened, and started pulling the cylinder up.

"Have you seen my brother-in-law this evening?" she asked. She was indulging herself in silliness, letting her mind wander to a ridiculous place imagining Melvin and Madge Lee as an "item." It was better than dwelling on Hal's eyes staring up at her from his lifeless body laying in the dirt.

"Oh yeah, I was supposed to tell you. Mel called, he's staying at Madge Lee's tonight. Said not to worry about him."

"What?" Jada pulled her hands from the clay, distorting her cylinder a bit, and stared at Irina in disbelief. "Doesn't Josia live there too?"

"Yes. But they have a guest bedroom." Irina smiled mischievously. "Or maybe they don't. Either way, I doubt Si has the balls to try and tell Madge Lee what to do. It would be useless anyway. Mel isn't married is he?"

"Well no."

"Neither is Madge Lee."

"But..." Jada found herself struggling to get her mind around Melvin's whirlwind idiocy. In her mind, sharing the same bedroom was more than being smitten. Not that she had legitimate objections; they were grownups after all. If asked, she would have to agree her misgivings were foolish, short sighted, and arrogant. Nevertheless, "Madge Lee's what? Age-wise?" she asked. "At least eighty-something, right? And Mel, I think he's only about sixty-five or so." *Yes, twelve years older than Terry.*

"And what," Irina chided, "do you think they should do? Shrug their shoulders and dismiss their feelings because of their age differences?"

"Well….no." Jada didn't know what she thought. She did know, however, that just as her life was sorting itself out a bit, everything was again turning around, turning over, and bouncing this way and that. Nothing made sense. And minor as it was among recent events, this wasn't the Melvin she knew.

Or, and this thought embarrassed her, had she just been so imperceptive, so turned into her own grief that she had failed to realize Melvin had also lost someone dear—his brother—and needed as much comfort and coddling as she did, maybe even more? Heck, he'd grown up with Terry. And on the lighter side, why wouldn't Melvin have sexual desires just like most everyone else on this planet? Silently she went back to the clay, something she could touch and feel. Something she knew was real, unchanged. Clay. Its seductive power was an old and friendly companion.

Irina also fell silent, seemingly mesmerized by Jada's throwing.

After a bit, Jada stopped and sat back. Her cylinder needed to dry a little before she attempted to shape it.

Irina took the break to ask, "Am I bothering you?"

"No, I'm actually glad for the company," she answered and gave her an encouraging smile. "Did Nick ever use a hair-dryer or propane torch to dry his pieces? I didn't see one around."

"I never saw him use one."

She would just have to wait for her pot to dry a bit naturally before continuing. So she focused her attention on

Irina. "Did you ever meet Darcie? And their two kids, Marta and Devlin?"

"No." Irina turned away for a brief moment of thought. "You've probably figured out by now I'm a loner. Hell, I'm close to being a hermit if it wasn't for my residents. And, you've probably also noticed I don't spend a lot a time on social niceties."

Jada made an appropriately tactful noise.

"So I haven't had that many 'romances' in my life." A remembrance evidently surprised Irina, causing her voice to catch for a second. When she spoke again, her tone was level. "So from the beginning I was blown over. I didn't think about his wife, his kids. I was awful. A fool in love, as the saying goes. Or is it a song?"

"Lasting loves are few and far between," Jada's sister-in-law Solina had often proclaimed. Solina also made a point of telling her on several occasions that Terry was an extremely lucky man to have "landed" her. *"He's so materialistic, Jada, I'm amazed every time I see you two that you're still together."*

Terry had been materialistic, Jada agreed, but she also believed there were worse personality flaws a person could have besides a touch of greed. She also knew sisters and brothers had their own way of seeing each other. *No*, she had not been a blind fool in love.

Irina continued, "I couldn't think of anything but Nick. And the sex—well it was phenomenal. At least to me."

Jada touched the bottom edge of her pot. It was drying at a rapid rate. She remembered the dry clay on Nick's hands and pottery wheel. *He must not have been dead very long before I saw him.* As she continued to listen, Jada began shaping her pot from the inside with a curved flexible red-rib.

"Then one day," Irina said, "Darcie came to pick him up and she had the kids with her. So young, so cute, so small. I didn't meet or play with them, but it was like a slap in the face.

What the hell was I doing? Fooling around with a gall-darned married man." Old anger re-surfaced, hardening her face. "You'd think I was a besotted teenager, for Christ's sake."

"You stopped it then?"

"Yes."

Jada pushed the rib too hard, too fast, and it went through the wall of her pot. "Oh well," she said philosophically as her creation collapsed upon itself.

"That's how I felt at the end of our affair," Irina said with a wretched little sigh. "I had built up his importance in my life so much...and all the while, I knew in my heart it couldn't have lasted. I knew I was just one of many. I even kind of figured he was seeing someone else already."

"Think. Do you have any idea who Nick might have shifted his attentions to?"

"God, I wish I knew." Irina sighed slightly. "I think it was someone in class. I'm pretty sure of that."

"Where's that psychic ability of yours when we need it?"

"You know I really wish I could turn it on and off. I get all these useless premonitions, crap I can't put to an event or person, and then when it comes to something really important, some information I need, nothing."

Jada almost asked her about the dream nonsense earlier at Josia's office, but decided to just let it ride. The dog stirred, stuck her nose in the air, sniffed, then dropped off to sleep.

"Strange dog," Jada said. "She seems to sleep an awfully lot."

"I know you don't want to hear this again, but she was waiting for you. I think she was really tired, you know, a-tired-from-life kind of thing. Now she's found you."

Jada ignored what she considered nonsense. "Did Nick ever mention anything about Chicago?"

"No. Why?"

"Just trying to make some sense out of everything that's happened. Since you're here, what's the story with Josia? I mean with his marriage? He never talks about a wife, not that I've talked to him that much." The clay on her hands was drying quickly; she needed to wash up. *Something there, something nagging at me, what the heck is it?*

The dry air and subsequent quickly drying clay also explained why the sculptured heads she noticed out back were still wrapped in plastic. An extremely slow drying time was needed to keep the medusa like tendrils surrounding the heads from drying too fast. She was coming to appreciate how different potting in the desert was versus her home ground of Seattle. *Former home ground.*

"Would you like to hear the other dream I had? The one about you?" Irina asked.

Seeing the earnestness in Irina's eyes, Jada didn't have the heart to make light of her fortune-telling. "Sure," she answered in an upbeat tone while wondering why she didn't want to talk about Josia's wife.

Quite abruptly, Irina seemingly changed her mind. "Nah, never mind, I don't think it's important. Maybe some other time. Sorry I even brought it up. On your question about Josia, it's probably best you ask him, he's sort of touchy about it."

With that, Irina headed back to her cabin, leaving Jada to her pottery and her thoughts.

Irina had had ample time to relive her dream foolishness and near collapse earlier in the day; and what had been so important suddenly seemed more like just plain silliness. What did dreams mean anyway? Real psychics actually see the future. Indeed, sometimes she believed she was psychic, and sometimes she thought she was just plain crazy. Part of it was Madge Lee's fault, always telling her to follow her instincts.

A lot of people probably had dreams about fires. And the dream on the boat, the one where Jada was with a man, and then that man became two men, then one man dies, and the other man tries to drown Jada. *No,* she wouldn't bother the poor woman with any more of her psychic BS. Jada had enough on her mind trying to find Nick's killer.

Once outside and heading back to her own cabin, she bemoaned to the stars, "What a helluva long day."

Jada continued to throw, screwing up a lot, completing a few nice shapes, but mostly re-experiencing the feel, the smell, the sensual texture of clay.

Several times as she worked, her mind went back to Nick—the not-so-perfect man. She hadn't known him, but her senses wanted to. What had he thought of ceramics? Had it still been a joy to him? And what was he thinking that nanosecond before the bullet entered his brain and he ceased to be?

Answers did not come, and after another hour passed, she decided to call it a night. She cleaned up the wheel, emptied her slurry bucket, and washed and dried her hands. *Washing my hands...again, something.*

Experience told her, she would just have to wait. Whatever was bothering her would come, in time. Then she locked up, for what it was worth given recent happenings. Locks were close to useless at the Red Rock Inn. Finally she and her dog headed out toward number-two.

Jada had missed the sunset, but the moon rising in the east kept the night from being totally black. *Chicken, chicken.* She was glad for her dog's company. *Yeah, I guess it's official: my dog.* Resignedly she gave her a name.

"Come on Tasha," she said, doing a test run. The dog's response was an enthusiastic tail wag, a nibble on her jeans, and a couple punctuation barks. "Tasha" had obviously met with her approval.

The air was cool, not yet cold, the wind gone still, and not a sound to be heard anywhere. For a moment Jada was overcome and enveloped in the sensation of being the only person on the face of earth. Involuntarily, she shivered. If she had not realized it right off, it was becoming increasingly apparent desert life was not for her.

Still, no bogeymen grabbed them, no goblins of the dark jumped out into their path, and most to the point, no gunshots cut through the night. But who the hell had been nosing around her cabin, carrying a gun this morning?

Once back, Jada unlocked the door to number-two quickly. Tasha charged right through the door, heading for the middle of the bed, and Jada scooted-in almost as fast after her, re-locking the door quickly behind them.

She laughed, first at herself; and next at the ludicrous security at the Red Rock Inn & Cafe. The lock on her door was the kind you found on low-end bedroom doors with a flimsy center lock-knob. The key probably hadn't been changed since Irina bought the place. No dead bolt, no chain, no window locks. She might as well put an invitation on the door: "Come on in."

An *invitation* of a kind was waiting for her on the wobbly little corner table masquerading as a desk. The envelope was small, square, and made of thick parchment type paper. She fingered it, feeling the texture. Nice. It was addressed simply, "Mrs. Beaudine," in pen and ink calligraphy. The lettering was perfect. She opened it, expecting—heck, she didn't know what she was expecting. Another party invitation maybe?

Inside was a folded bevel-edged note card. It read:

Some say life is lived in the mind. And how you think,

Inevitably determines
How you view who you are. What I see in the desert,
Is a flight from reality,
Is a painting brushed to my taste,
Is dust-demons chasing at my heels, Is heat cleansing my soul,
Is mine alone.

Instinctively Jada knew the poem was meant as a present, and she immediately knew which inmate at the Red Rock Inn and Café had left it. Yesterday's note had been a threat-while tonight's, from a different author for sure—was a gift.

Either way, both, friend and foe had come and gone at will. Why did Irina bother with keys at all?

Extract from Lyle Elliott's Letter to his Home Office
January 8—Almost Midnight

I'm not sure where to start. There's been another murder and a fire.

I told you earlier how I believe Terrence Beaudine tried to contact his wife today. I know, I know, I didn't get a good enough look, and I'm not positive it was Terrence, but who the heck else would be trying to get in her room? I'm guessing the Police Chief thinks it's the murderer, especially since whoever it was shot off his gun. I have to admit I find that a puzzling thing for Terrence to do. I've never pictured him as the gun-toting type, no, Beaudine is the sneaky, slimy, behind your back type of scumbag. Anyway, I was there, but I just didn't get a good enough look to go to the Chief with what I know. And I couldn't take off after him. Would have given myself away.

So I checked out of the Red Rock today, and before you ask, yes I checked back in. This time as the "old geezer," you know, the getup with the faded jeans, work shirt, and the big white beard and long white braid.

I think things are about to come down soon. He's going to have to make his move, and I'm going to be there.

This darn murder thing though is getting in the way. I must admit, I am a little curious myself. I told you this pottery teacher guy was knocked off, then this guy, Hal Morton from the studio gets killed. He was sort of the number one helper—been there since the beginning.

From what I can pick up he was a blackmailer so I'm pretty sure he knew something about the murder and was putting the squeeze on. Big mistake. Beaudine found his body. I swear to God, it's like she's a magnet for dead bodies or something.

Then there was a fire this morning. I know, I know, it's crazy around here. Somebody torched the Morton place. Obviously the murderer, and probably to get rid of blackmail information, at least that's how it's looking to me right now.

Chief Rhodes and Beaudine had interviews with most of the class people today. Don't know what came out of them except for the Berrys. Two of the people are this ditsy husband and wife duo, busy-body types. Turns out Samuels at the office knows them and they believe a spurned ladylove killed Williams. Seems he was quite a ladies-man—good-looking I'm told, tall and thin. I heard Ms. Hughes—she runs the Inn—call Williams a "perfect man." My money is on him not being so perfect, and that's what got him killed. But, I'm keeping my nose out of it, none of our business, just nosey. Unless maybe there's some connection down the road. Don't see how.

By the way, would you do me a favor and check my snail mail? It's been a long day, Ham.

Lyle didn't mention the second white car he thought was appearing too often. Maybe a Toyota? He just couldn't be sure yet. Heck, everybody in this town seemed to be driving a white car of some kind.

Ally was confused, and she didn't like it. This was not a time for doubt. But so much was happening and she had seen some things the last couple days that didn't make sense. She was sure though, the Beaudine woman was behind it all; and soon, very soon, she, Allison King, would exact Terry's revenge.

She lay in her darkened motel room, the drapes and window open so she could feel the night—her gun on the bed beside her. And again she tapped its finish with her fingernails. Her long vampish nails were real, but hard as fake ones, and she had become fond of the staccato sound they made against the gun's surface.

For the time being, she would just have to continue to stay at the Best Western, follow, and seize her opportunity when it came. Everything would fit into place soon.

Tasha woke Jada up at 3:00 A.M. with several sharp mean barks. She had evidently heard or smelled something she didn't like.

Jada peeked through her bedside blinds. Nothing. The moon was straight above in a black clear sky, giving the Joshua trees around the place ghostly shadows. But nothing seemed to be moving.

Nonetheless, Tasha jumped off the bed and barked again, by the door.

Quietly and cautiously, she got up, then silently crept to the front door and peered out front. Still nothing. Tasha sniffed along the bottom edge of the door for a moment, then abruptly lost interest and jumped back in bed. Jada also sat down on the bed and waited, listening.

Nothing. She waited some more, maybe fifteen minutes all told. Still nothing.

Since losing Terry, well over a year now, Jada had struggled to reach a point where she could take her destiny into her own hands, no longer controlled and manipulated by others. Not that she felt a complete master of her emotions; and for sure there were those moments—sudden and often puzzling-when the golden prize of what she had finally come to want to be herself, would evaporate, leaving her in a wash of loneliness, fear, and anxiety.

This was one of those moments. Still in control, though, and with forced calm she laid back down and felt for the poem tucked under her pillow. It was still there, its presence inexplicably comforting.

Eventually she managed to fall off again—albeit an uneasy sleep—but thankfully, sleep nonetheless. It had truly been the longest of days.

Amused, Josia had watched as Melvin Beaudine and his Mother had said their goodnights and gone upstairs, supposedly to separate bedrooms, sheepish grins and conspiring eyes unavoidable on both their faces.

That had been five hours ago.

Still he sat, outside on the dining room patio, wide-awake, staring into a moonlit star-speckled desert sky. He wasn't a stargazer by nature, but even he could appreciate their prodigious twinkling across the heavens above him. A couple more hours and it would be dawn, the stars would be gone, and he would probably still be awake.

He was thinking, of course, about Nick Williams and Hal Morton. He figured Darcie Williams had killed her husband because of his numerous affairs, *or* Irina Hughes had lashed out at her lover when she found out he was dumping her. Praying didn't come naturally to Josia, but in this case, he came close in his hope Irina wasn't involved; but he wasn't about to take bets on her innocence—despite what he had cavalierly told the Beaudine woman. And Morton, he guessed, was killed because he was blackmailing one of his two prime suspects.

Bottom line though, he didn't have anything to prove a case against either one.

Still, he sat. Indeed, it had been a caffeine drenched day, but his insomnia was more tied to the fact that losing didn't sit well with him. In two more days, maybe three if he called in more favors, the case would be out of his hands; and he certainly wouldn't be able to fault that decision. Two murders in *his* town and he didn't have once piece of evidence worth a damn.

Maybe his mother and her new boyfriend would turn up something in San Francisco. He doubted it. The Beaudine woman seemed to be a smart cookie, and tough to boot. Maybe she would have a brilliant insight. He doubted that even more.

"What a damn long day," he said to the crickets that liked to hang around the trellis at the end of the patio.

PART TWO
Muddy Waters

Chapter Six

Thursday

"Did you sleep okay last night, Mrs. Beaudine?" Manny set a pancake and egg platter on the counter in front of her. "Because I thought I saw a fox out back late last night. They don't come around often, but occasionally we get one. I yelled at it though. Nothing against foxes, I just don't want them hanging around the Red Rock."

"When was that?"

He cut five fresh oranges and started pushing the halves down over an electric juicer. "Oh around three or four. I lose time when I'm on the Internet. I shouldn't have stayed up so late."

"Jeez, you've hardly gotten any sleep." Then, on second thought and in deference to his youthfulness, she said, "Well, maybe you don't need as much as I do."

He finished up the orange juice and put it on the counter for her. "You're wrong there, Mrs. Beaudine."

"Manny why don't you call me Jada? Please."

"Sure thing." He grinned. "Like I was saying, I need a lot of sleep. When I do something stupid like that I pay hell for a

177

couple days until my body gets back to normal. On the other hand, the phone line is so slow, the middle of the night is a great time to get on the Internet."

"So you were up with your light on? Right?"

He nodded.

If by a lengthy stretch of the imagination someone had been out there last night, maybe Manny had scared him or her away?

Jada took a welcome swallow of fresh juice and refrained from telling him about the two large shoe prints she had seen in the rough sand and gravel outside her front cabin window this morning. It was something to think about. On the other hand, those footprints could have been there for ages and she just hadn't noticed.

He left her to wait on an elderly man who had just come in and taken the first table from the door. The same table the Hassidic-garbed man had chosen yesterday. Jada was left to eat alone. The pancakes, smothered in butter and homemade blueberry syrup, were excellent. What a treasure Manny was. Poor Terry hadn't been able to cook worth a damn. She wasn't much better. *We had managed though.* She drained her orange juice.

"Want another?" Manny was back behind the counter. "I'm squeezing one for Mr. Cox." He inclined his head toward the first table. "No trouble to do a few more oranges."

"That would be great. I don't think I've ever had such sweet orange juice. You didn't put any sugar in this did you?"

"Nope. I have a cousin who lives in Lindsey and she's got twenty acres. Small orchard, but she treats her trees good. Best oranges in the valley."

She asked where Lindsey was and what valley he was talking about.

"East and North of Bakersfield. You go up Highway 65."

Jada shrugged and wondered why she had asked in the first place. "Well," she said, while lifting her newly filled glass in a minor toast. "Wherever the town of Lindsey is, I salute your cousin." She drained her glass in one attempt. Sweet, aromatic, smooth.

He smiled broadly. "I'll tell her."

She finished the rest of her breakfast with leisure, yet thoughtfully, as Manny went about the business of feeding the old man, and then Mrs. Shoecraft who came in later, escorted by Linda.

It had been a rough night for Jada, and with the morning light, no new insights regarding murderers had materialized. One very important realization, however, had made its way to the forefront of her consciousness while brushing her teeth. Lyle Elliott. So after a final cup of tea, she left Manny another generous tip and went to the first table and sat down next to the old man. He was finishing off scrambled eggs and ham.

"You know, Mr. Elliott, or now Mr. Cox," she said. "Your disguises are pretty good, but you don't fool me. Although the Rabbi outfit did have me for awhile."

She had caught the "master-of-disguises," between mouthfuls. So when he coughed in surprise, choking was relegated to a noise issue only. "Ah. Ah. What?" he sputtered.

Jada gave him time to drink from his water glass. "You know it doesn't bother me anymore, Mr. Elliott. Actually, I should probably call you Lyle by now, we've been doing this dance so long. Over a year, in fact." She forced her voice to remain calm. "Hounding me, following me, innuendoes, suggestions, and then right before I left Seattle—your outright accusations. There was a time there when I hated you, you know."

Clearly speechless, he stared at her, his mouth not quite agape, but close.

"But then I came to realize you're just doing your job. And unfortunately, I'm your job. God, do I wish Terry had never taken out that million dollar policy. If I had known he was doing it, there's no way I would have let him." *No amount of money can bring him back.* "But I tell you, it still galls me, galls me very much, that you think my husband capable of faking his own death. You just didn't know my Terry."

He let out a resigned-sounding sigh, and fell back against his wooden chair back. "You know Mrs. Beaudine, you always seem so honest, so believable, but I know the truth. Evidently we don't see the same person."

"You don't *want* to see the real Terry. It's all a matter of money to you and your company, isn't it? If you knew my Terry, the real *Terry*, you'd know he'd never do something like that."

Lyle held his tongue, evidently realizing that though she seemed calm enough, there was fire in her eyes. They had faced off before, and she knew he was not a stupid man.

"And," she continued, in a tone calmer than she felt. "You certainly don't know *me* if you think I would have anything to do with something like that."

In a soft level voice he said, "I'm sorry. But I know he's out there. I think I've seen him."

She was no longer angry. For the first time ever, she felt sorry for Lyle. He was so wrong, and so implacable—a man trapped by his own ridiculous theories, unable to see the truth. "You're a deluded blind man. And I pity you." Odd, how those things happened, responses changed, emotions shifted.

Lyle was quiet for a moment, then he smiled. And the look in his eyes told Jada he never imagined he would ever smile in her presence.

In turn, she had never seen him smile, and felt an emotional tinge of something. She had no idea what caused the feeling, or what it was, but her response—leaving the café in a huff and banging the door loudly behind her—if not clear in its reasons, was definitely energetic.

Jada went back to her cabin, put out food for Tasha, brushed her teeth again, left a note asking Mrs. Chacon—hoping she could read English—to let Tasha out if she would. Then she got into her car and headed into town.

While performing these practical tasks, Jada felt a sense of extreme urgency building from within, and propelling her forward into this murder investigation. She now cared very much about finding the person who murdered Nick Williams and Hal Morton. And there was something else, unpleasant and unfortunately familiar. She had gone halfway into town before recognition occurred. It was the smell of evil, in disguise as usual. But there nonetheless.

They were in the everything-room, and Gabe's eager face and antsy behavior betrayed his difficulty in waiting to debrief Josia on his interview with Star Thomas. He had learned something from her and could barely wait to spill it out. With a touch of fondness, Jada likened him to a pot of soup on the edge of bubbling over.

Josia, either oblivious or indifferent to Gabe's distress, insisted on going through his coffee ritual before they started. The peons, that would be Gabe and herself, would just have to wait. She wondered if Josia knew how irritating his behavior was? And, if he *did* know, were his actions on purpose? Maybe he took perverse pleasure in being a jerk?

To be fair, he looked like hell. Face drawn, eyes bloodshot—a man in need of a good night's sleep. She almost felt sympathy for him, but her night hadn't left her in a generous frame of mind either.

After Josia saturated his coffee with a satisfactory amount of cream and sugar he sat down across from Gabe and next to Jada. "So," he said. "What have you got?"

"Mrs. Thomas had just gotten home from work a couple hours before I got there this morning," Gabe said looking at Jada rather than Josia. "I was going to see her yesterday afternoon, remember? No one was home, so I went back this morning."

Jada nodded and smiled.

"She works nights sometimes at the base. I expected her to be tired and not wanting to talk to me, especially since I missed the first appointment yesterday when we went out to the fire at the Morton place. But she greeted me at the door, had coffee and cinnamon buns waiting."

Josia raised an eyebrow. "I swear to God, Gabe, you always get the good ones. She was waiting for you, huh? How old is Mrs. Thomas? A looker?"

Jada bit her lip, kept her mouth shut, and continued smiling pleasantly. Her desire for information out-weighed her need to put Josia in his place.

Gabe cleared his throat and continued in a professional tone, "Mrs. Thomas is forty, tall, taller than I am, maybe five-nine. Shoulder length hair and nice looking for her age. And she was nice."

A hesitancy at the end of his sentence prompted Jada to ask, "Except?"

"Except she was really angry at Nick Williams. But I'm jumping ahead." He consulted his notebook. "Let's see, did I mention she had insisted I get there after her husband Phillip had gone off to work?" He looked up at her. "But you know that already, it's in our notes."

Notes she had yet to read.

"So I figured she didn't want her husband to hear what she had to tell me."

"And you were right, right?" Josia asked.

"Yes, Sir. Seems Mrs. Thomas had a few things she wanted to say about Nick Williams that couldn't be said in front of Mr. Thomas. Which is funny though since she didn't seem worried what she told me would get out. Like she didn't care."

"Maybe she doesn't care if he knows but she doesn't want to tell him herself?" Jada said. "She was having an affair with Nick, right?"

"She said their affair started a couple weeks after class started and they were still seeing each other when he was killed." Gabe took a deep breath. "She was supposed to get there early that morning, right after she got off work but she had to work overtime. Next thing she knew, Timothy Berry was calling to tell her Nick was dead."

Josia shook his head. "So Williams, at least some of the time in the last three years, was having simultaneous affairs?"

Amazement, envy, or disapproval, in his voice? Jada wasn't sure.

"That's what Mrs. Thomas said," Gabe answered, and went back to his notepad, this time quoting. "'The SOB was a womanizing prick.'" Again he took a second to clear his throat; this time looking like he needed time to remove the taste of Star's offending words. "She said the first time she took it in stride, but when he started seeing Ms. Hughes, she hit the ceiling. Seems she thinks Ms. Hughes is loony and his dating her was the last straw. An 'affront' she called it."

"She did, did she?" Josia said, with an unmasked touch of anger.

Unprofessional, Josia—you're letting your guard down. Jealousy maybe? Or just trying to put the pieces together like she was and coming up with an answer he didn't like. Irina found out about Star Thomas, got there early, and that was the end of

Mr. Nick Williams, the "perfect man." She was sure Irina was tough, but was she also ruthless enough to shoot a person point blank? And would she, over another woman? It didn't fit what she had seen of Irina so far.

Josia moved on. "Does Star's overtime alibi check out?"

"So far. I've talked to two of her co-workers, both saw her there, and one says she was working with her in a conference room until she left, about nine."

"What about the morning Hal Morton got killed?"

"She was at work again."

"Anything else you think we should know without reading your report?"

Gabe allowed himself a small self-congratulatory smile. "Well yes."

"And that is?"

"Mrs. Thomas said Mr. Morton tried to blackmail her. She recorded the telephone conversation and gave me a copy of the tape. He was going to tell her husband. She told him to go..." He gave Jada a quick look. "Well to go jump, sort of. What she actually said was a little rougher. It's on the tape. She said he never called her again."

"Well, well." Josia leaned back and put his hands behind his head. "Seems like our Mr. Morton was a slimy bastard with no balls. Throw the dirt out, if it works, great, poor sucker on the hook and money coming in. If it doesn't stick, so what, just their word against his. Nothing ventured, nothing gained. Wonder if she told Morton she'd gotten him on tape?"

"She said she did. Said he wasn't too happy about it either, but what could he do?"

"Tell her husband," Jada said. "Blackmail is a dangerous game. I think it would be a good idea if we had a little conversation with Phillip Thomas, don't you? If Thomas found out about it, he might not be the kind of man to take to Morton trying to blackmail his wife."

"Yep," Josia agreed. "Probably wouldn't be that fond of Nick Williams, either, now would he?"

"Are you going to tell him about his wife?" Gabe asked anxiously. "That is if he doesn't already know."

"I think we'll see what Mr. Thomas wants to tell us first."

Again, that sense of urgency Jada had experienced earlier grabbed at her. "Corissa James's husband, what was his name?"

"Ted," Gabe said.

"Chief, *Si*, I think—no—that's not right. I *feel* we also need to talk to Ted James this morning."

Josia gave her a scrutinizing look, potentially intimidating in its intensity; but her mind and attention were elsewhere, thinking—postulating the very beginnings of a theory. Problem was, no motive.

From Gabe's perspective, looking in on Josia and Jada's interaction and speculating whether the two liked or hated each other—there was only one thing he could tell for sure. They were not idling in neutral.

Barely believing what was happening to, and within him, Melvin Beaudine had pinched himself several times this morning.

"Refill, Mel, dear?" Madge Lee topped off her champagne flute from an iced glass decanter resting on a silver platter—itself sitting regally atop a three-level marble bathtub surround. She had told Melvin she considered the contents of the decanter the most perfect mid-morning pick-me-up known to humanity. Orange juice and *Dom Perignon*. "Was I not correct about this hotel? Excellent rooms, excellent service, excellent view. Wouldn't you agree?" From their near penthouse suite, views of San Francisco, the "city by the bay," poured in from almost every window.

Melvin most definitely agreed; and despite a lightheadedness that had appeared rather suddenly after his first glass of champagne, gladly accepted a refill.

"This tub is fantastic," he said. From the pulsating jets of water tickling his lower back, to the bubble machine on Madge Lee's end frizzing the water, Melvin had never seen or experienced anything like it. Overhead European shower jets hung in an intricate pattern, waiting to shower them with cleansing spring water—according to the brochure—when they were ready to rinse off. "Madge Lee, you know how to live."

"At my age, one certainly should have learned a few things." Her eyes twinkled with mischief. Indeed, she further explained, she had discovered a few years back while helping her son, that to her utmost joy, she loved traveling. Most to the point, she loved staying in top-drawer hotels. The luxury, the pampering attention, the food. And why not? If she didn't enjoy herself now, when would she? Besides, more often than not, she was successful at the work involved. She knew she was a clever old cookie, so why not use her brain and enjoy herself in the process? "And," she continued more seriously, "we've put in a hard morning. This is just an afternoon revitalization, then it's back to the phones. Maybe a visit to City Hall if we can squeeze it in."

Melvin wiggled his toes in the warm sudsy water and received a reciprocal wiggle from Madge Lee. "You think the information we're gathering might help?" He certainly hoped so. Jada was a wonderful gal in his mind, but she was always in the middle of something or other. Terry used to complain about it, joking mostly, about wishing he'd married a nice quiet stay-at-home type of woman. God, did he miss his brother. Even though at times, Terry had been an out-and-out bastard.

Intuiting his thoughts, Madge Lee asked, "What was Terrence like?"

"Well, I loved Terry a heck of a lot," Melvin answered with remarkable truthfulness, given Madge Lee wasn't a family member. Frankness with outsiders was another Beaudine family no-no. "But he did have several unpleasant aspects to his personality. Greed was probably the worst. He wanted it all. He was a lot of fun to be around though." He stopped there. He needn't mention the gambling; and there were some other items about Terry he thought were best left unsaid. Some things only he knew. Events from when they were children and Terry didn't get his way. Kid stuff.

"Jada does not strike me as a materialistic being," Madge Lee said. "To the contrary, her aura speaks to a generous spirit, possibly even to a fault. At the same time, she doesn't show her emotional side easily. Keeps her own counsel, I would guess."

"Hey, you're pretty good at this stuff." He smiled. "That's her alright. But you see, that was the beauty of it, they complimented each other." Terry had lucked up there, finding Jada. In truth, Terry had always been the lucky one. Do whatever the hell he wanted, the consequences be damned; and sure enough, everything usually came out just fine. "Actually, I'm not sure if I ever really knew Terry."

"I like your Jada. Something about your sister-in-law is psychically compelling. At the same time, my senses are making me quite wary of Terry Beaudine's spirit." She rubbed her toes this time along Melvin's inner thigh. "It's been building since I first met Jada, then you."

Melvin was beginning to not care about Jada or Terry for the moment, but he managed to ask, "You think we'll be able to help her?"

"I'm positive we will, Mel," she said. "I do think we will have to go to Chicago to accomplish our mission. But even though we're in this for your Jada and my Josia, the one I'm really worried about is Irina."

"Irina?" Melvin let himself slide down lower into frothy bubbles.

"The poor, poor, dear. How could she have been so foolish as to fall for that horrid Nick Williams? But she did, and now he's dead, and she has a substantial motive, no alibi, and of course, easy access."

He closed his eyes. "You don't think your son would really arrest her?"

"No. But the County and State folks would. That's why we have to get this thing cleared up. Fast."

"What are you expecting to dig up in Chicago?" He was finding it harder and harder to concentrate on Jada and murder suspects.

"Something tells me Nick Williams's past is the key to his murder. And I think we'll find that information in Chicago. I have a couple contacts there, private eyes I've done business with before."

The woman was a wonder. Such talk, private eyes and such. And what a lovely English accent, quite melodious to his American ears. "Think we should rinse off and get going?" God, he hoped not.

"No hurry, Melvin, now is there?"

The Thomas house turned out to be an upscale custom job on the side of a hill near the Red Rock Community College and looked like it had been chiseled out of the rock surface.

The parts discernable as house rather than rocks were angular and glass. From what Jada had seen of Red Rock City at large, and even in the upscale Thomas neighborhood, this house was "over-the-top" in a big way.

In harmony with his home and surroundings, Phillip Thomas was tall, thin, and angular—a frame meant for hanging trendy Gentlemen's Quarterly styles on. His features were strong without being rough. Jada thought him good looking in a classic sort of way; and if you judged by the house, he was also a prosperous young man. However, after a very few words, she chalked Phillip off as an arrogant SOB, and consequently unattractive in personality and looks.

Earlier, when she and Josia arrived, Phillip invited them into his palace, and eventually into the living room, with words and body language seeped in condescending tolerance.

His distaste for lesser beings was so palpable, Jada expected Josia to jump on him without hesitation, guns blazing. Instead, she heard Josia purr, "Really nice of you, Mr. Thomas to see us this morning. I know you're a busy man. By the way, this is *some* house." A low whistle. "Quite a view you have up here. Did you design it yourself?"

Phillip, ego clearly on his sleeve and now adequately massaged, was drawn right into what she quickly realized was Josia's "honey to a bee" routine. "Yes, Chief. I did design it myself. The hill presented quite a challenge, even for someone with my experience."

She watched as Josia listened attentively, awed and oohed, while Phillip chronicled the two years he spent conquering the hill, the Red Rock City building department, and conventional architectural wisdom. And while Josia fawned, Jada took time to take in their surroundings, trying to take measure of the man from his taste and possessions. Was he capable of murder? Would his choice of lamps or rugs tell her?

She was sure this was *his* house, not Star's. The sleek chrome and glass furniture, the eclectic mix of oriental and modernistic rugs, the Chinese prints and avant-garde paintings, the glass and ceramic sculptures—all of which Jada figured were from prominent artists—spoke to Phillip's architectural taste.

The end result of what she saw was a statement of unashamed ego projected through ostentatious prosperity; which Jada translated as a life focused on power.

She understood power, the desire for it, and the length human beings would go to achieve it. Jada had had to deal with powerful people in her past; and consequently recognized it by sight, touch, and smell. *Power and murder.* She had seen those two drives linked before. In Phillip's case, it was much too early to speculate with any certainty, but she was definitely on alert.

He took them over to a glass expanse opening to the Western horizon and a view of Red Rock City below. The town wasn't much, but Jada thought the view would be quite nice at night, the city lights twinkling against a dark desert sky.

Josia was saying, "You've done a nice job here, Mr. Thomas. Is there somewhere we could sit and talk for a moment? I have a few questions I need to ask you. Routine, you understand, but I would be negligent in doing my job if I didn't."

"Certainly, Chief, Mrs. Beaudine." Phillip indicated a leather love seat and two matching chairs in an alcove tucked in to their right. He did not however offer refreshments, another checkmark against him in Jada's mind. "How can I help?"

"You are obviously a man of the world, so naturally, I would be interested in your opinion of Mr. Williams and Mr. Morton." Josia leaned forward, solicitously, his body movements indicating eagerness to hear the great man's opinions.

"Well, that's easy. Nick Williams was a fraud and an ineffectual womanizer. Morton was a despicable blackmailing sleaze-ball."

"Fraud? How so?"

"It was obvious to me the man was older than the young-potter image he was trying to project. I'm also something of a linguist."

"Ah." Josia raised an appreciative eyebrow.

"And I am quite positive he was born and educated, at least in the early years, no farther West than Chicago. His vowels were not precisely the Atlantic coast, but he did not learn English on the West Coast."

"Interesting."

"Oh yes, I would also say Nicky-boy was hiding something."

"Any ideas what?"

"Afraid not, Chief," Phillip said. "If I had known he was going to get killed and we were going to have this discussion, I would have paid more attention." His words were said through a smile, but also with sarcasm, and slightly veiled so as not to slap you in the face, but clear enough.

Josia seemed not to notice. "And Mr. Morton?"

Phillip sighed resignedly before continuing. "We come to the real reason you're here, correct?" he asked. "To find out if I knew my wife was having an affair with Nicky-boy and if I knew Morton tried to blackmail her."

He is sharp, Jada acknowledged while simultaneously wanting to smack him right across his arrogant kisser. Amazing, that, she instantly realized. Her temper and anger were indeed her downfall, but seldom did she have an inclination to actually hit someone.

Josia just smiled and kept his mouth shut and waited.

"Well, I did," Phillip finally said. "Obviously."

The silence among them, though short in actual duration, had the emotional impact of hours. A speck of incertitude had crept underneath Phillip's veneer of self- assuredness. She could see it in his eyes and hear it in his voice when he said, "Star, of course, didn't know I knew." He cleared his throat.

"Of course." Josia said through his same smile.

"What she saw in that…well, let's leave it at that, shall we?"

"I'm afraid I can't, as you suggest, 'leave it at that,'" Josia said, and sat up straighter, eyes sharper, his whole demeanor crisper. "Where were you Sunday night January fifth and Monday morning January sixth until around eight in the morning?"

Resentment flashed in Phillip's eyes, but just as quickly disappeared. "I have no alibi. I was at home, here in bed until six A.M. which is my customary wake up time. I was still here when Star came home around ten. She had worked overtime. Not that I expect you to give credence to a husband and wife alibi."

"You're right, I don't. Now for Wednesday morning, January eighth, from about four until eight. Again, where were you?"

"As before, Chief, at home in bed."

"Do you own a gun, Mr. Thomas?"

"Several."

"A twenty-two, or a thirty-eight, or a forty-five?"

"All three, and a Ruger nine-millimeter."

"I need to take them with me. Is that a problem?"

"None, Chief. I'm a cooperative citizen. I will not insist you come back with a warrant."

Again, the smile. "Thank you, Mr. Thomas," Josia said.

"I could have killed them, you know?" Phillip said quietly. "My wife is a very attractive woman. I'm not surprised other men take an interest in her, or that she would fall for frivolous flattery. But Nick Williams, of all people? The man was nothing. And Morton, it was inconceivable he would try to blackmail my wife, then come to me when she refused his demands. He was absolutely unbelievable." He shook his head. "My wife is a weak woman, but even she had the common sense to stand up to Morton. Oh, I could have killed them." Some of Phillip's initial bravado seemed to be returning. "But I didn't." He left unsaid in words, but made crystal clear with his facial expression and eyes, *"And if you think I did, you better damn well have indisputable evidence, or your butt is mine."*

While Josia and Phillip went to collect his guns, Jada studied the picture of Star in an eight-by-ten silver frame on their sleek black marble fireplace mantel in the main part of the living room. It was a lively face with intelligent eyes and a small but strong chin. Definitely attractive, and not a weak looking woman by any stretch. What the heck did she see in Phillip, Jada wondered?

And again, for one of the multitudinous times in her life, she marveled at the wondrous mystery of love.

They dropped Phillip's bagged handguns back at the office for Gabe to get to the lab. While there, Gabe informed Josia that a Mr. Lyle Elliott had stopped by to see him. He didn't know why. Mr. Elliott had declined to tell him the purpose of his visit-but he would stop by again tomorrow.

"Probably wants to sell me something," Josia grumped.

Jada bit her lip, refrained from comment, and focused on organizing her thoughts for their next meeting with Corissa's husband.

The James household was out the south end of town in a sparsely populated area Josia explained was dicey when it came to water. "Some spots you hit it, some you don't. Guess James got lucky."

They did not talk much on the drive out, about a fifteen-minute ride, except for a couple curses from Josia addressing what he perceived as ineptitude on the part of fellow drivers, and two short exchanges initiated by Jada. One on Red Rock City topography and the water situation, and one on Phillip Thomas as a viable suspect.

She was tired, and from the look of him, Josia was too. Still, she made her second attempt at conversation because she wanted to get a measure on her own distaste of Phillip. Was it logical, or just one of those chemistry clashes humans sometime have? Her weariness made her blunt. "I thought he was an arrogant, egotistical ass. I was glad to get out of there."

Evidently equally tired, Josia's responding chuckle was weak. "Didn't like him, huh, Mrs. Beaudine?"

"I thought I heard you move on to 'Jada.'"

"Well, sorry about that, Mrs. Beaudine."

"Jada is fine."

"And so is Si, which you called me back at the office. Remember?"

Of course she remembered; he didn't have to rub it in. "Not only didn't I like Phillip Thomas on a personal level, but when it comes to the business of murder, it's sure easy for me to see him in that role."

"Wishful thinking, or some hard facts?"

"You're right, I would like it to be him, and I don't have any hard facts. But you have to admit, he's got the personality for it. And, he's got a darn good motive—his wife was fooling around with Williams. On top of that, his alibi sucks."

"Yeah." Josia's weariness came through in his voice. "It wouldn't bother me a damn bit to haul his butt in. Jerks like him bring out the worst in me. But I've seen a lot of his kind, and I don't think he's got the balls to kill anybody. All bullshit bravado with nothin' behind it."

She thought he was wrong about Phillip's capability to kill. Yet, she found herself warming to Josia for the moment and heard herself saying, "By the way, I thought you did a nice job with him."

He grumped by way of thanks and turned the cruiser off the pavement down a gravel road that felt like a washboard. "Hold on," he mumbled before turning silent for the five more miles of bone rattling, stomach destroying agony before finally pulling into the James driveway.

Jada didn't hesitate to get out. She needed her feet plunked back down solidly on *terra firma* to stop the rolling in her head and gut. Desert dirt roads left a lot to be desired.

The house turned out to be a new and expansive two-story adobe style structure sitting quite alone on the side of a long slope that headed out of town toward Highway 395. The view was again of Red Rock City, but from a different angle than at the Thomas place. Jada instantly and instinctively liked the house and its location; but she also speculated they were about to enter another pricey piece of real estate and she better get ready to once more deal with a house-proud egoist. And even though it was getting harder and harder to fight her fatigue, she marshaled her thoughts—*gathered her wits* as Terry was wont to quip—because she believed talking to Ted James was going to somehow help her fit the pieces together. In fact, she intellectually considered him, along with Phillip Thomas, a prime suspect.

Nonetheless, she liked Ted from the moment he appeared at the door. A bit shorter than average, rounder than most, and with thinning hair, he wasn't on first glance another GQ model candidate. Within seconds though, his dancing and curious brown eyes, generous smile, and warm inviting mannerisms spoke to Jada of a kind and curious man with a benevolent spirit. To her eyes, a rather nondescript man became attractive.

"Chief Rhodes, Mrs. Beaudine, I've been anxiously waiting since your call. Sometimes people have a hard time finding us, and even when they know where we are, they don't want to come down our dirt road." He laughed pleasantly. "I see I shouldn't have worried. You're a policeman after all," he said. "If you can't find us, who can?"

Inside, Ted asked if they would like some refreshments out on the patio and refused to take "no" for an answer. Once he got them settled around an antique wrought iron table in an enclosed and heated patio room, he went back inside to quickly return carrying a huge tray containing a pitcher of lemonade and an assortment of tea sandwiches. "I made the lemonade, and Cori made the sandwiches before she left."

"Very nice of you both," Josia said. "Sorry Mrs. James couldn't be here."

Jada knew that in truth, this was just the circumstance Josia had wanted. Ted James alone.

"If we had known."

But Corissa had known.

"Absolutely no problem, Mr. James," Josia said, evidently wanting to be up-front and congenial—at least to start. "To tell you the truth, Mr. James, I was hoping to talk to you alone." He smiled. "You know, to get your perspective of Mr. Williams from an outsider. We've already interviewed your wife at my office."

"I think I understand." Ted rubbed his chin thoughtfully. "I was thinking about Cori's class just this morning, and Darcie Williams in particular. I've been there a couple times myself, so I've met Nick and Darcie, and, well, I just can't imagine losing your spouse." He shook his head. "We've sent Mrs. Williams a sympathy card already, but you know nobody can say anything that will make it all better."

Oh god, how true. The loss is forever. Jada had to quickly look away, out into a colorful flower garden surrounding the patio.

He continued, "Please call me Ted. That is if you're comfortable with first names. Mr. James sounds like my dad."

Josia smiled congenially. "Ted it is then. You were saying?"

"My wife is quite artistic. She decorated our whole house. But until she found ceramics, I don't think she had a good outlet for her talent and energy." He pointed to a concrete pedestal at the corner of the patio. On top sat a large sculpture head, abstract, contorted, and quite unique.

"I've seen your wife's work," Jada said. "In the back room, at the studio. I had wondered who the sculptures belonged to."

"They're very time consuming, and they take a very long time to dry I understand." Ted cleared his throat and took in a deep breath, then released it. "Well anyway, that ceramic class was wonderful for Cori. I've watched her become so much more confident over the last few years since she started. Nick Williams did wonders bringing her talent out. I am truly sorry somebody killed him." His face saddened. "I'm sure Cori would say the same if she wasn't with her mother."

"Your mother-in-law lives in town?" Jada asked. Ted sighed sadly. "Well, yes, and no. Unfortunately Ruth sometimes feels the need to check herself in to, well, I'm really not sure what to call the place. Not really a nursing home—there are a lot of young people there—but not a spa or resort either, because some people there are going through a stressful time emotionally and need some medical assistance." He smiled wryly. "One of those exclusive pricey places," he said. "It's real nice. Outside of Palmdale." He looked at Josia. "And you know it's Mrs. Dominic now. Ruth remarried a couple years back. Really nice guy, he's very devoted to her."

"So," Josia said, bringing him back to Williams, "You think Nick Williams and the ceramic class had a positive effect on your wife? I have to admit, Mrs. James seemed a little skittish at the office."

"I'm not surprised," Ted said. "Cori, well…Cori had a tough time of it in some ways as a child. You see Billy McNichols abandoned Ruth and Cori when Cori was very young. I gather money was tight and she didn't have all the advantages she wanted, like nice clothes and college." He turned his head to look at Jada. "Not that they went hungry; I don't think it was as bad as that. But anyway, I think the whole experience left Cori with a bit of an inferiority complex and she's not comfortable at all around authority figures."

Josia stretched and helped himself to a second glass of lemonade. "This is good," he said. "I appreciate your openness about your wife. Though I doubt it has any bearing on these murders. But you seem to be a perceptive person." He leaned forward toward Ted. "Is there anything you or your wife picked up at class that might be of help to us? Let me say, I'm asking you about your wife because she had a hard time talking about it at my office."

"Have you talked to the Berrys?"

Josia nodded while Jada turned her head to hide a smile. *The infamous nosey Berrys.*

Ted said, "The reason I mention them is they seem to know everything about that class."

Josia then asked him where he had been during the time of both murders. He was in bed asleep with his wife until she got up and went to class.

"Wait," Ted amended. "On the morning Mr. Morton was killed, I was alone. Cori got up even earlier so she could go visit Ruth."

Did he own a gun?

"Heavens no."

On the way out Ted insisted on a quick tour. The layout of the house was functional and aesthetically pleasing, with rich Southwest colors on the walls, travertine marble tile floors, and furniture that accentuated the pueblo feel. What Jada found the most appealing were the small court gardens outside almost every room. Each had a theme—flowers, cactus, fruit trees. They looked like inviting places to sit and enjoy the passage of days, even now in winter.

"Cori is a wonderful gardener, don't you think?" Ted asked. "Here it is in January and she's managed to have flowers in bloom in several gardens. She scoured the nursery catalogues, you know. Ruth helped her a lot too, both women like flowers and I understand Ruth grew a lot of home vegetables when Cori was a child."

As they left, Josia said in an earnest tone, "Nice house. You did a good job."

"Thanks, but I can't take any credit." Ted chuckled. "I'm just lucky to be in this house. Amazing that we found such a great architect and then a good builder. And Cori did all the decorating. It's a little posh for me, and a little isolated, but the longer I'm here the more I like it."

Jada's thoughts went to Corissa James and what a lucky woman she was to have a husband like Ted. A husband who loved her, a husband still alive and able to tell her how he felt. Indeed, she stood and stared out into Cori's winter garden for several long minutes while Josia and Ted moved on, their voices barely registering on her conscious ears. The interview with Ted James had opened some emotional passages with Jada that she had thought were cemented closed for good. She was caught unaware, and for several moments had to catch an emotional breath.

Even though a year had passed and she had successfully gotten out of Puget Sound and its memories, she still missed Terry and still loved the thought of him. And felt utterly lost without him. For this moment she was still able to push it back; but once she surrendered, let herself "feel" again, Jada realized the emotion that would sweep over her, just like in the past, would still be a tidal wave and maybe impossible to control this time.

Such knowledge surprised her, and she was not ready to deal with the implications. Not today at least. She had a murderer to catch.

On their way back to the office, Gabe called and informed them Irina was also on her way to the office. They needed to hurry and get back. It was urgent.

Jada was immediately skeptical, but she knew Irina needed to be heard. Over time she had come to view the world as a complicated and oftentimes mysterious place. She doubted Irina was *actually* psychic, but *something* was going on. Irina was visibly shaking and Jada guessed in marginal control of whatever was happening. They were finally all standing in the parking lot of Josia's office. Irina, Jada, Josia, and Gabe.

Irina said, "I know you two think I'm crazy. Hell, I think I'm crazy, but I just can't get this picture out of my mind." After a quick look to Josia, she continued, "This has happened to me a couple times before, and, well, I've ignored it." She took a deep breath. "And what I had seen, happened."

"What's going to happen?" Josia demanded.

Even though her comments generated his question, Irina slid right by an answer. "But Madge Lee says I shouldn't ignore my insights. So, that's what I doing. I'm telling you. And if it's like before, whatever I'm seeing is happening right now, or real soon." Her voice quivered as she next looked to Jada and Gabe for support. "We got to do something."

"Look, Rina," Josia said with unmistakable impatience. "Could you just tell us in plain English what the hell you think is gonna happen?"

"For Christ's sake, Si," she spat the words out. "If I knew that, do you think I'd be standing here in this friggin' parking lot making a fool of myself?"

He clamped his mouth shut into a hard line. Jada fancied she could hear the gnashing of his teeth. Nevertheless, despite his obvious displeasure, or possibly because of it, she determinedly stepped forward and took both of Irina's hands into her own and said gently, yet resolutely, "We'll figure it out." She gave her hands a squeeze. "Let's go inside for a minute, have something to drink and calmly talk this over. How does that sound?"

"That sounds great, but you don't understand. We have to do something now. NOW!"

"Alright." Jada capitulated and let her hands go. "What is this 'picture' you can't get out of your mind?"

Irina closed her eyes, dropped her head forward a bit, and steadied herself against the fender of Josia's patrol car while Gabe supported her other arm. What an odd sight, Jada fleetingly visualized from a perspective of looking down upon their scene—the three of them standing out there in the parking lot communing with a crazy woman.

"It's two children. Yes, a girl and a boy, and they're playing a game, a game they always play, same place, same time every day." She closed her eyes for a second. "But I can't tell what the game is, I can't really see that part. Then it all goes wrong, horribly wrong, and they're falling into a big hole, an abyss, but I can't see what's at the bottom. I just know it's something really bad."

She took another deep breath, now leaning more heavily on Gabe for support. "I can't see the game, but it's something special, like...like something they know and no one else does.

"Oh yeah, and they're wearing dresses, they're both in identical dresses, those sailor collar dresses from the old days, no, no wait...she's wearing a dress and he's got on a little boys sailor costume—"

Jada blurted out, "The Berrys. It's Penny and Timothy. Si, Gabe, can we go there now?"

Josia did nothing except stare at the two women.

"Look, Si," Jada said. "We can't just ignore what's happening to Irina. The worst that will happen to you and your precious police department is you'll waste some gas. And later you can make a lot of jokes at Irina's expense." She wanted to grab him by the arms, give him a good shake. "I know you're tired, we're all tired. But if she has had these before, and they've come true, we can't just ignore this." She sighed impatiently. "And I'm sure it's the Berrys she's talking about."

Jada didn't view herself as having strong spiritual or mystical leanings, yet that sense of urgency she had felt all morning had now become fiercely intense. She had to do something.

Still, Josia stood staring at them while Gabe, holding Irina's arm, watched the drama unfold.

"Alright, forget it," Jada said in a flash of anger. "Come on Irina, my car is right over there, let's go ourselves. Where's a cop when you need one?" She grabbed Irina by her free arm and made movements to direct her.

"For Christ's sake," Josia said with irritated acceptance. "You're loony as a jay-bird, Rina, you know that don't you? *And* my mother encourages you in this lunacy. And now, you've got another female," he rolled his eyes at Jada, "defending your idiotic behavior. But if anybody is going to go to the Berry house in connection with these murders, it's going to be me."

In the end, the Red Rock City Police Office was left in Beth's capable hands once again, while they all headed out to the end of Brown Road in Inyokern—sirens blazing and lights flashing—Jada up front with Josia, and Irina and Gabe in back.

*   *   *   *   *

"I can see them in there," Gabe insisted. "They're just lying in bed. Can't they hear us?"

Josia pulled out his gun and used its butt to break the window. Quickly he covered his fist with his county-issue handkerchief and smashed the window further—it was double paned and not yielding easily.

"Son-of-a-bitch," he cursed. "If they're dead…" He didn't like what he could see in the Berry's bedroom. Timothy and Penny were both lying on their king-sized bed as if asleep. But not really. Instinctively he knew there was something wrong with the way they were resting, the awkwardness of their positions and the subtle but unavoidable look of plasticity to their bodies.

"Wait," he yelled to Gabe. "You smell that?" The unmistakable odor of propane.

"We got to get them out," Gabe shouted.

"I know, just go carefully," he said. "The gas." A quick glance to his patrol car confirmed what he hoped was happening—Jada on the phone, getting help. "The whole place could blow." He didn't have to explain to Gabe, everyone in the desert knew what propane could do.

"I'll go around and come through the front door even if I have to shoot it down and risk ignition." Gabe was gone before Josia could approve or disapprove.

"Good kid," he murmured to himself while he continued trying to make an opening big enough to crawl through and not slash an artery in the process. The smell was awful. He needed to hurry. "Where the hell is that ambulance?"

*   *   *   *   *

In the patrol car, Jada willed herself not to get out. She knew she needed to stay with Irina who was now vacillating between shaking and moaning. Josia and Gabe would know how to help Timothy and Penny. They didn't need her, even though she wanted to be out there with them. She wanted to know what was going on. Even from the car, she could smell propane. "Oh my God, the whole place could blow. We're too close." She slid over underneath the wheel. *Thank goodness.* Josia had left the keys. Trembling, she managed to start the car and back out of the driveway, out onto the road.

There wasn't much danger to surrounding houses. There weren't any.

"Jesus, Jada." Irina had her arms crossed over her body, hugging herself, rocking back and forth. "I should have come earlier. I waited too long. I was so afraid of making a fool of myself."

"Stop it," Jada demanded sharply. "You can't lay a guilt trip on yourself. You did the best you could as fast as you could."

If I had only insisted Terry not go on that boating trip. If I had only put my foot down. She could taste and smell fear and guilt surrounding her; Irina's, her own, even Josia's and Gabe's. She wished praying came easy. It didn't. She could hear Josia and Gabe yelling. At each other? At the Berrys? Maybe they were alive. She wanted to go help.

"I'm fine, Jada. Go help them," Irina said in a surprisingly strong voice.

"What...how?" *She must have seen it on my face.*

"Just go."

However, once she had rushed back up the driveway, she wasn't sure what to do to help. Miraculously, Josia and Gabe had pulled Timothy and Penny out of the house onto the gravel out front where both were frantically performing CPR on two limp bodies. Jada feared the worst. But all she could do was stand helplessly, watching and hoping.

She heard between counts, Josia asking Gabe, "Did you get the gas?"

"No time," he answered after his next count and before putting his mouth back over Penny Berry's. It was her only chance; the breath of life.

Without thinking, Jada took a deep breath, covered her own mouth with one hand, held her nose with the other, and rushed into the house through the door Gabe had broken open. She headed toward the back, searching for a kitchen. In the background she could hear a steady ominous hiss. *Escaping gas.*

Her first thought, the stovetop. But no, the stovetop and the oven were both electric. What then? She rushed through the house, stumbling several times in her haste. Their place was comfortably furnished, but frilly and jam-packed with furniture, curios, and boxes. *Stuff everywhere.* Stuff she didn't take the time to look at. Finally back in the living room she found it.

Propane logs in the fireplace. Luckily she found the shut-off at first look, a valve on the side of the mantel near the floor. By now the smell was almost unbearable. As she turned the knob, the hiss died. Jada knew though, it was not the time to hang around being self-congratulatory. The house was loaded with gas. It could still blow.

Quickly she stumbled back outside. In the distance, at last, she could hear the wail of sirens, moving fast. Irina had also gotten out of the car and was sitting on the ground next to Josia and a still breathing Timothy. Jada could see a steady shallow movement of his chest, back and forth, back and forth. Irina was holding his hand.

Josia had dropped back on his butt on the grass, the look on his face a mixture of exhaustion and anger.

Gabe still worked over Penny, diligent and methodical in his task. Jada dropped down on the ground next to them, and taking a cue from Irina, held the woman's hand. It was warm, a good sign. *Why oh why would someone want to kill the Berrys?* Almost immediately, the answer came to her. *The diaries.*

Then Josia said, "Why has some bastard tried to kill the Berrys?" He sighed, then answered himself. "The diaries."

Jada shot him a glance, who returned her look with a barely perceptible nod of the head.

The diary hunt did not begin until after the ambulance attendants rushed Penny and Timothy off to Red Rock City Hospital with Gabe and Irina in accompaniment. And not until Fire Chief Charlie McNeal and Ed Lowell, owner of Red Rock Propane, had inspected the premises and declared the house safe to enter.

For a very long time, Josia and Jada looked everywhere. They found nothing. Finally the two gave up and headed to the hospital. Jada was disheartened, exhausted and hungry. She figured Josia was too. But neither she nor Josia wanted to stop to eat. Not until they found out if Penny and Timothy had survived.

Back at the Red Rock Inn Mrs. Chacon entered Jada's room to clean. She didn't bother with a key; if you jiggled the doorknob just the right way, the lock popped easily. She let Tasha out for a stretch, dusted and made the bed. Then when she started to do the bathroom, she heard Tasha barking, close, and mean-like.

"Ay, Dios mío!" She went outside to see what all the commotion was about. What she saw were the spinning rear wheels of a late model white Ford, burning rubber and spitting dust back down the drive away from number-two. Tasha was running after the car, barking steadily.

"Mamma," Manny came running from the café. "Are you alright? Who was that? What happened?"

By the time Tasha returned, a good fifteen minutes later, the two had pieced together what they thought had happened. They figured while Mrs. Chacon was cleaning, the same man Manny had shot at yesterday had tried to get in Jada's cabin again. "He must have driven in from out back, from the desert. I would have seen him otherwise." Manny was sure no car had driven into the Red Rock's driveway. He had been in the café all the time cleaning up after lunch and watching. Jada's questions about what he'd seen during the night had not gone unnoticed by the sharp young man.

"Call Chief Josia, Manny. Bad things are happening here," Mrs. Chacon said in excellent English.

"Yes, Mamma, I'll go call him right now."

He didn't tell his mother he had seen the new guest, a Lyle Elliott, drive off after the car and the dog. He would still alert Josia. Funny thing, though, about Mr. Elliott. He seemed so familiar, yet he couldn't remember actually having met the man before.

Linda Lowry had a new poem. She couldn't wait to put it in Mrs. Beaudine's room—but when she saw Mrs. Chacon, she hung back. She had immediately taken to Mrs. Beaudine, but she hadn't made the same spiritual connection with Manny's mother. Not that she didn't like Mrs. Chacon. But she just knew Mrs. Beaudine would understand her poetry. She was a kindred spirit.

Besides, Linda was embarrassed, her clandestine actions were so childish. She hadn't even told Mrs. Shoecraft she'd left a poem for Mrs. Beaudine, and she told Mrs. Shoecraft almost everything.

Then she saw the white Ford come out of the desert, real slow and quiet-like. She was no fool and hid behind the old rusted-out water tank. She was sure the driver hadn't seen her. Linda however, got a good look at the stranger before he reached number-two and Tasha started barking.

Yep, a real good look.

On the way to the hospital, Josia wanted to talk, so Jada let him.

"Do you remember a movie called 'Paths of Glory'?"

"Sort of...Gregory Peck?"

"No, Kirk Douglas and Adolph Menjou. It's a war movie, and Adolph is a French commanding general who's a real SOB and screws up and kills his own men and then has some innocent men executed to cover up and Kirk Douglas is the only honorable man in the whole group." He held up his hand to hold back her questions. "Remembering the plot exactly isn't important. What's important is when I was a kid and I watched that movie, which, let me tell ya, is a real tearjerker, I thought how horrible and cruel military officers were and the whole world would just be a-okay if we just got rid of all the bad generals. The answers for a kid are so simple."

Now intrigued and interested, Jada waited silently. "Now that I'm the age I am and have lived the life I have—you know I had several tours of duty, I was in Nam near the end, and here I am a Police Chief. Obviously my perspective when it comes to the military and law enforcement has changed from when I was a kid."

She immediately jumped to the simplistic and erroneous conclusion that Josia, like many, had just become more conservative with age.

"What I have grown to understand is there are people in this world, everywhere, not just the military, but in regular institutions, in the government, in churches, in factories, in offices, on condo-boards…whatever. Wherever people join to do any goddamn thing, there are those people who will lie, cheat, steal, destroy other people, do whatever is necessary so they come out on top. Even kill."

Profoundly aware of the truth Josia was speaking, and a tad surprised he was the one doing the saying, Jada sighed in kindred resignation. "You can't get away from 'em," she said, then shivered. Still, she was not convinced Josia's life truths were the answer in these two cases. Especially when it came to Nick Williams. The way he was killed was personal. Revenge more likely than self-preservation or control.

The rest of the trip to the hospital was completed in silence. Jada wrestling with her own disappointments and demons; and she figured Josia was probably doing the same.

Gabe was waiting for them at the Emergency entrance.

Josia parked quickly, but before they got out, he turned to her and said, "What I was trying to say back there is I want you to leave town. I want you to go back to Irina's place, pack your bag and continue on your merry way to Atlanta. I'm sorry I asked you to stay." Before continuing, he turned to look out the windshield at Gabe for a second. "Whoever killed Nick Williams doesn't give a damn about human life and will wipe out anyone who gets in the way." He shook his head and frowned. "I'll be real pissed at myself, Mrs. *Beaudine*, if I have to identify your body on a slab at the hospital." He then held up his hand before she could protest. "But I know you're gonna do whatever you damn well please, no matter what I want. You're just like my mother. Willful. All I ask is you watch your butt. Got it?"

She didn't know how to respond. Should she be angry he was trying to tell her what to do, or pleased that he cared? It didn't matter anyway, because he quickly walked around the car to open her door. Both avoided eye contact.

As they walked toward Gabe, Jada searched the deputy's face for signs of how Penny and Timothy were doing. His somber young countenance was emotionless.

"Well?" Josia demanded as soon as they were in earshot. "How are they?"

"Mr. Berry is in intensive care, but the doctor says he's doing real good," Gabe answered. "His chances of coming out of this are good. He says we just have to wait."

So why aren't you smiling with joy? Oh, do I hate hospitals.

Gabe's face turned grim. "But he's not so happy about Mrs. Berry. She's still in ICU and on life support...." He let the rest of whatever he was about to say float away on a freakishly warm afternoon breeze blowing through the emergency entrance canopy.

"Where's Irina?" Jada asked.

"She's in the waiting room. Says she's not going to leave until Mrs. Berry is alright."

"I'll stay with her," Jada said. "Are you going back to your office?"

Josia's response was weary and resigned. "Nah," he said before stretching and rolling his head from side to side. "Gabe, could you do me a big favor? Get Beth to help you if you need to."

"Yes, Sir."

Looking much too tired to make his mouth move, Josia however managed a small smile that said, how lucky he felt to have Gabe. "Could you start the paperwork on this and coordinate with Charlie and the medics who came out there?" he asked. "Then notify the Bakersfield gang and get a forensics team out to their place. It's going to be their case soon anyway."

A frown showed how much Josia hated the sound of that last statement. Nonetheless, he added, "I'm not about to jeopardize any more innocent victims because of my pride. A couple more days, maybe just hours, and that's it."

"I'll get started right now."

"What I'm going to do," he said, "is go get some food, bring it back here and wait it out. If you're hungry too, stop and eat. Nothing else we can do for the Berrys right now."

Melvin had moved past pinching himself to accepting his good fortune. What a lucky man he was for finding the phenomenon of Madge Lee at this stage of his life. He wished Terry were here to share his good fortune; and with that longing his dead brother's handsome face appeared vividly in his mind's eye—with his dark hair, piercing almost black eyes, and perpetual wry smile. Then, for the first time in his sixty-plus year life, he became fully aware of, and simultaneously able to accept the fact Terry had not been such a good brother.

Terry wouldn't have given a damn about his finding happiness with Madge Lee. It had always been about *him*. And for a moment of unvarnished introspection, startling in its clarity and unexpected pain, Melvin was almost moved to tears by the failure that he now realized had been his and Terry's brotherhood.

Fortunately, he had no time to dwell upon his startling epiphany, for Madge Lee, like her son thousands of miles away, was also thinking about food and drink, and quickly brought Mel back to their current reality.

"He's back," she said.

The chauffeur Madge Lee hired for the day pulled up to the curb with his Mercedes limousine to whisk them off to their dinner destination. They had finished up their afternoon with a trip to Fisherman's Wharf and both were carrying chic designer bags containing chocolate masterpieces. "A little after-dinner snack," Madge Lee explained.

"Where shall it be, Mel?" she asked. "China Town, or something further down the Pier? Our hotel also has an excellent restaurant. Do you have a taste for anything special? Seafood? Italian?" She waited for his answer while the chauffeur, a polite young man named Peter Tinsel, opened the back door and got them comfortably ensconced in the rear of his limo.

Melvin knew Madge Lee had used this particular limo service before and thought Peter an excellent driver. Prompt, courteous, and he liked his style. His limo was painted a tasteful chartreuse, if that was possible, and Peter himself wore a paisley uniform, including cap and shoes. Even in San Francisco, by-passers stopped for a second look.

She had explained Peter's father was a successful San Francisco lawyer who very wisely had insisted his son work his way through college, at least partially. When he had asked his son what type of work he wanted to do, Peter had promptly responded he wanted to drive a limo. How better to roam the city, meet interesting people, drive a cool car—and while waiting for his clients, study for school; which he correctly speculated would be most of his working time.

To achieve that end, his father leased the limousine for three years and gave Peter the keys with instructions that it was up to him to make the payments, pay the insurance, etc. Then make enough to pay at least half the fortune his tuition would cost.

As it turned out that was five years ago, and Peter had paid all his tuition from his limousine earnings. Now in USF School of Law, he was still driving, studying, and making a buck. Madge Lee was of the opinion Peter was going to make a damn good lawyer when his time came.

Melvin also knew Peter had driven Madge Lee around town many times in the past and felt comfortable being part of her "little adventures," as she called them. So it wasn't surprising that once Peter had gotten in up front, he offered his opinion. "If you're into seafood, my favorites are *Vino e Cucino Trattoria* and *Pesce*. If you like oysters there's always *Swan Oyster Depot*."

"They all sound good to me," Melvin said, and smiled in anticipation. "How about we leave it to you?" He didn't know a darn thing about San Francisco restaurants. All he knew was he was having a grand ole time with Madge Lee and whatever and wherever, it was fine and dandy with him. What a woman, what an adventure. *And to heck with Terry anyway.*

"Yes," Madge Lee said, agreeing with Melvin. "You choose."

Peter pulled into traffic as several street-side onlookers stared amusedly as he drove away. "What's the scoop this time, Mrs. M?" he asked. "Hope it's not another murder." Peter spoke loudly so his voice would carry to the cavernous back of his stretch limo. He only used his digital intercom with unfamiliar clients.

"I'm afraid it is, Peter," Madge Lee said, also speaking up. "Mr. Beaudine and I are trying to gather information on the background of several people."

"Suspects?"

"Actually, the victim and his wife."

Mel knew through Madge Lee that Peter could re-tell every Perry Mason episode, having watched them literally hundreds of times. If the rather serious young man had a passion, it would be Mason as portrayed by Raymond Burr, with Barbara Hale as Della Street.

"Wow," Peter said. "You know Gardner's plots often hinged on the victim's past."

Mel figured he was talking about Erle Stanley Gardner, creator of Perry Mason.

Madge Lee said, "Yes, you're right. Sometimes, though, it was a suspect who had the mysterious past."

"Can you tell me about this case?" Peter asked.

On their way to dinner, Melvin listened, enraptured as Madge Lee explained to Peter who he and Jada were, about the murders of Nick Williams and Hal Morton, how Irina was high on the suspect list, and everything her son had told her about the class members.

"So," Peter said, "you and Mr. Beaudine want to find out what you can about Darcie and Nick Williams. See if there's anything in their backgrounds that connects up with any of the suspects. Is that right?"

"Yes," Melvin answered. "Today was mostly about Darcie, right, Dear?" *Only two days and it was "Dear" instead of Madge Lee, and on her side, "Mel dear" instead of Melvin, or even Mel.*

"Yes, all about Darcie," she said.

Traffic was smooth, so Peter had no problem continuing their conversation. "So what did you dig up on her?" he asked. He had explained earlier when he'd picked them up at the hotel, that he wasn't sure how or when—but sometime in the future, what he learned about how people behaved and what motivated them would come in handy in the courtroom.

"Darcie Williams," Madge Lee repeated the name then closed her eyes and leaned her head back. "From the County records we found out a few facts. She came into this world as Darcie Preston—born at St. Lukes Hospital in 1968 to Joseph and Theresa Preston. Both her parents are now deceased, her father from a heart attack, her mother from a stroke. She has one aunt, a Ms. Ann Streete who lives in San Jose with her partner Ms. Tilly Gibson, no siblings, and no cousins. Darcie went to school in San Francisco, stayed at home all the way through college at

San Francisco State. Then she moved to Berkeley for graduate work. We also found a marriage license for her to a Mr. Nicholas Williams. Couldn't find where they had an apartment in Oakland, but we did find a Nicholas Williams with a business license and home address in Berkeley."

Melvin whispered, "You're wonderful." And then slipped his hand into hers.

She squeezed his hand, stopped for a couple seconds to take a breath and moisten her lips. "Seems to check out with the info Darcie gave Jada and the dates seem okay," she said. "Still waiting for confirmation from Berkley that she got a Ph.D there, though I don't think they would have hired her at the base if her educational credentials weren't accurate."

Melvin added, "And none of Madge Lee's contacts could dig up a criminal record at the state or county level for either of them." Because of a hand signal from Peter, Melvin raised his voice even more. "We're going to see Aunt Ann in the morning. She was shocked to hear Nick had been killed. Evidently Darcie hasn't yet called and told her about his murder, and she was real nice about seeing us. After that, we're heading to Chicago, right, Dear?"

"Yes, I don't know what more we can do here."

Melvin suggested, "We could go up Telegraph Avenue first when we're on the other side of the Bay tomorrow morning. Could be that Pottery Shop is still there. Different owner I'm sure, but maybe they'll remember something about Nick Williams."

Madge Lee caught Peter's eye in his rear view mirror and smiled. "Are you available in the morning?"

"Wouldn't miss it for the world."

She's good with everyone. Melvin marveled yet again. Yep, he was darned lucky.

In fact, later that evening he brought up their whirlwind romance over a midnight pizza snack in their suite.

Melvin thought Madge Lee summed it all up perfectly. "At our ages, Mel dear," she said. "Who wants to wait around? 'Time is short' as the phrase goes. An American saying and sentiment, I'm quite sure. Nothing hurries a true diehard old-school Brit—which I no longer am."

At first, Red Rock City Hospital felt to Jada more like an oversized clinic than a fully-functioning hospital.

She knew little about medical equipment, but after closer inspection, all the essentials seemed to be present—big shining machines and a lot of contraptions on wheels loaded with pumps and monitors. Mainly though, and most importantly, there seemed to be an abundant supply of doctors, nurses, technicians—people in green or white scrubs—scurrying around doing what people are supposed to be doing in a hospital. *Keeping folks from dying.*

There were the usual painted lines on the floor; the two-tone walls with the middle metal trim; the inadequately marked closed doors you were always being directed to and were scared to open for fear you were in the wrong place. And heaven only knows what you might stumble into behind the wrong door. Then there was the hospital smell. Universal. Unmistakable. Pervasive.

She found Irina in the emergency waiting room, alone, slumped in a plastic and chrome chair that was bucket-shaped and hard—made in the millions for waiting rooms just like this one. She looked miserable and dejected.

"Hospitals suck," she said on seeing Jada. "And these chairs suck. And if Penny doesn't pull through I'll never forgive myself."

Jada tried to pull a chair closer to Irina, then realized all the chairs were bolted to a bar framework. "You're right. These chairs do suck." She sat down and found out the chairs at least swiveled. "Don't do that to yourself. You did not try to kill the Berrys. Someone else did. This is not your guilt." *Could I really have stopped Terry from going out that morning?*

"Why would somebody try to kill them? It doesn't make any sense."

"The diaries." Jada proceeded to tell her about Penny and Timothy's obsession.

"So they must have told the murderer," Irina said. "And the murderer figured, or knew even, that one of the two had written down something incriminating? Is that what you think?"

"That's the best we can come up with for now."

Irina rubbed her eyes, long and hard, then dropped back in her chair. "Like who he was fooling around with."

"You think it's one of the ladies in class who killed him?"

"Hell, at this point I don't know what I think. I'm the one who called Nick a 'perfect man,' remember? Can't trust my judgement, that's for damn sure."

"You knew something was happening with the Berrys."

"I had a bad dream," she said. "You connected it with Penny and Timothy. If it weren't for you…"

Jada gave up. She knew from personal experience there was no consoling the guilt-ridden. She herself would live with the blame, rightly or wrongly, for Terry's death for the rest of her life. Looking into Irina's face, Jada hoped her new acquaintance would not also end up saddled with such a burden. Funny how she'd come to like this strange woman in such a short period of time.

They continued to wait together, in silence. At one point an intern, who looked to Jada to be pushing the ripe old age of twelve, stopped for a moment to assure them everything that could be done for Penny was being done. All they could do now was wait.

After about half and hour, Josia came back with a sack of burgers and fries. Following him was a smiling nurse rolling an upholstered swivel chair for him to plunk his butt in. He thanked her with a wink, and she responded with a kiss blown on air.

He was still in uniform and Jada thought he looked like hell—and figured she didn't look much better. She said, "It's been a long day. Thanks for the food."

Irina raised an eyebrow, but kept her thoughts to herself.

"And it ain't over yet." He pulled over a small table from the other side of the waiting from and spread food and napkins around. "There's ketchup packages for your fries if you want 'em." He unwrapped a burger and started to take a bite, then put it down and sighed.

The three sat and waited for another three hours; and as night fell they passed over into that netherworld beyond tired, where one is still awake, but so numb you're barely functioning. They never touched the burgers.

Finally the child masquerading as a physician returned, and from behind a smile of relief declared Penny Berry past the crisis point. She was still in intensive care, but she would make it.

As they were leaving, Jada's brain forced her mouth to work enough to point out, "You know, Josia, we haven't even talked to Marie Shipley yet."

"I know."

"First thing in the morning?"

"Yep."

"Meet you at your office?"

"Yep."

Lyle Elliott's voicemail message to Hamilton Wolfe
January 9th — 10:00 P.M.

"The Beaudine woman found me out this morning. I've checked back in at the Red Rock Inn & Café as Lyle Elliott. If you need to contact me, you'll have to call my cell. I'm going to bed.

"Oh yeah. And somebody tried to kill Timothy and Jill Berry today."

Chapter Seven

Friday

Josia forced himself to patiently wait until Lyle Elliott finished. Not that he had had much choice. Besides, Lyle was turning out to be an interesting man with an interesting story.

"So, Chief Rhodes, that's how I ended up here." Lyle sighed lightly. "I know it sounds crazy, but yes, I followed her all the way down from North Bend in Washington. And now, the woman is in the middle of another murder investigation and I'm afraid Terrence is going to back off and not make contact until your investigations are concluded." He cleared his throat and fixed a firm gaze on Josia. "But don't get me wrong, I'm planning on waiting the Beaudines out, hanging around until you get everything wrapped up." He paused for second before finishing, "I assure you though, I'll stay out of your way. I'm only interested in bringing Terrence and Jada Beaudine in on fraud charges."

Josia had found Lyle waiting on his office doorstep. It turned out he had been there from the crack of dawn. Luckily for

Lyle, Josia had experienced another night of elusive sleep and had chosen to go into his office at the insane hour of 5:30 A.M.

Night coverage for Red Rock City was handled jointly by the County Sheriff's Department and the California Highway Patrol. A financial wizard on the Red Rock City Chamber of Commerce Board had figured out this arrangement solely on the basis of cost. Why keep the office open all night and employ two more people if they could get some other taxpayers to help foot the night-shift bill? Heck, that money could better be spent putting more stoplights on Red Rock Boulevard.

In truth, during the two years since they started the program, things had gone smoothly. Most night incidents were vehicular violations anyway—easily handled by the CHP cruisers already out there. On a personal level, Josia certainly appreciated not working nights. Besides, although the office was closed, he and Gabe were technically always on call if something unusual popped up.

After he had opened the office and got the coffee machine going Josia listened to Lyle's story with increasing interest and astonishment. This was definitely a new wrinkle. For sure, he had felt there was something squirrelly about the Beaudine woman, but he certainly wouldn't have figured her as a con-artist. And why would she do it? Wasn't the woman supposed to be filthy rich? Seems like that was in one of the articles.

Still, he reminded himself, he had seen stranger things. Indeed, suspicious by nature, he believed almost *anyone* capable of taking a walk on the wild side *sometime*, given the right set of circumstances. And for some people, there never was enough money. "Besides your belief Mrs. Beaudine is involved in screwing your company over," he said, "do you think she could also kill someone?" *Damnit*, he hoped not.

Indeed, during several of last night's quiet and sleep-illusive moments, he had recognized a tiny piece of his psyche was actually attracted to the screwy broad. Not that he would ever admit it to anyone else, nor that he needed another female complicating his life. His mother, Irina, and his wandering wife Helen were quite enough for one man to deal with.

Damn Helen anyway. Why couldn't she have just talked to him? Wasn't that what women liked to do? She was an additional reason he wasn't sleeping at night. He still missed her. He could understand her walking out on him. Hell, he was no prize, but leaving her dogs? How could she just abandon them like that? Her goodbye note had not only been a huge surprise, but also totally inadequate. And it pissed him off he still wanted her back.

He had researched through his buddies far enough to know she had been living somewhere in Victorville for awhile, *with* someone, before disappearing to parts unknown. One day, one day soon, he would try finding her. Not yet though. He was afraid of what he would say, or even do.

Lyle was saying, "No, I don't think Jada Beaudine could kill someone, but I certainly think Terrence could." Taking a breath, he knitted his brow thoughtfully for a few seconds. "But in reference to *your* cases, nothing I've seen or uncovered indicates any involvement, much less a motive, for either of them."

"Hmmm." Josia mulled over Lyle's last words. "You sure you don't want some coffee?"

Lyle shook his head. They were back in the everything-room where Josia's high-tech brew machine had just buzzed. He got up immediately. It was the second pot of the morning, but he needed more coffee as soon as he could get it.

Lyle asked, "You wouldn't happen to have a Coke in that refrigerator?"

He had instantly endeared himself to Josia. By his way of thinking, a man who drank Coke for breakfast had to be okay. He smiled and fetched Lyle a cold can.

Then, while Josia settled himself back in his chair with a fresh cup, Lyle said, "Small place you have here, but it's nice." He took a long swig of Coke. "You probably don't need much room anyway, just the three of you, right?"

"Yep." Josia leaned back in his chair. "You notice anything strange going on at the café since you've been there?" He held back a smile that wanted to come forward—a matching smile to the one he'd forced back when Lyle had earlier told him about his disguises. Grown man running around playing dress up. And as a rabbi? If Lyle had been an undercover-cop, now, that would be a different story. But an Insurance Investigator in disguise?

"Like what? 'Suspicious actions' kinds of things?"

"Yeah, 'suspicious actions' kinds of things."

"Anyone in particular you have in mind?"

"Nope, any of the inmates will do. They're all loony-tunes out there. It's just whether or not one of 'em is crazy enough to think they can get away with murder."

Between sentences Lyle had inhaled his Coke. Now he smashed the can and tossed it overhand, basketball style, into a brightly labeled recycle bin next to the refrigerator. Then, with eager eyes and an intent frown, he leaned forward across the table. "Like I said, I intend to stay out of your business, but if you're asking my opinion, heck, I'm glad to give it."

Josia smiled and sat up straighter. Something about Lyle he liked—even though he dressed up in disguises. *What the hell.* "Yeah, Lyle, I would appreciate your put on the mess I got here."

"The way I see it, Nick Williams's murder was personal, real personal. I think whoever did it wanted him to know who they were, probably spent time telling him—him sitting there at that wheel thing, a gun pointed at his head, the murderer looking him straight in the eye. I'd say real hatred was behind it. Otherwise, you're looking for a cold-blooded maniac. I guess there's more and more of them around these days, but I doubt it in this case."

"Yep."

"Somebody in that pottery class or at the motel."

"Yep. You *are* aware Irina calls it an 'Inn,'" Josia said before taking another long appreciative swallow of coffee.

"And the *distinction* that has for the Red Rock?"

Both men snickered.

"Ain't much of a place is it?" Josia agreed.

In a more serious tone, Lyle said, "I hope it isn't Ms. Hughes. I like her."

"Yep."

They traded a few more wisecracks, a few more "what ifs," and a few more "yeps" and "unhuhs" before finishing up. As Lyle was leaving, Josia offered him another Coke which he gratefully accepted.

After Lyle left his office, Josia sat for a bit, thinking. Indeed, an annoying prickly feeling tickling the back of his mind was telling him—this game had a joker in the deck. *Maybe even two.*

On the whole, Lyle was glad he had come. He liked Josia, though he figured the Police Chief thought he was an obsessed crazy-man when it came to Terrence Beaudine. And to be fair, why should Josia believe him? In over a year he hadn't come up with a single piece of evidence that proved Terrence was still alive.

Well, what the heck, he'd done his duty as he saw it. Rhodes had been informed and forewarned.

Lyle put on his sunglasses the second he stepped outside. It had become a habit over the last few days as he struggled to get used to the blazingly bright desert sun.

* * * * *

Despite the horrors of the previous day, Jada woke up refreshed and eager to get going. It felt good, like she had a purpose in life again. *Almost.*

Outside it promised to be another sun-soaked winter day in the Mojave, and the smell of sand and eucalyptus was expected, familiar, and for the first time, intriguingly comfortable.

Last night, she had rushed into her room to catch a call from Melvin and Madge Lee detailing their Bay Area adventures. Telephone call completed, she had dropped across her bed fully clothed and slept like a rock—Tasha at her side.

Now it was Friday morning, and the start of her sixth day at the Red Rock, if you counted Sunday night when she had pulled in. She didn't yet know who killed Nick or Hal, but was excitedly optimistic she soon would. *Something has changed.* She didn't know what—just that the future, and her solving this murder, didn't seem so bleak.

Not that the senior citizen lovebirds, Madge Lee and Melvin, had come up with any great revelations; *and* not that there was anything new from the lab; *and* Josia certainly wasn't any closer than she in figuring it out. Maybe it was the spark of enthusiasm emanating from Madge Lee and Melvin she found contagious? Maybe it was as simple as getting a good night's sleep. No dreams about Terry for once.

Then again, just maybe, her enthusiasm and good humor were involuntary reactions to the smell of coffee and pastry finding its way from the café back to cabin number-two. *God bless Manny.*

But first a shower, then breakfast, then meet Josia and head out to talk to Marie Shipley, the last member of Nick's class. On her way to the shower, Jada found a new poem on her desk.

Tonight the wind is high, The air is cold,
The sand devils are jumping, And strangely, I am at peace.

Jada smiled, and her mood lightened even further.

After breakfast, however, *after* Manny told her about the "visitor" and Tasha chasing the car, her good humor and excitement were immediately doused with a wash-bucket size portion of reality. And fear stepped to the forefront of her emotions. *How quick my life and emotions can flip-flop.*

"Beth called a deputy in from Lone Pine since you guys were busy," Manny told her.

"Did the deputy find anything?" Jada asked, trying to hide her apprehension.

"No, I'm sorry, nothing. I watched him make a mold of a tire track. But that was it."

The thought someone might have been around again last night, trying to—she wasn't sure what. *Maybe trying to kill me.* Not only was she uncomfortable, but it didn't make any sense. There was no reason for anyone to want to harm her; she was a stranger for goodness sakes.

"Don't worry, I was on the Internet most of the night and I kept an eye out. Nobody came around again."

She smiled gratefully at Manny and hoped he could tell how much she appreciated his caring. Especially since he'd only met her a couple days earlier. She knew such immediate emotional connections, like Manny and Irina, were rare incidents, and she should consider herself lucky. Nonetheless, Manny on watch or not, she decided to take Tasha along with her. She would just have to make sure she stayed in the car and out of the sun. *No,* she didn't want her new found canine friend inadvertently getting hurt. *Chasing cars, of all the damn fool things. Stupid dog.*

Josia dropped the letter from Craig and Sons, Attorneys-at-Law on his pristine desktop, took off his reading glasses, the five-dollar kind you buy off the rack at any drugstore, and rubbed his burning eyes.

"Can't lawyers ever talk in plain English, for Christ's sake?" he asked Gabe. "And I swear they're using smaller and smaller print all the time."

He dropped back into his swivel chair and crossed his long legs atop the edge of his desk. His movements, emphatic in their execution, added punctuation to his irritation and weariness. Since his little dawn talk with Lyle, he'd been running solely on coffee. Abruptly, he switched topics. "You think the Beaudine woman knows about Lyle? More importantly, you think she knows if her husband is alive or dead?"

"I don't think Mrs. Beaudine is involved in anything Mr. Elliott thinks is going on."

"Why not?" Josia demanded peevishly. *Because you think she's nice?* Immediately, he was sorry for his tone. A year ago he would have just said whatever he was damn well thinking in whatever tone of voice he damn well wanted. But recently— among some other painful self- realizations—he'd come to see that underneath Gabe's "eager young deputy" veneer was a thoughtful and smart kid. One day he'd make a damn good cop. So he needed to curb his penchant for aggressive sass.

"Because *young* Percy Craig, that's the son in the law firm—"

"Who is how old?"

"One-hundred-and-two."

Occasionally Gabe displayed a sense of humor, usually of the droll understatement variety, and Josia laughed appreciatively. "So, the young Mr. Craig said?"

"That when he read the will to the group, he thought Mrs. Williams was going to fall off her chair. He even quoted her, said her exact words were, 'That can't be, we were always trying to make ends meet. How could Nicky have all that money and not tell us? Five hundred thousand dollars? It just can't be.'"

Josia was not convinced. He'd seen a lot of good actors and actresses during his time on the force. *Cui bono* remained tried-and-true in his universe of motives for murder. "Who else was there?"

"Mrs. Williams brought her children and her sister. That was it."

"So, only two beneficiaries. Mrs. Williams and—"

Through their office glass Josia watched as the front door opened and a sour looking teenager and his tightlipped father entered and pulled Gabe away from their conversation. Turned out Dad was making his offspring pay for a parking ticket out of his own money. From both their expressions it was clear words had recently passed before coming in. Josia sighed, took his feet off his desk—probably didn't look very professional—picked the letter back up, and reread the sentence that really ticked him off.

Besides the Legacy passing to Mrs. Darcie Williams, Mr. Nicholas Williams also left $50,000 to Ms. Irina Hughes to be used for the refurbishing and expansion of her ceramic lab.

Fifty-thousand dollars would be a lot of money to Irina. Hell, it would be a lot of money to everybody he knew. "Damn," he cursed under his breath. Where the hell did Williams get that kind of money?

Also on his desk was the lab report on the guns he'd lugged in from Phillip Thomas and Leroy Ames. Nada. Not the murder weapons.

He cursed again, and his thoughts again jumped to Jada. Maybe he'd just ask her right out if she'd conspired with her husband. *Probably not.* His cautious streak held him back. He would not mention Lyle's visit. A seed of doubt? Maybe.

It was more probable that Lyle, likable as he seemed, was an obsessed insurance investigator who liked to play dress-up.

On their way to Marie Shipley's—Gabe left holding down the Fort, and Tasha comfortably ensconced on the backseat of Josia's police cruiser—Jada listened as Josia filled her in on Nick's will and the ballistic results.

When he finished, she asked, "Have you heard about the man snooping around my room yesterday and scaring Mrs. Chacon?"

"Yes."

She caught him taking his eyes off the road long enough to give her a quick assessing look, and wondered what *that* was about, but didn't pursue it. Crazy man.

He continued, "Beth filled Gabe in yesterday evening and Gabe filled me in this morning. There was also a faxed report from Norm out at the Lone Pine sub-station waiting in my machine this morning."

They fell silent.

Traffic was surprisingly heavy for a Friday morning in a town the size of Red Rock. Further, he was forced to slam on his brakes—almost throwing Tasha off the backseat—when an elderly man driving a big older model white Oldsmobile, his head barely visible above the steering wheel—moved into the intersection at the posted speed limit, but slower than a pickup truck driver behind him figured he should. The younger pickup driver swerved around the Oldsmobile in the middle of the intersection causing several cars, including Josia's, to almost collide. *Not good;* and Jada could see Josia was most assuredly not pleased. The siren and lights went on and it was a full block before the pickup driver finally pulled over. She figured a reckless driving ticket was a sure thing.

She was also not pleased. Jada wanted to interview Marie Shipley. That sense of excitement and urgency, admittedly tempered by a sizable dollop of fear-driven caution, was again gnawing at her gut. But by the time Josia ticketed the driver with an old-time scolding thrown in for good measure, and the young man, a new naval enlistee finally pulled away from the curb at a chastened five mph—a full half-hour had passed.

Ally almost panicked.

That stupid fool kid in the truck getting pulled over by that hot-headed Police Chief had forced her to pass the patrol car and risk being seen before she was ready. She was able, though, to keep an outwardly cool demeanor while sneaking a look at the Beaudine woman sitting in the passenger seat. She needn't have worried. Jada was turned sideways away from the window, fooling with something in the backseat.

"I'll get you witch," Ally hissed under her breath.

Out of nowhere, tears for Terry came again, but she didn't attempt to wipe them away until she had turned into a side-street. From there she made a U-turn so she'd be back facing the main drag. Then she pulled over to the curb and waited. Though her heart ached, she was not about to lose her prey now.

She was wiping her eyes when it passed, so she couldn't be sure, but darn-it, *that sure looked like the same white Ford again.*

For a second she considered following the strange car instead of trying to situate herself for a clear shot at Jada. "No, I need to keep on track." *The Beaudine witch is who I want.*

Ally pressed the button to lower her window with her left-hand, while tightening her right-hand around the grip of her ever-present Bantam .44 on the seat beside her. But almost immediately she realized it was a stupid idea to try taking Jada down with a handgun in the middle of traffic.

I'm not thinking straight. "Damn," she cursed and wished for her dad's rifle. A blue-metaled Remington lever-action-repeater, the rifle had been expensive and her father's pride and joy. He had taught her how to shoot it, and she still remembered its name—"Trailrider." Ally sniffed regretfully. She'd had to sell the rare rifle to help with funeral expenses when he'd died.

The Beaudine woman was not making this easy. *Another reason to hate her.*

Marie Shipley, at the age of seventy-something, comfortable in her skin and surroundings, was quite aware of how she looked—sturdy and round. Lately, she had taken to wearing broad brimmed straw hats adorned with colorful headbands and bows that added to her aura of "comfortableness" and complemented her customary wardrobe of long jumper-styled dresses.

Her state of ease had been long in coming. Born in the mid-1930's in Chicago, as a child she experienced wartime America, big-city style. Then as she grew, watched and participated, her country, indeed the world, had also grown, verily exploded—fueled by baby boomers, their children, their suburbs, their automobiles, and the roads to drive them on.

Oh, and those airplanes. How quickly they conquered the skies above. Then "plastic" in its thousands of manifestations marched in, challenged only by ribbons of concrete rolling across the land; then, alas, the computers and their bedfellows. Marie and her husband Martin had kept up with it all—pushing, stretching, and stressing with the rest of humanity.

But her world as a child, more precisely her parent's world—her mother, a Polish immigrant later naturalized was a professor at the University of Chicago, and her father was a physician at Bob Roberts Hospital at the same University—had revolved, evolved, and transpired in a radius of maybe twenty square blocks, if you didn't count the occasional trip downtown to the "Loop."

Grand days, albeit in a small world. Time marched on. She grew up, got married, and the years flew by. Then, in the '90s her Mother and Father had passed away, within two years of each other, and she and Martin by that time had arrived at a transitional point in their lives. They wanted to flee the big city with its constant clinkety-clank of other human beings, the increasing government encroachment in their daily lives, constantly rising taxes, and horrendous traffic—leaving no time to enjoy. With trepidation they had landed in Red Rock City. That had been ten years ago, and neither of them had ever looked back.

Today she was looking forward to seeing Madge Lee's son again, and she definitely wanted to meet this new woman, Beaudine, was it? Yes, she remembered from newspaper clippings she had dug up after that first morning at the ceramic lab.

In addition, Madge Lee's comments about the woman had been most intriguing. Marie decided to wait for them in the garden. Yes, she would clean up her lily-bulb bed while collecting her thoughts. In line with her advice at that first evening meeting at the Berry house, she needed to decide just how much she was going to tell her visitors. *Ruth Dominic*, now quite vulnerable, was a longtime friend and needed to be protected.

The Shipley house was a rustic-looking two story log building secreted among traditional ramblers in a residential neighborhood off Mojave River Boulevard. Jada and Josia found Marie in her back garden. Again, Tasha was clearly quite comfortable stretched out on the backseat, and with the windows open the temperature was definitely cool enough for Jada not to worry.

The moment Jada passed through the wooden arched gate on the side of the house, she was astounded by what she saw. Before her unfolded a winter oasis of vividly colored botanical delights—magically flourishing in an otherwise faded and dry desert world. She was taken aback, frozen for a moment at Marie's garden gate, almost mesmerized, staring at the plants, miniature trees, and flowers before her. Most of which, except for the roses, she'd never seen before. And such lovely fragrances.

Josia, on the other hand, proceeded forward without pause to talk to the woman on her knees patting down mulch near the back door. "Mrs. Shipley," he said, and extended his hand to help her up. "Remember me? Madge Lee's son. And this is—" He looked back to see Jada still standing at the gate. He cleared his throat loudly and gave her a pointed look.

"I'm sorry," Jada apologized as she scooted in to join them. "It's just your garden, I mean, it's so beautiful." Her words sounded gushing and silly to her own ears, so out of character for the person she perceived herself to be. But it was true. Marie had created something special.

Josia sighed audibly.

Marie laughed. "Of course I remember you, Josia. Still no time to 'smell the roses' I gather." Her voice was melodious and as pleasing to Jada's ears as her garden was to her other senses. The bucolic picture, the smell, the sound of birds—even now in winter, made you almost think the world was a lovely place. Marie had made herself a place where she fit; and Jada chased away a transient tinge of envy. Would she ever fit someplace?

"I'm sure these murders are heavy on your mind," Marie continued. "Still," she said, and turned to her. "So nice to meet someone who appreciates my handiwork, Mrs. Beaudine." She took off a well-worn garden glove and offered her hand. Her grip, mirroring Jada's own, was firm, sturdy. "My husband agrees more with Josia when it comes to garden aesthetics. Martin humors me though and does a lot of the heavy work."

Jada smiled, she couldn't help it. Marie Shipley, like Madge Lee, was infectious. "You know my name?"

"Of course, Dear. Madge Lee has told me all about you. I have hot tea, lemonade, and soda pop inside." Easily she slipped her arm through Jada's. "Let's go inside to the kitchen, sit down and relax, and I'll answer all your questions. So nice to have visitors, especially when Martin's off looking at petroglyphs and artifacts." She waved her free hand gracefully. "He's with some museum people out in the desert. Personally, I think it's an elaborate excuse to go riding around in jeeps."

Once inside, the three of them comfortably seated around the Shipley's kitchen table, drinks in hand, cookies on the table, Josia seemed to relax a tad.

"You know, Josia, your mother's entrance into our lives was a godsend. Here we were newcomers, didn't know a soul, just bought this house, which as you remember needed tons of work."

Jada was pretty sure his memory of the Shipley's move to Red Rock City was vague, but she watched as he smiled and nodded encouragement for Marie to continue. She figured that, like herself, Josia felt they were close to "something" and shared her sense of urgency. And though she was not yet ready to admit to a premonition, Jada felt talking to Marie would be a turning point.

"Another person who helped us settle into the community in the early days was Ruth Dominic. And when her daughter showed up in class, well, I was so pleased."

"Ruth Dominic?" Josia said the name like he'd never heard it before.

Jada knew he couldn't have forgotten Ted James mentioning Ruth. She certainly hadn't.

"Yes, Dear, don't you remember her? Maybe not. I remember you were off to France for awhile, then it was England, wasn't it? You may not have actually met her. But your Mother, Ruth, and I did quite a few things together."

Jada feigned the same ignorance of Ruth and Corissa that Josia had started. "Corissa James? Is she Ruth's daughter?"

"How clever of you, Mrs. Beaudine."

"Please, Mrs. Shipley, call me Jada." *Good grief, the woman has wrapped me around her little finger in a matter of minutes. She and Madge Lee—a matched pair.*

"Certainly, Dear. Of course you must also call me Marie."

Jada smiled. How easy it was to be around Marie.

"You two just help yourselves, there's plenty of lemonade and cookies. Your Mother says you're a coffee fanatic, Josia, but I'm afraid Martin and I don't keep any. Would you like some tea? It's nice and hot."

"I'm fine, Mrs. Shipley." He said her name with deference. Jada guessed generational sensibilities would make it hard for him to call his mother's friend by her first name. She also figured he was dying for a hit of caffeine laced with sugar. He continued, "You were getting ready to tell us something about Corissa James."

Marie smiled for a moment, evidently remembering. "Actually I know Cori as Corissa McNichols. You see I knew her as a teenager, watched her become a young woman over the last ten years we've been here. She's been married awhile now, at least a couple years or so, and I've met Ted James. She got lucky there. But I still think of her as little Cori McNichols."

"So you knew Corissa was going to take the class too?" Jada asked.

"Well, no, actually I didn't. The last few years I haven't seen as much of Ruth as I would like. Especially after she married Stan Dominic." Marie's smile turned into a self-accusatory frown. "My fault entirely, always some reason not to drive out to their place. Then with Ruth continually being hospitalized, or rather hospitalizing herself...don't get me wrong, it's nice, but Crestwood is still a hospital. So it was a surprise when Cori showed up at that first class. Of course I was delighted to see her. I thought it was just what the child needed."

Child? "In what way?"

"Before I say more," Marie's face took on a stern look, schoolteacher-ish in its demeanor. "I want both of you to understand why I'm telling you all of this. I don't like gossip of any kind, never have, and never will. But there have been two murders now, and if there's any chance little Cori might get hurt...." She spread her hands in explanation. "I would never forgive myself if I knew something and didn't tell you."

"You think you know something that will help us?" Josia pressed in a serious tone.

"Not necessarily. But you two are experts. You may hear something that will send you down the right path. That's why you're here, correct?" She paused for a sigh and a deep breath before continuing. "Madge Lee assured me you don't think I'm a suspect, and that maybe I could tell you all about the students."

"Exactly, Mrs. Shipley," he said. "No way I could imagine you killing someone."

Jada knew he was lying—*everyone is a suspect.*

He added, "And you and Mother are exactly right, I was hoping you may have seen something, or heard something."

"Good. Now, I've thought about how to go about this." She smiled, her round genial face alight with enthusiasm. "Why don't I start with Nick Williams. He was our teacher, and the first victim."

Jada and Josia nodded. Jada remembered Irina's handwritten appraisal of Marie on the class list. "Smart cookie," it had said.

"To begin with, he wasn't the carefree *bon viveur* and harmless ladies' man some might suspect. We all knew he had a wife and two children, for goodness sake.

"His looks were fair, but what I saw in his face were the eyes of a predator. And there was a nuance in his look that said, 'I'm so smart, and you're so dumb.' I believe he thought there was very little he couldn't get away with. And I'm guessing there was something in his past—something he *did* get away with."

"Something worthy of blackmail?" Jada asked.

"Exactly," Marie said. "And Hal Morton was just the type to try something like that."

"But that doesn't make sense," Josia demanded. "Nick didn't kill Morton, he was killed first. So even if Morton was blackmailing Nick, *who*, and *why* would anyone kill Morton?"

"I'm sure you two will figure out the connection," Marie said with confidence.

"So," Jada said. "You didn't like either man?"

Marie looked thoughtful. "I guess I didn't, not really. Seems uncharitable now, since both are dead. I did like Nick's work though. Especially his vases—so nice."

Her love of pottery drew Jada down a compelling tangent. "Then I'm assuming the porcelain statuettes of children and animals belonged to Hal?" She remembered his sanding one that first day. Jada thought them excellently made, and the intricate under-glaze painting of the features and clothes was quite good. But they weren't her cup of tea. *A compelling aspect of ceramics,* she mused. *There was something for everyone.*

"Yes," Marie answered. "Those are Hal's. That was the great thing about our class. You got to see everyone's work. I just loved it." She expelled a resigned sigh of acceptance. "Too bad it's over."

Josia's facial expression and body language said he didn't give a damn about a bunch of clay crap; he just wanted to catch a killer. "So how come you're so sure Nick was, what did you call him, a predator?" His tone also made it clear he wasn't looking for more of his mother and Irina's psychic nonsense.

"Because I've seen those eyes before in others." Marie's tone of voice was indulgent. "And I heard things."

"Like what?"

"For one, he and I were talking about how everyone has some unpleasantness in their past which they aren't proud of. And how those things come back to haunt you. Now, don't ask me how or why we were talking about that. It just came up like so many discussions in class. When you're all sitting around watching the teacher throw something, you just start talking."

Jada remembered similar class days from her own past. Good days—another life almost. A life she had achieved some comfort in. A life with Terry.

Marie continued, "And Nick said something like, 'he had never done anything in the past he was ashamed of.' Sure sign to me, he *had* done something quite unpleasant." She was thoughtful for a moment, evidently trying to make a decision. Finally Marie said, "Then there was that Wednesday afternoon...a class member was late leaving, going out the back door, and Nick was standing in the kiln room yelling at that person. 'You're wrong! You've got the wrong man.' Then I heard the back door slam. I was in the lab room, so I couldn't see who left. I didn't hear a car start, but most of the cars were still in the parking lot. Everyone had gone over to the café for lunch. I figured the person headed over to the café too."

"You don't know who it was?"

"No, sorry."

Jada could read in Marie's eyes that she had an idea who it was, but she was going to make them work that out for themselves.

"What about the rest of the class?" Josia asked. "How about Hilary Giles?"

"All I can tell you about Hilary is Martin and I are very fond of him. His son's death was a horrible, horrible tragedy. But I never perceived Hilary harboring any animosity against Nick or Hal. Of course I have considered the possibility Nick was somehow involved in the death of his son. But, I think if Hilary found that out, he wouldn't be able to hide his feelings. His pain is so immense."

"Leroy Ames?" Josia asked.

Now this is good, Jada thought.

"Straight-arrow type, okay guy, I think. Personally, though, I find him a self-righteous pain in the ass. The type that's a good citizen, which is fine, but also the type who would view anyone not doing things his way as 'deviant.' Martin and I owned a condo once. Leroy's the perfect type to chair a condo board. Rule-maker and enforcer."

Jada thought Marie was being a little hard on the man, though she'd only met him once. "You think he could kill someone?"

"Most definitely, without blinking an eye."

That statement silenced all three of them for a moment. Then Jada asked, "Corissa James? Was there anything else you wanted to tell us about her?"

"You've met her, right? Such an odd mix of timidity and," she searched a couple seconds for the right word, "resentment."

"What do you mean?"

"Ruth and I talked about Cori, when we were still visiting every week or so. You see Cori is a bright girl, but she didn't have many advantages. Like taking classes as a child. You know—music, drama, dancing. I guess the thing nowadays is soccer. Then there wasn't money for college. Ruth worked hard, sometimes two jobs, but still, it was hard making ends meet. I think at times it must have been rough for her. For them both."

"I gather there was a Mr. McNichols at one time," Josia said.

"Oh yes, Billy McNichols. I never met him. He was long gone when Ruth and I met. But she sometimes spoke of him, but seldom in Cori's presence. She was very careful about that. You see, he left them 'high and dry' as the saying goes, when Cori was very young. I also think there was some scandal involving money."

"And you think?" Josia pushed.

"I think Cori would have been impressed by Nick's worldly charm, even have an affair with him. The poor girl is not very experienced." The expression on Marie's face showed relief in the telling. "So she might know something. I don't know what, but whatever it is, Cori might be in danger."

"Like Penny and Timothy Berry," Jada said softly. Star Thomas had been next on Irina's list. "What about Star? An affair also?"

"Definitely." Marie sighed heavily. "You might also be well served, you two, to talk to Ruth. She has been in this town longer than I have and she just might be able to give you more information about the people in the class—especially Hilary, the Berrys, and Star." She blew out a sad whiff of air. "Ruth's at a place called Crestwood. But please, keep in mind, she is not a well woman."

Josia nodded, then asked, "Have you met Star's husband?"

Marie eyed him quizzically. "No, sorry."

Jada added, "And Corissa's husband, Ted. Could you see him as a murderer?"

"Yes," she answered simply. Then she asked, "Penny and Tim are going to be alright, aren't they?"

"Looks like," Josia answered.

"They are annoying sometimes, but really, the two are nice through and through."

The pottery, something about the pottery. "What was your work? You know, which pieces in the drying room?"

"You didn't guess?" Jada shook her head.

"Mine were the tall thin sculptures."

"Oh yes," Jada smiled. *The ones that looked like giant phallic symbols.*

Back outside while getting into Josia's cruiser, Jada said, "So, you've lived in France and England?"

"A long time ago."

Interesting, she thought, but left it at that. If he wanted to be a jerk and not talk about it, fine. The hunt for a killer was tops on her agenda anyway.

"I think we need to talk over what we've got," he said.

"Agreed."

"Back at the office?"

"Yep." *Son of a gun,* Jada berated herself, *I'm beginning to sound like him!*

* * * * *

After they left, Marie took the time to make herself a fresh steaming pot of strong black tea, sit a bit, and think. Madge Lee was right, the Beaudine woman was unusual looking, and there was something about her aura, something unsettled, a turmoil of the spirit. Maybe a touch of loneliness? She certainly didn't act like she was filthy rich. And Josia, still irreverent, brusque—unhappy. Too bad.

Fortunately Madge Lee was out there on-the-road, investigating, as she called it. God, that woman was a treasure. And now she had a boyfriend, Melvin—Jada Beaudine's brother-in-law of all things. That was good though, a man to keep an eye out for her, not that Madge Lee needed much protecting. Madge Lee had come through in the past when Josia was stuck— hopefully she would come through again.

Well, she had done her part, reluctantly, but it had to be done. Such an old and dear friend, but murder is murder, no matter how good the motive. So, she took another moment to pray Josia, Jada, and Madge Lee's combined intelligence would put Nick and Hal's killer behind bars—no matter how personally painful.

Jada wondered if she would think back on that prayer in the ensuing days and question the wisdom of asking God for anything, ever again. How did that hackneyed saying go? Oh, yes, *Be careful what you ask for.*

Melvin hadn't known what to expect. Madge Lee had stated quite clearly Aunt Ann and Tilly were "partners," which he read to mean lesbians. Or was "gay" the right term now for women too? He tried to keep up, but Melvin didn't have much experience with this part of Americana. Whatever the correct terminology, Melvin thought Aunt Ann and Tilly were wonderful.

In their seventies, the two ladies lived in an old farmhouse on five acres in the hills east of San Jose surrounded by fancy developments of grandiose homes inches away from each other. As their area had boomed, they had refused to sell all their property, but enough of their farmland had changed hands for them to now do whatever they darn well wanted; and what they wanted to do was travel, garden, make preserves, and develop Internet web sites.

So Melvin, Madge Lee, Aunt Ann, and Tilly—after the two ladies got over the shock of Nick's death—whiled away a sunny Friday morning eating quiche, sipping Australian Chablis, and chatting about a lot of things; the world, the stock market, the Internet, and Nick and Darcie Williams.

Later, when he and Madge Lee placed a conference call to Josia and Jada, they spent quite a bit of time—clearly managing to exasperate Josia in the process—talking about how charming and cute the two ladies were. When they did get down to actual information, it seemed meager. Nevertheless, meager or not, Melvin considered it a glorious morning well spent.

Before heading to Crestwood, Josia insisted on stopping by the office to check on things. Jada was quite certain "checking up" was a euphemism for satisfying his caffeine addiction. He needed to replenish. Tasha needed to stretch anyway, so what the heck.

Fortuitously, after Jada gave Tasha a walk and Josia brewed a fresh pot, Melvin and Madge Lee called in while they were at the office. Jada and Josia took the call in the everything-room on separate extensions.

After they hung up, Josia, demanded, "Well, what do you think of that?"

"Mmm," Jada answered cautiously. "I'm not sure what to make of it. You said your Mother has helped you in the past, right?"

"That she has."

"And that she's pretty sharp about things?"

"Yep."

"Well?"

"Damn." He slapped his hand on the table. "I thought maybe she'd have something. Sounds to me like she's just been sightseeing with that accountant brother-in-law of yours."

"Ex-accountant," she said. "I was hoping too."

He got up, refilled his cup, stretched, and massaged his knee.

"Still sore?" she asked.

"Nah." Then with a sigh he dropped back down into his chair. "We've still got a couple minutes before we head out to Crestwood."

"Well," Jada tried to keep her tone neutral. "You never know when there's something there and you just can't see it. You know, if you look at things from a different perspective...or you'll find out something else that will make the pieces you have fit." She was grasping for anything to re-fire the enthusiasm they had both shared earlier.

He smiled through a smirk. "Okay, I'll go along with your Pollyanna spin on the 'nothing' my Mother has come up with. For Christ's sake, we already knew Darcie was raised and went to school in the Bay area and that they met in the East Bay and he had a shop on Telegraph."

"But now we have it confirmed."

"So?" He shrugged.

"We could at least stop looking there." She thought back over what the lovebirds had said. "What about the new owner of Nick's old shop, that Clint-something guy?"

"He confirmed the year that he bought the shop from Nick which tied to Darcie's story of when they moved to Red Rock City. Is that what you mean?"

Jada shook her head. "No. He said when he bought the shop from Nick there were no lenders to be paid off because Williams had bought the place with cash."

"That's right." Josia raised an eyebrow. "Which means Nick had some money when he came to Berkeley. And he was how old then?"

"Thirty-something according to his wife, but more like forty-something if you believe Penny Berry." She rubbed her eyes, then decided she needed some water and got up and helped herself from the refrigerator. It gave her some time to connect some dots. "If Penny is right and Nick has a 'history' back in Chicago, that adds a few years. Maybe we've got..." *What?*

"Maybe we've got a guy who wants to land a younger woman so he lies about his age. And his past. So what?"

A lot of people would like to run away from their past. Me, for one. "Yeah," she begrudgingly agreed. "I'm just looking for a nugget."

Josia drained his cup, then leaned back in his chair and put his hands behind his head. "If we use your analogy and insist on finding a piece of gold, I'd say the stuff Tilly said about Nick was revealing. I guess since she isn't direct kin, she didn't feel obligated to whitewash his character."

"Yeah," she agreed. "What was it Madge Lee said Tilly called Nick?"

"A strutting little tomcat that drove like a maniac."

The face of the dead man Jada had seen hadn't told her anything about his personality or character. All she knew was he

246

was a potter. *And potters are all nice good people. Right?* "Nick could have been a real bastard as far as we know. Irina and Darcie will never tell us the truth because they probably can't see the truth. You met him, what did you think?"

"I only met him once," he said. "No impression. Wish I had paid better attention. What did you mean about Darcie and Irina not seeing the truth?"

"Love. Does stupid things to people." She felt she had been one of the lucky ones, knowing Terry so well.

Seemingly out of the blue, and apropos to nothing she thought they'd been discussing, he asked, "So, is there anything to what this Elliott guy thinks about you and your husband?"

Anger flashed within her, and she shot back an equally intrusive counter-question. "Why did your wife leave you?"

Josia humphed sardonically. "Because I'm a jackass. But if you're going to get all huffy over a simple little question, I guess we better get going to Crestwood."

"I guess we'd better," she snapped.

Jada was not sure exactly where in the high desert they had arrived. Indeed, she had attempted to track their passage from Red Rock City to Crestwood, but after passing a Rosamond exit south of Mojave on I-14, she had lost her bearings.

Nonetheless, somewhere south of Mojave and North of Palmdale, the Crestwood Convalescence Home now stood before them, five stories tall with two sizeable wings, and boldly identifying itself with a sprawling tower-to-tower sign. And in the harsh afternoon light, the massive structure cast several eerily long and geometrically thin shadows across the surrounding landscape. A stark still-life snapshot in time that Jada found surprisingly menacing, and she momentarily fancied the image would have made a striking black and white frame in an Orson Welles movie.

Tasha was asleep in the backseat, and even though the area was cooler than Red Rock City, Jada was still concerned about the heat. But a healthy breeze was stirring the air, and they found a parking spot in the shade under a clump of large Palo Verde trees. They left all the windows half open, and "let sleeping dogs lie."

Crestwood's front entrance was a center courtyard adorned with a large, round Mediterranean-styled fountain which was surrounded by generous lawn areas and accompanying patios furnished with distressed wood chairs and tables. The views from all sides were fair, ranging from the San Bernardino mountains to the South, to rolling high desert to the North.

Once inside, they were informed Crestwood's facilities ranged from spacious two bedroom apartments to studios, and there were single rooms with around-the-clock medical services or nursing. It wasn't mentioned, but Jada figured there was also a locked ward somewhere on the grounds.

Crestwood evidently wasn't quite a hospital, nor was it a nursing home. For some, it was a place to stay many years, for others, only a safe "rest stop." Marie Shipley had called it a hospital, and Josia, expectedly, called it a "nut house." Jada wasn't yet sure what she thought about the place.

Stan Dominic met them in the foyer dressed in middle-of-the road quality tan sports slacks, shirt, and shoes. He was a pleasant-looking man of average height and build, innocuous in features and demeanor. Jada—unkindly she knew—found his face flat, bland, and quite uninteresting. A man easily forgotten in a crowd.

He extended his hand to Josia and attempted a small smile that more closely resembled a grimace. "Stan Dominic, Chief Rhodes." Quickly he let go what looked to her like a very thin handshake. "Ma'am," Dominic nodded toward Jada without actually looking at her. Then back to Josia. "Are you absolutely positive you have to talk to my wife? And today?"

Josia said, "I appreciate your coming out here to meet us on such short notice." His tone was empathetic, but firm. "Unfortunately I've got a murder investigation on my hands, and I do need to talk to your wife. I wouldn't have insisted otherwise."

Stan shook his head skeptically. "I don't know what Ruth can possibly tell you about what's happened." He sighed resignedly. "But if you must, I imagine there's nothing I can do to stop you." He gestured toward French doors to their rear. "There's a comfortable sitting room for visitors. Could we talk before I take you out to the West patio to see Ruth? She likes to be outside as much as possible, even in cool weather."

"Sure," Josia agreed with a shrug.

Jada quietly followed the two men into a large and comfortably furnished room stuffed with arm chairs, loveseats, and couches, all arranged in groupings to facilitate conversation. It was nicely done, but she hated places like this. Admittedly the Crestwood was "high-end" and a lot of the people were there by choice, wanting to live the rest of their lives in a protected environment—probably a doctor and nurse on twenty-four hour call—dining room level meals—nice furnishings. Still, she hated it. *Why is Ruth here?*

After they were seated, Stan didn't take long to get down to business. "I can see by the look on your face, Mrs. Beaudine, you're wondering what kind of hideous man I must be to send my wife here."

Jada felt her cheeks warm and hoped it didn't show. She answered frankly, "I was wondering why Mrs. Dominic was here. Is she ill?"

"That's a difficult question." He sighed wearily, clearly conveying his thought that this was well trodden ground, but he would endure and go over it again for them. "I think Ruth is perfectly fine and should be home with me where I can take care of her doing normal everyday things. The real world. Cori, my stepdaughter, does not agree. She is convinced Ruth is near 'breakdown' stage and virtually dragged her here. My wife of course humors her." He spread his hands in resignation. "And frankly, who am I, to say for sure? Maybe the rest is actually good for Ruth."

Josia asked the obvious. "What does Mrs. Dominic's doctor say?"

Stan let out a short derisive laugh. "Doesn't know, now does he? They're all like that, you know. Nowadays you have to tell them what's wrong. At least he's been willing to try different medications. She doesn't have Alzheimers or anything like that."

"Does Mrs. Dominic act ill?" Jada pressed.

"I'll let you be the judge of that," he said. "The reason I wanted to talk to you first is, I wanted to give you some background on Ruth. I don't think she's ill, but Ruth has been despondent lately. I think circumstances have just worn her out over the years."

Jada knew there was more; Stan just needed the time to tell it.

"We've been married five years, now. For me, it was love immediately." He smiled slightly, remembering. "And I knew even then that Ruth's mind would wander. You know, she'd start remembering the past and just kind of leave us, mentally that is, for a bit. But I figured, so what, who's perfect?"

Jada was warming to Stan, but she could tell from the expression on Josia's face he was wondering why Stan Dominic wasn't confined in here with his wife.

"I mean, I don't mind. Who gets hurt? No one. I can take care of her."

"But Corissa doesn't agree?" Jada asked.

"No. It's not that Cori has anything against me, it's just she thinks Ruth needs medical supervision."

"Why?" Josia insisted.

Stan hesitated and cleared his throat nervously before answering. "Ruth has physically wandered away a couple times."

"When was that? And where did she go?"

"Oh, a couple years back, and we don't know where Ruth went. She was only gone a few hours, but she came back, don't you see, she came back."

Jada leaned forward and asked gently, "Can you tell us what it is in your wife's past you think is causing all this? I gather you want us to be delicate in our questions, right? So what is it we need to know?"

"It was that rat first husband of hers." Stan's heretofore bland face came alive with anger. "Abandoned her, don't you know? She and the little one. Didn't leave a penny—nothing. That Billy McNichols was a right out bastard!" He spat out the last word.

If looks could kill, Jada thought, and another quick glance at Josia's face confirmed his mind was leaning in the same direction.

Stan continued, "She had to raise little Cori all by herself. No wonder the poor girl doesn't think much of herself. Low self-esteem the shrink calls it. Cori's smart, you know, but she never had the advantages. Wish I'd known them then."

Calmly, but seemingly from left field, Josia asked, "What do you do?"

"Do?"

"You know, what's your occupation?"

"I'm an archeologist. I work for the university. Unfortunately I'm out of town a lot. I like fieldwork, going to the digs—" he cut himself short. "I guess to be fair to Cori, that's one of the reasons she keeps bringing Ruth here. I'm gone so much."

"Where were you last Tuesday and Wednesday?"

"Actually, Chief Rhodes, I was in Ecuador. I just got back yesterday."

A hefty-looking nurse with a large lettered nametag of "Jeremy" escorted them to a rear garden where Ruth McNichols Dominic waited. The garden grounds, like the front court, were a pleasant oasis with well-kept grass, numerous trees—old, heavy branched, and strategically placed for summer shade; and a couple flower gardens still displaying a few courageous winter blooms. Nothing like Marie Shipley's amazing horticultural achievement, but nice.

The temperature was cool enough not to worry about Tasha out in the car, but warm enough to still enjoy the outdoors. *January.* Jada shivered thinking how cold and rainy it was this time of year back in Seattle. Yet, she missed it.

In the middle of this peaceful area sat Ruth, cozily attired in a red and blue knitted sweater, wool skirt, and incongruous fleece lined high boots. A wisp of a woman, with a small round face surrounded by twenties-style curls, she had positioned herself in the center of a love seat. Jada guessed Ruth should be around forty-five, fifty max—yet something about her demeanor, particularly the way she held her body, put one in mind of a little old lady in her eighties or more.

The three of them, Jada, Josia, and Stan arranged themselves on the wicker furniture around the woman. Stan made the introductions, then sat back, tight lipped, and stiff. *Damned if I'll participate;* his body language was emphatically clear.

Ruth had a soft light voice that carried easily on air as she spoke. But the personality emerging from behind the voice seemed neither thin nor weak. Indeed, just the opposite. It was clear from beginning introductions, that regardless of her diminutive size and waif-like aura, Ruth was not the addle-brained and hypertension-racked woman Jada's mind had conjured up. She also seemed undisturbed by their appearance out of nowhere, and glad for the company without being overly eager. Most importantly, she appeared quite competent to discuss the matter at hand.

"I read about Nick and Hal's murders in the newspaper," Ruth said. "I didn't know either man. Odd," she tilted her head charmingly and looked to Stan, "that I never went to his class. Marie kept trying to get me to go, said I'd be good at potting. I doubt that, but it did sound like fun." She smiled, possibly at the thought of her friend Marie. "And after Cori started, I kept meaning to accompany her. She told me about the class and how much she enjoyed it." Ruth then tsked with a shake of the head. "But the picture Cori painted of Hal Morton was not a pretty one, I must admit. To be murdered, though…just doesn't seem right." She patted the curls above her right ear like a young girl preening for a beau.

Josia hesitated and looked to Jada. She took his meaning to take the lead, and asked, "Did Cori also have an opinion about Nick?"

Ruth smiled playfully at her. "Of course she did, Mrs. Beaudine. That's why dear Marie sent you all the way out here to talk to me. She called me, you know. Marie that is. Said she'd sent you to talk to me. Stan didn't want me to." She bestowed a most beatific smile his way. "Stan does worry so."

His eyes smiled at her in return, but his jaw and lip-line remained firm. No, he obviously could not control his wife, but he would not participate in this badgering of his beloved.

Jada asked lightly, "So Marie sent us here for…what?"

Ruth turned her gaze to a point in the distance for a moment of thought, then back to them. "You know why I come here?" She held up her hand to Stan. "I'm fine Dear, I want to talk to these people. I want to do whatever I can to help find who murdered Nick Williams."

"Why do you come here?" Jada asked gently.

"Because Crestwood is its own world. There is no past here, nor is there necessarily a future. Mainly I can live in the present, a lovely present, a present of my own making. I do so like the forties and fifties. Don't you? Such a simpler time. Values and roles were clear." She stretched out her hand and took Jada's. "Sometimes I get weary of the world we live in now."

For a second, Jada caught a flash of frailty and fear in Ruth's plain round face. Then just as quickly she saw strength and determination in their place as Ruth continued, "Cori was infatuated with Nick Williams. There. I've said it."

"By 'infatuated,' do you mean having an affair?"

"I think she might have been."

"She didn't say she did?"

"No, but she went on and on about him. How good he was, how he paid special attention to her."

Jada gave Ruth's hand an encouraging little squeeze.

"You see," she continued. "My Cori is easily flattered. What is it young people, say? Something about self-esteem. It's my fault you know. I wasn't able to give her the best. You do know about Billy, my first husband?"

"We'd like for you to tell us."

Ruth then told her story—about marrying Billy McNichols in Chicago, Illinois, then having Cori a couple years later, and how wonderful it was. Billy worked at The Chicago Board of Trade and was a rising star. She of course stayed home and took care of Cori. "What a mother should do." When Cori was only two, it had all fallen apart. Billy disappeared never to be heard from again. Yes, she tried finding him; yes she even hired a private detective. Nothing.

Jada was about to ask Ruth why she was worried about telling them her daughter was infatuated with Nick when she noticed Corissa peering at them from the glass doors leading to the patio where they sat. "There's your daughter, Mrs. Dominic." Corissa did not look happy. "Did you tell her we were coming to talk to you?"

"Cori is excitable," she said. "I didn't want to get her upset. She's so protective. Stan wanted me to tell her."

Jada had never seen someone actually "wring their hands," but Corissa was doing just that as she rushed over. "What are you two doing here?" she blurted out. "Why are you pestering my mother?"

Stan sighed but didn't rise. Instead he looked to Josia, his expression saying, *"You wanted this meeting, now you deal with her."*

Josia stood up. "Now, now, Mrs. James, there's no need to get excited," he said. "No one is pestering your mother. Just a few questions, you must understand that. I have two murders to investigate."

"But my mother has nothing to do with them," Corissa said, her voice strained. "Who sent you here anyway?"

Jada heard a shrillness in Corissa's voice that frightened her. The girl was near hysteria. She knew she wasn't skillful in the nurturing arena, but in what Jada considered her most soothing voice, she said, "Cori, it will be all right." She took the young woman's hand in hers; it was ice cold. "Come sit next to me." With her other hand Jada patted the spot on the wicker love seat next to her. "We were having tea and your mother was just telling us how important you are to her." *A small lie.*

Her words seemed to calm Corissa a bit. "But why are you here?" she asked in a more even tone. "Mother doesn't know anything about anyone in our class except what I told her."

Josia said firmly, "Yes, we now understand that, and we were just leaving." To Ruth he said, "It was very nice meeting you, Mrs. Dominic." Then he smiled one of his best and added, "And don't worry about your daughter. We'll find who killed Nick Williams and Hal Morton soon."

Jada couldn't believe he was ending the interview. She was sure there was more to be learned from Ruth and Cori if they would just press them a little more. But obediently she followed his lead and left as graciously as he did.

Back in the lobby though, she demanded, "Why did you stop? We were just beginning to get somewhere. I'm sure of it."

"There was nowhere 'to get.' Don't you see?" he said. "Mrs. Dominic is worried her daughter was involved with Nick and consequently is going to get killed too. And Corissa James is worried—"

Jada finished his thought, "Her mother is involved somehow and we're going to find out how and why."

"But I don't think...," his voice trailed off.

"I know it's hard to imagine Mrs. Dominic shooting anyone."

"Hmm."

Jada waited.

"Tell you what," he said. "Let's make a little stop before we leave."

His detour was to the administration office—fifty feet or so off Crestwood's main lobby. There they learned from Ms. Pertence that Mrs. Dominic was free to come and go at will. They did indeed lock the doors after dark and didn't reopen them until 8:00 A.M. the next morning. But there was a bell, and guests such as Mrs. Dominic could just ring and the watch-person would buzz them in or out.

After Josia pushed, prodded, and cajoled, she consulted the logs for January second through the fourth. On the second, Mrs. Ruth Dominic had left at 6:00 A.M. for an early breakfast in town. Then on the evening of the third, she had checked out for an overnight back home, and hadn't returned until noon the next day.

"But," Ms. Pertence pointed out in an annoyingly superior tone, "Mrs. Dominic often goes out for an early breakfast, and likewise often goes back home to be with her husband. Mrs. Dominic does as she wishes."

And, Jada, finished in her mind, *pays you guys a pretty penny for it.* Generous Stan, who Jada guessed was footing Ruth's Crestwood bill, was definitely making up for her earlier days of poverty.

An hour later Josia dropped Jada and Tasha off at her minivan in the Red Rock City Police Office parking lot. Josia was hungry, but she didn't feel like company. Again, another day had become exceedingly long.

Consequently, after a quick "See ya later," Josia headed back into his office, and Jada started digging her keys out of her canvas bag while thinking about what to do next. Head back to the Red Rock and pull her thoughts together? Eat maybe? Hopefully Manny was still dishing up chow, and if Irina was around, she could run some questions by her. Irina should be able to fill in some background information on Marie and Ruth.

To those ends, once back at the Red Rock, Jada stopped at the café before heading to number-two. Tasha decided to remain stretched out on the backseat. Manny was still serving lunch and Irina was supposedly in her office. The surprise was Corissa waiting for her in the back booth.

"I was wondering if you'd be coming back for lunch," Manny asked when Jada arrived. "I made chicken fried steak and mashed potatoes. Want some, or would you rather have a burger?" He leaned across the counter and lowered his voice,

"Mrs. McNichols-James is waiting for you." He made a gesture with his head. "Said she needs to talk to you right away."

Jada didn't know what chicken fried steak was, but she figured anything Manny cooked would be tasty. "Sure, Manny, I'll try your chicken. I guess you can bring it to me back at Corissa's booth."

"Actually, Jada, it's beef—" he started to clarify, but she had already turned her back on him to go talk to Corissa.

She quickly slipped into the booth facing Corissa. "Manny said you're waiting to see me." She could feel excitement rushing through her body. Whatever the reason, Corissa's wanting to talk to her was bound to reveal some new information. Maybe, just maybe, it would be that final little piece to bring it all together.

"Yes, I was hoping you'd come back here this afternoon." Corissa sat slumped in her seat, shoulders drooped, and her eyes red and swollen like she had been recently crying.

"I'm sorry we upset you earlier," Jada said, placating her. "But we really did need to talk to your mother and I really don't think she minded."

Corissa again seemed anxious and on the edge of emotional collapse. "My mother isn't well," she said. "I just can't bear to see her hurt anymore."

Jada choose her words carefully. "What do you mean?" It seemed to her Corissa was a more likely hospital candidate than Ruth. "Who's hurting your mother?"

"Oh, not now." She straightened up a bit. "Stan treats her like a queen."

"You mean your father, then?" Jada felt she needed to tread lightly. Corissa seemed more and more like a ticking time bomb. But she couldn't get a handle on what was sending her farther and farther into such a state of nervousness.

"He treated her miserably, you know. She was left to bring me up alone. I guess you know that already?"

"Yes." Jada waited.

Corissa brought her hands up from her lap and started chewing on the fingernails of her left hand. The nails on both hands looked ragged and low.

Jada continued to wait.

"Stan and mother are very protective of me."

"Yes, they both seem very fond of you." Jada was getting an inkling of what had compelled Corissa to come to the Red Rock. "You're worried either your mother or Stan killed Nick?"

Corissa caught her breath, then released it slowly. "Yes."

"But Corissa." Jada leaned forward to engage direct eye contact with the young woman. "What possible reason would they have to kill Nick?"

Tears began to flow from her already swollen eyes.

"Because...."

Again, Jada patiently waited.

"Because of me."

"You?" Jada's tone was more demanding than she would have wished, but the young woman had become exasperating.

"Yes. I let it slip one night."

For goodness sakes. "Let what slip?"

"Make Chief Rhodes leave us alone," Corissa said with a sudden forcefulness. "Make him leave us alone." She jumped up and rushed out of the café, bumping into several counter stools on the way, and before Jada and Manny could take in what was happening, she had started her car and shot out toward the highway—leaving the slam of the café door still ringing in their ears.

"Hey," Manny called out uselessly. "You didn't pay."

Jada picked up Corissa's check from the table. "I've got it." There was something extremely wrong with what Corissa had been trying to get her to believe. There was just no motive for Ruth or Stan—or even Corissa—to kill either man.

"Boy am I glad you came back," Irina said as she came out of her office, apparently unaware of the histrionic scene that had just transpired. She slid into the booth across from Jada in the spot where Corissa had been sitting. "What the hell have you and Josia been up to all morning?" She looked and sounded tired and worried.

Even though the days were few since meeting Irina, Jada was becoming reluctantly fond of this loony woman. "You look terrible, Irina," she said. "Are you all right? Josia is doing everything he can to find out who killed Nick." The apprehension she saw in Irina's eyes compelled her to add a little white lie. "He doesn't believe you had anything to do with the murders. You do know that, right?"

Irina smiled gratefully. "That's nice of you to say. But I know he thinks it's possible I killed Nick out of jealously. But he just can't believe I would also kill Hal." Her eyes pleaded for Jada's agreement. "Could he?"

"Of course not. We talked to Marie Shipley and Ruth Dominic today." She proceeded to fill Irina in on morning events.

"Madge Lee and Melvin might still come up with something," Irina said when she finished. "They're going to Chicago tonight, right?"

"Yes." Jada was not optimistic.

"I sure hope Darcie didn't know about Nick's affairs."

"You don't want it to be her?" She clarified. "The murderer that is."

"No." Irina shook her head, then abruptly squinched up her eyes and pursed her lips. "What was your husband, like?"

"What?" Jada demanded. She had been caught unawares. "What does Terry have to do with anything?"

"Oh, I don't know. Nick was evidently a flawed man." Irina sighed. "I've been wondering all morning why I bothered with him. Why couldn't I see him for what he really was? From what you and Si have told me about your interviews, everybody else in class saw him for what he was. Even Star. How could I be such a gall-darned fool?"

Lyle Elliott's words came back to Jada. *"We don't see the same person, Mrs. Beaudine."* No, Lyle was wrong, she had not been deluded about Terry like Irina had been about Nick. "I always felt Terry was the right man for me," she told Irina. "You know, 'soul mates' I've heard it called. It wasn't like we were completely alike. Heck, in some ways we were a lot different. But some fundamental stuff we shared in common." *And Terry gave me a world to be in. I belonged for once in my life.*

"Like what?" Irina asked. "I can't imagine someone who would be like me."

"Well, you're right, it wasn't like we were 'alike,' more like, well..." Jada struggled. "I know, here's an example. I've always been a loner, only child thing I guess. And Terry was the same, even though he had a sister and brother."

"But you liked being with each other, right?"

"Sure. But we didn't entertain that much, or join groups. We were enough for each other." *If you didn't count the gambling.*

"I understand the 'alone' part," Irina said. "It's not the same as lonely. I guess you must know that. But I never lost someone who carried a piece of me with them, like your Terry must have. Are you lonely?"

"Yes." Jada was surprised at her own candidness, and immediately fell silent.

"Here's your lunch," Manny announced with flourish as he slid a platter of food in front of Jada. He had plated a golden colored chicken fried steak patty on a swirl of country gravy, and surrounded his entrée with lightly sautéed baby carrots and garlic mashed potatoes piped in the shape of a rose. He cautioned, "This is *beef*, Jada, not chicken—in case that's important to you."

"Oh?" Jada asked.

"It's called chicken fried steak because of the way it's cooked," Irina explained.

Jada said, "Looks good." She knew Manny was an excellent cook, and by now she was getting hungry. Whatever it was, she'd try it.

"You hungry?" he asked Irina. "I can whip up another plate, real quick. You haven't eaten since breakfast."

The front door slammed and Lyle Elliott came in. With a nod toward Manny he quickly sat down at the front table.

"Be right with you, Mr. Elliott," Manny called out. "Well, what do you say Irina? I think you should eat something."

"Okay," Irina said, and Manny happily headed off to also take Lyle's order.

In the meantime Jada tasted a piece of meat. "It's delicious."

"Do you think your Terry ever had an affair?" Irina asked.

Jada's fork clanked as she dropped it onto her plate. Irina rushed to explain, "It's just that he sounds so perfect. While Nick," she scoffed ironically, "wasn't exactly the 'Perfect Man' like I said." She peered at Jada. "But maybe your Terry was."

Jada tried to keep her voice calm. "So?"

"So, if you and Terry got along so well, you know, *simpatico*, and he was always faithful and worked hard...Jesus...the man was nearly a saint."

Jada sighed through a small wry smile. *How can I hate this woman?* "Everything wasn't perfect, but no, I'm sure he never slept around." Something Jada heard in her own voice prompted her to add, "Although once there was a neighbor I wondered about." She shook her head vehemently. "But whenever I thought about it seriously, there was just no way." *Terry loved me too much to fool around with Allison King.*

Irina changed the subject. "Are you going to Nick's funeral in the morning?"

"Yes, are you?"

"Yeah. Jada…"

"Yes?"

"How much longer does Si have before the County takes over the investigation?"

"I think he's already run out of time. I really don't know why the County Sheriff or the State Police haven't descended on him already."

"The State's almost broke, you know that, right? As for the County, well that's an equally bad situation. And I think Si has a damn good reputation."

"Hmm." Jada wasn't convinced or impressed.

"I just can't imagine anyone in the class killing Nick and Hal. And trying to blow up Penny and Tim." She leaned back against the booth's wooden back. "What a crazy damn mess."

Manny returned with a plate for Irina. "Jada, that Mr. Elliott at the first table wants to talk to you when you finish eating." He couldn't hide his curiosity. "I didn't know he knew you."

She was not interested in discussing Lyle Elliott with Manny or Irina. She pushed her plate toward the end of the table. "Thanks, Manny." She dug into her canvas bag and pulled out a twenty. "This should cover for Corissa and me."

"More than cover—let me get your change."

"No, keep the change." She suddenly felt weary. Would Lyle Elliott never give up? "Irina, I'm going to let you eat in peace," she said, and got up.

Irina eyed Jada curiously but didn't voice objection to the abrupt end to their conversation.

Jada went to Lyle's table, sat down across from him, and said, "Well?" Her tone was surly and antagonistic.

He turned his head and looked out the window. "I know you don't want to believe me," he said. "But I'm sure your husband is in town and trying to contact you."

Jada leaned across the table, lowered the volume level of her voice and angrily forced her words through clinched teeth. "For Christ's sakes, Lyle," she said. "I'm telling you for the last time, as far as I know, Terry is dead. AND, I have not been involved with him in any scheme to defraud your insurance company." She leaned even farther across the table. "Not now, not ever." She could feel tears of anger and frustration trying to assert themselves, but she refused to give him the satisfaction of seeing her cry.

"I saw your husband this morning," he said, his voice still calm. "The fact is," he added in a surprisingly gentle voice, "I'm telling you what I saw so that you will be careful. You may be in danger. Are you so sure you know the real Terrence Beaudine?"

Furious, Jada rose from her seat and stretched across the table until her face was inches from his, "Screw you, Lyle." Then she grabbed her purse and headed for the front door.

Lyle, Manny, and Irina watched in amazement and alarm as Jada stomped out—banging the door behind her hard enough to make the door frame and front windows rattle in her wake.

Corissa's exit had been a whisper compared to Jada's.

Lyle visited his Best Western room to take a nice long hot soak in the bathtub. He wished for his Jacuzzi tub back in his Seattle condo. He'd done a lot of serious thinking back in that tub with its pulsating swirl of hot restorative bubbles. After his soak and before packing up to head back to the Red Rock Inn and Café, he also took the time to send a quick note to Hamilton.

Lyle Elliott's email to his Home Office
Friday—January 10th –9:00 P.M.

It's been a tough day, Hamilton. I have to think.

PART THREE
If Only…

Chapter Eight

It was Saturday morning, the day of Nick Williams's funeral, and Lyle could barely see where he was stepping. It was still dark, but he wanted to find a good spot and get settled before anyone else arrived. After he had emailed Hamilton, instead of rushing off, he had stayed up until midnight, thinking, formulating. He never made it back to the Red Rock, and was definitely tired this morning, but simultaneously quite invigorated.

Fortunately he had brought along a flashlight. He figured darkness was snake-time and he didn't want any confrontations with a sidewinder on its way home from "work." He finally found a small hillock far enough back from the actual gravesite not to be noticed, but close enough to watch with his binoculars.

In the off chance he'd be recognized, he'd chosen his favorite sixties retro disguise—the superannuated hippie photographer. He even set up his tripod and camera; just in case someone became curious, he wanted a plausible story.

He had also parked his car way on the backside of the cemetery so the Beaudines would not know he was there. Yes, he was still sure there were two Beaudines in town. This was an important day. He felt it in his bones. Terrence would show his hand, he just knew it.

Not as early as Lyle, but Jada also woke up before daybreak. Indeed, it wasn't long before she could see from her bedside window a vague tint of red and orange peeking above the horizon. The promise was there of another glorious sunrise followed by another day of clear skies.

She doubted it ever rained here. Manny had explained about arroyos and flash floods, but Jada found it hard to imagine. Atlanta would be quite different. She wasn't sure if that meteorological fact was good or bad, but Atlanta was going to be her new home. Not this god-awful place.

Damn. She had been so easily sidetracked, and now everything had become so complicated. Just a few days earlier it had been so simple—drive to Atlanta and buy a house near her relatives. So much had happened since, two murders in fact— and Lyle Elliott was still dogging her tracks. Part of her felt disheartened and put out, especially since she couldn't figure out who killed Nick and Hal, or convince Elliott he was wrong about Terry.

In fact, by leaving Seattle she had changed everything— yet changed nothing.

From the canine perspective, Tasha seemed eager to start the day and the moment Jada's eyes had opened, she plunked herself as close to her mistress as she could get without actually sitting on her; and there she remained, staring at Jada, dog drool barely missing her nose.

She scratched Tasha's ears and patted the dog's nose fondly. "I expect you're hungry and probably want a walk, huh girl?" Jada was also hungry, but the thought of walking over to the café and talking to other human beings was not appealing. Especially after yesterday's door-slamming snit, and then her hiding out the rest of the evening.

And the moment she had stepped outside into dry desert air yesterday afternoon she regretted letting Lyle piss her off so easily. His claim of seeing Terry, however, was insane; and she was beginning to think his obsession with them was mentally unhinging him.

She had spent the rest of the afternoon napping with Tasha, and the evening talking to Solina and watching poorly-received local TV. All the while, in the background, her mind churned away—processing, she hoped.

Her telephone had rung several times, and figuring it was Irina or Manny, Jada hadn't answered. Eventually, she went to bed, rather early, without dinner, then slept surprisingly soundly.

Now it was another day, and funerals sucked. The beautiful sunrise and sunny weather would not make everything okay. She sighed heavily and decided to call the café—better than walking over—on the chance Manny was already up and prepping in the kitchen. It wouldn't be that bad talking to Manny. It was Irina and Lyle that Jada was in no hurry to face again.

Manny was there and she asked if he could send over tea and a Danish. His response was outrage. "Heaven's no," he said. "Have you forgotten? Today is Nick Williams's funeral. You can't face a thing like that on an empty stomach."

Oh, no, she hadn't forgotten. "But I don't have time to come over and eat." *And I made such a scene yesterday.*

Manny seemed to acquiesce, but by the time she had showered and was ready to leave, a wicker basket lined with a couple of bar towels awaited her on number-two's patio table. His idea of breakfast suitable for a funeral morning was a large container of half frozen orange juice, a thermos of tea, a thermos of black coffee, four hard boiled eggs, two warm English muffins loaded with butter and jam in a special heat-retaining container, some slices of cold ham and cheese, a couple of Danish, some donuts, four or five wedges of watermelon (in the middle of winter!), and two dog biscuits.

She loaded Tasha, tucked the basket on the floor in front of the passenger seat, noticed Manny had also stuck a camp table and folding chairs in the back, then headed out to Red Rock City Cemetery. She wanted to be there before anyone else arrived.

How had Manny known the perfect solution?

In Seattle Jada had attended more than her share of funerals; and more often than not, they had taken place under closed-in grey skies accompanied by drizzle and bone-chilling winds. Those memories were not pleasant—miserable weather forcing everyone to slog across grass soaked cemetery grounds to end up huddled in disheartened little groups under huge black umbrellas provided by the mortuary. On top of that, the large branching cedars and hemlocks, so popular in Puget Sound, never failed to deepen one's feeling of sorrow. She had never found shelter or solace under their heavy damp canopies.

Especially that day at Terry's memorial. Understandably, she was not fond of funerals. *Who is?* Some things, though, you have to do, and Nick's funeral was going to be quite a different animal. First off, the sun was shining, the air was calm, and the temperature was already drifting up to a forecasted seventy degress. Just another sunny January day in the Mojave.

Second, she was there to catch a killer. It didn't take her long to find just the right spot for "funeral watching." To Jada's right, a group of sparrows was making a fuss in an Oleander bush, and to her left several Athol pine trees offered a modicum of shade cover for when the sun rose higher in the sky.

Good spot she decided, and undid the fold-up chair and camp table she'd dragged along from the car, placed her picnic breakfast within easy reach on the table, then plunked herself down and prepared to wait.

Like Lyle, she was on a small hillock. But she was closer to the anticipated action, with a good view even without binoculars. She could clearly see the parking lot and the gravel path leading to the gravesite where a canvas canopy had been erected. A freshly dug grave awaited Nick's casket. If she had turned around, Jada might have seen Lyle camped out on the rise behind her. At that distance, though, and with his disguise, she might not have picked up who he was.

Alert and inquisitive, Tasha sat down at her side, as tiny birds, some with orange breasts and a few with splotches of blue, dipped, dived, and darted from spot to spot—all the while chirping and chattering. *Life.*

She and Terry had had a friend who was a bird watcher. Taylor knew all the names, common and Linnaeus category, all their habits and habitats. She wished for Taylor now—he would know about these desert sparrows. In truth, she was guessing the cute little things were sparrows. Maybe they were finches.

Eventually and unavoidably, the gravesite overwhelmed her thoughts. "So much to life," she said to Tasha. "And all you can grab is such a little piece in one lifetime before you end up being lowered into that hole we're looking at."

That had so bothered Terry, the shortness of it all. So much he had wanted to do. Not that he'd complained much, at least not to her. She remembered Ted James and what he'd said about Corissa feeling she had been shortchanged when it came to opportunities. Jada thought it unfortunate Corissa was churning her emotions on past regrets, when she had so much in the present to be happy about.

Terry had also felt that way, sometimes. But you can't change the hand you're dealt, she would tell him; and he would unfailingly reply that you also needed to play those cards to your advantage. Should she have forced herself to be more adventuresome? Gone along with one or two of his crazy schemes? Would it really have hurt her that much? What good is money without happiness anyway? Questions she had asked herself many times over the last year. Answers she could be happy with had yet to come.

One sparrow with a bright orange breast dared to come and land a couple feet in front of them. Tasha seemed not to mind, so Jada broke off a piece of donut and tossed it gently the bird's way. "Probably a mistake, Tasha. She'll tell the rest and then they'll be scrambling all around here." Of course Jada had no way to tell its gender, but like many, she spoke of birds as female.

But, no, the little bird kept her song-box quiet and patiently waited for additional scraps. "Now there's a bird, Tasha-girl, that knows how to play the hand she's been dealt."

The sound of a car engine caught Jada's attention and she watched as a Red Rock City police cruiser pulled in and parked next to her minivan. It was still half an hour before the funeral procession was expected to arrive.

Josia Rhodes got out and headed straight towards her. He was out of uniform and wearing a half-smile for once.

"You had the same idea I gather," she said when he was in earshot.

"I bet you wondered why Manny put two chairs in your car."

"You talked to Manny this morning?"

"Yep."

"I left the other chairs in the minivan; you'll have to go get one." She dug her keys out of her canvas bag and tossed them to him. "There's plenty of food. Although if you had come any later I probably would have given the leftovers to the birds and Tasha."

He sighed and rolled his eyes skyward before walking back to the parking lot and retrieving a chair. Once back and settled with food and drink before him he said, "Thanks for bringing all this by the way."

Jada's initial instinct was to give him some sass. Instead, she chose to call a truce this funeral morning. Besides, they both were after the same thing—catching a killer. She did not, however, politely wait until he finished eating to start asking questions. "Why is this funeral so early in the morning, do you know? Usually they come from a church mid-morning or later."

He answered between devouring an egg and starting in on the fruit. "You see that little building over there behind the main office? The one with the small cross on the door?" He waited for her to nod. "It's a chapel, and they plan on having a short nondenominational service there. Then pallbearers will carry the casket to the grave site."

"Relatives?" she asked referring to the pallbearers and thinking they should talk to them next. Maybe they could shed some light on Nick's past. "What idiots we are." *Of course Nick's family would know something about his past.* "We should have been talking to his—"

"Before you get started beating yourself up, Gabe already checked that angle. Williams was an only child, parents deceased, no surviving aunts, uncles, or cousins that we could find except Aunt Ann, who's actually Darcie's aunt. The pallbearers will probably be funeral home employees."

"Oh."

"Darcie got this all together fast," he said. "The ME just released his body. Hal Morton's body is still at the coroner's, waiting. I understand his body is being shipped to a cousin somewhere in Maine." He put some ham and cheese on an English muffin.

"But suppose we, *you*, find something later on and you need to check—" Jada caught herself—autopsies weren't an appropriate subject to discuss while eating.

Her sensitivities however were evidently not Josia's sensitivities. Between bites he said, "The Red Rock Inn & Café is a desert shantytown motel, but I have to give it to Manny, the boy sure knows how to put a meal together. Even when it's just English muffins and cold-cuts." He only paused for a few seconds between the topics of food and autopsies. "Regarding Nick and Hal's bodies, they keep photographs, computer imaging files, tape recordings, certain organs, and tissue samples. The morgue is high tech these days, at least in the major cities."

"Manny's not a boy, you know. He's older than he looks. And the 'they' you're referring to is the ME and the forensics lab folks?"

"Yep."

"Do you think Irina killed Nick and Hal?"

"Nope."

"Might be good if you told her so next time you see her."

He stopped eating long enough to give her an inquisitive look that was not-so-friendly.

She rushed to defend herself, "It's none of my business how you two get along. I'm just passing along info."

He smiled. Barely. "Okay, you're right, next time I see her."

"Which is in about two minutes. She just pulled into the parking lot and is heading up here."

He looked out toward the parking lot, tsked irritably, then sighed, and finally mumbled, "If I'd wanted to have a party."

In the end it turned out not exactly like a party, more like a picnic wake. Irina had brought another chair and another basket containing Cokes, booze, wine, more cheese, and French baguettes. She also brought news. Someone had tried to sneak onto the Red Rock Inn property again; this time just as Jada was leaving. Manny had been watching number-two ever since he dropped off the basket. *"'Just had a feeling,'* he said. He also wanted me to tell you, Si, he was pretty sure it was a man and that the car was white. He couldn't get the plate, still pretty dark when Jada headed out."

"I better call in and get Gabe out to interview Manny. Or maybe I'd better..." He let the continuation of his thought become nonverbal and unceremoniously got up and headed to his cruiser.

The two women watched as he made his way down the hill to the parking lot. "He looks awfully tired," Irina said while getting settled and pouring herself a glass of Bordeaux even though it was only eight in the morning.

"Yeah. You know, he told me this morning he didn't think you killed Nick or Hal."

"Thanks for telling me that. But I'm figuring it's gonna be the Bakersfield boys and girls soon. They don't have the history Si and I do."

Jada didn't push—after all, it wasn't her business. Soon the parade of mourners would be arriving and they would be scrutinizing everyone, trying to pick a murderer. But for now, it was a surprisingly nice moment, what with a gentle morning breeze, good food, Irina, and Tasha; and for a few moments she let herself forgot why they were there.

After a bit, and seemingly without any previous connection, Irina asked, "Have you ever wondered why I don't have satellite TV at the Red Rock? You know Manny got his own, and so did Mrs. Shoecraft. You probably think it's because I'm cheap, right?"

"Mrs. Shoecraft?" Jada took a second to marvel at that tidbit. "I have wondered why you put up with such lousy reception. But, no, I don't think you're cheap. Just the opposite. I think you're very generous with your resources." She hesitated, searching for just the right words. "And with your spirit."

"I dated Si for awhile before he married Helen. You've probably guessed that, or maybe he even mentioned it." She laughed—quick, short, and humorlessly. "He would say I'd never have anything. His exact words were, 'You'll never have a pot- to-pee-in if you just keep on givin' it all away.' Sometimes Si can be a sorry SOB."

"Well...." What could she say? "None of us are perfect." *Not even The Perfect Man.* Then trying to lighten her mood, Jada returned to the topic of TV reception. "So, why *don't* you get a satellite?"

"Because I got tired of watching sitcoms, dramas, hell, even commercials that were always portraying a life that isn't real. Nothing is like it is on TV. Relationships, family, friends, food, whatever...it's a fantasy world they're selling...and what happens is you start measuring your own life against what you see." She took a hefty swallow of wine. "You know, why aren't I rich and famous, why aren't I having backyard barbecues where everyone's happy and singing and laughing. Why don't I have kids gleefully sitting around the breakfast table eating cereal and telling me how much they love me? You get what I mean, it's a bunch of crap they're trying to ram down our throats."

Jada was caught unawares by the emotional slam in the gut Irina's comments dredged up within herself; and it took her several long moments to regain composure.

"Jada?" Irina's voice was worried. "Are you alright? Is it something I said? I was just shooting my regular old BS, you know."

Jada wondered if she would ever be able to tell anyone her own secrets? Probably not. Even Terry had known so little.

Fifteen years, and she had never told him the details of her past. *None* of it like the sitcoms. *None* of it like the commercials. Eventually she managed a smile. "No," she said. "It was just how right you are, about TV and stuff."

Both women blew out long sad breaths before Irina refilled her goblet. Then Jada decided wine in the morning was a darned good idea and reached for a glass of her own.

Ally was happy again.

She had followed Josia out of town, figuring he'd be hooking up with the Beaudine woman before the funeral. She had kept her distance and pulled off onto a dirt road about half-a-mile before the cemetery, then she had taken a gamble the road led around to the back—and her hunch paid off. She found Lyle Elliott's car.

She was pleased and amazed at her own cleverness, and thus encouraged, continued to follow her instincts and parked a short way back from his car. Next, she cautiously took the narrow footpath she hoped led to the backside of the cemetery. She certainly didn't want to run into Elliott. But like him, she hoped to find an unobtrusive hillock where she could keep an eye on Jada.

It had been an awful year for her—often feeling like she was on the edge, not knowing where to go, what to do—her world completely shattered by Terry's death. Still, even now, the last couple days hadn't been that great, living in her car almost, surviving on fast food, Pepsi, and Tylenol. No picnic for sure.

But she knew her moment was near. She just had to keep the evil woman in her sights until that moment. That moment of sweet, sweet, revenge. Her gun was always with her, either at her side on the car seat, or in her bag as it was now. Ready.

She saw Elliott first, tucked away on the side of a small hill. Then she saw Jada, in front of him. *Ha!* And who was the smartest now? *She was.*

Silently and quickly she picked a spot at an angle from Elliott where she could see him and Jada without being noticed unless they turned around and really tried. A smile spread across her face as she brought her binoculars up to her eyes, captured Elliott, then Jada in its lenses, and savored her future moment of revenge.

According to Terry, Jada had always insisted on the "finer things." He had told her many times how Jada always had to have the best—luxury all the way. Yet, he never had any money to spend on himself or her, always having to take her to cheap, out of the way places. The woman kept Terry on an allowance, of all things. An *allowance* for a grown man.

Ally hadn't cared about the money so much, just being with him had been enough; and talking about all the things they were going to do. Terry and his wonderful ideas.

Oh, the high flyers he knew. They all greeted Terry by name when he had taken her to Vegas that time. And unlike the cheap motels they usually went to, they had stayed in an unbelievable suite, and he had played at the special tables in a private room. A weekend she would never forget.

Remembering now, she caught herself almost wanting to cry. *No, not now.* There'd be plenty time to cry when it was all over, and that would be soon.

She had stayed on Jada's trail even when she had to follow that police car, all the time worried the Police Chief would catch sight of her. But after a year, she must have become pretty good at this following business. She even stayed out of the way of Elliott. The fool. Imagining Terry was still alive. She certainly would know if Terry was alive or not.

What a crock, thinking her Terry would run off with his own wife. Maybe there was a hereafter. She doubted it, but maybe. And, if there was, her beloved Terry would instead be waiting for his evil wife so he could send her straight to hell. Instead of crying, Ally's smile broadened as she continued to watch Elliott watching Jada watching the now arriving mourners.

On the other side of the cemetery a white Ford Explorer pulled in, its driver looking for just the right spot.

Having knocked off two bottles of California Bordeaux in half an hour, Jada knew she and Irina were a wee-bit tipsy. The effect of so much booze so early in the morning was to subdue both women; and after some minimal back and forth on murderers and motives, conversation waned until only a companionable silence remained.

Funeral aside, it was a glorious morning, a unique experience, and a thought-provoking snatch of time. She was also surprised at the feeling of ease she now had with Irina, especially since she barely knew the woman, actually for only a week.

Had so much happened in just a week? It couldn't be. Two men dead. One being buried today, tissue samples from his body in some impersonal lab freezer somewhere; the other body still on a hard cold slab in a morgue drawer waiting to be shipped across the country.

After a bit, Josia returned from his cruiser, and Irina uncorked a third bottle. The three then waited in silence. And sipped.

Eventually a black van pulled into the parking lot and six somber-faced hefty men in black suits got out and trudged into the small chapel, while two more made their way to the burial canopy. Then right on time, a modest funeral procession led by a traditional shiny black hearse pulled in.

Behind the hearse a limousine pulled up and parked.

Darcie Williams — dressed properly mournful in a chic black suit, hat, nylons, and pumps, and accompanied by a middle-aged woman Jada didn't recognize, also in black, but less stylishly dressed — got out and headed toward the chapel.

"Who is that with Darcie?" Jada asked as she secretly noted that if you looked closely, it did appear Darcie was developing a little pregnancy pouch. She speculated the two current Williams children had been left at home with a sitter. Wisely, Jada thought, since they were both young and wouldn't understand. Too young to find out people die.

"Don't know," Irina answered.

"Gabe would know," Josia said. "My guess is Darcie's sister."

She could for sure see sorrow and concurrent denial encompassing Darcie's face. So sad. Nick's widow looked in control, composed and strong, but inside, turmoil. Jada knew, she'd been there.

Still, sad or not, Darcie had the most to gain from Nick's death. A half-mil estate was quite a motive; and in lockstep with Josia, she thought *cui bono* was not an idle idiom.

Surprisingly — she figured they would still be too weak — Timothy and Penny Berry followed the family limousine in their Volvo wagon. They got out slowly, dressed in matching black suits, and struggled to follow behind Darcie and her companion. Jada knew they were technically murder suspects, but her heart just couldn't wrap itself around them as murderers. Besides, someone had tried to kill *them*.

Leroy Ames, his wife Cynthia, and Hilary Giles arrived together in a burgundy Nissan minivan. Leroy had driven and Jada guessed the car belonged to him or his wife. Based on

Hilary's earlier comments, and reading between the lines, Jada speculated his wife Emily hadn't come because she was agoraphobic. Losing a son certainly could do that to a person. Again, so sad. However, Leroy and Hilary could not be ruled out as murderers either. Especially Leroy, if Marie Shipley was to be believed. But what motives?

The last car, a white Ford sedan, contained Marie Shipley as driver, and Corissa James as passenger. No Martin Shipley, no Ted James, no Ruth or Stan Dominic, no Star or Phillip Thomas; and Jada guessed Marie had come mainly to accompany her friend Ruth's daughter.

So in the end, few had come to publicly mark Nick's passing; and for Jada, his funeral turned out ironically and frustratingly anti-climatic.

Ally had tried several times to aim her pistol at Jada, once a hair away from pulling the trigger, but she was just too damn far away. *If only* she still had her father's "Trailrider."

If only. Jada would now be dead.

Instead, like the others, Ally could only sit and watch the small funeral assemblage. Ally kept her post until Josia, Irina, Jada, and finally Lyle all left. She would have preferred to follow Jada immediately, but she couldn't run the risk of Lyle seeing her.

Damn, damn, double-damn.

After the funeral, driving back down Highway 395 then I-14, about a mile before she would arrive back at the Red Rock's driveway, Jada pulled over onto the side of the road, stopped the car, and turned off the ignition. She needed to breathe a moment. Alone.

She recognized what she thought was Lyle's car as he passed her, and for a moment was afraid he was going to stop. He didn't. She hadn't seen him in the funeral procession, but thought he must be coming back from there. But where at the cemetery was he? And doing what? Had he been disguised as a corpse?

Jada laughed for a few seconds at her impertinent thought. However, her moment of light-headed amusement at Lyle's expense quickly evaporated as she got out, then walked to the front of her minivan and looked around in all directions at the endless rolling hills, the million balls of scrub brush, the ragged Sierra foothills, the smattering of Joshua trees, the cluster of stucco shacks that made up Irina's world.

From the landscape picture surrounding her, a torrent of past snapshot memories came freely; living pictures of places she had been, people she had known, moments in her past that had wiggled their way into the synaptic recesses of her mind and had waited there patiently—until this moment.

She found it puzzling why these particular experiences had remained while so many others had vanished. But there they were: the charming Victorian in Copeville and the octogenarian bachelor who ran it; the sprawling two-story hanging on the side of a hill in Santa Barbara with two curious Dobermans standing at its huge wrought iron front gate; the vacant hacienda cottage tucked in a rocky crevice in Truth or Consequences; and the stick-house on the Rock Port shore with its pesky sea gulls swirling around above. And there were also the pottery shops and studios, the numerous classes and workshops—she could still smell the clay, feel the slip and grit, even taste the ceramic dust.

But never in her mind's eye or sensory memories from her past, could Jada conjure up a place and a life like the one surrounding her here—this place and this life of Irina Hughes.

And as it had happened with Jada in the past, from nowhere and from everywhere, but probably triggered by one of her memories, the significance of the "hand washing" presented itself to her conscious mind. It was a detail that had bothered her from the start. Before Jada could further explore her insight, she heard the sound of tires crunching gravel. She looked to her rear. A small white compact car was pulling onto the shoulder behind her.

"Darn." Jada figured it was a Good Samaritan stopping to help. Not what she wanted or needed. She quickly headed for her passenger door, then bestowed a little wave of appreciation and a gracious smile toward the stopping car and its driver. Within seconds she started her minivan and drove off.

She hadn't seen her Good Samaritan clearly, but after a second quick look through her rear-view mirror, something about the receding image of the little white car and its driver seemed vaguely familiar.

Overcome with an all-encompassing blind rage, Ally beat her fists on her steering wheel and cursed her bad-timing. *Seconds too late!*

"I could have killed her just now!" she screamed. "I could have killed her!"

Hot angry tears came in a flood.

* * * * *

"I don't care what that lady claimed," Melvin said, savoring his mug of steaming spiked coffee. "That wind on Michigan Avenue froze me to the bone."

The morning weather-woman on cable TV had forecasted thirty-five degrees as the daytime temperature with the possibility of snow flurries. The arctic freeze Melvin had experienced that morning had been far below that mark. Now, he and Madge Lee were cuddled together on a settee-lounger under a quilted throw in front of a substantial fireplace in their suite atop the Peninsula Hotel. Room service had just left, leaving them two silver pots; one filled with freshly brewed coffee and the other containing creamy rich hot chocolate. Keeping the liquid restoratives company on a huge oval silver platter were two snifters of warmed brandy, and an assortment of iced *petite fours*.

"It's the wind chill, I'm sure, my dear," Madge Lee responded with a pat on Melvin's naked knee underneath the throw.

"We are warming up nicely though, aren't we?" An appreciative smile found its way across Melvin's face while his eyes glimmered lazily in pleasant accompaniment.

It had been a productive morning for them despite the cold. A visit to the Cook County Department of records, Loyola University, and Michael Reese Hospital had provided the investigative duo with quite a bit of information. In fact, their morning had been so fruitful, they'd treated themselves to a stroll through the Art Institute and a light lunch in the Institute's Garden Restaurant.

As it turned out, Penny Berry had been on the mark with her suspicions. Nick indeed had a few more miles on him than he had claimed to his wife. With his social security number they had back-tracked to his university record and then to his birth certificate which showed him to be forty-six years old. But neither Melvin, nor Madge Lee would have guessed they would also find a name change, a previous wife, and a kid for goodness sakes.

"We should call Josia and Jada, don't you think?" Madge Lee snuggled in closer to Melvin.

He responded in kind.

"Plenty of time for that call later this afternoon, don't you think, Sweetheart?"

"Plenty of time."

Eventually Melvin and Madge Lee's call did get made; and after Jada hung up on her end, she sat for a long time on the side of her bed in number-two stroking Tasha on the head and staring out the window—but not really looking—thinking. Finally, all the "bits and pieces" were beginning to fit together and Jada thought she knew who had killed Nick and Hal.

Jada watched as Josia crumpled his hamburger trash into a ball. "I don't think I'm going to pull this one off," he grumped while shooting the ball at the wall above the garbage can—trying to make a basket. He missed and the bag rolled under the table. "Damn," he cursed. "Oh well, game over."

She had driven into town, again with Tasha, all the while undecided as what to do. She now had to make a decision. Take a chance and let him in on who she thought was a murderer—or pack up, leave town, and let him figure it out on his own. *What the heck,* she finally decided, *the jerk doesn't like me anyway.* So why should she care?

So Jada explained who she thought killed the two men.

When she finished, Josia sat quiet for several long moments, staring at her through narrowed eyes. The longer he stared, the more foolish she felt. *I should have known better.*

Finally, he looked away toward the front counter and said, "You know, my Mother was right about you."

Here it comes.

"You're one damn smart lady."

She smiled, then was immediately peeved at herself.

"It brings together a lot of info we've collected," he continued. "Maybe it's enough to take to the ADA, but I don't think so, and I don't want to blow this. It's just theory. We need some hard evidence."

Gabe appeared in the doorway. He was holding a five-by-seven manila mailer envelope. "Miss Marshall from the fire station just dropped this off for you, Chief." He handed the package to Josia.

As Jada watched, the world went into slow motion as the package traveled through time and space from Gabe to Josia. She thought that whatever it contained was information crucial to wrapping up these murders.

"They did one last sweep of Mr. Morton's burn-site before the garbage crew comes tomorrow to clean up," Gabe said. "And they found what's in there."

Josia opened the padded envelope and pulled out a set of keys. Jada got up and went over and stood behind him as he went through the set, dirty, sooty key by dirty, sooty key. Again, it was like time slowed, causing it to seem like he was taking forever to accomplish such a simple task. Finally, he came to the last key and they smiled in unison.

"You know what this is, don't you?" he asked, then answered himself. "A safe deposit key."

A safe deposit key with the name of the bank, "Red Rock First," conveniently chiseled on its face. Jada expelled a breath she'd been holding, and time snapped back to its regular pace.

Josia said, "Let's go." He jumped up from his chair, almost stepping on Tasha and knocking Jada back against the wall on his way out the door.

But as she hurried to follow him, in an abrupt change-of-mindset she inexplicably envisioned a forewarning—containing no detailed particulars or underlying logical understanding—but with the clear feel that she and Josia were both wrong. Indeed, there was a whisper in the back of her mind that hard evidence would play a very small part in apprehending Nick's killer. And just maybe, the role of that envelope would instead be a catalyst for other events to follow.

Red Rock First Bank was located on a side-street about two miles down the main drag with a posted speed limit of twenty-five mph and two stop signs to further slow travelers. Consequently, it turned out to be a ten minute excursion from Josia's office.

On their way there, to Jada's later shame and chagrin—she figured Josia's too—neither noticed the white Explorer following their patrol car, or the white Escort following the white Explorer, or the white Corolla following the white Escort. They again didn't notice the white-car brigade when they left the bank ten minutes later, a box full of Hal Morton's blackmail "goodies" in their hands.

Right before they pulled back into the Police Office parking lot, Josia's police-band crackled on. "Chief, it's Gabe." Jada couldn't miss the urgency in his voice.

"What's up?" Josia answered.

"I've got Mr. Elliott on his cell phone, says he's following the white Ford Explorer that took off from Irina's place Thursday—the one shooting off the gun around Mrs. Beaudine's cabin. He's got a plate number. I'm sending it into DMV while I'm talking to you. He needs assistance now."

Josia switched on the lights and sirens. "Got it. Where's the SOB in the Explorer now?"

"Mr. Elliott says he's right behind you."

Josia cursed vehemently, and Jada couldn't stop herself from turning around to look. What she saw was a white SUV careening to the right, heading down a side street they had just passed, wheels smoking. She couldn't see the driver, except it looked liked a man wearing sunglasses. But squinting, and leaning to the side, she did recognize Lyle Elliott's Escort in pursuit.

Jada had never had any desire to participate in a car chase. But here she was, doing just that. She couldn't stop her heart from racing or control her short and shallow breathing. *Fear.* She pushed it back. *Excitement.* She let it surface.

"Call the State Patrol immediately," Josia barked into the radio. "Get Beth in, and you get out here too. We're heading west on Bowman, it's gonna be gravel soon."

"Yes Sir." Click.

"You have on your seatbelt?" Josia demanded of Jada.

"You betcha." She was surprised she could talk. "Lay down, Tasha," she commanded to the backseat without looking.

By now they were going what felt to Jada like sixty miles an hour down a side street and coming to an intersection with a stop sign. Ahead of them a rolling cloud of impermeable dust moved down a gravel road on the other side of the intersection.

Josia seemed calm enough, and two cars coming into the intersection from both sides managed to stop in response to his siren. But as soon as they crossed the intersection and hit gravel, her body, despite the seat belt, bounced up and down in a washboard rhythm. Then the road narrowed to one stingy lane with rough desert terrain confining them on both sides. She found it awful.

"Damn dust," Josia swore. "Keep your window and vents closed."

She had already figured that one out. "I can't see anything."

"Damn." Josia slammed on the brakes sending them bounding over rolling dust mounds to their right but successfully missing Lyle's Escort sitting in the middle of the road, the car's left front end tilted, crippled.

Josia was finally able to stop after turning his cruiser around almost 180 degrees and bouncing off several Joshua trees. Consequently they were able to see a previously unseen white Corolla, now hastily turning around in the road by backing up, then quickly lurching forward. The mystery driver— Jada couldn't tell if it was a man or woman—successfully completed the turn and headed back from where they had all come, bumping and bouncing at some outrageous speed, sending even more dust into the maelstrom whirling around them.

Jada suddenly felt wretched and thought she was about to puke. She didn't.

"Who the hell was that?" Josia started to follow the Corolla, but his motor stalled. Once again he cursed.

"Whoever it was got out of here fast." Realization of what just had happened came to Jada. "What about Lyle?" She pushed against her car door with her shoulder—which she was surprised to find extremely sore.

Her door was jammed. "Lyle," she said again. Then, "Oh my, god. Tasha." Terrified, Jada dared to look in the backseat. But Tasha was clearly not a dumb dog and had hunkered down on the floor in the corner between the back and front seats. Jada sighed with relief.

"We've got to get to Elliott." Josia slammed his shoulder against his door with considerable force. The door finally gave and he was able to get out. Jada and Tasha were able to climb across the seat and get out after him.

Lyle was still sitting in the driver's seat and he didn't look good: there was a nasty gash across his forehead she knew would require stitches, there was a smaller cut over his right eye, and his lower lip was bleeding and already beginning to swell.

Bottom line, he looked like he'd just come out of a boxing ring—the loser. On the good side, he was alive and able to speak.

"Don't let him get away." His breaths were short and choppy. "I know it's Terrence Beaudine...I've been after him too long to let..." Then he passed out.

While Josia used his handheld to call for an ambulance, Jada wanted to grab Lyle's limp body and shake some sense into it. *Why wouldn't he let it go?* "Lyle Elliott is a stubborn man," she told the world, angry and frustrated. "And he's obsessed. My husband is dead. I don't know how many friggin' times I have to tell him that."

"Could be," Josia said clicking his phone off. "But I do want to know *who* was in that Explorer. And who was in that Corolla."

"Where does this road go?"

"To Highway Fourteen. The Explorer is long gone." Anger, the heavy-duty variety, flashed across Josia's face. "And so is the Corolla." He looked away, kicked the dirt vehemently, then walked toward the back of the car, his back to Jada.

As she waited for him to "get-it-together," she *tried*, quite unsuccessfully, to figure out who the heck was in the Explorer and who was in the Corolla. She knew neither were Terry, but then, who really *were* these people mudding the waters she and Josia had made crystal clear just a few short minutes ago back in his office?

* * * * *

It took awhile to get Lyle on his way and the cars sorted out, but then Jada insisted on going back to Josia's office and going through Hal Morton's papers. The results were frustrating, and much like Nick's funeral, anti-climatic. Hal had been neat and orderly in his blackmail record keeping. Handwritten notes on a prospective victim, signed no less, were stapled to supporting documents he had dug up. *What a slime bag.*

Copies of Penny and Timothy's birth certificates were there along with a quickie family tree. There wasn't a note on Hilary Giles, but there was a copy of a newspaper article about his son's accident. *Odd? Did Hal know who had killed Hilary's son?*

His notes describing Star and Irina's affairs with Nick were surprisingly detailed. *Had Hal hired a private detective, or slithered around in the dirt by himself?*

There was nothing on Leroy, Corissa, or Marie.

After several reads they both concluded there wasn't anything new to be found in his blackmail stash; and Jada, though she left her feelings unexpressed, was deeply disappointed and depressed. There was nothing remaining for her to do but go back to the Red Rock.

Indubitably Josia would be handing over the case tonight or tomorrow—better to ask for help versus having it taken away; and she figured she would be packing up and heading out Monday morning at the latest. Beliefs and hunches didn't count with ADAs.

Maybe Melvin will be back by then.

What made her heart and mind ache most was the knowledge Nick and Hal's killer would probably get away. Hopefully down the line Josia would call or mail her the outcome. She left him Solina's address and phone number in Atlanta.

One bit of good news did come in while they commiserated—Lyle was okay and had been released from the hospital.

Then with the sad acceptance it was all over, she finally left his office and headed back to the Red Rock. No white cars followed her.

After Jada and Tasha left his office, Josia stared for a long time out the front window at the spot where Jada's car had been parked.

Gabe wisely left his boss and friend to his own counsel. Josia knew this was a good thing, because he was not a happy man. After a few more minutes, he picked up the phone and dialed the Kern County Sheriff's Department. Time to officially turn this case over.

As soon as Jada and Tasha returned to the Red Rock, Manny and Irina tried to make her eat—meatloaf and twice-baked potatoes—drink some wine, and sit and talk with them. She obliged by filling them in on the safety deposit box keys and the car chase. But eat, she couldn't. She had nothing left. Not physically nor mentally, and the very thought of food made her nauseous. Tasha, on the other hand, devoured several hotdogs Manny steamed for her and tanked up on cool bottled water.

While Irina and Manny badgered Jada and pampered Tasha, Gabe called them with the news Lyle had stopped in at their office, looked awful but seemed fine, and was heading back to the Red Rock.

Finally, Irina and Manny ungraciously gave up on getting Jada to eat. However, Irina insisted on walking her back to number-two. Once back at her cabin Tasha headed for the center of the bed and zonked out in seconds, while Irina gave the room a once over.

Jada was as tired as Tasha, still a smile came as she watched Irina check under the bed and in the closet. "What are you doing?" she asked. "Pretending to be a bloodhound? That's what I have Tasha for."

"Tasha is laying down on the job." There was a forced lightness to her voice. "And things have gotten just too damn crazy around here."

Jada sat down on the bed. "You're right about the craziness, and I think Josia has given up because of that. And because he doesn't have any evidence. On anyone. And he doesn't want anyone else getting hurt." She paused for just second. "I'll probably be leaving tomorrow."

Irina turned to her, and seeing the look on her face, Jada added, "I'm sorry I haven't been able to help you."

"But it's got to be one of the class members we saw this morning at the funeral, remember. I know you can figure out who it is."

"Maybe." She was pretty darned sure she knew who had killed Nick and Hal, and the knowledge saddened her deeply. But she had no proof; and she could be wrong. For sure, she didn't want to hash it all out with Irina.

"I need to rest now," she said. "Can we talk later? Please."

Irina put her hands on her hips and gave Jada a put-out and put-upon look, but refrained from saying anything more. She did deliver an exaggerated sigh, then left without further word.

Jada flopped on the bed next to Tasha and expected to drop off immediately just like her pooch. To her surprise and consternation, sleep did not come. Instead, she lay there, stroking Tasha's head, reliving the events of the day—and of the we ek. The murders of Nick and Hal had taken her mind off her own goal and sidetracked her actions. Last week all she had wanted to do was escape. Her dream—to find a safe harbor with her sister-in-law. *Just a Sunday ago.*

If she had just stopped for gas in Tehachapi, or headed toward Mojave instead of Red Rock City. *If only.*

Jada also needed to accept and conquer the resurfacing emotions initiated with seeing Darcie Williams's face at the funeral—an all too vivid reminder of her own situation. Her own loss. A loss she had been dealing with for so long. A loss she thought had eased.

No, the unavoidable truth was she still missed Terry. Maybe in Atlanta—maybe then and there she could finally move on—with a little help from Solina and Neal. The thought of her sister-in-law and brother-in-law conjured up visions of Melvin and Madge Lee. What an unlikely paring. Maybe that was the *good* to come out of this misadventure. Happiness for Melvin?

Finally Jada dozed, fitfully and only for a few moments. For outside another golden sunset—this one laced with broad brush strokes of red—was developing and filling her window with color.

Real sleep insisted upon being elusive. She didn't want to go over to the café, however, and interact with Irina and Manny again. TV reception was atrocious as usual. Consequently, with no appealing alternative, Jada decided to go to the studio and throw a couple pots. Who knew when she would have another opportunity?

It would take her some time to get set up in Atlanta. Besides, throwing pots was something Jada liked to do, not something she had to accomplish. Or something someone else was forcing on her—like so much that had happened since Terry's death.

Yes, she would trudge out into the dark desert night to Nick's studio. *The center of it all.*

Tasha opted to remain in bed, on her back, legs in the air, most probably dreaming the dreams of the "Just."

The air was cold and dry—the sky was now turning from red to black—and some stars were beginning to make themselves visible. After Jada walked past the reach of cabin number-two's scanty porch light, she wished she had made Tasha get up and accompany her. Fortunately, the flashlight—courtesy of Irina—she had grabbed from her car lit her way further, and a nightlight above the studio rear door helped her navigate into the kiln room and drying area.

Quickly she found the light switch, and as she passed the ceramic projects wrapped in plastic, it came to her at last where Nick's murder weapon had been hidden, and she cartoonishly slapped her hand to her forehead. "Of course! How could I be such an idiot?" Unfortunately, when she attempted to find the sculpture in question, it was gone.

"I'm too late," she said to Nick's hushed ceramic lab. *Still no proof. Still just a theory.*

Thus, again empty-handed in the evidence department, she was left to existential sighs and light moans of disappointment as she found some clay and wedged a four or so pound hunk until its consistency felt smooth and pliable. The clay was cold, but bearable. And it was good therapy. The clay she tried this time, probably selected by Nick to meet dual needs of throwing and sculpting, was a high fire general purpose red stoneware which felt good to her touch.

Once her clay was prepared, Jada got together a slurry bucket and tools, chose a wheel and stool, and then, finally ready to throw, slammed her clay down on the wheel, smoothed the slightly asymmetrical mound, and started to center.

As she moved the clay through her hands she thought again of the parade of possible suspects she'd met over the last week. Darcie Williams, the now affluent grieving widow; nervous and excitable Corissa and her sweet doting husband

Ted; Corissa's fragile waif-like mother Ruth and her new husband Stan; the forever grieving Hilary and Emily Giles; the promiscuous Star Thomas and her egocentric husband Phillip; "Mr. Upright" Leroy Ames and his nondescript wife Cynthia; the smart and immensely likable Marie Shipley. People she barely knew, suspects all.

And of course there was Irina Hughes. Her new friend. One was a murderer.

Jada sensed a new presence before hearing or seeing her. "I thought you might still be here," she said into the open studio, not knowing exactly where her visitor was.

"I saw you come across from your cabin." She was standing behind Jada.

"You came to retrieve your gun."

"Yes." Corissa McNichols-James moved around to where Jada could see her, a .22 magnum pointed at Jada's head. "You knew it was me from the first, didn't you?" As before, Corissa's voice was volatile, her emotional state most probably in lockstep. However, this night, Jada heard and felt a tinge of cold determination underlaying Corissa's words.

Indeed, she turned her head and looked up into the young woman's eyes and saw a mouse backed into a corner. She spoke as calmly as her racing heart would allow—she knew this mouse would bite if provoked. "Well, you washing your hands bothered me the very first day. It seemed strange that you'd be washing your hands when it didn't look like you'd done anything yet with clay." Jada surreptitiously inhaled a calming breath. "Then in your interview with Chief Rhodes you confirmed you hadn't started anything, so why wash your hands?"

"Hah!" Corissa's laugh bordered on shrillness. "That's the flimsiest thing I've ever heard. That can't be all?" Carefully and slowly she took several more steps until she was directly facing Jada sitting at the pottery wheel. The gun was still pointed at her head. "My hands were just dirty, that's all. Without this gun you have nothing, *nothing.*"

Jada needed to keep her talking. She had not forgotten Nick's lifeless face, deformed and destroyed by a bullet. This child-woman was deadly.

"You're right, I really don't have anything to take to Chief Rhodes. You can keep the gun, I don't care. I'm no threat to you, my hunches don't count." As she talked, Jada continued to cone the clay up and down, smoothing it, aligning all the particles in the same direction. She couldn't seem to stop.

"No, you won't talk, not if you're dead. I sure don't want to kill you. Mother likes you, you know." Corissa seemed a little more in control of her emotions talking about her mother.

"I like your mother, too. It was because of her you killed Nick, right?" She was uneasy pushing Corissa to talk about the murders, but the alternative—until she came up with something better—was being shot.

Corissa's mental pendulum continued its swing and her demeanor became dead calm, her tone almost clinically factual. "I killed him because he was an evil bastard."

Jada went for the big one. "Nick was your mother's first husband, Billy McNichols, your father." She held her breath. "Right?"

Corissa spat out a harsh, "Huh. He thought he was being so cute, changing his name that way. 'Billy' to 'Williams', and 'McNichols' to 'Nick.' He even tried to make love to me you know?"

Jada held her tongue.

"If I hadn't mentioned my mother's name, we would have never known. You should have seen his face when he realized I was the daughter he deserted. I couldn't believe it either. My own father. And after what he had done to my mother and me." Corissa's eyes, so deceptively housed in her cherubic countenance, flashed hatred. "You know he stole almost a million dollars from the company he worked for? Left my mother with the shame of it." Her mental pendulum swung. *Whoosh.* "I hated him all those years," she almost screamed the words.

"And after you shot him?"

"I slammed his head down into that precious pot of his. I wish I could have done more."

Jada wasn't sure if she had a better chance of escape with Corissa in hysterics or Corissa in control of her faculties; so she waited, continuing to fiddle with her clay and trying to figure out how to overpower her without either of them getting hurt. "Why did you kill Hal?" she asked as calmly and non-judgmentally as her emotional level permitted.

"I didn't kill Hal. I was at the airport picking up Ted, remember?"

Jada didn't challenge her, though she knew Corissa could have easily killed Hal and then gone to the airport. "Why did you put the note on my pillow? I was leaving anyway."

"What note?"

"You torched Hal's house?"

"Had to be sure."

"And the Berrys?"

"They didn't die, now did they?"

"But you tried to kill them. Was it for their diaries?"

"Of course. The nosey busy-bodies. God I hated those two gossipy idiots. Always dressing alike. But I didn't know what they had seen or heard. Once I found out who Nick really was, I made an awful scene out back." She actually smiled, as if this memory was a pleasant interlude. "That was the day before I killed him." Then, quite easily—*whoosh*—Corissa's mental pendulum swung again. She smiled and asked, "For awhile did you think mother had killed him?"

"Yes."

"Mother wouldn't hurt a fly. She never even talked bad about him all those years she had to raise me on her own." In an instant, her voice had turned mean.

Jada wondered why she hadn't seen the bitterness underpinning Corissa's instability from the very start. It was so palpable now.

"*If* I'd just had a few of the advantages," Corissa continued, bitterness and regret saturating her words. "I could have been someone, done something. Instead—"

"Your life isn't terrible, you can't think that. I met your husband, Ted. He's such a nice…" Corissa wasn't listening, only telling.

"Mother had to grow vegetables instead of going to the grocery store like everyone else. She bought my clothes at the Salvation Army and Goodwill." Her gun never wavered, but she had clearly moved to the edge of a mental precipice. "Now I'm a wife to a mediocre man, living in a dust bowl trying to be a town. No future, not even a past I'd want to tell anyone about. I could have been somebody." For a second, and only for a second she waved the gun around dramatically. "An actress, a singer, a writer, even a physician or an engineer. *If* we'd only had the money. If he hadn't deserted us. No. I'm glad I did it. He deserved to die."

Think, Jada. Think. And keep her talking. "Just look at your pottery and sculptures. They're coming along so nicely. You should be proud of that."

"Do you know he said my sculpture heads stunk? Oh yeah, my heads stunk! He didn't think much of my pots either. Didn't keep him from wanting to get in my pants though."

Jada couldn't think of anything to do but continue to listen, wait, and pray that somehow an opportunity would present itself. She feared the worst though. She had no weapon, while the gun in Corissa's hand, admittedly only a .22, was becoming larger and uglier as the seconds ticked by.

Corissa and Jada both heard it at the same time, the bark of a dog coming closer, fast. For a second Corissa was distracted, distracted enough to look away from Jada toward the door and the sound of barking and a woman's voice calling Jada's name. Jada took the opportunity to push hard with both hands on the base of her mound of clay while simultaneously stomping hard on the peddle of her wheel—sending the wheel-head revolving in high gear and her mound of clay flying off.

The clay didn't hit Corissa, couldn't have actually, but it caused her to duck in ignorance and turn away as she got off her shot—which fortunately missed Jada, but unfortunately grazed Irina's left arm as she rushed in. Nonetheless, in the confusion, Irina grabbed Corissa by the arm with her injured hand, seemingly mindless of her own fresh gunshot wound. And with her still functioning right hand and arm, started pounding on Corissa.

Under her attack Corissa's gun went flying, eventually hitting the floor and sliding underneath a back table.

For her part, Tasha took a broad four-legged stance and barked her head off while Irina, with only one serviceable arm, continued swinging and punching at the young woman. Irina was losing. But as Jada was collecting her wits enough to rush over and help—from the doorway, gun pointed—Josia Rhodes forcefully shouted, "FREEZE, Mrs. James! I don't want to shoot you. Hands up. NOW!"

Only a few seconds passed before Jada and Irina stepped back, and Corissa collapsed to the floor, weeping like an injured child.

Jada spent the rest of Saturday night until the wee hours of Sunday morning waiting at the hospital for Irina to be released. Her hero Tasha spent the night snoozing in the back of her minivan.

Irina would be alright, and so would Corissa. In fact, the doctors said Irina could go, but admissions had yet to deliver their "release" stamp of approval. So, the two women sat in the same room they had waited in to hear about Penny and Timothy a few days earlier—again, waiting. Probably in the same chairs.

Irina's left arm was in a fancy blue sling and several pharmacy bags full of heavy-duty painkillers sat on her lap. For all her toughness, Irina turned out to be a sissy when pain was involved. "Damn hospitals," she cursed. "The only thing they really care about is getting their hundred-dollar aspirin fees." Her initial shot of pain killing drugs had kicked into effect and she was consequently returning to form. "What the—" she caught herself before uttering whatever profanity was in line to pop out, "heck is taking them so long?"

"I don't think getting upset will help matters." Jada gave Irina's hand an encouraging squeeze. *Where the heck did Josia go?*

Earlier, Irina had immediately called Josia when she had heard Tasha barking her head off in cabin number-two. It had then taken Irina a few more seconds to figure out where Jada was, then run out to the studio. Josia had arrived at the Red Rock within minutes of her call, albeit out of uniform, looking bedraggled, put upon, and genuinely apprehensive.

Fortuitously, he always carried his firearm and had been already heading to the Red Rock to talk to Irina. His official reason why—to warn her. He would be handing the case over in the morning and she would be coming under closer scrutiny than he had given her.

Then when it was all over, after the medics left with Irina and Corissa, everyone at the Red Rock, including Mrs. Shoecraft, had wanted to load into the various cars languishing around the Red Rock and come to the hospital. Josia, though, had requested—insisted actually—they could not help, and should remain at the Red Rock. There had been a lot of grumbling, but after he had promised to call every half-hour everyone had finally trudged off to his or her respective cabins. All but Lyle Elliott. In the end, Jada, Lyle and Josia had followed the ambulance to the hospital in Josia's cruiser.

After *one* hour of waiting, a then nearly catatonic Corissa had been released into the custody of the Kern County Sheriff. The pendulum of her mind had come to a dead standstill. Along with Corissa went her .22 for analysis and the task of calling her mother Ruth and her husband, Ted. Josia had promised to show up in Bakersfield for full statements with Jada and Irina in tow as soon as the hospital gave the OK.

After *two* hours of waiting, Josia and Lyle declared they were going outside for a smoke. Since Jada had never seen either of them smoke, she didn't know what the hell they were doing.

After *three* hours of waiting, Irina had finally appeared, subdued, arm in a sling, definitely alive and well, but surprisingly reluctant to discuss what had happened.

Now, *four* hours later and well into a new day, Irina was able and willing to give the hospital hell. Jada considered that a good sign. "If you're so psychic, how come you didn't know she was going to shoot you?" Jada joked.

"I did know, I just wasn't fast enough. Just because I'm psychic doesn't mean I'm quick." Then with a little smile, Irina added, "Honestly though, I didn't rush out there just because I had a premonition. It was because Tasha was barking. She knew you were in trouble."

"I should have been better prepared." In fact, she couldn't believe how utterly stupid she had been. She figured Corissa had killed Nick and Hal, and near the end, she had even figured out where the murder weapon was—hidden in Corissa's medusa head sculpture. So she should have guessed the screwed-up Corissa might still come and try to kill her. "God," she paused for a second to make sure she had her emotions in tight control before finishing with, "I owe you, Tasha, and Josia my life. Thank you."

Irina looked away and responded softly, "You're welcome."

The returning Josia cleared his throat from the doorway. "Ready to go? We've got an hour's drive ahead of us and at least a couple hours of questioning."

"Do I have to go?" Lyle asked from somewhere in the hall behind Josia. His disembodied voice sounded disjointed and oddly despondent to Jada's weary ear.

"Yes."

Jada asked, "Where have you guys been?"

"Drinking," Josia answered quickly.

Too quick, but Jada was much too tired to push it. Heck, maybe they *were* drinking, she could use one herself. But where did they find booze at this time of the morning?

Josia never told anyone the main reason he had been heading to the Red Rock Inn & Café that night. He had had a "feeling." God forbid it ever got out to his mother or Irina that Josia Rhodes had acted on a premonition.

He would tell Jada about the second accident later when she could handle it—had no choice. Gabe had called with the information about the crash and urged he and Lyle, who was still reeling from his own smash-up barely half-an-hour earlier, to come quickly. They had gone immediately.

A CHP officer and the medics were already there when they arrived. It was a one-car rollover. Terrence Beaudine's white Explorer rested precariously, upside-down and mangled, in the ditch near the end of Wild Wash Road.

It was not a pretty accident sight, even for an experienced trooper like Josia. The gas tank had exploded, demolishing most of the Explorer and Terrence. His ID had miraculously survived.

Josia had to admit that Lyle, the stubborn SOB, had been right in believing Beaudine had faked his own death in the icy waters of the San Juans. But not this time. *No doubt this time.* They had his body—dead on the scene.

Josia and Lyle had readily agreed, they wouldn't tell Jada where they had been and what they had seen tonight until after the paperwork in Bakersfield. And when the time came, Josia would do the telling.

Lyle Elliott's email to his Home Office
Sunday—January 12—1 AM

Well Ham, looks like we're going to have to pay after all.

I can tell you for sure that Terrence Beaudine is now dead and I don't see any way of getting out of paying out to the widow. It's a sorry situation.

I was wrong about the Beaudine woman, though. Doesn't seem she was involved. And if she was, I sure can't prove anything now with Terrence dead. The stupid idiot rolled his car. All that scheming to appear dead, then die anyway in an avoidable car accident.

Dumb.

Also turns out Corissa McNichols-James, that's the squirrelly young woman I told you about, killed Williams and Morton. She also tried to asphyxiate this ditsy couple. I'll give you all the details when I call you tomorrow.

Planning on hanging around to make sure everything checks out on Terrence and then I'll head on back to Seattle. There are a couple things that are still bothering me.

After finishing his email and sending it off with a sigh, Lyle turned off his computer, and stood, causing pain in his back and both knees; then stretched his lanky frame, causing even more pain.

He knew most of his current discomfort was from the car crash out off Bowman Road. It had obviously taken a heavier toll on his body than his ego permitted him to admit. He certainly could have stayed in the hospital, but that would have been another affront to his dignity. He was also aware that besides being banged up a bit and looking like hell with the stitches and bandages, he was extremely weary.

And at the same time, he didn't feel anything emotionally. He knew he should. Relief, anger, resentment? *Something.* Today was the culmination of a long hard job. Indeed, he had been following Terrence Beaudine for over a year. He should feel some sort of emotion. *Just too darned tired,* he guessed. *My mind must not be able to grasp it's over.*

He walked over to his Best Western room's picture window, pulled back its nondescript floor to ceiling drape, and looked out into the lonely blackness surrounding the hotel. Besides his own reflection, haggard and drooped, he could see a light mist floating on the night air. Or was it fog? Lyle wasn't sure what to call the desert haze creeping in.

A car pulled into the motel's parking lot, its headlights fuzzy and haloed, its color and make unidentifiable in the hazy night enveloping the motel. *Was that the same white Ford he'd seen pulling in earlier? Nah. Couldn't be. And if it was, so what?* He let the heavy drape fall back into place.

He wondered what Jada was doing. Then unbidden, and surprising in its intensity and disconcerting implications, Lyle was momentarily overtaken by an emotion he had never experienced in his whole life, nor could now put a name to.

Allison King, once finally cocooned back in her room at the Best Western, buried her head in her pillow and cried with uncontrollable abandonment. She didn't care if her mascara ran, if her blood red lipstick smeared, if her sexy silk blouse wrinkled. None of it mattered any longer.

If she had only known he was still alive...*if* she had only known. To grieve for Terry a second time was almost unbearable.

And it was all the Beaudine witch's fault.

Chapter Nine

Sunday for Real

Back from Bakersfield and after a couple hours of sleep, Sunday started again for Jada, this time with a crimson sunrise she felt she could finally really appreciate. For at last, it was all over.

She figured there would be plenty of time to catch up on her sleep in Atlanta; now was the time to get going. Quickly before she could really think about it. So after an early breakfast at the Red Rock Café—she would miss Manny quite a bit—Jada went back to her room and started getting her few things together.

But before she could get out of number-two and back on the road, Josia knocked on her door.

Once inside, and before Jada could think about or comprehend the significance of his uncharacteristically subdued manner and tone of voice, he informed Jada that Terrence had indeed been alive. But he was now actually dead—for real.

For Jada, from that unspeakable and wrenching moment, the passage of time became a horrid foggy blur as she tried to take it all in. And cope. It became a day of reverberating shock, of duties painfully accomplished, of conversations poorly executed and half remembered, of blurry car rides back and forth from the Red Rock Inn into town, of meals eaten only at the insistence of others—and the ache all day of Terry on her mind.

The worst of course was identifying Terry's body. The burns were so severe. Melvin and Madge Lee were on their way back, but too late for him to assist with the task at hand. It was not easy. And Jada knew it would be even harder for Melvin. In some screwy ironic sense, and somewhere deep in the recesses of her now wobbly mind, Jada was glad she was available to identify Terry. Not Melvin.

The jewelry, the ID, the notebook—all Terry's. And, what was left of his hair.

Of course there would be tests made by the ME, maybe even DNA comparisons if she might still have something back in Seattle. If not DNA, dental records for sure.

Irina, her arm still in bandages and a sling, but doing fine, comforted Jada as best she could. Manny tried pumping her up with food and drink. Even Lyle made a point to offer his condolences. He had made it clear several times that no matter how much he had wanted to catch Terrence, he had not wished him an end like this.

Eventually, evening came, and everyone finally left her alone, back to their own lives and immediate responsibilities. And Jada found herself and Tasha again sitting on number-two's makeshift patio. Jada in the peeling white wicker armchair, and Tasha stretched out lazily on a grass mat next to her. Together they watched the western sky above the Sierras fade to black another night.

Her body was spent, her thoughts haphazard, sad, weary, even optimistic—uncontrolled. She had run from Seattle to escape her past, her grief, herself. She had so desperately needed to find a place where she belonged. On the way, she had hit a bump in the road called the Red Rock Inn & Café. More like a mountain than a bump, but she felt she had almost made it to the top.

Being part of solving Nick Williams's and Hal Morton's murders had felt so sweet—even though she hated that poor Corissa had been the murderer. Then Josia had told her about Terry.

Now, being able to accept the truth that Terry had been alive all this time was a horrendous emotional boulder she would have to climb over and get past. It would not be easy. In fact, she felt like crap and barely able to cope.

So, once again, Jada fled to throwing pots in Nick's lab as therapy to manage her emotions. Somehow, some way, that singular ceramic island Nick had created in the Mojave, had become for Jada not only a refuge of sorts, but also a touchstone for her sanity. Her Mojave misadventure had started there—much had played out and been revealed there—and her desert sojourn was now ending there. A final session of restorative throwing.

Indeed, Jada almost felt like the lab was calling her to say good-bye. Were Nick's or Terry's ghosts there, beckoning her? She doubted that and shook her head at such foolishness.

"Too long around Irina," she mused.

Though, in the condition her mind was, Jada felt a little apprehensive about trudging out to the lab in the dark. And as usual, Tasha opted to snooze it out in the middle of the bed. Jada almost insisted she wake up and accompany her, but her dog looked so cute, so comfortable—she didn't have the heart to disturb her, and decided once again to "let her sleeping dog lie."

* * * * *

From her entry days into the world of ceramics, Jada became immediately enamored with pitchers and bottles—seeing, throwing, and touching them. For her, shape and form were primary. Not that glazes weren't important, but to her mind the glaze conceptually came after the form, and its function was to complement and enhance, not overwhelm. She decided to try a pitcher; she didn't feel strong enough again in her throwing to pull-in the neck of a bottle. A pitcher would be more forgiving.

Nick's ceramic lab—she would always think of it as his—was silent. Peaceful. She left the lights low, only flipping the switch for the hanging fixture over her wheel. Maybe here her mind would be able to absorb and make sense of today's happenings in dimmed quiet. She had just centered and started to pull a cylinder when she heard a voice from her side.

"Well, Jada Beaudine, you're certainly a hard woman to kill."

What! She hadn't heard a warning sound before the voice. Nothing. Jada looked up from the wheel directly into the muzzle of yet another gun. This time a 9mm revolver held by her very much alive husband, Terrence Beaudine.

She had never fainted in her life, but she came immeasurably close that second when she saw his face. The same dark eyes she had looked into for so many years twinkling mischievously. That same trademark smile of his, a tad off center, crocked, and seductively teasing. Unrestrained and colliding emotions instantaneously flooded her. Jada wanted to jump up and smother him in hugs, she wanted to kick him in the balls, she wanted to scream, she wanted to cry.

In the end, she just stared at the gun's muzzle and Terry's face—paralyzed. What she was seeing and hearing was incomprehensible. "Terry?"

"This isn't how I planned it, you know," he said calmly with no hint of awkwardness or chagrin. In fact, the timbre of his voice was still as smooth and melodious as the first day she'd met him. His eyes though, appeared darker, more intense than she remembered; and psychologically, the gun made him seem taller and bigger.

She heard herself inanely stammer, "You're alive." And within milliseconds of speaking those words, a rushing stream of memories flooded back to her—good and bad. Accompanying tears, no longer controllable, flooded her eyes.

"You state the obvious, my dear," he said before allowing her a twitch of a bemused smile. "No. Don't move."

My god. Jada's mind wanted to comprehend. *He's serious, deadly serious.* My husband is trying to kill me!? She swiped her eyes with the back of her hand. "Terry," she managed, "I… don't understand. Why? What's happening?" She sounded like a jabbering idiot. She felt like a fool.

He laughed lightly and the gun barrel vibrated slightly. "I guess I do owe you an explanation. You won't understand, of course. You never did understand about my ambition, about wanting more, about control." His eyes seemed to morph darker, harder. "Greed is a dirty word to you, isn't it?"

And that's when she heard it for the first time, and saw it in his eyes. Bitterness, hate. *Had it been there before and I just hadn't noticed?*

"But you know, I was ambitious enough for the both of us. *If* only…"

"*If* only what?" Jada heard herself demand even though she was barely cognizant her lips were moving, or that her voice was audible.

"*If* only you weren't such a…goody-goody. You know what it was like living with you?" His voice, embittered and mean, lashed out at her. "You were never there to support me in the ways a man needs if he's going to be a success, now were you? No, 'do-it-the-right-way Jada,' content to just sit out there in Carnation, let the rest of the world go by. Sure you had money

311

already, but what about me? Huh, what about me?" he spat the last sentence out. "And all those years, wasted. I could have done so much if you'd helped just a little. Instead I had to turn to outsiders for help. They helped me alright. I even had to turn to another woman."

Nausea, violent and uncontrolled, swept over her. Jada had no idea what to say, what to do—her mind was numbed by incredulity. This couldn't possibly be the same man she had spent fifteen years of her life with, the same man she had hitched up her fortune with, made love to, built a home with, laughed and cried with.

"Nothing to say, huh?" He inched a bit to her left. "I know you're dying to know who she was, aren't you?" Then he laughed loudly and with pleasure. "You didn't know, did you? Allison King." He whispered the name.

But Jada heard it quite clearly.

"You remember her, don't you? Stupid bitch, but she served her purpose."

An affair. This is a nightmare. He's moving to get a better angle on my head. Jada doubted Tasha would be coming to her rescue this time. No, she was on her own.

Now a sneer accompanied his anger. "Tell me, did you think in your wildest dreams I was still alive? Did you?" He wagged the gun in her face for emphasis. "I bet you actually thought I was dead."

Jada thought she heard door hinges squeak. But he didn't seem to have heard anything. No doubt wishful thinking on her part, she knew her mind was stumbling. She managed to say, "You were here that afternoon in the studio, right after Nick was killed, weren't you? You called my name."

"Ah." He smiled, now looking quite pleased with himself—his expression saying this was turning out more like he had envisioned. "Now you're starting to think. More like the Jada I know, the Jada who always had to make sense out of everything, the always-logical Mrs. Jada Beaudine. Making sense out of this, huh? Are you?" His voice had gone past mean, to nasty.

Evil. The "evil" Josia had talked about, and she had felt.

"I was going to try to reason with you then, but that damn Hughes woman came ploughing out here and I had to leave. Then…well, then things changed."

That warning note on my pillow was to try to get me back on the road. "You tried to contact me a couple times at the cabin. Was it you shooting off the gun?"

"Actually I wasn't trying to hurt anyone, not then. Just figured the gun would slow the idiots down." He scoffed harshly. "There was still a chance to convince you then. If that asshole insurance prick hadn't gotten in the way." Terry took a step closer to her, the muzzle of his 9mm still demanding her attention. "I do believe I'm going to have to take care of him before this is all over. He just won't leave it. Stupid ass."

How had I ever loved this man? Jada thought she heard a sound again. Someone breathing? No, a true rescuer would have already put a stop to this insanity.

"Why, Terry? Why?" Jada could barely recognize this person as her husband. *Everything Lyle had said was true. What a fool I've been, what a fool.*

"For money, of course. You only knew about my legit debts. Bankruptcy would have fixed that. Gambling debts, now those don't go away so easy."

"You *did* fake your death." *And left me holding the bag.* "I'd collect your insurance then you'd get the money from me and then kill me?"

"No, no…not at all, not at first. It was for the two of us I did it. We'd take the money, disappear to some island somewhere where they didn't care who we were. Meet some people, have some parties, the high-life at last." He smiled, evidently reliving for a second the old dream. "We could have had that before, but I let you have your way. This time, it would be *my way*. I just knew I could talk you into it after I reappeared." His smile disappeared as quickly as it had come. "Of course I'd have to get rid of Allison. She's a determined little firecracker, and she'd find us, I know. She was great in the sack, but not the kind of woman you want to spend the rest of your life with, if you know what I mean." Terry looked to Jada and waited a couple seconds as if he actually expected her to understand. "It would have worked, too, *if* only Lyle Elliott had left it alone. No. He just wouldn't drop it."

"And if I hadn't agreed with your plan when you miraculously returned from the dead?"

Terry made a noncommittal guttural sound, tilted his head the slightest bit, and shrugged philosophically. "Academic now, isn't it?"

She still couldn't emotionally comprehend that Terry was behind all this, but mentally, puzzle pieces were coming together. "So when your creditors," *mobsters no doubt*, "realized what was up—"

"They were going to kill me, at first. Fortunately, we were able to work out a deal."

Oh my God.

"They had a little matter they wanted me to take care of."

"The body in the car," she whispered.

"On the mark as usual. You haven't lost it." He sighed heavily and said the name, "Tommy Max."

A memory of the APB poster for Thomas Max on the police station "Wanted" board flashed across her consciousness. *Evidently you didn't rob mobsters and get away with it.* The police were looking for a newly deceased man. Jada felt her connection to reality slipping.

"Now my dear, I'm sorry, but if you think you'll wear me out by talking…"

She watched as he firmed-up his stance and leveled his pistol. She said more to herself than Terry, "You killed, Hal, too, didn't you?" *And I blamed Corissa.*

"He saw me lurking around the studio and tried to blackmail me. I figure he must have come back looking for something. He didn't even know who I was, but figured I had something to do with Williams's death." Terry rolled his eyes in disbelief. "Now I think he was looking for the murder weapon. Stupid fool. And slimy. Won't be much missed, I don't think." He smiled remembering. "He came back later and so did I." He took the time for a short derisive laugh. "See that bag?" With another slight tilt of the head Terry indicated an overnighter in the shadows by the front door—then waited for Jada to follow his instruction—never taking his eyes off her. "It's full of money, Jada. Three-quarters of a million, give or take. They pay well for 'clean up' jobs, even when you owe. With the insurance money it could have been almost two mil. We could have shared, but now it's too late for you." He cleared his throat and again stiffened his arm. "Time's up."

Jada felt herself rise up from behind the wheel—jump actually—and propel her entire body through a dreamlike tunnel of space and time. Directly towards Terry. Something within had snapped. And though Jada knew her mind was tricking her into believing she could stop him, her entire body was nonetheless taut with resolve—her hands ready, willing, and seemingly capable of strangling the *man* she had once so loved.

In that nanosecond of insanity; anger, disgust, incredulity, egoism, mental fatigue—all that and more, propelled Jada into action. So what if he was pointing a gun point-blank at her head? She still had enough remaining mental clarity and intrinsic self-respect not to be Terry Beaudine's willing victim.

I will not go easy into that "good night."

But before she could actually reach Terry, Jada heard his pistol cock, saw the short quick flash from the muzzle of his gun, heard it fire—*but then*—within another ethereal wisp of slow-motion time, she next saw an exaggerated expression of disbelief and horror overtake his face—then become fixed as if in stone. A face that now included a one-half-inch hole in its forehead.

Terry fell straight backward to the floor with a sickening thud, his gun leaving his hand and careening away from her, somewhere into the depths of the dim ceramic lab. And she landed on her knees on hard concrete floor. Barely a foot in front of him. Pain shot like a spear through her groin, and instinctively, even though red clay caked her hands, Jada grabbed for her face, then her heart. *I'm not hit?*

Indeed, from the shadows of the back doorway, and before he had gotten his own shot off, Allison King had shot Terrence Beaudine point blank in the forehead with her fancy .44 Smith & Wesson. The man who wouldn't seem to die had finally moved on.

Allison, without second thought, next turned her body and gun toward Jada.

Jada's mind and body moved into shock, no longer able to function.

"At last," Ally hissed, straightened her arm, and prepared to kill again. "The pleasure of killing you is all mine."

But in one fluid act, Lyle charged into the studio from Ally's rear, carrying a plaster throwing bat from the back storage room and hit her squarely on the back of her head. The blow sent Ally smashing to the floor with another sickening thud; and her gun, like Terry's, skidded across the floor—almost to the exact spot Corissa's .22 had come to rest just one night earlier.

*   *   *   *   *

316

Lyle did not want to further beat up on a woman, or worse, be forced to kill her, which he would do to save Jada. He had his .38 Smith & Wesson with him in his inside jacket pocket. However, using it was the last thing he wanted to do.

What he did want to do, needed to do, was get Jada, Terry's gun, along with the gun belonging to the crazy woman, *and himself*, as far away from the studio as possible. *Fast.*

He grabbed Jada by the arm. "Come on, we've got to get out of here and call the police." He yanked her up from the floor—she was surprisingly light—then grabbed Ally's gun from the floor and stuffed it in his right front jacket pocket. He couldn't see Terry's 9mm. He would have to leave it.

"Ouch," Jada cried out.

"Sorry," he mumbled while pulling her toward the back door. "I don't know how long she'll be out." He shook Jada like a rag-doll. "For goodness sake, that woman just killed Terrence and was about to kill you. You've got to get out of here!"

Jada was clearly in limbo-shock, but she stumbled after him as he almost dragged her to the backdoor. On the way, he saw Terry's gun under a stool, scooped it up, and stuffed it in his left jacket pocket.

He knew his prints would be on both their guns, but it couldn't be helped. And comically, if humor could be found in such a circumstance, he felt like an old-west gunslinger. *Three guns, for Christ's sake.* But again, it couldn't be helped; he had to get those weapons out of that crazy woman's reach. He surmised she was connected to Terrence in a deep emotional way, but in all his year-long investigating, he had never crossed paths with her until Red Rock City. *I'm slipping.*

And seeing Terrence in the flesh for those few seconds had been such a surprise. Of course he'd looked at his picture many times. But the man in person was so nondescript-looking, so plain. Mediocre.

What had these two women seen in him? Lyle allowed himself a second to muse that his mother had been right about one thing at least. Love was not comprehensible.

Not until cold and dry desert-night-air slapped Jada in the face did she again start to remember the fact her Terry had tried to kill her—was now dead—killed by some crazy neighbor-woman she could barely remember. Who had in turn tried to kill her.

It was too much to wrap her mind around.

Fortunately Lyle didn't let go of her arm, he just kept pulling her forward into the darkness. Finally, somewhere out in the desert in back of the lab, she felt him release his vice-grip as he dropped to the ground on his butt, panting heavily.

Her arm and legs throbbed, and her head pounded with pain. She could taste and feel baby dust-devils of sand dancing in the blankness surrounding them. And it was cold. Dark. Like that first evening, so few days ago, when she needed a place to stay. Just for the night.

On the ground, his hands fumbling and shaking, Lyle managed to unclip a cell phone from his belt and breathlessly call Josia. She heard him, but wasn't able to listen. His words were beyond her comprehension. She dropped to the ground next to him, her body and mental capacities exhausted. And her shoulder hurt like hell.

I'll be alright, I'll be alright. Jada searched for a mantra to keep her sane as she tried to force her mind to come around, to comprehend. But stray images and bits of words and sentences were ricocheting and colliding around in her brain. She felt like she was crying, sobbing in fact, but in reality she wasn't. Just shaking.

Lyle put his arm around her.

She might have heard the squeal of car wheels in the distance. She did hear the shot. Then the squeal of tires again. Lastly, she heard Tasha barking, then Linda Lowry's voice, then Manny's, then others from the Red Rock—all heading their way.

Chapter Ten

Down the road a bit

Ally liked the silver blue Chrysler minivan she had purchased off the used car lot on the outskirts of Tucson. Nice leather seats and all the extras.

She also liked the black Altima she traded the minivan in for in Atlanta. Even nicer.

No more low-end white compact-cars for her.

She thought maybe she would next head south around the coast of Florida, or maybe head north up the Atlantic seaboard? She had the money to do whatever she wanted, and Ally was beginning to enjoy cruising the good-ole US-of-A. And it would take time before the stupid cops would stop looking for her. Best to keep moving for awhile.

Indeed, it would also take a big walloping piece of time for her to forgive herself for believing Terry had actually loved her. *Bastard.*

Ally patted the attaché case on the seat next to her and took consolation in the one-hundred dollar bills bulging its sides. Even better than a gun as a traveling companion.

Maybe she would even get a motor-home.

Okay, she knew she'd been stopped from killing the evil Beaudine woman, but after a few days and some thought, even she had finally realized what a liar Terry had been—to both of them. *Real bastard, now wasn't he?*

Her father, rest his soul, would forgive her for not killing the woman. And her mother, again rest her soul, would applaud her for smiting Terry Beaudine to hell. Several escaping tears surprised her; but she was driving, no time for such nonsense.

Ally was thoroughly glad she'd killed him. It was odd though, how her burning desire for Terry had turned to hatred. And murder. In a matter of minutes. *Him saying she wasn't the kind of woman to spend the rest of his life with—that had done it. If he* just hadn't said that. Life was funny sometimes, now wasn't it?

At least she was the one who had ended up with the money.

She pulled down her visor and looked into its fancy lighted makeup mirror, pursed her lips, and re-appraised what she considered her perky and pouty little features. A new shade of lipstick might be in order, and maybe a dark sultry chestnut color hair job?

Jada Beaudine certainly could also do with a makeover. Big time. Of course with asymmetrical features like hers, boyish almost, she thought there wasn't a lot that could be done. And that funny short red hair—looked to Ally like peach fuzz.

She flipped the visor back up and fondly contemplated her new makeover. A road-sign appeared on the side of the road: "Jacksonville 30 miles." It was a glorious southern Spring morning and life was to be enjoyed. Now wasn't it?

She patted the attaché case again. It was crammed full of money, Terry's hard earned blood money just waiting to be spent.

Finally, the days were noticeably longer, plenty of evening available for a grand sunset featuring Sierra foothills capped with brilliant streaks of burnished red and deep tangerine, with the in-betweens and edges lightly washed with powder blue and pink. Jada thought she had never seen anything like it before—while simultaneously knowing she had. *My first evening in the Mojave.*

Chairs had been dragged over for the occasion from all the Red Rock Inn and Café cabin patios, and like their occupants, were an eclectic mix of styles.

To Jada's left sat Irina—the one who had embroiled her in all of this—then the introverted young Linda, and next to her Miss Shoecraft. To Jada's right sat Josia, then Lyle, then Manny, and finally Madge Lee and Melvin—holding hands between the chairs and making goo-goo-eyes at each other. All sitting in a ragged semicircle facing the West, watching the sun depart for the day.

Tasha was stretched out comfortably at Jada's feet, and taking her cue from the humans, looking expectantly toward the horizon.

It was a party of sorts. This was Jada's first night back.

Irina and Manny had brought along several bottles of chilled vino, cheese, sliced salami, crackers, olives, pickles, even deviled eggs, and set them up on a camp table to their rear.

She knew that even though she'd been allowed to return from Crestwood, she was not yet well—still trying to re-grasp and regroup, and succeeding, she hoped. Slowly.

Over her winter days at Crestwood, Josia, Lyle, Marie, Madge Lee, and Melvin, all had come calling, making the appropriate noises about what a shock she had experienced— barely masking their fear and apprehension regarding her mental well-being. Marie had stayed the longest on her visits, sometimes just holding Jada's hand, not bothering with words.

And Melvin, she knew, was also still in shock, though Jada was sure Madge Lee was right there with him, comforting and consoling. Solina, Neal, and the children had come out from Georgia—for Terry needed to be finally buried. He was cremated actually, and Solina took the ashes back to Georgia.

Irina had said straight out on her first visit to see Jada at Crestwood, "You thought your husband was dead, then he re-appears, then he evidently dies again, then he returns-from-the-dead and tries to kill you. *Then* his ex-lover kills him and tries to kill you. Who wouldn't go bonkers?"

Bonkers indeed.

Manny and Mrs. Chacon with Tasha in tow, had also visited several times, and brought food along with their comforting words.

"The red's getting even deeper over there." Irina pointed to the Southwest. "See? It's gonna end up one of those deep bright red ones tonight. I just know it."

Jada said, "There was a moment there when I didn't think I'd be here to see another one of these."

"More than *one* moment, if you remember," Irina chided.

Josia said, "Thinking you're gonna die, seeing your own mortality up close and personal-like, well that changes a man." He let out a small self-deprecating chuckle. "Or a woman. Guess I should start using 'person' more often."

Jada noticed an uncharacteristically chagrined look accompanied Josia's new found words of wisdom, and she smiled. It felt good. Then she thought of poor Ted James and Ruth and Stan Dominic. What a tragedy for them; and her smile faded. Corissa was still awaiting trial, but she did have the best defense attorney Ted and Stan could buy.

Irina was right about the sunset. What had started as a subtle hint of red in the southwest sky was developing into a crimson that deepened as it spread across the horizon in front of them—overwhelming the remaining pastel edges of pink and blue.

"Mrs. Beaudine," Manny cautiously asked. "You are okay now, right? I mean with talking about it?"

"I'm just fine," she lied. "What do you want to know?"

"From what I can figure so far," Josia butted in, "Allison King followed Jada here from Seattle." He shook his head in wonderment of what he'd just said. "The woman must have really hated you."

"I hardly knew who she was," Jada said quietly.

"You didn't catch her?" Manny asked Josia. "We heard you go after her and then the shots."

"No I didn't catch her," Josia admitted tight lipped. Not only had he not caught her, but neither had a three-state manhunt brought her back. Allison King had effectively disappeared from the face of the earth.

"She took the money with her?" Manny pressed.

"Yep, she got away with all the gall-darned money." Understandably, Josia was not happy about this particular aspect of the whole mess, and Jada was surprised he hadn't peppered his answer with profanity.

"And you, Mr. Elliott," Manny asked. "How did you know to go out to the lab?"

Lyle smiled and looked at Linda Lowry. "I wish I could take credit for that but Linda here came and got me. I'd just arrived from the Best West...well, just gotten back from town. And my cabin is next to hers, you know."

Linda looked down at her hands folded primly in her lap while Mrs. Shoecraft beamed lovingly at the young woman.

Lyle continued, "She was delivering one of her poems to Jada's room when she saw Terrence following her to the lab. She had seen him before, lurking around Jada's cabin, and then when he checked to make sure Jada's door was closed tight that night, we're guessing to make sure Tasha couldn't get out since your locks here suck, Linda knew something was wrong and came and got me."

Jada felt overwhelmed with how much she owed these people, and a warmth she hadn't felt in a long time flooded her being. She almost cried.

"Well," Lyle summed up. "Terrence Beaudine is now really dead." Then quickly, clearly remembering the impact on Jada and Melvin, he said, "I'm sorry, Mel, Jada, I didn't mean the way that sounded. I know this is horrible for you both."

Melvin nodded, indicating no offense taken.

For Jada, however, what had happened with Terry and her could not be wiped out with a few weeks of rest and a couple bottles of wine. His face—with a bullet-hole in his forehead still haunted her dreams in cabin number-two.

But to Lyle she responded, "It's okay," and managed a smile in his direction. "It's hard to get mad at a man who saved your life." Lyle, the man who had actually known her husband better than she and doggedly tracked him for over a year—had come to visit her at Crestwood almost daily. She wondered if he'd quit his job to stay there?

The people sitting around her were still mysterious in many ways. Maybe understanding would never come, shouldn't come—because that's the way life is. Less mysterious though, now that she had experienced a few—but still wondrous—her Mojave sunset was turning out spectacular. Crimson red, velvet orange—deep, vibrant, mesmerizing. And tonight's brilliant show, Jada fancied in an unexpected wave of awe and reverence, was in memory of those they had lost.

"Are you packed?" Irina asked.

"Yep, guess I'll be checking out in the morning."

Both women laughed, and she wondered if Irina's large and marvelously luminous green eyes were twinkling.

Still, Jada did know she would be leaving one morning, one morning soon—but not tomorrow.

Author's Note - 2016

Death of a Perfect Man was my second novel. I so enjoyed writing Jada Beaudine's Red Rock Inn adventure, and during this second-edition editing, I realized how much I still like Jada and her friends.

I also still remember the first day my husband and I drove up California's Highway 14 and saw the signs for Red Rock, Inyokern, and Ridgecrest—marking a new desert chapter in our lives.

This opportunity to share Jada's tale a second time is a wonderful experience.

Madeline (M.M.) Gornell's mystery novels include—PSWA awarding winners **Uncle Si's Secret** and **Lies of Convenience** (also a Hollywood Book Festival honorable Mention), **Death of a Perfect Man**, and **Reticence of Ravens** (a finalist for the Eric Hoffer 2011 fiction Prize, the da Vinci Eye for cover art, and the Montaigne Medal for most thought provoking book). Her next book, **Counsel of Ravens** (a London Book Festival Honorary Mention and LA Book Festival Runner-Up) is her first sequel, and was a continuation of Hubert Champion's Mojave saga.

Rhodes The Mojave-Stone is her latest novel and a San Francisco Book Festival Honorary Mention. She continues to be inspired by historic Route 66, and **Rhodes The Mojave-Stone** reflects that continuing fascination.

She lives with her husband and assorted canines in the Mojave High Desert near the internationally revered Route 66.